PP

BOOK STORAGE

Cores, Lucy Michaella,
    The year of December, a novel. Mc-
Graw-Hill Book Co. [c1974]
    406 p.

1. Clairmont, Clara Mary Jane, 1798-1879 -
Fiction. I. Title.

cs

The Year of December

The Year of December

a novel by

Lucy Cores

McGraw-Hill Book Company
New York   St. Louis   San Francisco
Düsseldorf   Mexico

Book design by Marcy J. Katz

1 2 3 4 5 6 7 8 9 B A B A 7 9 8 7 6 5 4

Library of Congress Cataloging in Publication Data

Cores, Lucy Michaella, date
    The year of December: a novel.

    1.   Clairmont, Clara Mary Jane, 1798–1879
I.   Title.
PZ3.C8122Ye   [PS3505.06673]   813'.5'4   73-19675
ISBN 0-07-013128-7

For Emil

ISLAVSKOYE

The country place that bored Evgenii
Was truly an enchanting spot;
A devotee of simple pleasures
Might have thanked heavens for his lot.
A manor house, from winds protected,
Stood in seclusion undetected
Above a river; meadows free
And golden pastures one could see
Flowering variously. . . .

Alexander Pushkin,
Evgenii Onyegin

Early in the morning of a summer day in 1825 a boy of eighteen stood at the window of his bedroom looking out into the garden. He was the youngest son of the ancient family of the Princes Volynski, spending the summer in their country estate near Moscow, young Prince Grigorii Petrovich, or, to his family, simply Grisha. It was an exquisite July morning, clear as a gem. The boy contemplated it gravely. His youthfully blunted features in spite of their pale look of illness held more than a promise of comeliness. His lips, full and well marked, had that special sinuous conformation which, even more than his snub nose and high cheekbones, was the true characteristic of a Russian face. He had been seriously ill the whole of the previous winter; his recovery had been a slow one and, for certain profound reasons of his own, that had suited him. This morning for the first time he felt that all-suffusing sense of well-being that seems to come with special strength after one has shed the last vestiges of a stubborn illness.

He moved away from the window, walking with a limp; one of his legs was wasted and ended in a clubfoot, with the toes lifted almost entirely off the ground.

"Up early, this morning, Excellency."

Fomitch, his valet, was already there to attend him, his big chin blue with overnight bristles, a graying cowlick rising in the back of his head like a pigeon's tail. There had been no need to call him. No matter how early or quietly his charge rose, Fomitch awakened too and rose up from his pallet in the dressing room to wait on him.

"What a splendid morning, Fomitch."

"God is good to us, a fine summer day, Excellency."

Grisha proceeded to dress with his help. Everything felt good this morning: as he relieved himself, he couldn't help smiling unconsciously at the robust drumming of the arcing stream hitting the bottom of the chamberpot; the water Fomitch poured out of the washing jug was marvelously refreshing on his hands and face; and there was a special newly ironed smell about the shirt the valet brought him.

Although Grisha would have died rather than expose his unsightly foot to anyone's eyes, he took it as a matter of course when Fomitch, kneeling, eased the hose over it. It was only old Fomitch: a comfortable presence that had always attended to his needs. He had always been there. It was from him and from his old nurse Tikhonovna that Grisha had got his first sense of identity and learned his Russian—with his parents he conversed mostly in French.

Later in the morning, accompanied by his elderly French tutor, Professeur Lachaine, he went to see his mother. Unlike the rest of the old-fashioned house, which was still crammed with dark unwieldy furniture dating back to Tsar Paul, the Princess's apartments were light and airy. Her sitting room was paneled in her favorite lilac silk, snowy muslin drapes billowed at the window, the furniture was pure Empire, all light woods and swan-neck curves. Only the bank of ikons in the corner, a host of dark-faced, gold-haloed saints, framed in darkened silver, showed it to be the room of a Russian noblewoman.

Grisha's mother, Princess Irina Mikhailovna, reclining with her customary languor on the chaise lounge, was talking to her housekeeper, a stately, comely woman in her forties. A towheaded serving girl stood before them, holding a gown reverentially aloft. Her thin arms trembled with the effort, setting the taffeta shimmering like a pigeon's throat.

The Princess's magnificent eyes, huge and somber in their shadowed hollows, rested on Grisha with their familiar expression of mournful inquiry.

"*Maman.*" He kissed her hand, felt her lips brush his temple and the quick flutter of her thin fingers making the sign of cross over him. "*Que le bon Dieu te bénisse, mon fils.*"

The housekeeper moved with swimming steps to the round rosewood table on which a silver samovar steamed gently, its polished surface dimming and brightening. A dismissing jerk of her kerchiefed head released the girl, who slipped by him, soft footed. He caught the uneven sound of her quickened breath, mingling with the rustle of the taffeta, and a whiff of soap and camphor and something else difficult to define. A look slewed toward him from beneath the lowered whitish lashes; then she whisked out through the door, the gown floating behind her like a green-and-lilac oriflamme.

The Princess glanced after her. "She is not doing badly, is she? Not too bright but willing. . . . See if you can polish her up a bit, Nikolavna, you're good at that."

The housekeeper, pouring the tea out for Grisha and the tutor, acknowledged this with a serene smile. Doe eyed and soft of bosom though she might be, she was feared like the devil himself by the household. Grisha once came across her as she was punishing a luckless housemaid and was repelled by the savagery with which those plump white hands inflicted blow after blow on the girl's steadily reddening face. He had never liked her since. "She is the niece of your Fomitch, you know," the Princess added, to Grisha.

"Yes, her name is Matryosha, isn't it?" Feeling color rising to his cheeks, he bent his head down over the cup of tea Nikolavna had handed him.

"No, no, she is Marie now. I couldn't possibly have a Matryosha waiting on me. And certainly not in Moscow. I am thinking of taking her there." The Princess gave her faint sweet smile. "*Ça lui plaira, n'est-ce pas, le bon Fomitch?* But never mind that." She drew her son down onto the tabouret, beside her. Presently she would proceed to cocoon him in a comfortable invalidish coze, eliciting all the minutiae of his receding illness, cataloguing all the symptoms —only one basic fatal defect, the one that could never be put right, would never be mentioned. "How do you feel this morning? Did you sleep well?"

Before he could answer, his tutor intervened: "Reluctantly, *madame la Princesse,* I have to report that Prince Georges stayed up very late last night. It was long after midnight when I woke up and saw that his candle was still burning. Needless to say I immediately went in and saw to it. . . ."

"Dear Monsieur Lachaine, I know I can count on you." The Princess smiling stretched her hand to the tutor in a gesture of gratitude. It was also a dismissing one. M. Lachaine kissed her hand and retired to the back of the room, where he drank his tea discreetly contemplating the neoclassical frieze of dancing nymphs skirting the porcelain stove.

The Princess laid her narrow hand on Grisha's forehead, smoothing back his hair: "Well, and what was it you were reading, Georges? So terribly fascinating that it kept you up the whole night? In spite of what we had agreed on, about your going to sleep early?"

Grisha grinned guiltily. "*The Fountain of Bakhchisarai, maman.*"

"I know, I know, *il est séduisant, ce Pushkin.* Confess now, he kept you awake far too long, didn't he?"

Well, that was true enough. Long after he had closed his eyes, Khan Girey's odalisques paraded on the inside of his eyelids, shedding diaphanous shreds of veils on their way to the pool.

[4]

But he is happiest, Zarema,
Who lies in love's luxurious thrall. . . .

He felt his whole face flaming up into one of those devastating blushes that plagued him constantly. If she only knew. . . .

Last summer he had made his confession to the village priest who had come to the house specially for the services. Outrageous fantasies and their unnerving culmination—the physical easement somehow as shameful as the rest; in the morning the faintest sympathetic smirk on Fomitch's face as he aired the bed—all this could be decently summed up in the ritual Slavonic you used on such occasions: "Forgive me my sins—impure thoughts, body's pollution." The sign of the cross swept over his bowed head, the old voice thickened with age and liquor absolved him in the name of God: "Pray, Prince, pray, mortify the flesh."

One good thing about the illness: it gave you respite from all that. Now it would begin all over again. Even last night. . . . "Well, *maman*," Grisha said with an uncomfortable little laugh, "from now on I'll read nothing but Karamzin's *Poor Lisa*, and that'll put me to sleep immediately."

"Don't be unkind, *mon chéri*. A dear good man and most devoted to the Imperial family, *ce cher Karamzine*," she said, referring to the court historian in the same tone that she had used talking about Fomitch. "Now your Pushkin is an entirely different matter—he was misbehaving all over Petersburg before he was sent away. . . . African temperament and African tastes. . . ."

She broke off as Prince Pyotr Andreich Volynski entered, still wearing his riding clothes. He was holding a letter in his hand, and he negligently dropped it on the little inlaid table by the Princess' chaise lounge.

"*Merci, mon ami.*" The Princess seized upon the letter with an almost girlish eagerness. By the way she plunged into it, forgetting their presence, Grisha guessed it to be a letter from one of her St. Petersburg friends. Not even the letters of his two married sisters or his brother Sergey, now serving with the Preobrazhenski Regiment, rated that special attention.

The Princess missed terribly that brilliant and dangerous city where the Volynskis had lived until their unofficial exile two years ago. Their palace on Nikitskaya Street, drafty and old-fashioned, was to her a sad comedown from the polished mansion on the

English Quay. As for the Moscow society, the Princess, used to moving in the highest St. Petersburg circles, found it cozy but provincial. The Muscovites were much too informal; they talked in Russian almost as much as in French; their balls were mere romps. Sometimes she felt she couldn't bear it. She would talk about returning to Petersburg, quoting friends' letters to show how much the Volynskis were missed, and pointing out how often various members of the Imperial family had alluded to them with kindness. To this her husband would merely reply with a shrug of his powerful shoulders. "Very kind of them all," he would say. "Nevertheless, the situation remains unchanged: *ça y pue fortement encore.*" The very sentiments that had been his undoing: Prince Pyotr Andreich once observed that the bad odor that clung to the Tsar's privy counsellor Arakcheev was due to the fact that the latter's duties included the emptying of the royal chamberpots. This remark was passed on. At the next reception Emperor Alexander was markedly cold, not to say brusque, the whole of the court followed suit, and the Prince, unused to that sort of treatment, decided to move to Moscow.

The Prince nodded to Monsieur Lachaine, gave Grisha his hand to kiss—as always, touching his lips to that well-kept white hand, Grisha was conscious of a timid, almost subservient desire to please—and eased his handsome portly body into one of his wife's delicate armchairs. Sipping the tea, which Nikolavna immediately served him with a low bow, he watched his wife's oblivious face with a slightly sardonic smile.

Grisha addressed him diffidently: "Was it Krasnobai you had out this morning, Papa?"

"Yes. He gave me a good gallop. Went over that fence in the south field like a bird. . . . Am I to understand that you have given up riding altogether? Do you intend to spend the rest of the summer with your nose stuck in a book?"

The tone was as indifferent as ever. Nevertheless Grisha flushed with pleasure: could it be then that his father missed their rides together? That had been their one point of contact, a time spent in a seldom attained state of mutual approbation. Grisha rode extremely well, and Prince Pyotr's cold gray eyes would warm upon him in unqualified approval: he would even talk to his younger son, for once, just as he would talk to the older, Sergey, bluff and unconstrained. Stammering a little Grisha said, "I was just going to ask—I mean, may I come riding with you tomorrow?"

"Oh?" His father's eyebrows rose slightly. "Think you're up to it?"

"Oh, yes, Papa. I'm really well now. In fact, this morning . . ."

"Very good." his father said, in English. "I'll expect you then. Don't oversleep."

"No, Papa, I won't," Grisha assured him, obediently switching to the same language. "I am—looking toward it."

"Looking forward to it," his father corrected him with a grimace. "Your English is getting rusty."

"I am sorry, Papa. Looking forward to it. I have missed it very much."

Horseback riding was better than anything else in the world, almost better than reading. He loved everything about it: the smell and the feel of the marvelous creature under him, the way all his strength seemed to go out through his loins into its powerful body, the smooth motion miraculously taking the place of his own ugly gait.

His father, disregarding for once his mother's anxious strictures, had him taught to ride when he was ten, and Grisha still could recall in every detail the first ride they had taken together. It had been harvest time, the meadows through which they rode were full of peasantwomen with rakes. Their colors were those of the wheatfield, golden, cornflower blue, poppy red, and they had bowed down before the riders the way grain does. Later, as they pulled their lathered horses to a walk, his father turned to him a boy's face, smoothed out by pleasure.

"Good boy!"

He used the Russian word *molodetz*, which expresses the utmost in jaunty excellence, and Grisha really did feel like a *molodetz*: the horse curvetted coquettishly under him and he sat it fine and straight, looking proudly about him. An idea struck him. "Papa!"

"Eh?"

"Perhaps they'd let me go into the cavalry."

Immediately he knew how stupid that was. His father's face froze. He said brusquely, not looking at his son: "No, it's the diplomatic corps for you. . . ."

". . . It seems," said the Princess, looking up from her letter, "the Emperor is unwell."

The Prince's teacup was sharply arrested midway to his lips.

"Anything serious?"

"Well, it's his leg again. He is in considerable pain. The Empress herself is nursing him . . . Catiche says"—the Princess's face was irradiated by her St. Petersburg smile, sly, vivacious, brilliantly amused—"that there have been no visits to *la belle* Naryshkina lately."

"He'll be back soon enough. It's just that old business with his leg, nothing serious."

An unfortunate remark. His wife's lips thinned, a rosy patch stained each sharp cheekbone. "Oh, no doubt about that, a wife is only good as a nurse. *Vous êtes tous les mêmes, les hommes. . . .*" Her voice trembled a little.

Grisha looked away, uncomfortably. Like everyone else, he was well aware of his father's philanderings. He had often overheard the grooms at the stables—a cheeky gossipy crew—making pungent comments on them ("A proper Turk, his Excellence, runs up every hill he sees!"—their laughter was indulgent, not unprideful); and sometimes, as he rode through their village of Andreyevo, a child scuttling from underfoot would fix him disconcertingly with his father's eyes.

He rose to his feet, and Professeur Lachaine, who had been patiently waiting in his corner, put his empty cup down and came forward with another one of his significant little coughs.

"Off to your lessons now?" Holding on to her letter, the Princess made a sign of cross over him with her free hand. "Don't work too hard. Don't let him get tired, M. Lachaine. . . . By the way, Georges, I am counting on you this afternoon for the Pomykovs—I refuse to entertain *La Pomykov* alone, she rattles on so. I don't suppose *you* are to be counted on, Pierre."

"Why not? *La Pomykov* may be a pretentious *bas bleu*, but Zahar Nikolaitch is a sensible man, I don't mind talking to him. . . . What else has Catiche to say? Have they all gone to the Tsarskoye Syelo?"

In the corridor, Grisha ran into the towheaded serving maid, Matryosha. She stopped and made a low peasant-type obeisance, which, evidently remembering instructions, she immediately changed into a curtsey, saying, "Wish you health, your Excellency," in her childish, slightly nasal voice.

Grisha stopped too. "Good morning, Matryosha."

"Ah, qu'est-ce que vous dites, quelle Matrioche? C'est Marie maintenant. Isn't that so, my dear?" said Monsieur Lachaine, lapsing into his terrible creaky Russian. A crooked tobacco-stained forefinger chucked her small round chin.

"Yes, sir, Marie," repeated the neutral little voice.

She had changed since last summer, Grisha saw. She looked plumper and sleeker in the full-skirted cotton dress that, being attached to the household staff, she wore now in place of the old combination of threadbare shift and sarafan. Two neat braids issued tautly from under the muslin cap instead of the single soft untidy plait he remembered. Only the way she stood before him, the droop of the flaxen head, was the same. The matured body still said, "Here I am, do with me as you please."

With a stiff nod, he limped away from her.

Hard to believe that at one point last summer he had found that inarticulate presence so exacerbating that he had considered seriously getting her somehow sent away. His winter's illness had taken care of all that. She was now a trifling ache, perversely self-induced and easily dismissed, a mere ghost of last summer's trouble.

Oh, that troubling summer—in some ways it had been worse than the wretched winter of illness that followed it. All at once he had found himself changing: his voice sawed up and down an uncertain register, his wrists shot out of his sleeves; his stride lengthened and his limp increased, as if his bad leg couldn't keep up with the general growth. Nor was it the only member to give him trouble: his very center of gravity seemed to have shifted downward to a specific area where all kinds of troubling new sensations eventually came to an embarrassing clammy resolution.

Even the statues in their park drew his unfocused longings. Once finding himself alone in front of a nude Flora or Hebe he had reached up to lay his hand on her marble breast. His heart beat tempestuously, the marble seemed to warm magically beneath his palm. Closing his eyes he was abandoning himself to a wild dream, when a sound roused him. Jerking his hand away, he saw his father walking toward him, a brace of dogs frisking at his heels. He

[9]

waited, scarlet faced. The Prince, impassive, merely nodded to him and went on, whistling softly through his teeth.

One day in August he was riding with his father, groom Fedka following at a distance, when, breaking through a stand of alder and birch, they came across the village pond, where peasant women were bathing. Startled, he reined in his horse and gaped at them. Most of them were naked, some in dripping shifts—all this seemed to turn on him, breasts, thighs, bellies, overwhelming and somehow menacing in their plenitude. His eyes winced away, and lighted on a young girl standing apart in the shallows, dreamily stirring the water with a cattail, smiling a secretive little smile as she drew circular ripples with its brown-velvet cylinder.

His father, edging his oversize bay gelding Krasnobai beside Grisha's slender-legged Nelly, surveyed the bathers unperturbed. "Splendid healthy animals," he remarked, gesturing with his riding crop as coolly as if he were looking over a promising herd of cattle. "Beauties, too, some of them. Hmmm?"

The Prince had spoken without bothering to lower his voice. The women saw them and submerged, giggling and splashing. An audacious voice shrilled, "Come on in with us, *barchuk*, we'll give you a bath." Their laughter was bold: he might be the Prince's son, owning them body and soul, but for the moment all that was discarded together with the clothes they had shed in bright bundles all over the grass.

"Women," said the groom Fedka with a companionable grin. "Give 'em a chance, they'll eat you alive, the cannibals. . . ."

"They frighten you, I suppose," said the Prince smiling.

"Scare me to death, Excellency," Fedka sang out gaily. And for a moment he and his father seemed to Grisha to share a sort of understanding, comradely and faintly salacious, as if they were members of a universal club as yet closed to him.

Once noticed by him the girl detached herself for good and all from her background. He began seeing her around. Going through the village he would see her scuttling across the dusty street, her bare legs twinkling under the coarse blue kersey of her sarafan, dodging into an *izba* with a quick backward look and a flick of an untidy flaxen braid. Once he found her even closer to home, right outside the park gates; she was leaning against a fence, rubbing one dusty foot against the other, as she listened, of all things, to his own Fomitch.

"My niece," the latter explained later, upon being casually questioned, "my own sister's girl, Matryosha by name, a nice enough little filly, brighter than the rest of that lot." The engrained contempt of the house servant for the land serf sounded in his voice.

And then unexpectedly she materialized right under his eyes, on the steps of the veranda, while his mother, dressed to go for a drive, looked her over twirling her white lace parasol. Beside the girl Fomitch stood, his solid body inclined, in a proprietary and protective pose, as if he were looking after both their interests.

"She seems a nice little thing," the Princess remarked. "I like to see pretty faces around the house." She patted the girl's cheek kindly with her gloved hand. The girl's eyes widened at her touch—they were, Grisha noticed, that special muted blue of a cornflower toward the end of its bloom—but she stood there dumbly, only panting stealthily through her parted lips.

The Princess frowned a little. "She is not half witted, is she?" she asked Fomitch. "Because then she won't do."

"God forbid, *matushka*, not a bit of it, just struck dumb by her good fortune like. . . . Kiss her Grace's hand, you dummy, thank her for her kindness." The girl gave a violent start and fell headlong at the Princess' feet.

"Thank you, your Grace," came muffledly from the crumpled blue kersey bundle.

A few days later, as Grisha sat in the garden reading Constant's *Alphonse,* Fomitch approached and in a low conspiratorial voice asked him to come along. "Something I've got to show your Honor."

"But what is it?"

"Just please to come." Fomitch wore an anxious grin on his face. Grisha's retriever Toozik, laying a bird down at his feet, would grin up at him like that, anxious and triumphant at the same time.

Intrigued Grisha closed his book and followed his valet into the wilder, older part of the park. On the other side of a rustic bridge arching over a stream there stood a small gothic pavilion. Nobody used this one any more. But it wasn't empty: Grisha, ushered by Fomitch into its shadowy interior, permeated by a nostalgic musty odor, saw that a cot was standing in the middle, fully made up. Matryosha, wearing nothing but a white shift, was sitting on it, her bare feet tucked up under her. A stubby red hand played nervously with a loosened plait flung over one shoulder.

Fomitch jerked his head commandingly at her and she got off the bed and stood next to it, clasping her hands together, her head bowed low so that he could see the childishly straight line of the parting. There was an air of total submission about her whole slender figure.

"You'll do, I guess," Fomitch said, giving her a swift but thorough glance of inspection. "I had her cleaned up, like, your Excellency. . . ." With another minatory nod to the girl—mind now!—he left them.

Grisha remained where he was, driven into the ground like a post. But his body knew: a stab of exultation and terror streaked through it, and the familiar ache at his loins focused and solidified.

"Matryosha," he whispered. The girl slowly lifted her eyes to him. Dilated, blindly blue, they clung to his face. Her hands untwisted and fell to her side. She just stood there, waiting. "Here I am, do with me what you will," every line of her utterly passive body seemed to say.

Grisha took a swift step toward her, stepped too heavily on his bad foot and lurched off balance. Matryosha's face changed: an expression of fearful curiosity appeared on it. Her gaze slid down to his foot and stayed there riveted.

And suddenly the little room lengthened, it was now miles long, and he knew he couldn't make it, he couldn't go shuffling all those miles toward her waiting figure. The impulse at his loins withered, he was cold and weak with the miserable ebb of it. He turned and hobbled hurriedly out of the pavilion.

Fomitch was patroling outside. At the sight of his master, his jaw fell open.

"You old fool, how dared you? How—?" Grisha said in a strangled voice, awkwardly striking at his amazed face. Fomitch didn't even try to duck; he merely waited, unblinking, for the blow to fall. Grisha dropped his fist and limped away from him, dragging his foot exaggeratedly in his haste. Fomitch followed, still stunned, shaking his head and blinking rapidly.

Halfway back, Grisha stopped. "And whatever gave you the idea? How did you dare . . . ?"

"For reasons of health, Your Excellency," Fomitch answered promptly. And his use of the phrase and the whole reminiscent

[12]

stiffening of his body—a sort of coming to attention—confirmed Grisha's suspicions. Instructions must have been issued. Transfixed with humiliation he remained mute, while Fomitch went on explaining: "A young man's got to grow up to his manhood, that goes without saying. I picked my own niece, Excellency, clean as a whistle"—a shade of grievance came into his voice—"nobody's laid a finger on her, just right for you. . . ."

First time for her too . . . Pity for the girl stabbed through his angry humiliation. Hustled out of her village, cleaned up, waiting to be deflowered by a stranger . . .

"Your own niece, and you bring her, like an animal, force her . . ."

"Force her? God forgive us, Excellency, why it's an honor for her, she never expected. . . ."

And that was true, there had been no fear in the wide-eyed stare she had bent upon him, just boundless submissiveness—not until she saw his foot. . . . His brief spurt of compassion was submerged in a flood of self-pity. Grisha sat down on the grass and took his head in his hands.

Fomitch stood over him, wringing his hands. "Your Excellence—Grishenka. . . ."

"Go away, damn you."

But Fomitch didn't go away. After a while he said in a cautious voice: "Didn't give yourself a chance, darling, is all. Look, that's how it is sometimes, the first pancake comes out a lump. Anything's hard at first, even pleasure. . . . You'll be getting it into 'em soon enough, never fear."

It wasn't until much later that Grisha recognized that his serf was doing as best he could, a father's job, trying to reassure and comfort his wounded manhood.

As far as his father was concerned, he never said anything about it at all, though presumably Fomitch must have reported to him. Grisha was grateful for the silence; it was bad enough to have still another inadequacy, a specially shameful one, chalked up to him.

He remembered his older brother Sergey telling him all about the mysterious business of "going to see women." There was a discreet establishment, it seemed, where knowledgeable ladies took care of you. "Not a bad thing the first time," Sergey had said, "you do feel a bit of a fool, you know, don't really know how to go about it. . . ." He had smiled complacently, passing his hand over the new, barely seeded blond moustache; one could see that that first ineptitude couldn't have been of a long duration or given him too much grief.

But that winter, when they got back to Moscow, Grisha never did get to go to the house with the ladies, because he caught a cold which became pneumonia with complications and was followed, after it became certain that he would live, by a long period of convalescence.

There had been a postscript of sorts: Sergey, sitting on his bed, in his green and scarlet Preobrazhenski Regiment uniform, good-naturedly trying to entertain the invalid with his chatter about his exploits and conquests. "Look close to home for the best, though. There's a little girl I found last month in our own Andreyevo—actually, she's your Fomitch's niece or something—simply lovely!" He kissed his fingers, his young rosy-cheeked face trying to assume a rakish man-about-town expression. "Young, shy, something fresh and untouched about her. . . . I love it like that, when they make you feel as if you're the first one. Not that I was," Sergey laughed wholeheartedly, his strong white teeth flashing. "You know what the old man's like: it seems he was there before me."

Grisha remembered Marya Ivanovna Pomykov from her previous visitations, a bustling woman in her middle thirties, so full of energy that she could leave neither herself nor her family alone. A small engine seemed to power all her movements, imparting a bounce to the modish curls beneath her bonnet and a twirl to her parasol, as she advanced toward them. Her husband, Zahar Niko-laitch, a smallish, swarthy man with an intelligent monkeyish face, could barely keep up with her.

The table with samovar and refreshments was set up on the veranda. The visitors disposed themselves around it, with a flutter and rustle of the ladies' lightly starched muslins. Introductions were performed: *my sisters, Catherine and Olga*—two young ladies, rosy-cheeked and mum—*our little Johnny*—a ten-year-old, accompanied by his tutor, a handsome young German by the name of Gambs, whom Grisha remembered from the summer before—*and Dunia*—a pigtailed mite of five in pink dress and pantalets who kept close to a thin dark young woman, apparently in charge of her.

"*Vous vous rappelez mon Georges, sans doute,*" said the Princess, indicating Grisha, who had stationed himself, as soon as he had seen them coming, on the other side of the table—a defensive maneuver he resorted to whenever he met new people. "And I remember Dunia very well, how she has grown!" she added, smiling on the little girl, who, all at once overcome by shyness, melted into the young woman's skirts. Grisha gave the latter a quick look: an extravagantly slim, long-necked creature, with black hair and eyes, which she kept modestly cast down, and a longish nose, with a tip faintly reddened by a cold—unquestionably the governess, she had that withdrawn, colorless, not-one-of-the-family look about her. The Princess smiled at her too, graciously: "I don't believe I remember you—you're a newcomer, are you not, Mademoiselle—Mademoiselle—?"

"Clairmont, *Madame.*" He was right then, the French governess. "I have only had the pleasure of becoming a part of this household this past spring." Her voice was charming, clear and resonant, the French extraordinarily pure. An expression of pleasure appeared on the Princess's face: like her son, she was sensitive to voices.

"And a most important member, *ma chère Princesse*, I should be lost without her." Madame Pomykov's voice sounded even more strident after that low pure utterance. "You know how I am, it is the most important thing in the world for me to see that my children are properly educated, and I have found such a treasure in my young friend here . . ."

Grisha's attention shifted to the other end of the table where politics were being discussed. "It looks," Zahar Nikolaitch was saying, "as though Poland has the knack of pleasing the Imperial family . . ." The Prince was listening to him with a special attention quite unlike his usual courteous indifference. Court politics still stirred him up. "I hear Grand Duke Constantine is swearing that he will never leave Warsaw. . . ."

"Well, he'll have to eventually, won't he?" The Prince was referring to the fact that the Grand Duke Constantine, as the eldest of the Tsar's three brothers, was the heir to the Russian throne.

"Well, Prince, one hears that his aversion to occupying the Russian throne is such that when the time comes, he might very well pass it on to Nikolai Pavlovich and just stay on in Poland as its viceroy."

He pronounced the Russian name of the Tsar's other brother with a marked French accent—a bit of an affectation, since the rest of his French wasn't all that good. Perhaps, Grisha thought with an involuntary smile, the strong-minded Marya Ivanovna had hired the French governess for her husband as well as for her children.

"Come, come, honored Zahar Nikolaitch. One doesn't renounce one's claim to the Russian throne that easily."

Grisha suddenly remembered the letter from St. Petersburg with its news of the Tsar's illness. "Is the Emperor seriously ill?"

His father gave him a blank look. "No, of course not, what makes you think so?"

"I couldn't help wondering, *mon père*."

"Because of our talk about succession?" said Zahar Nikolaitch turning his friendly monkeyish face toward him. "No, indeed, my dear young sir, not a bit of it, our beloved sovereign is perfectly well and will continue to be so, with our prayers. But when there is no natural heir, the question of succession is bound to come up from time to time. . . ."

"Nicholas First," said the Prince slowly, testing it. "Well, I for one would not repine at seeing him on the throne. An admirable young man, energetic and conscientious." His voice warmed; the Prince had a special affection for the younger Grand Duke, who, like him, abominated Minister Arakcheev.

Zahar Nikolaitch made a sympathetic little sound. Nevertheless Grisha had an impression that his attitude toward Nicholas was not as wholehearted as his father's. "Someone," he remarked neutrally, "I don't remember who, has described him as a mixture of Peter the Great and the army lieutenant."

"The Empress herself, I think." The Prince chuckled. "Well, it is true, he is even more committed to the army than the Emperor himself. One thing I would vouch for: *he* wouldn't tolerate even a shadow of sedition in the army. As it is, one is constantly hearing of secret societies springing up in it like mushrooms. Or perhaps," the Prince's voice hardened, "one might more correctly call them outgrowths of the one all-embracing secret society: conspiracy, you know, my dear Zahar Nikolaitch, is proverbially hydra headed."

"Conspiracy? I shouldn't use that term myself," said Zahar Nikolaitch soothingly. "Surely the most one could say is that a certain amount of liberal thought exists in the army."

"A certain amount of liberal thought," the Prince echoed sardonically. "One might as well say a certain degree of plague. Secret organizations have no place in Russia; they are breeding places for revolutionary activities. Why do you suppose Alexander has abolished masonic lodges?"

"And yet, my dear Prince, it was the same sovereign who had said once, *'il faut distinguer des crimes des principes de la révolution.'* A puzzling contradiction, *n'est-ce pas?*" Zahar Nikolaitch shrugged his narrow shoulders.

The Prince gave a chilly smile. "Frankly, my dear sir, His Imperial Majesty's ways are as mysterious to me as they are to—him . . ." He flicked a finger toward one of the footmen, a young boy, evidently just promoted, who, his breath inheld, his white-gloved paws spread out, was passing around a plateful of *zakusski.* "It's hard on a monarch whose early years had been tainted with a doctrine that he can't possibly put into practice. Alexander's early education with the Swiss La Harpe—" He shook his head and his look shifted toward the German tutor on the ladies' side of the table, whose entire appearance, the carelessly tied cravat, the dark hair a few romantic inches longer than was *comme il faut*—most of all perhaps the slight rapt smile hovering about his sensitively modeled lips—might to a censorious eye characterize him as another of those progressive Germans bringing seditious doctrines to undiscriminating Russian families. "Yes, indeed, your La Harpe has a lot to answer for."

"Or, from another point of view, not quite enough," said Zahar Nikolaitch, smiling. He picked up two walnuts from a dish and cracked them between his fingers. The shells fell all over his fancy paisley waistcoat. The Prince smiled back at him, his eyes glinting.

"Yes, I know you, you're a well-known *carbonare*, Zahar Nikolaitch."

"*Mon ami,*" came the Princess's voice from the other end of the table, "do listen, this is the most amusing thing. . . ."

The Prince turned toward her, his animation receding to his usual expression of courteous attention, not unmixed with boredom.

"I have been calling this young lady Mademoiselle Clairmont, and it turns out that she isn't mademoiselle at all but Miss. She's English."

"Oh, everyone thinks she is French," said Madame Pomykov.

The young woman gave a quick noncommittal smile, a mere flicker of white teeth between her pale lips. "I have been accused of being Italian too."

Certainly she was unlike any English governess Grisha had seen: rawboned strawhaired creatures, all of them, angular in movements, constricted in speech. His own Mr. Evans, gone back to

England for the summer, had been a stiff inarticulate stick of a man, knowing no language except his own and strictly dedicated to teaching it.

His father surveyed her too with an air of mild curiosity: as though something that he had taken for a goat unexpectedly turned out to be a deer. "One would never take Mademoiselle for an Englishwoman. Are you sure you are one?" he asked her in English, smiling.

"Perfectly sure, my lord," she answered in the same language. "I was born in London and spent my youth there."

"I was there is 1814," the Prince observed, "in Emperor Alexander's retinue. I daresay," he added with mechanical gallantry, "you are too young to remember this occasion."

"Indeed I do. I remember seeing Emperor Alexander appearing on the balcony of the Pulteney Hotel. We all thought he looked charming."

"Well, he's not as slender now as when you saw him in England," Madame Pomykov observed, with her boisterous neigh of a laugh.

The Princess shut her eyes briefly: she was pained by even the most innocuous criticism of the Imperial family. "His Majesty is still considered the most charming man in Russia." Having uttered this gentle rebuke, she turned again to Miss Clairmont. "You must miss your native land very much. It's a hard thing to be forced to go away from one's home, to be parted from one's friends." Her resigned sigh was obviously for her own condition. Both she and Madame Pomykov were talking French, and Miss Clairmont shifted to it effortlessly, without any carry-over of an English accent.

"Perhaps I miss my friends more than my native land, Madame. Although I own I find myself a little homesick when I am addressed in English as faultless as his Excellency's." She raised her eyes as she spoke. They were large and black, strongly outlined by thick dark eyelashes. When she lowered them, her face again became a sallow not unpleasing oval.

The Prince, who prided himself on his English, looked pleased. "English is one language one must speak well or not at all. . . . Ah, 1814," he went on nostalgically. "A glorious year for us. There we were, fresh from our conquests, greeted as saviors of Europe wherever we went, the Emperor regarded as an angel descended from above. . . . It was a triumphal march, everywhere. In England—it was a pleasant visit," he finished dryly.

Miss Clairmont gave another of her little smiles. "We are too phlegmatic and xenophobic to give a visiting monarch the attention he deserves."

"What about your own? I still remember your Prince Regent courting the populace like an actor—all *he* got was whistles. . . . We were talking of succession just now," he said, turning back to Zahar Nikolaitch. "What could be more ludicrous than the situation we found in England, with the son serving as regent while the reigning monarch was still alive?"

"But the poor old gentleman was quite mad," said Miss Clairmont.

The Prince said indulgently: "His Majesty Tsar Paul was reportedly similarly afflicted; yet there was no question of setting any of his sons as a regent over him. He reigned a complete autocrat until he died and his Majesty Tsar Alexander ascended the throne."

"Then perhaps replacing a demented ruler by a saner one is to be recommended for the sake of *his* survival as well as that of the people."

There was a little pause. Zahar Nikolaitch clicked his tongue, looking amused and apprehensive at once.

"I can't imagine what you mean," said the Prince icily. The lorgnette in his fingers rose like a weapon. He leveled through it a stern look at the young governess. In Russian society no one ever referred to Tsar Paul's unnatural death.

Miss Clairmont, nothing abashed by having committed a grave social solecism, sustained this look with something like relish. Her sallow cheeks were stained with pink, her eyes brilliant. She was no longer plain—as if being the center of attention, even if disapproving attention, nourished her. And then, with a flicker of something like alarm in her black eyes, she turned it all off: her animation flagged, sank, disappeared totally. Casting her eyes down, she was silent.

The Prince let his lorgnette drop. "Young women mustn't talk politics."

"No, *mon Prince*. What must they do?"

His father shrugged, all at once bored with it, "Oh—charm and instruct us, of course," he mumbled with a polite grimace, "beautify our lives like the flowers you so charmingly resemble. . . ." With a final little bow he turned back to Zahar Nikolaitch, ready to resume their man-to-man talk, which was so much more interesting and rational.

The Princess, tactfully filling in the pause, began to talk about the Andreyevo gardens, which were her pride and joy; she spent a great deal of time planning and improving them. "I should particularly like *you* to see them," she said kindly to Miss Clairmont. "They are laid out like an English park, you see. We've had an English gardener especially brought in for them. You must tell me what you think."

"Miss Clairmont might also tell us what she thinks of Grisha's English," the Prince intervened. "Why don't you take the young ladies on a tour of the garden, Grisha?"

"*Oui, mon pere,*" said Grisha, bracing himself. There was always that uncomfortable moment when he would have to leave his post of safety. On those occasions his limp became exaggerated, and, do what he might, he couldn't help watching for its effect on those who saw it for the first time. As he limped from behind the table, Madame Pomykov's face went stony, and she looked past him at her sisters. "Forgot to warn them," Grisha thought wryly. But they were well brought up; after the first unguarded moment, their round pink faces assumed the unnatural blankness he knew and feared. Only the little girl, leaning against Miss Clairmont's knees kept upon him the unswerving stare of childish curiosity.

The governess wasn't looking away either: her dark eyes lifted to him, widening in unabashed attention. Her lips parted: was she about to be awkward again and comment on his limp? She didn't, but her eyes stayed on him: all listlessness gone, vivid with interest, she watched his lurching progress, as if it were an intricate fascinating maneuver.

All at once he was furious. Intolerable! He would ask her exactly what she meant by it: the very words he would use, couched in the iciest, most crystallinely impeccable English he could summon, formed themselves on his lips: "My limp seems to interest you, Miss Clairmont: haven't you ever seen a cripple before?" But as he looked fully upon her, her whole expression changed, softened, melted in such complete understanding that for a moment he had the unnerving feeling that he had spoken aloud. An unutterable tenderness swept across her face; incredibly an answering message sped back to him: "Never mind, my darling," said clearly those luminous eyes, those parted lips. Before he could take it all in, it vanished, and she was again the correct Miss Clairmont.

His mother's narrow hand on his sleeve detained him. "No, I don't think I'll let you, *mon enfant*. . . . Georges has been very ill, you see," she said to Madame Pomykov with that half-sorrowful, half-defensive inflection which she always used talking about him to strangers. "He really mustn't overdo."

Madame Pomykov exclaimed in sympathy.

"I'm perfectly well, *maman*," Grisha said, flushing. "No reason why I shouldn't take a little walk."

"*Mon ami*, it's not a little walk, and it's the hottest time of the day. The doctors were very definite about it. . . . I will trouble you to take my son's place, Monsieur Gambs," she said, turning her tired smile on the German tutor, "you know your way about, I think, from last summer."

"Yes, I remember your beautiful gardens very well," said Monsieur Gambs, smiling and bowing gracefully.

The moment the enigmatic Miss Clairmont was out of sight, her employer launched into a detailed description of her virtues and accomplishments. Miss Clairmont taught the children not only French and English but also Italian; she was, besides, an accomplished musician. "And she comes excellently recommended. The Zotovs met her in Vienna and engaged her as a companion for their oldest daughter. The only reason I've been able to get her from them is that Betsy Zotov is getting married and so has no further need for a *dame de compagnie*."

Grisha looked after the group that was proceeding toward the park. The children frisked ahead, happy to be freed from the adults. Monsieur Gambs had given his arm to Miss Clairmont and was saying something to her. And suddenly she turned her head and looked back at Grisha, directly at him, unsmilingly, and again he had that sense of attention beamed full upon him, some sort of intense communication in a language that was as yet strange to him. Puzzled, faintly resentful, he watched her out of sight.

Claire's Letter to Mary, July 10

    . . . This letter will only go to you if I can arrange to have it taken by two English ladies of my acquaintance who are going back to England. Until then I keep it under

[21]

lock and key, just as I keep my diary. The Russians are not only a curious race but also a race of curious people. On the national level there is censorship and scanning of all letters going out of the country. On the domestic level, there is that terrible inquisitiveness that takes no heed of anyone's wish to be private. Everybody reads everybody else's diary, and everybody knows that; the young ladies of the house when they get angry at each other leave their diaries open at the latest entry, so that the culprit should know exactly what is being thought of her.

As a precaution I've been doing some double bookkeeping. There is a diary that I've kept that anybody can sneak a look at—and there is another, written in code and shut away out of sight, in which I give myself the pleasure of pouring my heart out. I suppose you think this is silly. But my experience in Vienna, where the police spied on Charles and me because of our background, has made an ineradicable impression on me—you don't know what it means to know that you're being followed, that your papers are secretly looked at. It has made me cautious and secretive. Besides, as you know, my only hope of earning a livelihood is my present occupation—and there is little chance of continuing with that if it becomes known that the charming, retiring, demure Miss Clairmont, that special jewel for which Marya Ivanovna Pomykov is envied all over Moscow, is a Monster Issuing from a Den of Godwinish Principles.

If my letters get to you, well and good. Otherwise there is my *other* diary. When we are together again, I shall read you—not all but most of it. Anyhow, enough so that you will know exactly what my Russian life was like.

The Pomykov household is a mass of contradictions. On one hand the children's heads are crammed with *souvenirs d'histoire* at breakfast, dinner, or whenever Marya Ivanovna can get hold of them—and she is capable of sitting up until all hours discussing Kant with me and Hermann Gambs—on the other, whenever Madame loses her temper, she lays about her with a heavy hand among her domestics, who submit with the dumb fortitude of serfdom. She makes me think of Catherine the Great who, in spite of her fine intellectual correspondence with Voltaire and Diderot, had no scruples about putting the final touches to the complete system of serfdom in Russia.

Yesterday we went for a visit to the estate of our neighbor, Prince Volynski (a very old name, that, as you can tell by the title of *Knyaz* or *Prince*—the title of *Graf* or Count didn't come in until Peter the Great, with his predilection for the West). The Prince is a virile, arrogant male animal. The Princess is somewhat older, overdelicate, overnervous, sapped of vitality—presumably by him. Marya Ivanovna tells me that she has given birth to fourteen children. Only four survived. The misery of going through the double peril of giving life and seeing it lost! I know it only too well. . . .

Yes, of course, you know it even better than I. Wilmouse, little Clara, that poor tiny baby in London. Remember how we wept together over the pitiful little body? And your poor breasts still full of milk. . . . I think I died a little every time with you. . . . And then, then I died really and truly when my own child. . . . No, I can't.

Their youngest son was there. Young Prince George—at least I think so. These Russian names! His father calls him Grisha, his mother calls him Georges, as does his French tutor. And I—I suppose I would call him George, in English.

He is lame. Isn't that strange, Mary, that he should be George and lame? At first he was a silent attentive presence effacing himself behind a table, and then when he had to move—oh, that look, the look I know so well, quick, mistrustful, angry in advance. It brought everything back to me—all the rest of the day I kept remembering things. . . .

(Added the next day.)

An interesting new development. We've been asked back to the Volynskis'—an unprecedented piece of attention, according to Marya Ivanovna. Later it was explained.

I had another opportunity to look at Prince Georges. Poor boy—sensitive, diffident, deeply, resentfully conscious of his defect. Oh, hating it—

The father talks with pride about his other son who is in the army. The mother defensively enlarges on how well her Georges will do in the diplomatic corps. Well, of course—where else will he go with that leg? Anyhow that will be his career, therefore special attention to languages; therefore, since they have no English tutor this summer, would the clever quiet self-effacing Miss Clairmont with her special pedagogic gifts be kind enough to oblige the Volynskis in the matter of having daily conversations with the young man?

She would.

The Pomykov house was as unlike the polished Andreyevo mansion as it could be—an untidy, sprawling structure with a weathered almost shabby look. The groom who took Nelly wore a rumpled *kazakhin* not completely buttoned; inside the house, an elderly butler, in a faded buff livery, didn't seem too sure of how and to whom to announce him.

"His Honor has gone to Moscow. Her Worship Marya Iva-novna—I don't know if they're up yet—please to wait." He stumped out, shrugging his jacket to rights.

Grisha sat down on an elongated sofa covered by two long pallets of striped calico and looked about him. There were the inevitable busts on top of massive bookshelves, vases standing on doilies bordered by chenille fringe, pictures covered over with muslin, summer style, to keep them from getting dusty—everything very ordinary. Somebody was playing the piano in the next room, repeating one passage over and over again: the passionate notes surged up to a point, stopped as if blocked, and went back again to the beginning.

Presently Monsieur Gambs, the German tutor, strode quickly into the room, the little Pomykov boy trotting alongside of him. "You've been made to wait, I am so sorry," he said in French, smiling and holding out his hand to Grisha. He too had a slightly unbuttoned look, with his shirt open at the collar *à la* Lord Byron, his hair romantically tousled. No tutor in the Volynski household would have been permitted to look like that.

[24]

"To tell you the truth, we all stayed up until three in the morning—just talking, you know—so Madame Pomykov is making up for lost sleep."

"But if Miss Clairmont . . ."

"Oh, she's up. The Instructors of Youth," he said with comical emphasis, "must be on hand to instruct, midnight discussions or not." He motioned with his handsome head toward the door from which the music came. The player, having apparently eliminated whatever obstacle had been impeding the progress, now surged on to the conclusion of the phrase ans swept on triumphantly. "That's Miss Claire playing, you know. She is a superb musician, as you can hear. . . . I'll take you to her, Prince."

Miss Clairmont hung oblivious over the keyboard. Her movements as she played were strong, almost ungainly, quite unlike the genteel swaying of young ladies performing sweetly at parties; she bent to her task like a rower making his way upstream. The little girl Dunia was curled up in a large armchair next to the piano, together with a large white Persian cat. Lulled by the music she lay there motionless, sucking dreamily at her fingers, her pale blue eyes unfocused. The cat purred inaudibly, its furry throat vibrating, its paws kneading the chair cushion.

Miss Clairmont finished her passage and got up from the piano, patting absently at her slightly disarranged black hair, and smiling at her listeners.

Uneasily Grisha braced himself against another disconcerting look that might emanate from those dark eyes. But she greeted him with courteous impersonality that reassured and, unaccountably, disappointed him at the same time.

The minute she had risen from the piano, the children closed in on her, claiming her. The boy burst into excited speech, a mingled babble of Russian and French pulsing from his stammering lips. "À l'étang—Monsieur Gambs a promis—a big old carp—nous l'avons vu . . ." The little girl crawled off the chair, batting her sleepy eyes, and leaned against her, staking out a claim. Miss Clairmont drew her close with one hand, putting the other on the boy's thin shoulder. "No, stop it, Johnny—you must tell me what you want quietly; there's no hurry—I will listen." The babble slowed up and she nodded.

"Yes, I'd like to come down to the pond—I'm stiff from sitting at the piano. . . . Would you like to?" she said to Grisha in English.

[25]

"Or is it too difficult to walk that far with your leg? The pond is at the other end of the garden."

Nobody had ever commented on Grisha's limp that casually. For a moment his breath was taken away—then he was able to answer her with a casualness that strived to match hers.

"I can walk any distance."

"That's what I supposed, but I thought perhaps I'd better make sure," said Miss Clairmont serenely. She put a shawl over her shoulders and picked up a book from a chair. "Shall we go then?"

Oddly, as they went out of the house, he was aware of a sense of lightness and relief. Once, when he was ill, the sick nurse who looked after him, seeing him try to hide his wasted leg from her, said to him, quite simply: "Don't be ashamed of it, Excellency. God sends us all kinds of trials, have to bear them with a good heart." And then, too, after an initial flare-up of anger, he had felt somehow eased. Even the anger had felt different from the strangled muffled rage that would rise up in him at the quickly averted glances, the determined nonmention that made his limp an obscenity courteously ignored in polite society.

The Pomykov garden matched the house, a pleasant wilderness, again totally unlike Andreyevo's English gardens, with formally clipped trees and geometrically neat pebbled walks. Here the trees had a comically shaggy look. They passed by a huge oak spectacularly outspread, its magnificence domesticated by the several sets of swings hanging from its majestic branches. The children frisked ahead of them, shrilling away, as they dove in and out of pools of sun-flecked shadow. Glancing back, Grisha saw the white cat following them at a distance, leisurely and disdainful, its plumy tail waving gently. Miss Clairmont strolled on in an equally leisurely manner, questioning Grisha in English: How long ago did he stop his English lessons? Had he had opportunity to read much? What were his plans for the summer?

"It is quite clear, Prince," she said at last, "you're much too advanced for my other pupils. You're far beyond Pollock's *Cours de la Langue Anglaise*. What you need is a great deal of conversation. You and I will have to discourse together *constantly*."

"A form of Plato's dialogues?" asked Monsieur Gambs, smiling.

"Oh, no, that wouldn't do at all. Socrates does all the talking there, all his disciples ever do is say, 'Yes, Socrates. You've

certainly shown us the right way, Socrates,' in a most syco-
phantic manner. We don't want that sort of thing at all, do we,
Prince?"

"I hope I will be permitted to join in," said Monsieur Gambs,
"whatever the form. . . ."

He shared his sweet smile between Miss Clairmont and Grisha,
who suddenly decided that he liked him very much. "Oh, certainly," he said, smiling in his turn and blushing, "that is, of course, if
you think it won't bore you. . . ."

"Well, I am not so sure," said Miss Clairmont, coolly. "Your
accent is so terrible, darling Hermann. One must speak English
properly, you know, or not at all. . . ." There was a sudden change
in her voice, a slight nasal constriction, a clipped quality. With
mingled delight and alarm Grisha realized that she was very
delicately and adroitly imitating his father. "What I propose to do is
read English books and discuss them. I have an extensive English
library, which I brought here through the good offices of my former
employers, the Zotovs. . . . I remember," she said turning to
Monsieur Gambs, "the terror that struck through me when we
stopped at Memel and I saw some poor Englishman—a titled one,
at that, he couldn't believe this was happening to him!—having his
luggage ransacked by the customs officers. They confiscated all his
books and letters. If they had taken this from me—my dearest
possession. . . ." She raised the book she was carrying to her face
and laid her cheek against it tenderly. "But we went through
without a hitch."

Grisha peered curiously at the faded gilt letters under the slim
fingers that had tightened convulsively on the book. *REV——
ISL——?*

"*Revolt of Islam,*" said Miss Clairmont. "Yes, indeed, a very
revolutionary book by a revolutionary author—or so your censor
would call him. Incalculably corrupt to young minds. . . . But I
shan't corrupt yours with it—not yet, anyhow." As she slipped it
nimbly into her reticule, Monsieur Gambs transferred his smiling
gaze to Grisha, as if inviting him to admire this unconventional
devil-may-care Miss Clairmont with her revolutionary volumes
fortuitously smuggled past the censor.

"You see, Prince," she went on disarmingly, "I am terribly
intimidated by your father, I tremble to think of what would happen

if he knew that I gave this book to you to read. . . . However, I am sure we will find something perfectly suitable in my library."

"I wonder," Grisha said diffidently, "if you perhaps have—" He frowned trying to think of the English title, and finally brought it out in Russian. "*Abidosskaya nevesta*. By Lord Byron. I have read it in Kozlov's translation, but I should love to read it—originally. . . ."

"In the original," Miss Clairmont corrected him, mechanically. And it was as if this first step into her teaching duties changed her—her charming voice flattened, all animation flowed out of her face. "The title in English is *The Bride of Abydos*. By Lord George Noel Gordon Byron." Her voice was pedantic and expressionless. She added: "I suppose he is read a great deal by young people."

"Well, my sisters admire *Lara*, and my brother Sergey admires *Corsair*, but he thinks *The Prisoner of Chillon* is boring. But it isn't, it's very—moving. . . . I should like very much to read *Don Juan* in English."

Miss Clairmont inclined her head without speaking. Her averted profile was a bleak sallow cameo, with lowered eyelids and thinned lips. Was that the mien, he wondered uneasily, that would be presented to him during their non-Socratic dialogues?

They had arrived at the edge of a small overgrown pond that lay twinkling serenely within its frame of rushes. A couple of ducks circled it sedately, drawing faint glassy furrows after them. On the farther side two old men wearing their faded house-serf uniforms sat on the bank with their lines. As they watched there was a brief silvery commotion in the water, one of the lines tautened, and the children ran around to see the catch. Monsieur Gambs loped after them, boyishly.

Miss Clairmont stayed where she was, craning her long neck after them. She looked alien and mournful against the sunny landscape, like a migratory bird of unknown species that had briefly alighted in a backwater refuge.

Claire's Journal, July 12

How strange to feel that limping presence at my side again, to hear the halting step. I look into the boy's hazel eyes, so distrustful, so vulnerable, and I wonder: "Is that how *he* was at eighteen?"

[28]

Oh, dear, dear, dear, how badly I used to want to know all about *him*—how he was as a child, as a boy, a very young man growing up. I would have given anything to have been a part of his life then. And then afterwards, how I wanted *not* to know anything, to forget it all. I was *rigid* with the need not to feel. When the news came last year that he was dead, I tested myself coldly: no, I didn't care. Not about him or anything. And, devoutly to be hoped, would never again. Loving people is too hard on one—all sorts of dreadful things happen, they die, they kill you. . . .

And it really is quite possible and even comfortable to live on the surface, skimming the thin nourishment you need from the top of any relationship. When Tre—dear, vainglorious, piratical Tre!—wanted me, I was able to sidestep him, with only a flutter of complacent pleasure at landing such an exotic bird. Pluck a feather from his preening plumage and let him go—no love, please. . . . And Hermann, too—I told him immediately that I valued him immensely but couldn't love him—or anyone else. But that was all right—in fact, I know he was relieved. He was immediately able to put me on a pedestal. For the other thing he goes elsewhere. The other day going for a walk around the pond I flushed Dasha, the plump little laundress, half-dressed out of the old bathhouse. Soon after Hermann made his appearance, somewhat more disheveled than usual and fixed me with eyes full of agonized question. Did I see, did I guess? Needless to say, I obligingly pretended that I was blind.

He was, nevertheless, as gloomy as Werther the whole day. I put my hand on his sleeve and he drew back and said, "Don't. Today I feel as if the touch of my hand on the hem of your dress would soil you." Like all Germans, he is terribly sentimental and romantic.

My most satisfactory *cavaliere servante* is lovely Vasska, who follows me wherever I go, purring at a touch of my hand. When I go up to my bedroom at night, he comes right along. Marya Ivanovna says jokingly: "There goes Miss Claire and her cavalier." Upstairs, as I undress, he watches me intently with his chin tucked into his white ruff. When I am in bed, he springs onto it and arranges himself carefully at my feet. Then gradually he makes his way upward and stretches himself on my supine body. His paws knead my breast, his amber eyes glare gently into mine, until sleep closes them. I daresay that warm weight on my loins, the occasional tiny pang as his claws penetrate the blanket and dig into my skin, are responsible for whatever disjointed erotic dreams I have. My harmless little furry incubus—I don't think I'll want any other bedmate for a long long time to come. . . .

Claire's Journal, July 13

I find it extremely—oh, liberating! exhilarating, even— to write in code. At first it was hard. Not a natural way of writing at all—and then, in spite of it, I was still being careful, as if writing for posterity—or perhaps for the eyes of my inquisitive employer. But the other day, I came upon her as she was going out of my room, and she gave me the most comically reproachful, *thwarted* look, every line of her expressive countenance saying, "I didn't expect you to be capable of such mean subterfuge." I knew beyond doubt that she had ferreted out my diary and couldn't decipher it. The rest of the day she was quite short with me and kept making bitter little remarks about odiously secretive natures. She is such a funny one! Anyhow, it was a sort of test. After it, all the restraints seemed to fall from me, and my pen began fairly to skim over the paper. Why, I could safely write anything, anything at all. Even obscenities!

The trouble is I know very few. Incredible how prudish we were, how primly we used to filter out of our ears the obscenities we heard all around us. Let me own this: women like us, in the middle zone of society, find it impossible to use bad language. The drab on the street— and Lady Caroline Lamb—may spout it happily. But Mary and I—we may speculate without restraint, question the existence of God, and rock the accepted tenets of morality without any difficulty at all—but my tongue boggles at even the slightest impropriety and my hand slows up trying to write it in my own secret never-to-be-penetrated journal.

What, for example, is the vulgar word for the male member? Do I know it? Of course I do. I remember, when I was a little girl of ten, my little brother Willy, scarcely six, confided a secret to me: "You know what? I call my cock Clarissa." And me staring at him in horror and bawling loudly like the detestable little prude I was: "Mother! Willy is using bad language!"

And Geordie, saying to me in his nighttime voice, "Oh, my lovely cunt." There, it took me a small struggle to write this down, but I did it! As for me, I used to call him "my lord." It was exciting somehow: that feudal form of address which we were brought up to deprecate—to use it in the moments of greatest intimacy, to murmur slavishly in bed: "Oh, my lord." All kinds of meanings clotted together—I found it curiously aphrodisiac. And he too. Those particular words uttered just then were like a spur applied to a thoroughbred's side at just the right moment in the race to get him over the line. Though I was the one mounted, I was in control. . . .

For the first two weeks after Grisha had started his lessons with Miss Clairmont, his mother kept questioning him closely about the Pomykov household. Grisha admitted cautiously to the considerable informality prevailing there. He was perfectly aware that if the Princess were to visit there (as though she ever would!) she would probably be scandalized and repelled: "slovenly" might well be her judgment and "exactly what could be expected from Marya Ivanovna Pomykov."

The servants, instead of being confined to their quarters to be summoned at need, lounged all over the house desultorily redding up, untidy and sleepy. The Pomykovs themselves were equally relaxed. Zahar Nikolaitch, though impeccable in his appearance when he set out for Moscow, let down shockingly when he came back and went about in a peasant blouse and a Turkish fez. Grisha found that rather endearing, but he didn't think his mother would. More disconcerting was Marya Ivanovna's habit of emerging from her bedroom in generous dishabille to engage him in sprightly conversation. He would stand before her, trying not to look, until

[31]

Miss Clairmont, neat and composed, came to his rescue and bore him away to his lessons.

Their social life was very full. Neighbors came in swarms to drink tea or dine, casual visitors stayed overnight, and Zahar Nikolaitch, coming back from Moscow, would be sure to have in the carriage with him two or three more guests, who would doss down with the minimum of formality in the big rabbit warren of the house. Marya Ivanovna, an indifferent housekeeper, was frenetically hospitable. Her face shone with complacence when upward of thirty persons sat down at the table for tea or dinner.

The Princess was particularly concerned about the Pomykovs' social circle. "He's an avowed *carbonare* and she dotes on Rousseau—God only knows whom Georges can meet there," she would say to her husband. She listened with a certain haughty incredulity while Grisha obediently listed the Pomykov guests. She was unimpressed by the fact that Genichsta, a talented young composer and musician who was beginning to be known all over Moscow, would come up and play duets with Miss Clairmont. But she was reassured to learn that they were on good terms with their neighbor the Count Lapochkin, that General Mack was a frequent guest, and that Count Tolstoy came to stay the weekend.

The visitor who impressed Grisha most was of a different order. "I understand you are a great admirer of Pushkin, Prince," Zahar Nikolaitch said to him one weekend. "Well, a very close friend of his is visiting us today. Ivan Ivanitch Pushchin." He nodded toward a slender man of average height, with a pleasantly flat Asiatic face. He was wearing civilian clothes, but there was something military about his bearing: as he conversed with Marya Ivanovna, he flexed one knee and bent the other, keeping one bent arm behind him, in the same attitude of exaggerated attention, as young lieutenant Kakorchine addressing himself coquettishly to the young ladies at the samovar. Immediately that pleasant but undistinguished figure acquired in Grisha's eyes an aura of reflected glory. "Pushkin's friend, *maman, figurez-vous*! . . ."

The Princess was less than enchanted. "You and your Pushkin, Georges! They say he has written some positively scandalous verses—about his Majesty, no less! If his friends are anything like him . . ."

The arrival of Grisha's older sister in a delicate condition put an end to those catechisms. His mother's attention slipped from him, focused on the rounded protuberance that had become an adjunct to her daughter's usually trim figure. She now merely occasionally alluded to Islavskoye as "Georges' second home."

The Prince too was interested in Grisha's visits to Islavskoye. His inquiries however were limited to the educational aspect.

The house was full of young ladies, relatives of Marya Ivanovna, who periodically arrived with their governesses, and filled the house with flutter and noise. Grisha steered clear of them. They were all of them rosy round-faced gigglers who ignored him, reserving their attention for the young officers whom Marya Ivanovna swept up along with others into the net of her indiscriminate hospitality. Miss Clairmont impartially taught them all English. But since his level was far above theirs, his lessons with Miss Clairmont continued strictly à deux. The weather remaining superb, they usually took place in the garden, in a small wooden pavilion—which in Russian, aptly enough, goes by the name of bessyedka or "little conversation."

The little girl Dunia usually came along. She was a fragile, silent child, apparently greatly attached to Miss Clairmont, much given to twining and sidling and hiding behind skirts. She would lean against Miss Clairmont's knee and with her finger in her mouth fix Grisha with an attentive, enigmatic gaze. After a while he learned to disregard it, just as he ignored the fixed amber stare of the cat Vasska, who also stayed underfoot during these lessons. Dunia would listen to their conversation and suddenly burst into laughter, mysteriously amused by some combination of foreign sounds. For some reason the words "how many" caught her fancy. She seemed to endow them with a certain plaintive mesmeric quality and would go about her solitary games, mournfully crooning, "How many, how many," until all meaning washed out of the words.

Occasionally Monsieur Gambs would impetuously waylay them on their walks to read aloud a passage from a book or a poem. He was subject to such enthusiasms and had jottings secreted all about his handsome person; sometimes, when he read them in his pleasant sonorous voice, tears would come to his eyes.

Once, as he was leaving Islavskoye, Grisha picked up a scrap of paper from the grass, covered with writing that had the special contours of a poem. He took it with him to read, guiltily postponing until afterward his recognition of Monsieur Gambs' elegantly spiked handwriting.

. . . Ton nom peut vivre dans mon coeur . . .

Je veux y graver ton image;
Ton oeil voilé de souvenirs,
Ton âme enflammant ton visage
De haine pour de vains plaisirs. . . .

It went on in that vein. Grisha read it all respectfully. He was aware that Monsieur Gambs considered himself a poet—quite a few of the verses he read so emotionally were his own and it was commonly known at Islavskoye that he was working on a French epic poem entitled *Moïse*.

Grisha took the poem—he had no doubt to whom it was addressed—back with him when he went for his lesson the next time. The weather for once was overcast. He was shown into the second parlor and found it transformed into a combination of a bazaar and a zenana. Open trunks hauled down from the attic gaped with old-fashioned court dresses, crinolines, furs, parchment-colored laces, artificial flowers, and trinkets of every description. All the young ladies were there, burrowing into the trunks and posturing before mirrors with antiquated gowns held up against them; a small corps of house maids was picking up after them.

Monsieur Gambs's pleasant baritone declaiming French alexandrine verses rose above the feminine hubbub, and Grisha spotted him, with a book in his hand, inexplicably dressed in an oversize, fantastically embroidered Persian robe trimmed with sable. A slight nostalgic haze of camphor lingered about him. Two maids crawled at his feet pinning up the hem of this extraordinary garment while Miss Clairmont, standing on a chair, was winding a scarf around his head.

He broke off reading to greet Grisha. "We have decided to put on Racine's *Esther*," he announced. "Hence all this Oriental confusion. I am to be the villainous Amman, and Miss Clairmont will be Esther, with all these handmaidens to tend her."

"Marya Ivanovna has promised to stop on Loubianka and get us Oriental shawls," said one of the girls, who was carefully trying on a bridal pearl-seeded *kokoshnik*. The traditional Russian headgear hiding her French coiffure transformed her totally—suddenly a peasant bride right out of a village wedding looked back at her out of the mirror.

Miss Clairmont, having finished draping an impressive turban on Monsieur Gambs's head, leaped down lightly from the chair. "*Voyons,* perfect," she said, contemplating her handiwork with pleasure. "It's those Oriental arched eyebrows of yours, Hermann, they support a turban admirably." She lifted it carefully off his head. "I shall tack it down right here and now. . . . Do come in, Georges." (The formal Prince had been abandoned almost from the first. He had rather expected her to anglicize his name to George, but for some reason she adopted his mother's name for him, the sole gallicism in their otherwise English conversation.) "We were just waiting for you. We are all going to have an hour of English conversation with our Russian tea. Come sit here, next to me. Will you pour, Olga?"

The young lady in the *kokoshnik* took it off and, once again becoming a *jeune fille bien élevée*, took her place sedately at the table with the samovar, the others following suit. Monsieur Gambs, relinquishing his robe to the maids, leaned elegantly against the mantelpiece. Grisha swept a pile of clothing off the chair Miss Clairmont indicated, got his feet entangled in it and sat down rather suddenly. Flushing he looked around at the circle of rosy, round, interchangeable girlish faces. There was a pause broken by smothered giggles and Miss Clairmont, busy with Monsieur Gambs's turban, said imperturbably: "If you can't think of anything interesting to say, young ladies, offer nourishment. Catherine?"

One of the gigglers, suddenly very serious, said: "Will you have tea, sir?"

"Yes, thank you, Miss Catherine."

"Do you like—how do you say *varenye,* Miss Clairmont?"

"Jam."

"Would you like to have some jam with your tea?"

"Yes, thank you, I would."

The stilted conversation took him back to the nursery, with his sisters, at their favorite game "grown-up visitors." ("Will you have some cookies, Elizaveta Petrovna?" "Thank you, they are simply delicious, Sophya Petrovna.") Fighting over him. "He's *my* sick little boy." "No, my sick little boy." Their childish arms tight about him, they petted and bounced him on their bony little knees. Then, the game over, they would trip off, forgetting all about him. He would come stumbling after, crying to be taken along, and suddenly cruelty would flash on their faces. "Let's run away from Grisha." And away they'd run, laughing heartlessly. . . .

"I am so glad we're putting on a play." Miss Clairmont's voice fluted serenely through a conversational pause. "I have always loved anything to do with the theater, even as a little girl."

"Did you have plays in your house then?" asked one of Marya Ivanovna's pink nieces.

"Well, in point of fact"—her eyes narrowed with reminiscent amusement—"we did put on a performance of sorts. You see, we used to have quite a few exceedingly clever people come to visit—and very often we were asked to get up and deliver prepared lectures to them, from a lectern our father had made for us—all of us, even my little brother Willy. His chin used to just clear the top of the lectern."

The whole room fell silent respectfully contemplating the spectacle of learned tots holding forth from a pulpit made specially for the purpose by a fond and learned father.

"Mostly on philosophy. 'How charming is divine philosophy' was our motto. That's a quotation from John Milton, a great English poet of the seventeenth century. . . . My sister Mary was especially good at this. Her lectures at the age of eleven were really quite extraordinary. But then she was quite an accomplished little girl. . . ."

Monsieur Gamb nodded, smiling, as if he knew all about it, and something like envy darted through Grisha. He said, "I am sure you too were accomplished, Miss Clairmont."

"I am most obliged to your lordship for the compliment," said Miss Clairmont, smiling and inclining her slender body toward him. "My talents lay in another direction. I would usually be called upon to sing and perform on the piano."

"A Euterpe to your sister's Egeria," Monsieur Gambs observed. "It seems to me you must have been the best-informed young ladies in England."

"Yes, indeed we were a product of a very special education. Extraordinary care was lavished on it—philosophy, classics, language—just as though we were men. . . . But there was one bad thing about our education," she said, with a slight derisive smile. Her thickish dark eyebrows quivered and rose—a trick Grisha learned to recognize as a prelude to her wry witticisms. "Along with our—accomplishments, it gave us very expensive tastes in men."

"Oh, Miss Clairmont!" The girls cooed and tittered delightedly, enraptured by this bold Miss Clairmont, who, meanwhile, with her close-lipped little smile, took the few last stitches in Monsieur Gambs's turban. "You see, we were taught to venerate greatness above everything—so neither of us could be content with any but the very best. As a result"—she paused and bit the thread off between her white teeth—"as a result, young ladies, you see me here, a spinster, teaching English in a foreign country far away from home. . . . If you have finished your tea, Georges, I'll ask you to read for us from *Rosamund*. First volume, page 22."

But Grisha only had time to read aloud one page of Mrs. Edgeworth's excellent book—far below his level—when Madame Pomykov's voice was heard; she swept in triumphant in her going-to-Moscow plumage, followed by two footmen, with packages chin high. Those packages were deposited on chairs, adding to the pleasant chaos already reigning in the room, and girls crowded about them, clamoring happily.

Grisha and Monsieur Gambs escaped into the garden, where Grisha returned the poem to its author, owning blushingly that he couldn't help reading it.

"My dear sir, no harm done, I welcome your reading it," said Monsieur Gambs affably. "Just a little poetical offering for Miss Claire's birthday, which comes next month. I may add that better poets than I have written verses to Miss Clairmont. Still. . . ."

He regarded Grisha smilingly, his head to one side, waiting for comment, and Grisha suddenly felt almost pitying affection for him. Monsieur Gambs was an older man, an accomplished scholar, and plentifully endowed with social graces. But the eagerness with which he awaited Grisha's judgment on his poem made them equal.

"I enjoyed it very much, it's an excellent poem, Monsieur Gambs. . . . I particularly like that line about her eyes veiled with memories . . ."

Monsieur Gambs flushed girlishly. "Yes, that's rather good, isn't it? There is a certain air of noble mystery about her, isn't there?" Grisha agreed, somewhat doubtfully. There certainly was something about Miss Clairmont that inspired curiosity: he wasn't sure, however, that he would express that quality in such lofty terms. "This is a woman who has gone through ordeals that might have broken a lesser spirit, whose exquisite perception has been rarefied through suffering, who—in short, Prince, she's been through a very bad time," Monsieur Gambs said, dropping from the dithy-rambic to plain human sympathy and immediately soaring up again. "She who should be shining in her own firmament as a star among stars, to be displaced, thrust forth. . . ."

Entranced, Grisha saw Miss Clairmont revolving serenely to the sound of celestial music. Some silent convulsion, mysterious and disastrous, nudged her out of her appointed place: down, down she fell, her long black hair streaming cometlike behind her; then she reappeared, dimmed and subdued, on their horizon.

"I don't think it's too much to say that from her youth Miss Clairmont has been an intimate of some of the greatest minds in England . . ."

"Yes," Grisha interpolated eagerly, "when she was talking about the people who came to her father's house . . ."

"Exactly. As it happened, Coleridge was one of them—Lamb—you're not familiar with those names? And yet they are very important in modern English literature," said Monsieur Gambs, a touch pedantic all at once.

"More important than Lord Byron?" A thought struck him. "Do you suppose he too . . .?"

"Came to her father's home?" Monsieur Gambs's manner changed; in contrast to his previous warmth, it now became restrained, almost cautious. "Well, hardly. A member of English aristocracy would not ordinarily seek out a commoner, even if he happened to be the country's foremost political philosopher. . . ."

"Oh, is that what Mr. Clairmont was?"

"His name wasn't Clairmont. You see, Prince, he wasn't actually her father but her stepfather."

"What was it, then? Was he famous? Oh, Monsieur Gambs," Grisha blurted out impetuously, "I do wish I knew more about Miss Clairmont."

But Monsieur Gambs was shaking his head at himself. "Some-times," he said, "one gets carried away. I don't believe Miss Clairmont would relish a discussion of her background, no matter in what respectful and admiring terms it was couched. . . . Thank you, Prince, for your sensitive and gratifying criticism of my little poem."

As he rode home, it occurred to Grisha that in many ways Miss Clairmont dominated his imagination as much as Matryosha had last summer—though, of course, quite differently. He considered the possibility of silently worshiping Miss Clairmont, like a hero out of a Richardson novel. Adoration from afar was both romantic and safe. You languished in secret and wrote poems to the object of your passion and ran no danger of being rebuffed. The only trouble about this was Miss Clairmont herself. She simply refused to fit into the pattern of a Richardson heroine.

"Well, I certainly am no Sir Charles Grandison," he thought wryly.

He remembered, as he often did, that incredible look she gave him the first time they met: that incomprehensible, utter tenderness that had momentarily poured over him. That look never occurred again and, in fact, might have been pure imagination on his part. And yet, now and then, he fancied that he saw a faint reflection of it in her great dark eyes; that, behind the measuring look of a teacher assessing the material she had to work with, there was a secret speculation pertinent to him alone.

Perhaps it was fatuous of him to imagine this mysterious particularity: Miss Clairmont was curious about everything: she had admitted as much the other day, when he had stayed on after his English lesson to have tea with the Pomykovs. "I am afraid that is my besetting sin," she had said, "to want to know too much, about too many things. . . ."

"But isn't that true of all daughters of Eve?" Zahar Nikolaitch had countered with an indulgent smile. Turning away to talk to a guest, he missed Miss Clairmont's gnomic reply: "No, only of the daughters of Lilith. . . . You look puzzled, Monsieur Georges," she went on, turning to her pupil and automatically switching to English. "Don't you know who Lilith was?"

He had shaken his head, intrigued. The name had a seductive, Oriental story-book flavor.

"I shall tell you, then," Miss Clairmont leaned back in her chair, and wrapped her shawl closer about her. She was always cold in the evenings. Her long stay in Italy, she claimed, had melted all the British ice in her veins and left her vulnerable to the Russian cold. "You see, Adam's first love was not the housewife Eve, but Lilith. God made her at the same time as he made Adam, out of the same clay, and they were equals. But God, essentially a male principle, eventually became uneasy about the pair. There they were, free of fear and curious about everything, ranging all over Eden, always wanting to know about everything, and egging each other on to ask questions. Why? why? why? They were a danger to Him with their terrible curiosity and *no* sense of limitations whatsoever. And Lilith was the instigator, she was the one who led the way. So He banished her to another part of the garden, and He put Adam to sleep, commanding him to forget about Lilith. Then He made him a proper wife—out of his body, this time. And Adam did forget about his first love. But Lilith prowled about the garden, making mischief, biding her time. . . ."

She had a true story-teller's manner, that mesmeric cadence that draws a listener into complete absorption. Grisha was reminded of his nurse Tikhonovna, who was a remarkable story-teller, and used to keep him bound to his chair with her cozy long-drawn-out tales about Ivan Tsarevich and the Firebird, the wicked sorcerer and the Tsar-maiden.

"Occasionally Lilith managed to escape celestial surveillance and find Adam. And they *talked!* Just as they used to, speculating about everything. Eve never did, you see, she just listened. . . . Well! It was Lilith and not Eve who got Adam to taste the apple from the tree of knowledge. Adam and Eve were banished from the garden, and so was Lilith. But even on earth she went on with her troubling ways, luring Adam from Eve whenever she could, putting ideas in his head. And thus into the dull dough of Eve-begotten humanity there came the wild leaven of Lilith's seed. . . . Well, that's the parable of Lilith."

"I should imagine Adam would always want to be with Lilith," Grisha said thoughtfully.

"Oh, no, I don't think he did. Men don't really like intelligent women. But sometimes they can't help being for a time attracted to them . . . So you liked my story?"

"Yes, very much. Did you make her up—Lilith?"

"Not at all. You can find many mentions of her in old rabbinical literature," said Miss Clairmont, in her teacher's voice. "And the Bible mentions her once—not very flatteringly. Some have even claimed that she was an Assyrian witch. . . ."

"I like your version."

"Oh, it isn't mine. It was an idea of a very dear friend of mine, who was considering writing a new version of *Paradise Lost*. It was to be a very ambitious, daring work, dealing with women's capabilities. He was one of few men who wasn't afraid of handling that subject. It would have been his major work, a great soaring

[40]

poem. . . . But it never got beyond being an idea that he discussed with me. He died before he had a chance to write any of it," said Miss Clairmont, with a rigid smile. All at once it dissolved. Her eyes glittered, her longish nose and eyelids reddened, her whole face turned ugly with trying to hold back tears. "You must excuse me, Georges," she said in a low voice and, dipping her long neck down, rose from the chair and glided out of the room.

Claire's Journal, July 15

After P.B. died I tried to remember everything about him with unimpaired vividness. The way he laughed, for example; unable to stop, as though possessed with happy hysteria. His blue eyes would be suffused by laughing tears and a single hyacinthine vein would swell on his delicate temple. A certain delighted grimace he made, when he approved of something; I knew the mechanics of it, I could almost reproduce it on my own face, so dissimilar to his. I used to practice it before a mirror, so I wouldn't forget exactly how it was. . . . But it faded with time, it all faded; I no longer remember him with the same clarity. I can reproduce in my mind the sound of his laughter, sweet and shrill, but how much sweeter than shrill I can't exactly remember. . . .

Claire's Journal, July 18

I promised young Prince Volynski Coleridge to read. Later, looking through my books, I came across *Lamia*. Suddenly it all came back to me. Curtains drawn across the windows, darkly flickering flames in the fireplace, and Geordie's voice talking horrors. . . . We had been talking about demons and ghosts, and he said: "Did you ever notice that in every folklore all the worst demons are female?" I can still hear that soft voice (it always went soft when he wanted to hurt) going through the catalogue: the succuba that sucks out your breath, the harpy that pollutes your food, the nocturnal hag that rides you until you're lame—and then came that passage from *Lamia*:

Behold, her bosom and her side
Are hideous, old and foul of hue . . .
A sight to dream of, not to tell . . .

I glanced at P.B.: he had been listening, his face gone blank with that extravagant attention with which he always listens—used to listen—to things. . . . I saw then that Geordie was frightening him—the way his flesh began to flow away from his cheekbones, leaving them stark, and he turned so pale that even in the firelight one could see the freckles. . . . And then as Geordie's voice began to rise, P.B. made a crying face like a frightened child and leaped to his feet. . . . He recovered almost immediately, and said that the reading made him think of a story he heard once about a woman with eyes instead of nipples, and, as he had looked at Mary, he thought he *saw*—Mary promptly clapped her hands to her breasts with such an air of outraged propriety that we all broke into laughter. . . .

But later—we were walking back to our cottage from his villa, our shadows trailing sooty behind us in the moonlight—P.B. said: "He really hates and fears women—be careful, Claire!" Well—I thought I knew what set Geordie off into that queer anger—he had been thinking of that horrible nurse of his, he had told me about her, coarsely and loathingly: "Nobody was corrupted as early as I was," he had said, "I was just a budding boy and she used to play with my bud." I couldn't bear to think of him soiled by that sordid old memory, so I waited until everybody in the cottage was asleep and then stole back to the villa, running as swift and quiet as a ghost across the moony fields, to charm it away, to show him that his Claire was neither a witch nor a harpy, that she loved him. . . .

Claire's Journal, July 19

After everything smashed, I went away as far as I could—they wondered about my "compulsive emigration to the north," as Trelawny called it. Why Russia, so far from everything and everybody? I would have gone to the

Antipodes if I could! And yet, even here, in this totally alien land, so utterly different from England and Italy that I might be on another planet, even here, I find old landmarks, hear old echoes. It's like a dream where you break your heart because the images you summon up are not totally what you've lost, just inadequately like it.

Take Hermann—so painfully an echo of P.B.—the enthusiasms, the encyclopedic knowledge, the same enlarged way of thinking, even some of that zany purity. But, oh dear, not enough—just the difference between his "Ode to Urania" and the "Hymn to Intellectual Beauty"—just enough to bring the loss back. And my lame pupil, with the same fatal name. And even little Dunia—ah, Dunia, just the age. . . .

Just the age—but nothing like, of course. The other one was an imperious lordly child, with dark blue eyes and firm round chin, cleft, like *his*. This one is a pallid little thing, with clinging, sidling, sidelong ways. Their old nurse calls her *russalochka*. That means "little mermaid." Hermann explained it to me—the Russian mermaid is not at all like the buxom fishtailed Teutonic variety, but a cold pale sprite, born of river mists.

Claire's Journal, July 20

A Monsieur Pushchin came to dinner. I had seen him before but had taken little notice of him. He is a mild young man, in late twenties, with a rather sweet smile on his somewhat flat dark face. Doesn't talk much, but listens very well, for which reason, I suspect, he is a prime favorite with Marya Ivanovna. I had discounted him as a pleasant nonentity. But tonight Marya Ivanovna drew me into conversation with him—nothing significant, some point of information—and suddenly from under those modestly lowered eyelashes, there came speeding toward me a swift, practiced, frankly evaluating gleam, raking me up and down. It came as a surprise—I hadn't noticed anything like that in his conversation with the young ladies. But then one of the maids came in with a tray, and she too got this swift appraising up-and-down look. It occurred to me then that this gentle courteous butter-wouldn't-melt-in-his-mouth Pushchin was probably a very common sort of womanizer looking for easy conquests among his inferiors. Well, why not, wasn't Geordie like that too? Truly at ease only among barmaids—with them he never bothered with that weary old pose. . . .

At any rate, I was angry. A desire to retaliate, to get across to this man that a lowly governess isn't quite the inferior he thinks she is, overcame me, and when he looked at me next I met his look full, challengingly. Oh, dear me, what a mistake. It only got me a longer, fuller, more impertinent stare, plus a little smile that said quite plainly, "I'll attend to you presently, my dear, don't be impatient." Oh, infuriating. My anger rose another notch. And then, suddenly, came the usual weariness with it all—what do I care for this impertinent little voluptuary? What if he thinks me fit prey? What does it *matter*? Indifference hedged me about like a wall. The next time that impertinent stare just bounced off.

Later on Marya Ivanovna said to me, "Monsieur Pushchin asked me all about you." A faint jealous note soured her voice. Marya Ivanovna doesn't like anyone but herself to be noticed during her gatherings. She sees herself, I think, as a mixture of *Mesdames* Récamier and de Staël. The other day, at dinner table, seeing attention straying away from her, she brought it back forcibly by saying in front of assembled company in her loudest voice, "I am a perfect Messalina by nature." Zahar Nikolaitch, dear man, merely smiles at this.

She went on, "*Ce cher* Pushchin—he is the kindest man—just the type who can be counted on to dance with the wallflowers." I couldn't help a silent smile at this little needle, and Marya Ivanovna added: "But he is an eccentric too. At one point his whole family was terribly worried about him."

Seeing that she seemed bent on talking about him, I obliged by asking "Why? He does not seem the type to worry his family."

"Nor is he, really—the most devoted son, the tenderest brother . . . But, you see, he used to be in the army, and

[44]

doing remarkably well. And then he resigned. Do you know what he wanted to be? A policeman."

"A policeman?"

"*Oui, ma chère, c'est ça,* a plain ordinary policeman, *un quartalnyi*! It was with great difficulty that they talked him out of that. Instead he became an examining magistrate. . . . And that after making a brilliant career in the army! Brilliant!"

"But *why,* Marya Ivanovna?" All at once I was curious: it seemed so unlike the man. Marya Ivanovna merely switched her plump shoulders and said vaguely: "Oh, they are all revolutionaries in the army."

Monsieur Pushchin's name came up again during our English lesson: "I do like Monsieur Pushchin tremendously. You know, he is Pushkin's best friend." Here my little Prince went all starry-eyed. They all have a special feeling here for a poet named Alexander Pushkin. I have been solemnly assured that he is one of the world's greatest. "The equal of your Byron," they say, by which I daresay they mean that he is one of his many imitators. Hermann, who knows Russian quite well, does assure me that there is an unusual strength and clarity in his poetry. All I can say is that all this must be lost in translation, because when he tries to English it for me it leaves me cold.

"Imagine," Georges said, his hazel eyes round with wonder, "imagine being a friend to a real poet, a great one. . . . Why are you smiling? Did you know that Monsieur Pushchin is Pushkin's friend?"

"No. All I know about Monsieur Pushchin is that for some reason he wanted to be a policeman."

"Well, I know the reason, Miss Clairmont. It is because he wanted to show that there is no menial place for serving the people."

I merely stared at him, *bouche béante.*

"Zahar Nikolaitch told me so. That's why he left the army and became a judge: because he wanted to serve the people. I—I think that's very admirable, don't you, Miss Clairmont?" said Georges, in his serious young voice.

Wanted to serve the people. . . . that charming, demure

little woman chaser? People are eternally surprising, it seems. . . .

Arriving at the Pomykovs' one afternoon, Grisha found the house deserted except for old Pavel, Zahar Nikolaitch's elderly valet, catching up on his sleep on a trunk in the corridor. "They are all at the meadow down by the pond," he said languidly, dragging himself to attention, "having a picnic, your Excellency." Grisha went down to see, not perfectly sure of the location but directed halfway across the garden by the sound of voices. A child's joyful squeal reached him, as he limped hurriedly along the trampled path to the clearing from which the voices came.

They were playing *goryelki*. The whole household participated as well as the guests: there was Marya Ivanovna paired with Monsieur Pushchin, and Zahar Nikolaitch handfast with plump Anyuta from the sewing room. Miss Clairmont had paired off with Monsieur Gambs. He loped along with awkward plunging gait, and she ran at his side beautifully, like a dancer. Her black hair had tumbled down and was streaming out behind her. She shrieked with laughter when Johnny, who was being the tag, caught up with her and threw his arms around her narrow waist.

Something dark and sullen welled up from the depths of Grisha's soul. He watched for a minute and then turned and stumped away blindly, so enclosed in his unreasonable anger that he actually strayed off the path into the uncleared thicket. For a while he found a fierce, self-punishing satisfaction in fighting his way through it, savagely breaking off the black alder branches that whipped against his face. His rage was directed mostly at Miss Clairmont. The sight of her running and laughing was somehow a deep betrayal that made all her kindness to him seem like odious pretense.

Miss Clairmont was waiting for him in front of the house, winding her black hair up into a knot on top of her head, her breast rising and falling under the sprigged muslin fabric of her dress. He stared at her stupidly, completely thrown off balance by her unexpected appearance, and she said to him, speaking indistinctly because of the hairpins in her mouth: "I saw you going away . . ."

Grisha's face went wooden. Not only running around and laughing in that intolerable manner, but also spying on him as she ran! He said stiffly: "I was under the impression that this was the time for our lesson, but since you were otherwise occupied . . ."

He shrugged his shoulders and made a brief ironic bow, acutely aware that both the shrug and the bow were absurd, and the tone of the remark boorish, and that he couldn't help either. Disregarding it all, she said quickly, "No, wait," stretching out her hand to him. Her hair fell down again. With an impatient little sound, she wound it up swiftly, skewered the hairpins through it (her dark eyes compellingly holding him where he was all the while) and was again the neat Miss Clairmont.

"I called after you," she said, "but you wouldn't stop."

"*Il n'y avait pas besoin . . .*" Grisha began stiffly.

"English, please."

"There was no need . . . Since you were enjoying yourself . . ."

"Well, and so I was. But don't you know, my dear Georges—"

He waited, rigid: she would say now that she preferred being with him and he would hate her forever for having the presumption to lie to him out of pity.

"—haven't you discovered yet that I'd rather teach than play any time? I love teaching more than anything. . . . Well, come along."

Deflated, he meekly followed her to their *bessyedka*.

They read *The Rime of the Ancient Mariner* by Coleridge aloud and she drove him through the pages mercilessly, pouncing on every mistake, berating him for every bit of slovenliness in pronunciation. The reading over, she shut the book and looked at him, smiling. An answering smile shaped itself sheepishly on Grisha's reluctant lips. He was feeling rather silly. Now that the incident was over his reaction seemed inexplicable to him, a shameful childish tantrum over nothing. Was she going to scold him for it? But no, she merely offered him, as usual, his choice of subject for the rest of the hour. "What shall we talk about, Georges? I am at your service." She folded her hands in her lap, miming obedience.

"I don't know," said Grisha, comically at a loss. "I can't think . . . Unless I was to tell you the dream I had last night," he added, unexpectedly to himself.

"No, don't," said Miss Clairmont, hastily. Grisha bowed, discomfited. "Does she think I am going to tell her that I dreamed about her?" he thought resentfully.

Because it was nothing of the sort, but merely a recurring nightmare of his, which he both welcomed and feared. The beginning was delightful: by a gigantic effort of concentration, he

[47]

would rise out of his bed and flap heavily, like a night owl, out into the darkness. For a long time he would swoop and wheel over the sleeping earth, his heart full of exhilaration. Then the denouement would come, as he always knew it would: perhaps that very knowledge brought it on. He would suddenly find himself in the midst of a host of starlings. Chattering, clacking shrilly, they would zigzag about him, pecking at him with their sharp little bills, their small shiny eyes glaring wickedly, until the impetus of his flight faltered and he thumped heavily back into bed. "Birds," his nurse Tikhonovna would say, nodding her head wisely, when he told her about it, "that means money, wealth, my darling." But somehow he didn't think so.

"It's not a good idea to listen to anyone's dreams," said Miss Clairmont. "It tells you too much—then you're never forgiven." Her black eyes were kind and shrewd on him. "I don't want you angry with me for telling me your dream, Georges. Not now that we're getting to be good friends."

To his own surprise Grisha blurted out, "I wouldn't mind your knowing."

Miss Clairmont shook her head regretfully. "Yes, you would, Georges. You may not think so now, but you would. I'm speaking from experience. Once someone told me a dream he had. Then afterwards he could never forgive me. . . ." Her voice went low. "No, never . . . You see, dreams are so deep, such an important part of you. Being made to part with one is almost like a violation. And I did—I made him . . ."

"Made him? How could you, if he didn't want to?"

"Well, that was it, he did and he didn't. It could go either way. I—pushed him." One corner of her mobile mouth went down. "I meant it for the best, naturally. I knew how it tortured him. In the morning, hollow-eyed and wan, he would say, 'I had that damned dream again.' Hating it, fearing it. Stands to reason he would want to share the horror. 'Tell me,' I said, 'Geordie. It's neither necessary nor good to bear your burdens alone. It'll ease you to tell me. . . .' Well, I was right. After he told me, he never dreamed it again. . . ." She was silent, receded deep into herself, at once a spectator and participant in some hidden drama.

"Geordie," Grisha repeated, savoring the strange name, with its syllables harsh and caressing at the same time.

With a flick her eyes came back to him. "Yes, Geordie. That

sweet name out of his Scotch childhood that nobody else used. . . . His first name was George."

A small galvanic shock went through Grisha as the gruff British monosyllable, so unlike the soft Gallic *Georges*, struck his ear. All at once with every bit of him he wanted to hear more about this man, who had a name like his and strange dreams that it was dangerous to know.

He asked tentatively: "Is—is he the one who was going to write about Lilith?"

"The same who . . . ? Oh no." She gave a soft scornful chuckle. "No, it wasn't P.B. P.B. wouldn't have minded. Crystal clear—open—no dark recesses in him . . . And even if there were, he would have forgiven—he could forgive anything. No, it was someone else, quite different—a *clenched* man—grudging of himself . . ." She contemplated the specter darkly. Then, recalling herself, she gave the characteristic little shake of her whole person that brought her back to her everyday academic self. "At any rate, I no longer let people I care for tell me their dreams. . . . But one day, perhaps, if I think I ought to, I might tell you his." Walking into his mind with exasperating ease, she added, "No, it won't be a betrayal. You see, he is dead now." Bending her dark head to one side, she repeated musingly, "Dead." The word had a totally noncommittal sound.

"He too?" Grisha said, involuntarily.

"Yes, he too." Her large dark eyes rested on him, speculatively. Her face wore the expression he was to learn to know only too well: the blank look, just tinged with apprehension of someone who is conscious of being about to do something irrevocable, the merits of which had not yet been decided and indeed still are a matter of considerable doubt.

"No harm telling you about it right now," she said slowly. "Why not, after all? . . . It was a very real and detailed dream. He was in a huge room readied for some festive occasion. Chandeliers gleamed and tinkled, an unseen orchestra played delectable airs, and at the far end of the room, by a table laden with exquisite fruits and wines, a host of people waited for him to join them. All of them were people he knew well—his mother, his friends and admirers, his mistresses . . . oh, and his wife, of course. Not at all surprising, that." She stopped, pondering this statement with a grim little smile.

"Oh, he was married then?" Grisha said inanely, merely to put an end to that disconcerting silence.

"Yes, but estranged from his wife. In fact, she was the cause of his having to leave England. . . . It was perfectly natural for her to be there in that waiting group. But he also included all his mistresses, of which he had a considerable number. He was one of those beautiful flawed men who are disastrous to women. Every time he dreamed this dream—it was a recurring nightmare—he included another one of his lovers. . . . I still remember how relieved I was that I hadn't yet appeared there."

Oh so that's how it was, Grisha thought.

"Afterwards, he said to me, 'I suppose tonight you will be in my dream too.' 'No,' I said to him, 'Geordie. I'm not here to add to your nightmares.' And I didn't. . . . In his dream, he told me, he starts walking toward the assembly. And they are watching him all that time. Cold, silent, immobile, like a crowd at a funeral. . . . And gradually, *slowly*, he begins—not to hear—but *sense* laughter. Quivers of it run across the motionless faces staring at him—their shoulders begin to shake with it—another moment and a gale of it will sweep him away . . ."

The starlings swept, skirling, into Grisha's mind, pecking him down out of his dream.

"And then—and then comes the shameful part. His words—not mine—I still remember the grimace of self-disgust with which he uttered them. In his dream, he said, at this point he begins to shout and strike attitudes and declaim—oh, anything to prevent that terrible imminent laughter—and he keeps at it until finally he awakes in a rank sweat, sick with self-disgust. . . . You see, he had been born with a clubfoot and was quite lame. It was what he called his 'comic gait' as he walked across that room that he feared would make them laugh at him. And he would do anything to prevent that. . . ."

Grisha came to his feet as if stung, in an explosion of so many feelings that for a moment he couldn't focus on any and merely floundered in their turbulence. Through the ringing in his ears he heard her calm voice saying:

"Perhaps I am wrong, but that's not your trouble, is it? I don't think you worry about being laughed at, it is being pitied that you mind. Well, that wouldn't have bothered *him* much," she said with a touch of dryness, "he did quite a bit in that line for himself. . . .

But God! that corroding dreadful fear of ridicule that infested everything he did! What waste, what unnecessary suffering!"

Grisha said nothing. His feelings had sorted out and he was mostly conscious of a vast, all-engulfing, resentful embarrassment. But before he could bring himself to say anything, she spoke up again, crisply:

"Time to rehearse for *Esther*—are you going to stay and watch?" And rightly taking his disjointed murmur for refusal: "Then I must leave you. 'Til tomorrow, then!"

When he finally looked up, she was a mere white shape flitting away from him through the sun-permeated tunnel of the lime alley.

Claire's Journal, July 23

Why did I start talking to him *so*? I don't really know. I suddenly wanted to. I think it was the dumb fury with which he limped away, the dark look of rage, the formal words overlaying the deep resentment. It was almost as if *the other one* were looking at me through his resentful eyes. Even the words were the same . . . "Pray go on enjoying yourself." That's what *he* had said that day when he came into our cottage and found Mary playing Ranz des Vaches, and me dancing, whirling round and round with little Wilmouse in my arms. . . . A fatal resemblance— surely it couldn't be there for nothing. I was all at once possessed by a mystic sense of parallel, it seemed as though I was being given an—an opportunity. My weary indifference cracked and out of the crack there came a tiny, thin, tendriled plant; its name was curiosity. . . . And there I was again launched into one of those double-tongued conversations, in which one speaks not so much to the person one is addressing as to another, the unseen, wary listener lurking within. . . .

"Had a good ride, Excellency?" Fedka sang out merrily, springing to Nelly's head as Grisha rode her into the stableyard. He was one of the younger grooms, a handsome tall fellow, with a ruddy, faintly pock-marked face and liberally oiled yellow hair. His shallow blue eyes sharpened as he took the horse. "Pecking a bit on the fore, ain't she?"

"No, is she?" Grisha dismounted hastily. Ordinarily he would have been the first to notice the slightest hitch in his darling Nelly's smooth gait. But all during the ride his mind had been preoccupied with framing reasons to give his father for not going on with his English lessons. At the usual time for his ride to the Pomykovs', he had found that he simply couldn't bring himself to go, he still felt too churned up and uneasy after the conversation of the previous day. Instead, he had his excuses sent to Islavskoye and spent the afternoon riding.

Fedka gently lifted Nelly's foot—her foreleg arching elegantly as he did so—and bent his yellow head over it. A whiff of cheap pomade and sweat reached Grisha's nostrils. The thickish red fingers, decorated with several rings and glistening with blond hairs to the knuckle, prodded and explored with careful gentleness. Nelly stood still, whiffling peacefully into his hair. "You aren't going lame, are you, my darling?" Grisha said anxiously, stroking her velvety nostrils. "Just picked up a pebble, we'll have it out in no time, don't you worry, Excellency," said Fedka in a reassuring, older-brother tone. Grisha sighed with relief: like all Andreyevo grooms, Fedka knew his business.

Prince Pyotr Andreitch Volynski, a passionate lover of horse-flesh, kept prime stables both in Moscow and in the country. His grooms, all of them, were possessed of an almost mystic expertise in handling horses. They were treated almost as well as the thoroughbreds they tended. Like them, they were a handsome, spirited crew. In their demeanor there was nothing either of the servility of the house serf or the stolid resignation of the peasant. They bore themselves with gayety and pride, like men who belong to a special class and know it.

"All right, then, you take care of her immediately, will you, Fedyushka, my friend?" said Grisha beseechingly.

"Never fear, Excellency, right away."

A stealthy motion just beyond his area of vision attracted Grisha's attention. Turning, he caught a glimpse of a white kerchief among the bushes behind the stables; it went fluttering like a big butterfly in the direction of the main house. Fedka gave a complacent man-to-man grin.

"One of the girls from the house, Excellency, visits here sometimes, like. . . ." His face shone with simple, sated, animal sensuality.

Grisha's answering smile held wistfulness. All at once Fedka's life seemed utterly enviable to him: spending all his time looking after horses, seducing willing housemaids, not bothering his head about anything. . . .

To be like him, like his brother Sergey—whole, unmarred, uncomplicated. . . .

At the dinner table, Prince Pyotr Andreitch remarked to him, "I hear you gave your lessons a miss today. Lovers' quarrel, eh?" He gave an unexpected short bark of laughter. Grisha too smiled but with some bewilderment. "I shouldn't like anything to interfere with your English lessons now that you're actually beginning to sound like a semblance of an English gentleman."

Nor, Grisha realized, did he, after all. Now that he had recovered from the discomfiture of the day before, the idea of staying away from Islavskoye dismayed him. He would miss the sprightly social life in which he marginally participated. Zahar Nikolaitch with his quirky acuity, the sweet-tempered Monsieur Gambs, even all the pink nieces and cousins, had become imbedded in the fabric of his own life and so had that other half-disturbing, half-sisterly presence, that punctuated a sense of perfect safety with unexpected shocks.

Going to his room he ran into Matryosha in the corridor and was aware of the usual sore-tooth twinge—diminished but still there. He forced himself to stop and acknowledge her timid dip of a curtsey and "wish-you-health, Excellency," with a "Good evening, Matryosha—I mean, Marie."

"I'm Matryosha again, Excellency."

"Really? How is that?"

"Evdokya Nikolavna—the housekeeper, your Excellency—they said I don't need to be called Marie now that I am no longer waiting on her Grace."

"Oh, aren't you?" He realized now that he hadn't seen her around for a few days.

"No, sir. I am in the scullery now. Evdokya Nikolavna—they say my peasant ways are too rough for her Grace." There was an indefinable dread in the way she kept referring to the housekeeper, peasant fashion, in third person plural. Her small breast went up and down in an abrupt childish sigh.

She wasn't looking well, Grisha thought. The sleekness, the roundness were gone, she was again the skinny waif of a summer ago. There were purplish shadows under the speedwell-blue eyes and the small mouth was pinched.

"I am sorry," he said awkwardly.

"Thanking you kindly, Excellency." With another little bob, she was gone.

The next day Grisha arrived in Islavskoye at the usual time and found Miss Clairmont in the garden, sitting under the great oak tree with her book. Dunia was nearby playing with her dolls, scrupulously giving each a turn on the swing.

Miss Clairmont raised her eyes from the book she was reading and saw him. A surprised radiance flooded her sallow face. "Oh, Georges, I am so glad. Oh, do sit down. I didn't think you'd come back."

Disregarding his embarrassed protest, she went on earnestly. "No, you see, this is a fault of mine—I do too much—I presume. Nothing is more irksome than having other people's memories foisted on to one. I shan't do so any more. . . ." Her tutelary crispness came back. "You have finished reading Locke's essay, I believe. We shall have it as our topic of conversation for today. He distinguishes ideas in two distinct orders: what are they?"

Until that moment Grisha hadn't realized how much he wanted to hear more about the man who had his name and his limp and was similarly tormented. He blurted out in an agony of disappointment: "Aren't you going to tell me more about *him*?" With some effort, he added, "I—I don't mind your talking about lameness."

And immediately Miss Clairmont's face underwent one of those disconcerting transformations. Her dark eyes liquid with tenderness, she leaned toward him so swiftly that for a panicked moment he thought she was going to kiss him. But she merely laid her narrow hand against his cheek. The touch was light and quickly withdrawn.

"Wait, let me think it out."

Silence ensued, complete except for the peaceful buzzing of insects in the sun-distilled shadow, and Dunia crooning, "How many, how many," as she cuddled a doll. Grisha watched Miss Clairmont's still face, anxiously. What was she thinking? It was like sitting by the pond at the end of the garden. The opalescent changes, the minimal ripples drawn across its surface by the passage of some tiny over-water skimmer, the deeper, more deliberate furrow indicating the sub-surface movement of a fish—

one could sit for hours watching it, half-mesmerized by these sparse evidences of the complicated submarine life.

The surface trembled, broke up, a smile, frank and sparkling, fountained upward.

"I daresay this could come under the head of English Conversation—if you keep your end up, Georges, and draw me out."

"What does that mean, 'draw out'?"

"Make the other person talk, by putting pertinent questions. The expression comes from drawing a cork out of the bottle. The idea is that then the contents pour out in a gush and drench you. . . . How to begin then?"

"At the beginning, perhaps?"

She smiled approvingly at the diffident little joke. "I suppose," she said slowly, "it all began with my letter. To him," and was silent again until Grisha, obediently following instructions, prodded her with: "What did you say in it?"

"That I loved him, that I wanted, more than anything else in the world, to meet him. The usual thing—usual for him, I mean. Being an important poet he used to get thousands of letters like that. 'Whatever possessed me to let you in?' he said to me. 'For months I have avoided company. I've put locks on the door and drawn a pentagram on the threshold to keep the devil out. And yet you've managed to find your way in.'

"'But you yourself bade me enter, my lord,' I said. So complacent, so proud of my clever conversation, my clever letter." She wrinkled up her long nose in disgust and beat the air with her hands as if chasing away a gnat. "I still cringe when I remember that fatuous, romantic, unworthy *sham* of a letter."

"Sham? You mean you only pretended? You didn't really love him?"

"No, how could I? I had never met him." With a glance at his dismayed face, she added quickly, "No, no, it's not as bad as all that, not a *deliberate* pretense. I was only seventeen and one can persuade oneself of anything at that age. Today of course I am able to break that grand passion down into all its not so grand components—hero worship, a desire for adventure, vainglory. . . . Envy, too. Yes, much of this was based on just plain envy. Isn't it odd," she said with mild wonder, "this is the first time in all those years that I can admit even to myself that I was just childishly envious?"

"Envy? Of whom?"

"Of my sister Mary. I suppose I have always envied her. I never was a pretty child, and she was, and so damnably accomplished to boot. And her mother was famous, while mine was merely a good housewife, and her famous father was merely my famous stepfather. And her hair fell naturally into those soft spaniel ringlets—oh, I wonder if you understand how it all just seemed so unfair!"

Grisha nodded, the image of Sergey complacently splendid in his green-and-scarlet uniform flashing into his mind.

"And then," she went on, still speaking in humorously rueful tones, "to cap it all, there was the matter of P.B. We were such kindred spirits, he and I, so marvelously attuned to each other, each understanding the other from a look, a half-word. But in a most inconsiderate fashion, he fell in love with Mary and not me. . . ." A laugh escaped her, spontaneous, fresh, girlish. "Oh, how Geordie used to tease me about it in Geneva! 'I can just see it,' he would say, 'the flutter in that household when P.B. walked in, a gawky young Gabriel bringing glad tidings. Well, Mary got them, appropriately enough—poor Claire, having to settle for being a mere handmaiden!' "

For a fraction of a moment Grisha got the full sense of both the man who had said these words and the man of whom they had been said; a twin vision, swiftly gone, like a pair of rare birds swooping into the range of one's field glasses, hanging there for a split second and flashing out again.

The little girl Dunia laid her doll down and came over. She clambered on to Miss Clairmont's lap and, winding her thin arms around the governess's neck, tucked her head under her chin.

Miss Clairmont's arms tightened around the child's skinny body. Rocking her dreamily, she went on, musingly and seemingly at a tangent: "I know envy is supposed to be one of the deadly sins. Well, it isn't—jealousy is. Envy is merely venial. But jealousy— that's a harpy of a passion befouling everything. All the ancient demons of possessiveness rise up and crouch over their prey, shrieking 'mine, mine.' What right has anyone to say 'mine' about what can't be possessed? P.B. never would. For him there were as many levels of loving as steps on Jacob's ladder and he ranged them all as effortlessly as a seraph. . . . But Mary . . ." She broke off with a frown and a tiny headshake at herself. "Never mind that. . . . *I* had never been jealous in my life. Envious—yes. I will own to that. . . .

"You see, Georges, all the girls in our family—Mary, I, even pathetic little Fanny—were brought up for greatness. In full expectation of achieving it. And at first we had no doubt we could do it for ourselves. Why not—superior young women that we were? A young man with half our accomplishments would be certain of making his mark in the world. And then—little by little—it began to be borne in on us that it wasn't going to be that simple. The channels open to respectable but indigent young women were few—they all led to rather dreary backwaters. Teacher, governess, most likely of all a disillusioned young woman on a shelf, waiting for a nonentity to condescend to marry her. . . . Oh, everything in me rejected this.

"You know how I used to feel? As if I were outside a very exclusive club, where the special, the elite were supping on nectar and ambrosia, and here I was *starving*," she said with an eloquent gesture, her face hollowed out with remembered hunger. "And I couldn't get in, any more than I could into White's: only men allowed. No lady would even *want* to get in! And then instinctively I knew—Mary, too—that in the long run, if you are a woman, you will be permitted to achieve greatness only indirectly, vicariously, through a man whom you help to achieve his. . . . So you begin to look for someone who can do this for you. Not consciously or deliberately, oh no, but by an instinctive natural process like the blind groping of ivy tendrils toward a supporting tree. . . .

"*He* asked me once, 'Tell me, Claire, if I were just an ordinary obscure man without fame or talent, would you have fallen in love with me?' I still remember," she smiled musingly, "the anxiety with which he waited for the answer: it mattered to him very much, because, you see, by then he was beginning to care for me. . . ."

She paused and Grisha, too, found himself hanging anxiously on her words.

"I said, 'No, I don't think so.' Not the answer he wanted. But it has always been a matter of pride with me to be absolutely honest, and I knew, I *knew*, I could never have fallen in love with an ordinary man. No, it was specifically his greatness that attracted me to him. But what did it matter? What did it prove?" said Miss Clairmont, suddenly turning to him fully and speaking with such intensity that he knew that she was no longer addressing him but someone else, no longer there yet somehow not totally beyond the reach of that low passionate utterance. "When I did love him—love is all of a piece, indivisible, you can't isolate its various elements. It doesn't matter how one starts loving, ultimately one loves another person just because he *is* that person. And that means everything about him—not only the greatness but *everything*, the way he smiles, the way he makes love. Both the soaring poetry and the halting walk. . . . How he balked at believing that! That what he regarded with such moral horror was just an imperfection, nothing more—something that only made one love him more. . . ."

Grisha listened to this with skeptically thinning lips. He had heard that line of talk before: Jesus Christ was supposed to love you in spite of your deformities—in fact, he was assured, because of them: it was a sort of recommendation to His favor. But however Our Saviour felt, plain ordinary people felt otherwise. They shrank from ugliness. Even—Miss Clairmont was wrong about this—even people who loved you. His mother loved him devotedly. Yet, when he was ill, she was not the one to tend him, she left it to the Nurse, and he knew why: she was too sensitive, it offended her to look at his ugly botched-up body. When his feverish tossings dislodged his blankets, he remembered how carefully she kept her beautiful careworn eyes averted from his foot until Tikhonovna had drawn the blanket back over it.

Dunia, who had been nestling quiet in Miss Clairmont's arms, now stirred restlessly. Raising her small hand she put it against Miss Clairmont's lips. "*Dovolno*," she said imperiously and repeated it in French, "*c'est assez*."

"You see, Georges, she sees right through pretenses," Miss Clairmont said merrily. "She knows it's not an English lesson."

Rocking the child faster, she went into a little song, obviously a familiar game: the little girl's replies came with ritual readiness.

"*Es-tu ma petite poupée?*"

"*Non, non, non.*"

"*Es-tu ma petite chatte?*"

"*Non, non, non.*"

"*Es-tu ma petite fille?*"

"*Oui! Oui! Oui!*"

"Aha!" Miss Clairmont sprang lightly to her feet and swung the little girl around and around. Her blue dress ballooned around her,

Dunia's pink pantalets flew. The two finally collapsed on the grass, breathless and giggling.

On the way back to the house Miss Clairmont said to Grisha: "Last night I was remembering and writing down what I remembered of that first time I saw *him*. If you think you'd like to read it . . ." With an odd little self-conscious laugh, she reached into her reticule and drew from it a packet of notes. "Ordinarily I write my journal in code. But, for some reason, last night I didn't—it just came out in English, in a gush, I don't know why. . . . Yes I do." The black eyes came back to his steadily. "I suppose I really meant it for you, Georges."

Claire's Journal, July 24 (given to Grisha)

. . . That first time I saw him, I wasn't really seeing him. A dazzling image of a young god stood between us, blocking my view of him as he really was.

The height was all wrong, for one. I had expected him to be at least P.B.'s height—taller, because P.B. stooped so. But even standing arrow-straight, as he did to make the most of his inches, it was apparent that he was almost a head shorter. That was hard to accept. For a while I stubbornly addressed my remarks to the Olympian figure I had envisioned, and a small handsome man answered me in a shy soft voice, as hesitant as a schoolboy's. Later, when he became furious with me, oh, dear, what cruelties came out of that adorable curved mouth in that low musical voice—how it flayed me!

Even now I can remember vividly every detail of the way he looked as he waited for me at the fireplace, leaning against the mantelpiece. His profile stood out against the dark green wall as clear as a cameo—sharp, *sharp*—every hair in every ringlet painstakingly etched out on my receptive mind.

The room was grubby—spiderwebs in corners, fat gray fluffs of dust under the furniture—and there was a grubbiness about him, too. The small aristocratic hand on which he leaned his curly head was not only ink-stained (*ink-stained*! I said to myself in rapture, imagining line after exquisitely rhymed line flowing out of that schoolboy clutch) but also grimy. And his linen wasn't clean. That jarred me, I must say. My mother, a demon housekeeper—Papa Godwin always wore the snowiest of shirts—had instilled in me from childhood the belief that, come what may, one's menfolk had to be kept immaculately clean. . . .

Ah, but his beautiful face fitted into my preconceived image all right! He had the most seductively molded lips I had ever seen and they curled in disdain. Apparently at first he cultivated a sneer through sheer shyness, to face the world which didn't appreciate him, and then, when it did, the disdainful cast of the mouth stayed, most becomingly. And he was pale—oh, the loveliest transparent luminous pallor—it gave his eyes a darkly celestial color, bluer than blue. Altogether he looked totally beautiful there, against the dark green wall, like some exotic butterfly pinned to green felt for my delectation—a marvelous specimen of a modern poet. I was lost in admiration. But when I fell in love, later that same day, it was for a reason having nothing to do with his brilliant looks.

It wasn't long before I found myself in trouble. He had remarked, "Do you know, if I were afflicted by your brand of hero-worship, I'd be damned careful to stay away from its object. Confrontation is the end of illusion, don't you know that, you silly girl?"

And I began to explain to him very carefully that I had no use for illusion. When I worship someone, I want to know everything about that person, good or bad; and I particularly wanted to know all about him. "Everything," I went on, foolhardily unmindful of the darkling look he suddenly bent upon me, "the reality—the truth of you."

"Yes, I know," he said very softly, "that's what all of you come sniffing around for."

Disaster! One minute I was secure in my glory, sipping nectar on Olympus; the next, my temple of glory came tumbling down about my ears.

"The truth of you," he said, mimicking my rapturous tones. "The reality—was he really such a beast to his wife that she simply had to snatch up the baby and run? Did he really sleep with his sister—well, half-sister, but half is better than none?" More and more disgust weighted his soft voice. "Is he quite possibly mad? Is he? Was he? Did he? Oh, God, what a glorious world it is." And then, lightly, negligently—he might have been turning out a drunken trull who had followed him into his house out of the streets—"I think you had better hop it, my dear. I am not in a confiding mood today. . . ." And with finality, "Good-day." And the small white hand reaching for the bell cord.

Somehow I found the strength to bring out: "If you send me away, thinking *this* of me, I will not want to live."

I meant it, too. I could see with bitter clarity the bottle of laudanum that P.B. kept in his room, the contents of which would presently go down my throat.

I think he sensed that I meant it. He stared at me, arrested, and I began talking with the drunken zany eloquence of someone pleading for his life. In our family, I told him, we were taught to probe and question—that is why I had to analyze just what it was in his writings that so stirred and attracted me. Everything he wrote began to seem to me after a while like a magician's cloak—oh, dear, how it begins to come back to me, that desperate, artful, extravagant pleading!—the purpose of which is not to reveal but to take attention away from the magician. But it was precisely the magician that I wanted to know about, he fascinated me even more than his blindingly magnificent cape, I was charmed by the riddle of the inner man. That was what I had meant. As for the immoderate myths about his private life, they meant nothing to me, they weren't even marginally on my mind. . . .

At this point I saw with horror how monstrously insensitive of me it had been not to realize that they were bound to be in his. . . . But it had never occurred to me that he could care. Surely he must know—tempestuously I went off at a tangent—that, being what he was, he would be bound to be attacked. There was such an innate contempt for the existing order in everything he wrote, everything he did, that it couldn't but make them uncomfortable—that's why he was being attacked, not because of his wife. . . . He had been listening morosely, while I blundered on in my misery. And all at once he said, with the slightest tremor of laughter in his voice, "Do you know what your difficulty is? You don't know when to stop talking. . . ." With a gasp I did so, I knew it was all right, I was saved . . .

Oh, how carefully I trod for a while, how I watched myself. Once, I remember, I slipped. I said to him: "You have such a *nolle me tangere* air—as if you were carrying something secret and precious and were afraid to be jostled. . . . I wonder what it can be." And then in a hurry: "No, I don't. I don't wonder a bit! It's none of my business!" And that made him laugh. He had the most endearing laugh—it changed his whole expression, bringing something childlike and trustful into his face. . . .

When he got angry at me, all over again, it wasn't my fault. A barrel organ had been playing a waltz outside. It had a sort of pervasive banal appeal that tunes of that sort have, and I found myself unconsciously swaying to it. And immediately he was onto me like a tiger. He said to me in that gentle voice in which I recognized the already familiar ominous undertone: "Would you like to take a turn around the room, Miss Clairmont? Unfortunately I won't be able to partner you."

All during our conversation, even when he was raging at me, he had not moved from his position by the fireplace. Quite unnatural it was—as if he were posing for a portrait in the most effective attitude he could assume. But now, as if to underline his words, he detached himself from the mantelpiece, and went blundering and lurching across the room to the window. He had this quick running way of getting around, on tiptoe, stepping on his lame foot as little as possible and coming to a rest as soon as he could. My young Prince just stumps along grimly. But *he* so hated his lameness that it was almost as if he tried to change it to anything else—a blundering flight, a sort of wounded-bird skimming run—anything but the hated limp. And, as he closed the window, with a bang, he looked back at me.

Everything changed then. Until that second I didn't really *see* him. In spite of everything I had been saying about wanting to know him, I was really too busy thinking about myself and the impression I was making. But when I met that look,—oh, such a proud, wary, vulnerable look!—I forgot all about myself and fell in love with him.

How different everything became: all at once I seemed to be inside his skin, knowing all about him. He repeated, still on that strangely accusatory note, "I am sure you dance famously, don't you?" And I knew instinctively what to say. "No," I said, casually, lightly refuting the accusation, "singing is what I do best." And knew by the way his shoulders unstiffened that I had said the right thing. . . .

The swift impatient script might have been a code in itself, so hard it was to decipher. Grisha puzzled it out, word by scribbled word, while his bedside candle flickered and wavered, straining his eyes until the underside of his eyelids began to feel sandy.

Wild speculations rose up in his mind as he read. There had been a frontispiece in a certain book—where was it? In their Moscow library? He would send for it tomorrow—an exaggerated curl of the lip, a moody stare from under a corsair's turban, a small white hand on the pommel of an ornate eastern dagger . . .

After a while he became conscious of a sound barely penetrating through the closed door of his bedroom; something like an insect's high-pitched whine, but infinitely dolorous in the still night. Irritated, he climbed out of bed and went out to investigate. Two figures huddled together in the corridor, their shadows conferring darkly behind them: Fomitch, candle in hand, was talking to Matryosha. Arms thrown over her head, rocking from side to side, she wept bitterly, a thin, sad, little-girl plaint. At the sound of the door opening, she stared at him aghast between her slender forearms and fled down the corridor, her felt slippers making no sound.

"Stupid girl, waking up your Excellency," Fomitch grumbled angrily.

"It's all right, I wasn't sleeping, Fomitch. What was the matter?"

"Nothing to bother your Excellency with. . . . Those girls! 'Nobody to talk to but you, Uncle, nobody to open my heart to.' And tears! 'Ssh,' I tell her, 'not so loud, you'll wake up the young Prince' . . ."

"Never mind that. Why was she crying?"

Fomitch sighed. "That damned Nikolavna, Excellency, may the devil take her, has been making her life miserable, needling away 'til she's like to be driven out of her wits, poor little soul."

"But why? What's she got against her?"

"That I can't tell, Excellency, God knows what starts eating those females, when they get to a certain age. It's like they can't stand to see a pretty young face around them."

A certain careful opaqueness in his eyes reminded Grisha of something that he had overheard once: that Nikolavna once was one of his father's many mistresses. Well, and Matryosha too . . . With a grimace of distaste for both of them, he said, roughly: "I'll tell her to quit."

"God forbid, Excellency, she'll go for the girl worse than ever. I know her kind, like a cat with a mouseling. . . . Claw her to death, she would. . . ."

"I see." Into Grisha's mind came the memory of those plump white hands relishingly inflicting punishment. "I suppose I'd better talk to my mother."

Fomitch looked pessimistic. "Do no good, either. Her Ladyship your mother she just leans on that Nikolavna like she was a stone fortress, hears with her ears, sees with her eyes. . . ."

"She certainly wouldn't want her to mistreat any of her girls," Grisha said, getting back into bed.

Fomitch sighed, drawing the bedcovers tenderly over him.

"Best leave it alone, Excellency. Not fitting for you to get mixed up in women's quarrels . . . I've got some ways of my own. I'll talk to Tikhonovna, she's a wise old body, maybe between the two of us we can blunt her claws a little, the damned bitch. We've done it before. . . ." He smoothed out the counterpane, painstakingly arranging it so that the great elaborately embroidered "V" was squarely in the middle. "You go to sleep, sir; a young boy needs his sleep."

"Good night, Fomitch. No, leave the candle be, I'm going to read a little."

Obscurely troubled, he watched Fomitch leave the room. Sometimes, as happened now, he would sense among the servants a subterranean society with its own firmly established hierarchies, feuds, and alliances having nothing to do with their masters; it was disconcerting—like looking through a magnifying lens at a colony of ants and seeing that they were wearing human faces.

The next morning while Grisha was having a lesson with Monsieur Lachaine, he happened to glance through the window of the schoolroom—it gave on the back of the house—and saw Matryosha furtively making her way through the bushes of the kitchen garden. Reaching the side door, she stopped for a minute, smoothing her dress and setting her apron straight. She replaited a loosened braid, turning her head from side to side as she did so, and the movements added to his impression of a wild creature, fearfully on the watch, expecting to be flushed out of its covert. He noted her emaciated, feverish look, with eyes too bright and too large for the small face.

"*Ah, ah, vous revez, Georges?*" said Monsieur Lachaine, reproachfully. "*Faites donc attention.*"

Grisha returned to his algebra. Again, like that first time, when in the midst of his humiliation he had fleetingly felt for her, he saw Matryosha as something more than just a creature, not unlike Nelly, meant to minister to his comfort and gratification. He hadn't been able to use her. Others had. But for all that, it seemed, she had her own thoughts and feelings and agonies, having nothing to do with him.

He remembered that thin, lost weeping last night. Pity stabbed him and stuck like a burr.

Claire's Journal, July 25

The Russians are really unlike anyone else in the world. To the eye, to the ear, to the touch. Occasionally, to the nose. I have always had a feeling for them. There was a Russian colony in Florence who had quite taken me up. The Shuvalovs, the Vorontsovs, the Buturlins—all of them completely European, faultlessly Continental, not a touch of accent in their French. Yet the villas in which they lived seemed to have a special bouquet, just a little too strong, like perfume left standing too long, and beginning to be redolent of musk. I could almost see an outline of onion-shaped cupolas hovering over the Palladian facades. A Russian in his own habitat naturally makes himself even more felt. Running to irrational extremes. Gay and melancholy at the same time. Uncontrolled in his behavior—and yet, behind all that loose emotional abandon, there's a deep core of secrecy. Even the flirtatious Pushchin. In the middle of his inane compliments, something wild flashing at one through those Mongolian slits, and immediately sinking out of sight; no tracking of it to the lair, it's taken cover. . . .

And take Prince Georges—how infinitely more interesting than the English boys of his age. Except one, of course, and he is the one I never met, not until he grew up. Could I talk across a gap of years to an English boy, as I have been talking to Georges? It's the strangest feeling, as if my curiosity, my terrible curiosity about the other one, is being finally assuaged; as if I'm reaching into the beginnings and wrenching it all into a different direction. . . . A wild fancy . . . Am I going all fantastic and Russian myself?

Arriving in Islavskoye, Grisha noticed a change in tempo, a disorganization. The servants, usually indolent, ran around like stirred-up ants. He found Johnny Pomykov at the stables throwing pebbles at pigeons, instead of having his usual lesson with Monsieur Gambs. Then barely inside the door he was collared by Marya Ivanovna, who immediately entrusted him with an invitation to his parents to attend a performance of *Esther* two nights from now. "*Racine*, you know, not any of those new plays in questionable taste. I have sent a note to your parents, but I am counting on you, *cher Prince*, to exert your powers of persuasion—after all, by now you're quite a member of our little *congerie*. . . ."

Grisha, who could easily imagine his mother's indignation at being expected to travel to the home of comparative strangers to see a performance by a corps of tutors and governesses, merely bowed and excused himself to go to his lessons.

"Unfortunately, I can't tell you where Miss Clairmont is just now: *ci, là, partout!* But most probably in the theater. She and Monsieur Gambs are our tutelary spirits, you know. We are all completely in their hands!"

The Pomykov theater was a smallish building distinguished from the others by a pediment and a row of slightly crooked Greek columns. Inside, the gilt-legged chairs were piled up, and a manservant, rags tied about his feet, performed a sliding dance on the floor, polishing it to high gloss.

Miss Clairmont wasn't there. Only Monsieur Gambs was up on the stage, making a neat diagram to indicate exits and entrances. He explained to Grisha that Marya Ivanovna had suddenly decided to have *Esther* put on day after tomorrow, for her husband's birthday, instead of next week, as was planned. "Therefore panic and confusion everywhere! But I think Claire and I will be able to manage. We have done it before, after all. The difficulty is that I have to play Mardoch as well as Hamman, and there is almost no time to change."

It was clear to Grisha that he was enjoying every minute of the confusion, the small chaos which under his skilled direction would inevitably be soon transmuted into harmony. If there were several more parts for him to take, Hermann Gambs would keep and perform them all with the same combination of sparkling zest and German orderliness that characterized everything he did.

"If you'll excuse me, Prince, a few more notes." His pencil, sharpened to perfection, raced squeaking over the neat diagram.

"Monsieur Gambs," Grisha asked, "who is Godwin?"

Gambs started and broke the point of his pencil. Taking out a small silver pocketknife, he began to sharpen it anew.

"William Godwin," he replied, in the measured tones in which he gave his lectures on history, "is a well-known English social philosopher. His *Political Justice* expounds on the immorality of present institutions and enlarges on the utopia that will ensue when these are destroyed. He also believes in extending women's rights. He is considered one of England's foremost freethinkers. . . . May I ask you, Prince, why you are inquiring about Godwin?"

Grisha hesitated, not quite able to answer immediately. Last night's reading had left him bursting with questions. The most important one could only be put to Miss Clairmont herself. This one had just slipped out for no particular reason. A perfectly innocuous question. There was no reason, surely, for the tutor's grave look upon him. "I wanted to know who he was—besides being Miss Clairmont's stepfather."

"Ah, so you know *that*. . . . Well, you see, that is a fact which is not generally known—in point of fact, not known here at all, apart from me—and now, it seems, you." Monsieur Gambs's voice took on the implacable gentleness of one explaining facts to a backward child. "I wonder, Prince, if you have sufficiently considered the situation. Godwin's writings are considered revolutionary even in England. Here, as you can imagine, they would be regarded as no less than the works of the devil. If Claire's relationship to him became known, she would probably, in spite of Monsieur Pomykov's liberal views, lose her position here, and might not even be able to procure another. After all, a governess, a preceptress of youth, and here she is, harboring ideas which people fear without really knowing anything about them—Would she teach the children atheism? Disrespect for authorities? Such questions are bound to arise. So, as you see, Prince . . ."

The tutor spoke gently and reasonably, and Grisha listened respectfully; for all that, the two of them seemed to be all at once facing each other in a combative stance, Monsieur Gambs armed with superior understanding of the situation and the full weight of Miss Clairmont's confidence, while all Grisha had was the few pages in her uneven script. . . .

"Your lecturing voice, Hermann!" said Miss Clairmont, behind him, startling him. "What are you imparting so solemnly to my pupil?"

"Prince Georges," Monsieur answered unsmilingly, "wanted to know who William Godwin was."

Something indefinable colored his words: a reproach or a warning. Alarm leaped up in Grisha. Had he really done something wrong? Would she too turn that minatory look upon him? But Miss Clairmont merely divided an approving smile between the two of them.

"Quite right! I am sure you explained it all to perfection, dear Hermann. . . . Well! Great confusion reigning in the house!" Her face wore an expression that was mock-rueful and exhilarated at once, presaging some comical disaster. "Marya Ivanovna has invaded the sewing room, reducing both Esther's handmaidens and her own to tears. Also, she is sending down the big couch from the drawing room, which, she is persuaded, is the very thing."

Monsieur Gambs's hands passed slowly upward over his face, ending up in his hair. "No. *Ach, du mein lieber Gott!*"

"In fact, I think they are bringing it in through the back door right now. If you are lucky they won't be able to get it in."

Indeed, from the back of the theater there came dull thuds, as of an army bringing up a ram to breach a fortress. A rumbling basso belonging to Gerassim, the Pomykovs' huge coachman, said deeply: "Hold your end up, you son-of-a-bitch. Can't do it all myself." Monsieur Gambs dashed to the back of the theater, and Miss Clairmont laughed heartlessly.

"I shall now desert poor Hermann in his hour of need. . . . Come along, Georges." She caught hold of his hand and hurried out of the theater, not stopping—his limp grew exaggerated as he kept pace with her, but he didn't mind—until they came to the clearing, near the pond. She let go of his hand and then sat down on a bench, smiling at him. "I am so glad to see you, Georges. I need a little change from the alexandrine verse. . . ."

Not without a certain portentous solemnity, Grisha opened his notebook to where the pages of the journal she gave him lay next to his English composition. Offering them to her, he waited for her comment. She made none, merely tucking them into her reticule, as matter-of-factly as if it were a sheaf of some domestic notes.

Grisha could bear it no longer.

"Miss Clairmont, please, please. If you knew how I . . ." Impulsively he caught at her thin hands. "You said a poet, a famous modern poet? Who? What was his name?"

Not withdrawing her hands, she looked back at him with the faintest lifting of her dark brows. "Oh, he had all manner of names. It is the custom in England as well as in France to have several proper names," she went on, maddeningly tangential, "really a much more instructive custom than yours. What does one learn from the Russian patronymic? Merely the father's name. English names give one much more of a man's background. One of his names was Gordon, indicating, you see, his Scottish heritage: the Gordons are a very old family. And Noel—he inherited that name from his mother-in-law together with part of her estate. He hated her but he kept the name. . . . And—no," she veered abruptly, "I shall not say his surname. Not that you won't guess—or probably have already done so. . . . Now, let me see your composition." She gave him a sharp look. "Why the stricken expression?"

"Perhaps," Grisha said, faltering, "you don't want to talk to me about him, because you no longer trust me." He plunged on, miserably. "Because—when I asked Monsieur Gambs about your stepfather, Mr. Godwin, I was—making myself important. Showing him that you confided in me too." Yes, the careless intimacy of

"Claire and I" had irritated him; childishly he had been impelled to show that he too— "I fear I have perhaps made myself unworthy of any further confidence from you. . . ."

"How very Russian you are being, Georges!" Friendly mockery glimmered in her smile. "Such a huge *mea culpa*! No need for it, I assure you. I don't mind my friends discussing me. . . . And have no fear, I have every intention of talking about *him* again. . . . I suppose I am reluctant to name him because I don't want you to think of him as a famous English poet—only as himself, my impossible, cruel, driven lover . . ."

"I shall do so," he assured her eagerly. "I will only think of him as—Geordie?" He was and sounded doubtful. There was a private sound about the name. "No, I don't believe I could . . ."

"Well, that was my private name for him. No one else used it—nor did I call him by it when anyone else was there. In company he was always 'my lord'. . . . But he did have another, friendlier name. To Mary and P.B.—and me when we were not alone—he was"— a reflective smile slipped across her lips—"Albé."

"Albé," Grisha repeated, testing the name.

"Yes. Because of his title—those were the first initials, do you see? And also because one day when we were out sailing he sang us a wild song that he swore was an Albanian air—but that, I think, was a hum. . . ."

"A hum?"

"A joke . . . And now, Georges, I must insist on a proper English lesson, or *I* will begin to feel unworthy—of the generous salary your parents pay me."

At the end of the lesson, however, she relented and talked a little of her London days with him—with Albé. ("Though he wasn't Albé then, that came later, in Geneva. . . .") She had been little more than a bystander, in those days, floating dreamily on the edges of his personal maelstrom. He had been in the middle of a great change; finishing off his disastrous marriage, dismantling his life, getting ready to leave London. ". . . In that ridiculous carriage of his, which was made in the image of Napoleon's traveling coach." She shook her head, laughing. "Oh, that unbelievable carriage. I saw it when it arrived from Baxter's and was struck speechless. It had a *lit de repos*—a plate chest—a—one could live in it! And he was taking with him as many of his animals as he could cram in—and a retinue of some odd humans: his man Fletcher, of course, and a North Country page by the name of Rushton, and a Swiss servant, Berger, and an Italian doctor called Polidori, who was a fool but also foolishly devoted. 'To be surrounded by people who care about one, that's the main thing,' he said. But he sailed away without *me*," she said half-sorrowfully, half-playfully.

"Of course, I knew that I would see him again. I had no doubt of *that*. I belonged in his life—I knew that even if he didn't, every instinct told me so. And besides, I had already made my plans."

Her dark head tilted to one side, she seemed to contemplate the girl she used to be, as indulgently amused by her antics as though it was a harum-scarum younger sister. And that very impersonality of hers made her younger self come alive for Grisha: he *saw* her, a dark, intense girl, at once a *poseuse* and an artless worshiper; uncomfortably intelligent and given to comical blunders; and not so submerged in a grand passion as to be above making her plans.

"How I wish I had known you then!" he burst out, with real regret.

"You think you might have liked me?" Miss Clairmont asked on a note of impersonal curiosity.

"Oh, yes. It would have been so splendid!" He could have talked to this young Claire with even more freedom than to Miss Clairmont. She would have been even more truly his sister and friend: riding with him—he would have seen to it that she had a horse just like his Nelly—sitting out dances with him at the Moscow assemblies; talking to him about everything. . . . A semi-mournful it-might-have-been sort of gayety flared up in him. "I probably would have fallen in love with you," he said daringly and, inevitably, flushed.

"Would you? *He* didn't." Hooking her linked hands about her knees, Miss Clairmont leaned back against the tree, dreamy-eyed. With a little sigh, she finally allowed the past to reach her, bear her all the way back. "I made him uneasy. Some people are so terribly uncomfortable with themselves that they find it difficult to allow themselves to be loved—they fear a claim might be made on them. I was making no claims, however. I was so terribly grateful to him. Why, before he touched me, I was nothing, a soul wandering in a limbo, waiting to be born. I had a meaning now, I was alive, and all because of him. . . .

"And yet the very fact that I made no claims bothered him. He would say to me in that gentle voice of his, 'Pray go away now.'

And I would go obediently, leaving him by himself in that wretched house with the slovenly servants and a bailiff in the kitchen. . . . But he was glad to see me come back, I could see that. 'Sing to me, Claire,' he would say, 'I am blue-deviled today, sing to me. . . .' And I would sing him all his favorite songs. . . ."

With another deep sigh, she let her head sink back against the tree trunk behind the bench. Her eyelids drooped; her eyes glimmered darkly under her eyelashes. From that long, arched faintly vibrating throat there came a note, low and trembling; another followed, it rang stronger, surer, slowly shaping a song.

> *Plaisir d'amour ne dure qu'un instant*
> *Chagrin d'amour dure toute la vie . . .*

This was not the first time Grisha had heard her sing. Self-possessed, neat, standing composedly by the piano, from which the accomplished Monsieur Genichsta flashed his bright performer's smile, she too would perform admirably. But never like this, never before this plangent musical grief, this wild sweetness. As he listened, Grisha felt his eyes prickling with tears.

"Bravo!" sounded from the woods nearby. The singer and the listener both started violently. Miss Clairmont's eyes flew open and she rose, looking around, her face so young and bewildered that Grisha instinctively put himself between her and the newcomers, who, advancing out of the woods, turned out to be Zahar Nikolaitch and Pushchin. A young stable boy in a livery too large for him followed them carrying fishing rods. Zahar Nikolaitch, his sad monkeyish face suffused with feeling—he was a passionate lover of singing—merely nodded at Claire, smiling mistily. Pushchin, who had already shouted "bravo," continued to be vocal in his admiration.

"Will you forgive us for eavesdropping?" He spoke with easy gallantry, automatically falling into his characteristic stance of a military man making up to the girls. "Like Ulysses caught by the sirens' song, I simply couldn't move."

Miss Clairmont responded with a composed curtsey. "You are not to suppose, Monsieur Pushchin, that we end every lesson with a song," she said with a cool little laugh.

"How I should envy the Prince if you did!" Pushchin included

Grisha in another gallant inclination. "I believe I would give anything to hear you sing like that again."

"I daresay you shall," Miss Clairmont said, indifferently. "I perform any evening, whenever I am requested to do so." With a graceful sideways swoop, she picked up her books—it was a consciously graceful movement, Grisha noticed, as if in spite of herself she couldn't help responding to the warmth in Pushchin's almond-shaped eyes. "Well, I must go back to Thespian endeavors now. . . . Gentlemen." With another slight curtsey, she left them.

Pushchin looked after her, a little smile playing on his lips. "Remarkable, this little Englishwoman," he observed. "Sings like a nightingale, moves like a filly . . ."

"A charming young woman, the children adore her," Zahar Nikolaitch agreed. "Please have the goodness not to start anything in that quarter, honored Ivan Ivanitch. . . . We're going fishing, Prince. Would you like to come along and try your luck? The old pond is boiling over with perch."

They proceeded to the pond, Grisha unhappily conscious of his companions' slowed-down pace. Miss Clairmont was the only one who seemed to realize that he could walk as fast if not as gracefully as anyone.

"We've been talking about your hero," Zahar Nikolaitch said. "Ivan Ivanitch here was describing his visit to him. . . . Prince Georges is a great admirer of Pushkin," he added to the other man. "I know he's always longing to ask you about him, but doesn't quite dare to."

"Really? Why? I didn't know I was such a forbidding-looking chap," Pushchin said, glancing at Grisha with a gentle smile.

He was quite different in masculine company. There were apparently two Pushchins: one addressed Miss Clairmont—indeed all women—with predatory gallantry; the other, dropping all that nonsense, talked about his famous friend simply and lovingly. He described his arrival at the village of Mikhailovskoye, in which the exiled poet lived, so graphically, living through it all over again himself, that Grisha could visualize it all: deep snow scored with blue shadows, horses snorting out congealed puffs of steam, and the poet himself, scrawny and agile, in his nightshirt, dancing for joy on the stoop of his small house.

"It's so damned lonely for him, you see, and I could only stay

[73]

one day. But at least, caged or not, he still sings, my poor Cricket."
There was boundless tenderness in his voice. "God, the magnificent poetry stored in that curly head. . . ."

"Is he well?" Zahar Nikolaitch asked anxiously. Having arrived at the pond, he settled himself comfortably on a bench, opening the collar of his blouse and pushing his disreputable straw hat to one side to shield him from the sun. "He's been writing letters, I understand, complaining of an aneurism."

"Oh, he was just giving the authorities an opportunity to be generous and send him abroad. The request was duly shown to His Imperial Majesty and turned down: so Collegiate Secretary Pushkin is to stay where he is." Pushchin gave a brief angry laugh. "That's what they call him, you know, that's all he is to them, Collegiate Secretary Pushkin, Civil Servant of the Tenth Class. . . . I truly believe that ours is the only government that deliberately humiliates its poets."

"Yes, well . . ." Zahar Nikolaitch sighed. "Do you know Pushkin's 'Ode to Liberty,' Prince?"

"Yes, of course."

"And can recite it by heart, I daresay?"

"Oh, yes!"

"There you are, that's what it's all about," said Zahar Nikolaitch to Pushchin. "That poem has been handed all around: anything with a smattering of learning can recite it. And there's strong stuff in it. . . . Would you oblige me by reciting it, Prince?"

Grisha did so willingly, as always feeling the intense pleasure in the harmoniously marching lines, the clean steely rhymes. And yes, he hadn't thought about it before, but he could see how the lines about Paul's assassination could make uncomfortable reading. . . .

The crowned reprobate falls low . . .

That was Paul L.: everybody knew about him. And of course Alexander, all light and goodness though he was, was his son.

And that last stanza, stirring but injudicious:

. . . Wherefore, do ye, oh monarchs, learn:
No penalties, no recompenses,
No dungeons, no, nor altars, may

[74]

Gird you about with sure defenses.
Be ye the first to bow your heads
Beneath law's egis. . . .

"No wonder the authorities are annoyed," said Zahar Nikolaitch, who had been listening, nodding like a mandarin, eyes half closed with pleasure. "But he certainly knows how to put words together, the swarthy little devil. . . . And that's how it is with everything he writes: pure music."

"Unfortunately His Imperial Majesty has a tin ear," Pushchin remarked with a sudden unsettling flash in his mild slate-colored eyes. "Getting deafer by the day, too."

There was such cold dislike in his tone that Grisha turned to him in amazement, blurting out naïvely, before he could stop himself: "Don't you love the Tsar?"

He spoke with incredulity. He had been brought up in an atmosphere of adoration for Alexander that had endured from the Napoleonic days. And even now his father, out of favor at the court, never spoke of the Tsar except with veneration. It was inconceivable to Grisha that he could be otherwise than loved.

The last time he himself had seen the Tsar was three years ago in St. Petersburg, just before they had left for Moscow. He and Sergey, then a cadet in the Military Academy, riding their horses along the shore, they encountered him one day mounted on a handsome bay cob, all alone except for an aide following at a distance. Grisha bowed low, Sergey gave a military salute. Smiling, the Emperor acknowledged their greetings and passed on. Grisha could still remember every detail of that encounter: powerful stooping shoulders in the green uniform of his favorite Preobrazhenski regiment, smoothly barbered apple-cheeked face, and that smile—utterly captivating, shy and sunny at the same time, meant for each of them separately. Seeing that smile one could understand crowds weeping and calling out, "Our father, our shining sun," whenever he passed.

Afterward Sergey and he had looked at each other in incredulous rapture: "Did you see . . . ? Wasn't he . . . ?" And Sergey had burst out in a voice thickened by emotion: "I would let myself be cut into pieces for him."

Remembering this, he looked at Pushchin with bewilderment nearing indignation.

Pushchin didn't answer immediately. Profound sadness darkened his flat face. Presently he said in a quiet, self-communing voice: "Of course, I love him. How not? Always did . . . When we were in the Lyceum, we all adored him. We used to wait for his visits to the school as one awaits a meeting with a loved woman. We practically swooned every time he addressed us, like a bunch of lovesick schoolgirls. Our angel Tsar, the sainted liberator . . . And the dreams we used to build about him! We were going to live in a perfect society, headed by the ideal ruler, all injustices corrected, serfdom abolished, in a glory of freedom and trust . . . Well, *promettre et tenir sont deux* . . . But it's hard to forgive such a disillusionment after such a promise."

His voice hardened: he spoke of the promise, almost as though it was something between him and the Tsar, an engagement contracted personally, now gone back upon.

"But we do have reforms——"Grisha began.

"Do we?" Pushchin again gave that cold smile. "Well, let's take abolition of serfdom. A sale of a serf used to be advertised in public print. That is forbidden now. So now the term used is 'released into service.' That euphemism is what your charming wife looks for, Zahar Nikolaitch, when she wants to buy a cook. The point is, however you put it, human beings are still being bought and sold like cattle. Well, that's about the state of affairs that exists in all reforms. . . . Not to mention other benefactions: crushingly stupid censorship, police surveillance, systematic repression of liberal thought. I've heard," he said with a grimace of distaste, "that the Tsar has been keeping a little book with names of those even mildly suspected of liberalism. He consults it whenever anyone's name comes up for promotion. Quite a turnabout for a sovereign who had been called the Liberator in his time."

Zahar Nikolaitch sighed, his eyes on the stable boy, who, hunkered down in the grass, was carefully baiting their rods with worms out of a small pail. "He's aging. Mistrust comes with age. Also, I hear, he is quite obsessed with the idea of a huge conspiracy around him—a secret society whose members are *capable du tout*—not a comfortable feeling, you will agree, my dear Ivan Ivanitch."

"No, not very," Pushchin agreed quietly, "but one not unusual among autocratic rulers." His dark look was gone, replaced by his usual expression of mild good nature.

[76]

"Is there really such a society, do you think, Zahar Nikolaitch?" Grisha asked. He remembered now that his father too had talked of sedition in the army, a hydra-headed conspiracy, as he had put it.

"Well . . ." Zahar Nikolaitch put on his canny lawyer's face. "If there is a group of individuals who feel that the hand of government lies somewhat heavy on the people, that there is need for reform—something that the Tsar himself used to believe in his younger days—and if they get together privately to discuss ways and means for bettering the situation, there is nothing sinister about *that*, is there?"

"No, of course not," Grisha said, subtly flattered by the earnestness with which Zahar Nikolaitch addressed him.

"Of course, if it went beyond that, if there were an intention of overthrowing the government, or attempting anything against the sacred person of the Tsar . . . But that is unthinkable," Zahar Nikolaitch said, taking his baited fishing rod from the boy.

"Quite unthinkable," Pushchin agreed, taking his. There was a soothing note in his pleasant voice. He might have been giving a personal reassurance to Zahar Nikolaitch. "I myself am convinced there will be no uprising of any kind during Alexander's lifetime." Simultaneously he and his host cast the lines out into the lazily dimpling pond.

Claire's Journal, July 28

Esther produced with great éclat. Hermann was able to accomplish all his changes in good style. I must say that I enjoyed myself prodigiously, *actrice manquée* that I am. Perhaps I should have gone on the stage after all as I had intended to do before my life took a different turn. I might have become a second Mrs. Siddons!

To my great astonishment both the Princes Volynski made their appearance, the father bearing his wife's regrets with patent insincerity. There was dancing after supper. The Prince distinguished me by his attention. He congratulated me on my performance and wanted to know "what could possibly keep a young lady from dancing, when there was music to dance to?"

I merely smiled and demurred. What kept me from dancing was the sight of his son standing on the sidelines watching the dancers with a mask of indifference carefully fitted over his wistful young face. But I couldn't tell the Prince that.

"I used to be an enthusiastic performer myself," the Prince went on. I was sure, from the way he lightly stamped his foot and looked about him with a conquering smile as the musicians swung into a mazurka, that he still must be one. "Now I find it much more satisfactory to claim an old man's privilege and converse with a charming young woman instead."

As was to be expected, we talked about his son's progress in English. His Excellency was excessively flattering. He thought I was a superb teacher. He also enlarged on the great advantages of having a young man like Prince Georges exposed to the edifying influence of an accomplished and charming older woman. Particularly a young man of a retiring character and special sensitivity who because of his special problem finds it hard to form attachments.

I can be foolishly innocent sometimes. I listened to him, smiling and nodding and preening myself—nothing more pleasant for a teacher than to have her work praised—when I suddenly realized what he was getting at.

As I stared at him, he produced a well-bred grimace that had all the length of a smile but none of its fulness. He was sure I understood him. At first I was completely furious. Then the funny side of it struck me and I wanted to laugh in his face. I didn't, however—that would have certainly meant the end to our English lessons—and merely answered him politely. Afterwards, I even stopped being angry. I certainly intend to be of service to his son, although differently from the way he has planned it.

I must say I wasn't sorry to see father and son take their leave. For once, I was able to accept invitations to dance, which I did with great pleasure: I love to dance. I stood up for écossaise with Lieutenant Kakorchine, and a waltz with Monsieur Pushchin, who held me much too closely and told me that *"vous dansez comme une fée."*

Claire's Journal, July 29

It happened right after the second performance of *Esther*—but deep within me I suppose I had been expecting it all along. I was going up to my room, still dressed in my Oriental splendor, thinking of Geordie and his predilection for Eastern ladies—here I was, the intractable bluestocking, finally dressed for the harem. And suddenly I was taken hold of, pushed back against the wall—handled! There was that dark flat face, over me, keeping its usual expression, demure, a little smile on his lips, eyelashes delicately lowered—he has long, long eyelashes like a girl's—while his hands, ranging over my body, talked a totally different language. Shameless, they pulled up my spangled skirt, closed on my buttocks. Ruthlessly clamped to him, I felt the hard surge of his flesh against me, and when I opened my mouth—not to cry for help, no, nothing like that, just to produce a low sound of sheer surprise—it was closed by his. It sounds brutal and repulsive, but actually it wasn't—just knowledgeable and strong. And his lips were cool and fresh, soft like rose petals. . . .

Then there were voices. He stepped away from me and quite deliberately pulled down my rucked-up skirt. He also set himself to rights. A little wry smile accompanied his downward look and he glanced at me too, smiling, as if inviting me to sympathize with his predicament before he buttoned his coat upon it. The next minute he had decamped, leaving me rumpled and speechless on the stairs. When, a few minutes later, I followed him into the drawing room, he was there listening to Marya Ivanovna's chatter and lapping away at his tea, demure as a tomcat home from a foray over the roofs. . . .

I sat in my corner, conversing mechanically while I tried to sort it all out. It was so extraordinary, so offensive and terrible—wasn't it?—and the worst thing was that it was exactly what I wanted: a strong sensual jolt that pushed me right out of my passive continence of the last few years. And the Russianness of it—brutality and expertness strangely mixed—like the contradiction of the civilized sinuous mouth in the flat Mongol mask. I had never had carnal contact before with a man I didn't know. Even Geordie—and he had gone right to the point after relatively few preliminaries—still when we made love, it was the outcome of my knowledge of him, the summing up of what I felt. But this! At this moment—so unlike me!—I wanted to know nothing about him—the less, the better. I just wanted pure sensuality.

(Continued the morning of July 30)

A barely heard step in the corridor, a door opening just long enough to let him slip in, a blur of white moving toward me. The next moment he had slipped into my bed, and we were coupling, silently and savagely, breathing our suppressed cries into each other's avid mouths. It was wonderful, that silent visitation in the middle of the night, the searching artful hands, the muscular waist between my legs, the pumping vital strength that found its way into me; the strangeness and then the oneness as we dissolved mindlessly into each other. A moment later a breath of laughter in my ear—and I found myself echoing it. We giggled silently in the dark, hugging each other, slept briefly, and made love again, now leisurely, playfully, exploringly. Not a word was spoken.

He slipped out as quietly as he came. All that was left of that stealthy visit was a trace of mushroomy odor and a few dark tendrils of hair on the sheets. I got up and regretfully aired them out, washing the telltale sticky spots and then exposing them to the early morning breeze. The damp spots are drying out as I am writing this.

Claire's Journal, August 5

When I was younger, sleeping with someone was a big step—a final seal to an important relationship. But I don't even know this man properly, except as an expert lover. And that seems to be enough.

His recklessness infects me. In the evening, as he is carrying on a decorous conversation at the other end of the room, his glance finds me. A slight questioning lift of the eyebrow, a swift glinting motion of his eyes toward the door. And I slip away into the garden, unnoticed, and presently, in the warm summer darkness, he is with me, silent and urgent.

The other morning when I was taking a solitary walk in the nearby woods and he came riding by on his way to the Pomykovs'—I welcomed that happenstance lovemaking, right there, on the grass, the sun shining down on us, and his horse grazing placidly nearby. . . . But it's never a totally animal coupling—his hold on me is ruthless, shameless, and yet tender. Afterwards, my dress is carefully smoothed down, the gray eyes caress me with a fond smile, and there is an affectionate murmur of *"Akh ty anglichanochka moya"* as he leaves me. It's like a pleasant erotic dream, wanton but not sordid, that one remembers with a smile as one comes luxuriously awake.

Let me own it shamelessly: I enjoy it and it agrees with me. My mirror shows me looking younger, livelier, more like Claire of the Geneva days. Even my constant summer cold has disappeared without a trace. . . .

An exciting experience, without depth or meaning: faceless pleasure, unobscured by longing or regret; a sense of physical well-being—it's enough for now. For once, let it be just that, a simple sensual experience, as uncomplicatedly pleasant as bathing in the pond on a hot day.

Like many children set aside from their peers by a handicap, Grisha as a child was a voracious reader, a player of solitary games, an architect of fantasies. A swan regally gliding on the Tsarskoye Syelo lake would address him in a woman's voice, granting three wishes; and he himself, shooting a toy arrow from his bow and following it to where it fell, would become Ivan Tsarevich off on one of those mystic quests on which younger sons were being constantly sent.

Later, reading *Ruslan and Ludmilla*, he would be enchanted to find himself again in that fairy tale world:

A green oak by the seastrand standeth,
Engirdled by a golden chain;
And on that chain a learnèd tomcat
Walks round about and round again.
Goes to the right—he tells a story,
Goes to the left—a song he sings;
Great wonders!—a wood demon roams there,
A mermaid on the branches swings. . . .

It was plain to see that Pushkin must have had a nurse like his own Tikhonovna. . . .

She no longer told him her fairy tales, even when he came to visit with her in the little attic room where she sat, deaf and failing, busy with the family linen on which her gnarled old hands embroidered fantastically ornate initials. But her place, it seemed, was now taken by a thin dark bluestocking of an English governess past her first youth, whose accounts of her past life held him spellbound in the same way. Fitfully recounted during English lessons, garden walks and afternoon teas, they had a certain meandering continuity. He was beginning to feel as at home in her past as he used to be in the fairy lore of his childhood.

One day he found her sailing paper boats at the pond with Dunia and Johnny, and she said to him: "P.B. adored sailing paper boats. He used to make them out of unpaid bills and discarded poems." She had a way of starting all her stories in that abrupt confiding way, bringing him to instant attention. "I remember—that was soon after Albé had left England—we came to a pond during one of our long walks in Hempstead—just the two of us, Mary had to stay home with the new baby—and anyhow she didn't like long walks—and he stopped at it to sail paper boats. . . . There was a mob of urchins watching him—P.B. had a way of attracting watchers with those odd childish pursuits of his, but none of them ever gibed at him. I think it was the totally unself-conscious way he did it. The way he did everything, not to make himself interesting or to provoke comments, but just because he felt like it. Actually a typical nob's attitude when you come to think of it. . . ."

"Nob's . . . ?"

"That's cant for nobleman. . . . P.B. was a baronet's son—unfortunately disinherited for his inconvenient views, so we were rather poor at the time. . . . And he never knew what he wore, everything was shabby and his jackets always pulled out of shape because of the books weighing down the pockets. But he didn't care. He was simply comfortable in his skin. . . . Geordie—Albé—wasn't. . . . Almost ready, *mon petit*," she said to Johnny, who came clambering up the bank to demand another boat to add to the fragile flotilla bobbing about in the water. She was silent for a moment, turning the scrap of paper expertly between her strong thin pianist's fingers. As she bent her head over her task, he noticed a tiny crop of glossy black tendrils running down the nape of her long neck.

He thought, not for the first time this week, that she was looking better than he had ever seen her look—even close to being downright pretty. The lovely summer had finally caught up with her, infusing her sallowness with ruddiness, making her habitually pale lips shine as if covered with some rosy salve. Noticing for the first time a tiny black mole right over the corner of her smiling mouth, Grisha remembered his father saying that a mark so placed was a sign of hidden sensuality. "There are all kinds of little signs like that," he had said smiling—he was talking to Sergey, naturally—"Keep an eye out for them and you'll pick yourself a good one."

Grisha blushed—this was Miss Clairmont, his special friend, his mentor, not to be slighted by grossly inappropriate thoughts like this. He pushed it out of sight. Giving Johnny the finished boat, she went on:

"All at once as I watched P.B.'s ridiculous little fleet blow across the pond, I experienced a change of mood. Until then I had felt no deprivation with Albé gone—I had even been happy, in a dreamy disorganized way, just thinking back to our London days together. But now panic struck me. I saw Albé sailing away from England never to return, with never a thought for me. . . . Right out of my life . . . It was such a terrible thought that I began to snivel quite unashamedly. . . . P.B. came back to me, wringing out his wet shirtsleeves, and said very seriously: 'Why are you weeping, Claire? Is it because this frail little bark is such a very apt allegory of our chancy existence?'"

A giggle broke from her.

"P.B. had a way of—of *metaphysicizing* the most commonplace occurrences. Once writing to a female correspondent, he asked,

'Are you capable of rising above the world and to what extent?'"

Grisha found himself laughing affectionately at a man he had never met. "And was she?"

"Dear me, no. It's a very difficult piece of levitation. . . . I remember that day particularly, Georges, because from then on I devoted myself in earnest to prying us out of London. . . . Not that any of us wanted to stay there—London was gloom and dirt and ill health and creditors dogging P.B. and dismal letters from Skinner Street upbraiding us for our fecklessness. . . ."

"Skinner Street?"

"My mother and stepfather lived there. Neither Mary nor I had been there for two years—not since the three of us made our escape to France." In answer to his inquiring gaze, she explained briskly: "When Mary ran off with P.B. they took me along."

Grisha's eyes stretched. Romantic elopements were a staple of everyone's reading. But ordinarily heroines leaving parental roof to join their lovers did so unaccompanied. He asked "Why?" baldly, realizing as soon as he said so that he was being rude. But she answered with equal simplicity.

"Because I knew French."

"Oh."

Miss Clairmont went on dreamily: "We had gone gypsying all over the Continent. It was our Grand Tour—shabby and disreputable, just like us," she said merrily, "but incredibly exciting and edifying. It kept us *aux cieux* long after we came back to London. Now, two years later, P.B. had no objections to repeating it. But it had to be done soon, soon! Every night as I lay sleepless on my bed, the ceiling of my bedroom with its cracks and stains would turn into a map of Europe. Staring at it desperately, I could see a miniature coach creeping like a beetle across the web of rivers and roads. Through Netherlands, along the Rhine, over the Alps to Geneva, stopping at certain predetermined places. If I was to see *him* again, if our paths were to cross at any point, our wheels too had to be set in motion, and that soon. . . . Well, it happened, it came off. We caught up with him in Geneva—actually we got there first and waited for him. Geneva . . . Dear place—lovely place. You must stop there, Georges, when you go to Europe—you haven't been abroad yet, have you?"

Grisha shook his head. Illness had prevented his taking the usual

Grand Tour with Monsieur Lachaine. He thought now, wistfully, that he would give anything to slip back into the past and take it, gypsy fashion, with them.

"Well, make sure you go there. . . . It's full of historical interest too, you know: Verney, where Voltaire lived; Vevey where Rousseau wrote *La Nouvelle Héloïse*—Clarens—they are all there. . . . I *want* to think of you there. . . . Yes, I had my Geneva summer, and I have it still, no matter what happened later. P.B. gave it to me, as he gave me everything I ever asked him for. . . ."

The revelations broke off here, because Dunia fell in the water. Grisha hauled her out and she nestled damply in his arms, a green lick of weed on one cheek, rubbing her sleek wet head against his sleeve, like a kitten. Grisha felt a flick of pleasure: the little creature liked him.

"My little *russalochka*," said Miss Clairmont with love, taking her from him. "Off to the house with you, to change. *Hop, allons vite.*"

Hand in hand they twinkled away among the trees, the child's skirling laughter coming back to him. Johnny galloped after them, whooping.

More oddities emerged in their next conversation, which took place in the schoolroom, the weather having gone gloomy and showery. It turned out that, their romantic elopement notwithstanding, P.B. and Mary weren't married. They merely lived together. "As you know, Georges, Mary and I were brought up as freethinkers; to regard marriage as an artificial restriction, shackling a naturally free mind." Miss Clairmont had reverted to her teacher's voice, crisp, didactic, setting forth a purely intellectual proposition. "Needless to say, P.B. shared those beliefs. To him, any law condemning people to cohabitation one moment after the decay of their affection for each other was a piece of intolerable tyranny. . . . As for Mary—well, there was a deep-rooted conventionality in her that eventually found its proper place." A faintly astringent note colored her voice. "But at the time we are discussing—yes, I will say this for her—she gave herself to the man she loved as freely as I did. Neither of us stooped to bargaining for respectability," she said with quick pride. "Does this shock you? Make you think less of us?"

Her tone told him quite clearly that she wasn't afraid of his bad opinion for her own sake, but simply because it would disappoint her in him. Somewhat disjointedly he tried to reassure her. Nevertheless he was conscious of some reservations.

It wasn't prudery: Grisha, brought up in St. Petersburg's brilliant and licentious society, could have no provincial illusions about the sanctity of marriage. He was only too aware of the fashionable illicit pairing going on about him. This cotillion went on in the highest circles. The Tsar himself led it: everyone knew the story of the beautiful Naryshkina encumbered by pregnancy as she made her low court obeisance to the Empress, both women knowing by whom she was pregnant.

But the unmarried young girls stayed on the sidelines, immune. Even in the careless licentiousness of the St. Petersburg court, virginity was respected. Once that frail barrier was breeched behind the respectable cover of marriage, they too were free to join the dance. Until then—

"My brother Sergey says that no honorable man would approach a pure young girl except with an intent to marry. He thinks it's"—he searched for the correct English word and settled on his father's favorite one—"unsportsmanlike."

"You mean, to spoil the value of the marital merchandise before it's delivered intact to the altar?"

This was pure cynicism. "No, it isn't like that, it isn't that at all," he said almost angrily. For once she did really shock him.

It really was different for a young girl. His thoughts went back to his sister's wedding: the candle-pierced church-dusk, voices lifted in plangent sweetness behind the *ikonostas*, flooding the church, so that it seemed to quiver on its foundations and rise up on that wave of solemn song. He remembered too the way his sister Sophie had looked, suddenly transfigured from the merry petulant girl she had been into something special and holy. No, the marriage ceremony was a solemn and beautiful ritual, a sacrament in the full meaning of the word: how could any girl go through it unless she was a virgin?

Miss Clairmont listened to him, gravely, as he struggled to get it all across to her. "What about the groom?" she asked. "I take it unspotted purity is not a requirement for him?"

Grisha couldn't hold back a grin: his brother-in-law had been a notable rake before his marriage. "Well, it's not the same for a man. . . ."

On the contrary: for a man, purity, all the preaching at confession time notwithstanding, was not a desirable commodity. Failure to jettison it as soon as possible indicated an alarming inadequacy. Again he saw himself stumbling out of the pavilion where Matryosha stood waiting, passive but repelled. . . .

Monsieur Gambs, entering the schoolroom to give his daily history lecture, with the usual retinue of pink-and-white nieces and cousins billowing at his heels, gave them a grave questioning look; and Miss Clairmont, gathering her books together, answered it tranquilly: "Georges was explaining to me the sacrament of marriage in Russia."

"I was thinking of our last conversation," she said to him the next day, after their lesson. "Naturally, my dear Georges, it's hard for you to imagine young people of about your own age, as we were at that time, deliberately challenging the usages of society. The thing is, I should hate you to think of us as—as a dissolute crew."

"Oh, no. I couldn't—I would never . . ."

"A lot of people did so regard us—in some cases precisely those whom one would least expect to. But we were neither unprincipled nor irresponsible. P.B. had the most highly developed sense of responsibility I had ever met. *He* would never abandon or betray anyone who trusted him. . . . Oh, how I miss him!" Her voice was the voice of a young girl grieving.

Unexpectedly to himself Grisha blurted out: "Sometimes it seems to me as though P.B. was the one you liked best."

Absurdly he minded. He wanted her to love the other one, the difficult lame one, best.

She tilted her dark head musingly, blinking the thick black eyelashes now beaded with crystal. "I've often pondered on the—the *untidiness* of love. For all my talk of kindred spirits, when I fell in love it had to be with someone irrefutably alien. . . . Cruel, so cruel to himself, but also to others, and secretive and thoroughly, for all his romantic airs, materialistic—in such petty unattractive ways too! When I began to hate him, I used to go religiously through that catalogue of meannesses. . . ."

"You began to *hate* him?" He stared at her, appalled.

"Oh, yes, quite bitterly. The greater the love, the greater the revulsion from it, you know," she said with a painful little smile. "In fact, I am afraid that I hate him still."

She had stressed her remark about P.B.: "*he* would never

abandon or betray . . ." With the slightest tinge of disappointment in his voice—these were commonplaces that he had not expected from his unique Miss Clairmont—he asked, hesitatingly: "Did *he*—betray and abandon you?"

To his relief Miss Clairmont looked startled and even a little affronted. "Good heavens, no. I'm no sniveling Clarissa Harlowe. I wouldn't bear a man a grudge because he had ceased to love me—or thought he did. No, I never considered myself *abandoned*—in either sense of the word," she added with a little sniff. For a moment she was silent. Then she said in a different voice: "I hate him because he murdered a being dear to me."

Grisha involuntarily crossed himself.

"Yes, murdered—it was murder—stupid cruel unnecessary mur—" She broke off, her face going greenish pale, all the new near-prettiness draining out of it. For a moment he thought she would faint. But instead she took a few swift paces to where Dunia, seated on her low tabouret, was dressing her dolls, and sank to her knees, burying her face in the thin little neck, straining the child's body fiercely close. The contact seemed to calm her. After a while lifting up her head, she was able to say almost in her normal voice: "I am sorry, Georges. Stupid of me . . . But I can't talk about it. . . . No, not yet . . ."

Claire's letter to Mary, August 8 (not sent)

You've wondered about P.B. and me. I've seen the question in your eyes and sometimes even wanted to answer it. Did I want P.B.? Did I have him?

Shall I answer now? Yes, I wanted P.B.—in the way you meant, exclusively, for me alone—only once. It was in Switzerland, the first time we went there. We had taken a boat out and were lying in it, drowsing, the three of us, I on the left, you on the right, each with her head on his shoulder. I remember that so well, and the peaceful look on his face, that's how it should be, love without chains, freely shared. And at all at once, perversely, I wanted him to choose. Lying there, with my cheek on the bony part of his shoulder—you similarly on the other side—I willed fiercely: turn to me, turn to *me*, knowing that the other side of him you were willing the same thing. Between us he lay, his slumbering spirit tugged one way and another. And then turned his head to you.

That was when the choice was made. What happened in England afterward didn't really matter. It was the final seal to the strange subterranean interflow of sympathy between us, a visitation, a night dream. The Annunciation might have been something like that, something dreamed, experienced on a totally different level from reality. Afterward we smiled at each other and went on as before. It didn't touch you at all.

But that time on the boat I had really wanted him for myself. . . . But you knew all that, Mary. You knew about your victory.

Claire's Journal, August 15

The other day I said to Prince Georges: "Shall we make a compact? You can ask me anything—any question—and I'll answer it with complete truthfulness. It's wonderful to know that there is one person whom you can trust, who won't lie to you." As soon as I said this, I felt a *frisson*. As if my own voice came back echoing to me over the years.

I can still recall every detail of that night at Villa Diodati. Lake Leman lay shimmering beyond the dark mass of the Sécheron vineyards; the warm wind had risen and was blowing the curtains inward into the bedroom where we lay embraced. His dog lay at the foot of the bed snoring cozily and occasionally awaking to scratch for fleas. . . . His voice saying sleepily: "That's how I like you best—a silken body warm in my arms—a dove's breast for my head—a siren's voice singing in the darkness. . . ." He dropped off to sleep while I sang, and that was unusual; he had never done so before. I held his slim body slippery with sweat in my arms, while the moonsquare crept away from the window. When it reached our bed he woke up and said to me pettishly, blinking in the cool brightness: "Are you still here? I don't allow people to watch me in my sleep." But the very fact that he had—I was filled with timid joy. I said: "But I am not people, Geordie. I am Claire and I love you so terribly." And I even ventured to say: "One must trust at least one person, Geordie. . . ."

He didn't answer that. He sat up in bed and reached for the coverlet, which he arranged carefully across his legs, before lighting the candle on the bedtable—a ritual he never forgot even after the most abandoned bout of lovemaking. Candlelight showed him naked from the knees up, and as always I thought with compassion how terrible it was that in his eyes all his beauty was canceled by what the coverlet concealed. Because he *was* beautiful. I loved to look at him naked, whenever he let me: "Please, ah, please, leave the light be, I want to see you." "Trollop," he would say gently, blowing the candles out.

He had such a lovely fine-grained body, as smooth breasted as a statue and as beautifully white—I can still see his whiteness glowing against brown me!—with that special clarified luminousness that made one think of alabaster. That was due, I believe, to his peculiar diet, mostly consisting of water. (Oh dear, the constant mixture of the beautiful and the silly!) He was deathly afraid of gaining weight and constantly waged battle against encroaching corpulence. They told me he was getting quite fat in Pisa, together with his little contessa, and I had been spitefully glad. . . . But in Geneva he had been a slim young god.

He said, abruptly: "Why should I trust you?"

"Because I love you," I told him, "because there's nothing I wouldn't do for you if you asked me."

That got me a heavy look from under his finely penciled brows. "I don't need anything from anyone. . . . I don't even *want* to need anything."

"But if you ever did . . ."

"Really? Anything? Reckless girl," he jeered. All the same something both doubting and eager flashed in his eyes.

"Anything—ask me for anything any time—I'll give you it, no matter how precious to me." Needless to say, what I had in mind at that time was merely my life. "It's good to know that there is one person in the world to be limitlessly trusted."

He was silent a moment. Then he sighed. "Bed talk—soft foolish harmless stuff—I shan't hold you to it."

"Yes, do, do hold me to it, Geordie. You shall see."

"Yes, we shall see."

It was a conversation repeated over and over again during that summer, our Geneva summer, like the variations in my favorite Mozart Sonata in A Major; where a simple folk song is repeated in major and minor, with rhythmic changes, crossed hands, everything. And always I answered steadfastly, reassuring him: "I do, Geordie. I will, Geordie. Try me, Geordie."

I knew he would have to. Try me, I mean. Just saying all this could never be enough for him. That's why I was able to bear two years of silence. And when finally that terrible letter came from Venice, I could read between the lines, I knew I was being tested. During the sleepless nights when I considered my answer to him, I could see him, across the Adriatic, starfrost on his auburn curls, saying with that dark look, that doubting smile: "Are you still the same, Claire? Do you still tell the truth? Make extravagant promises? Keep them?"

It had been taken for granted from the beginning that Grisha could ask Miss Clairmont about anything. It became apparent, however, that there was at least one subject on which she was not ready to be questioned, that last time, she had looked as though she would die of it.

He could only speculate about it on his own. Whose "stupid cruel unnecessary murder" had taken place? A being dear to her, she had said—someone, it seemed, she had loved as well as she had *him*. With a flutter of queasiness in his bowels, Grisha decided it must have been P.B. He was dead—was the other one responsible for his death? The more he thought about it, the likelier it seemed. There must have been a duel. . . .

He had often heard Sergey talking lightheartedly about the duels, which, though proscribed by law, were constantly taking place among the officer corps, as a form of exercise, an elegant and dangerous way of keeping oneself honed to a fine edge. It set up a troubling tremor inside of you when you thought of this deliberate intimate exposure of oneself to death at the hands of another human being. . . . The dark possibility haunted him.

Meanwhile Miss Clairmont went on talking to him in a completely natural manner of what she half-mockingly, half-nostalgically called her Geneva summer.

"For once it all had turned out as I had planned. At his first meeting with us, he had raised his eyebrows at me and said 'Nonsensical girl!' But for all that he was glad to see me. Even as he spoke he smiled, so I knew all was well."

"He knew then that he loved you?"

"Oh, dear me, no! He didn't even trust me. No, that came later. In the beginning he merely enjoyed having me there because—oh, I was available, I amused and pleased him. . . . Besides, at that time, I think, he was beginning to realize that he mightn't be able to return to England very soon, and he found himself valuing English faces, liking to hear English voices. Meeting P.B. was the important thing. He actually thanked me for bringing the two of them together." Her dark eyebrows gave the familiar sardonic twitch. "P.B.'s noble rank helped. Albé always had great respect for that—a mark of a parvenu, I believe," she said with an unkind little laugh.

"Parvenu? But he himself was nobly born, wasn't he?"

"His branch of the family was a minor Scottish one, not terribly distinguished. The title came to him quite unexpectedly by a series of fortuitous deaths—before that they weren't particularly noticed."

"I see."

The Volynski family, which went back to the old Moscow princes, also had a lot of insignificant little branchlets issuing from the main stem: "the suckers," his father called them. When they showed up, from the provinces, to pay their respects, one had to be particularly nice to them just because it was so easy to hurt their feelings and they were, after all, family.

"But I think he would have liked P.B. even if he had been a commoner—perhaps in a slightly different way, but he still would have. He found him stimulating and different. 'Now that the wave of enlightenment is receding,' he said to me once, 'and we are settling back into mediocrity, it's interesting to find an original like him stranded on the beach.'"

"Then," Grisha cleared his throat, "then he—Albé—liked him at first."

"Yes, from the very first meeting."

Yet there was the murder, afterward! Grisha felt a thrill of genuine horror.

Apparently there had been no premonition of the catastrophe; everything had gone on famously. The two men—the presumed victim and his executioner-to-be—walked in amity about the mountainside, bathed in the pellucid light, breathing the sharp clear air, and talked about everything in the world.

"I loved to hear them talk. And for once I was merely content to listen—would you credit that?" She made a small mocking grimace at herself. "Sometimes I would interrupt: 'I think what P.B. *really* means . . .' and immediately get a sharp set-down: 'Oh, are you there, truepenny? Explaining away what everybody really means? . . .' Even now I can hear those two voices, strophe and antistrophe, answering each other. *Light, light, light,* says one, *light and universal goodness, man was born to be good. . . . Darkness,* says the other, *guilt and darkness; who of us here would dare to look within himself? Not I . . .* So thoroughly committed to the dreary old dogma that holds us to be irreparably flawed, even as we leave the womb. . . . Well he *was* flawed in a way that he found unbearable. But he was impelled for certain dark reasons of his own to make out of a purely physical defect something like a moral horror and then hate the world in which such a thing could happen. . . . You don't feel that way, do you, Georges? Hold a grievance against the world because of your leg?"

She waited for his answer, and, as always when she spoke of his lameness, he went through the gamut of startled anger, resentment, grudging amusement at her direct ways, and that final strange lightening of spirit as he murmured: "No, I don't think so."

"I don't think so, either." Her serious look scanned his reddening face. "You have such a good face, do you know that, Georges? There is suffering there but no vindictiveness. . . . Well, Geordie—Albé—*was* vindictive. He felt deep within himself that he—together with the rest of mankind—was a—a bad lot, full of dark cruelties and lusts and all kinds of irredeemable evil. It was all part of his background: his early childhood was spent in Scotland, that land of morose Calvinism, where suckling babes are taught that they are sinners. . . . For a while I too"—her voice deepened somberly—"yes, I too was converted to his gloomy doctrine and agreed that it was a bad world. Not then—not in Geneva—much later. After the other voice in the dialogue was stilled."

How, Grisha questioned silently but intensely, *how was it stilled?* To his chagrin, Miss Clairmont stayed with the safe Geneva days before anything terrible happened and there was only talk.

"You mustn't think, Georges," she said to him earnestly, "that P.B. was an addled optimist who saw nothing wrong with humanity. He never denied the corruptibility of man: only his *inherently* evil nature. 'We are born perfect,' he would say, 'but immediately thereafter the work of outside corruption starts on our sound but vulnerable minds. Fear and guilt—that's what twists and cripples us from birth, not our evil nature. Fear and guilt—they are what make us both cruel and afraid, drive us into the madness of mutual hatred and the bloody absurdity of war.'

"And Albé countering, 'But fear and guilt do not just exist in the vacuum, they are part of the human make-up, aren't they?'

"'They are the effluvia of immoral self-perpetuating institutions,' P.B. would tell him.

"'Man-made, though! Man-bloody-made!' Albé would shout, and his small white hands would go plunging into the auburn ringlets. 'This is an argument that bites its own tail!'

"And the argument would go on and on, voices getting louder, hoarsening—oh, it's wonderful how heated people can become about their basic beliefs. . . ."

"I suppose that's why there are religious wars—and duels," Grisha said, the last word escaping him in a compulsive interrogative squeak.

Appalled at himself (but he couldn't help it, he couldn't!) he stared at her waiting. Now it would all happen again: the livid pallor, the near-faint, and perhaps, perhaps, unspeakable revelations.

"Duels," Miss Clairmont repeated, in a thoughtful colorless voice. And all at once, confounding him utterly, her whole face lit up, crinkled with laughter. Hysteria? But she said in a voice totally inappropriate to recounting horrors:

"I never told you about our silly duel, did I? Oh, yes, we had a duel and quite an event it was. . . ."

"Was P.B. . . . ?"

"Yes, he was involved in it, poor lamb." A spontaneous chuckle broke from her. "All of us were, in a way. . . . Have I mentioned a young man called Polidori? Dr. John Polidori? I believe I have. He came to Geneva as part of Albé's retinue. His first utterance upon arriving there was, I remember, to proclaim the lake too small for the mountains. He was the other combatant. Oh, what a farce it was!"

With something that he shamefacedly recognized as just plain disappointment, Grisha saw the unspeakable recede back into the unknown. But he should have known that Miss Clairmont belonged as little in the Castle of Otranto as she did in *Clarissa Harlowe.*

But then what did happen?

Claire's Journal, August 20

Came down to the parlor for the afternoon tea, and I found Pushchin deep in discussion with Georges and Zahar Nikolaitch. Pushchin was describing some of the enormities going on in the military settlements, into which thousands of unwilling peasants have been herded by Imperial decree. The Emperor's military adviser Arakcheev is in charge of them. It was a nightmarish account. Modern hospitals, kept strictly for show—and peasants all around them dying in an epidemic of bloody flux without a finger raised to help them. Specially trained midwives—and pregnant women whipped to death. Streets kept spotlessly clean—and grain rotting unharvested in the fields while peasants are kept trimming every tree to exact specifications. Couples paired by lot; women fined heavily if they fail to conceive or have a miscarriage or bear a daughter; whole families running away from these exemplary settlements, preferring to perish from hunger in the forests. . . .

"I've been told of a peasant woman dashing her newborn's brains out against the wall: 'You're better off dead than growing up here!' Meanwhile Arakcheev keeps bringing the good reports: 'Everything running smoothly, Your Imperial Majesty, your people are blessing your name for your goodness to them.' And His Imperial

Majesty is pleased, he never hears the groans of his people, tortured to death by the Old Faithful. . . ."

His voice never rose. But it deepened and vibrated, and a knot of muscles bunched stiffly in the angle of his jaw.

I stared with amazement. Was this my bland libertine? And then I remembered what Georges had told me once—that he had left the army "to serve the people."

"But it isn't his fault, he can't know what that beast Arakcheev is doing." Grisha, distressed and defensive about his idol.

I am fascinated by the tremendous personal feeling that the Russians have for their rulers. It's like a love affair: they abase themselves before the loved one, they pray for him, they find excuses for his excesses, they'll die for him—for him, *personally*—if need be. How different from the English. Imagine waxing passionate about poor old Prinny!

"But shouldn't he know? And isn't it a pity, Prince, that the Tsar of Russia should find it necessary to surround himself with people like the spy Benkendorff and the jackal Arakcheev?"

"Not a *jackal*," Zahar Nikolaitch remarked judicially. "You know what they say about him? Industrious as an ant, malevolent as a tarantula. . . ."

There was a pause. Then my Georges, almost in tears, burst out: "Oh, how terrible it is that these things are being kept from the Tsar! He is not a bloody-minded despot after all. If he knew—! Is there no one to tell him?" He swung toward Pushchin, almost accusingly. "You say there is a secret society pledged to correct injustices. . . ."

"You are mistaken, Prince," Pushchin murmured with his calm smile. "*I* never said that. . . ."

"Then somebody—you, Zahar Nikolaitch! Well, if, instead of meeting in secret and just talking, they would go directly to the Tsar. . . ."

"One of Arakcheev's most important duties," Z.N. remarked, thoughtfully regarding the tips of the red Moroccan leather half boots he wears around the house, "is to protect the Tsar from precisely such inconvenient incursions. . . ."

"I don't care—if I possessed proofs of such horrors, I would get them to the Tsar, even if I were to die at his feet for it the next moment!"

I must say that my pupil looked quite beautiful as he pronounced this piece of high-minded idiocy. The next moment, naturally, he recalled himself and went crimson with embarrassment. Both men looked at him with an identical expression of tenderness, Pushchin even murmuring some Russian pitying endearment under his breath.

"*Ah, jeunesse, jeunesse,*" Z.N. sighed. With his eyebrows climbing high and hollowed-out cheeks, he looked more like a wise old monkey than ever. "Of course, Prince, Emperor Alexander is not a bloody-minded despot. On the contrary, he quite earnestly desires the best for his people. But he is completely, irrefutably convinced that the only hope for their future lies in this very plan of converting the Russian peasant to an orderly military system. So, he will go on doing his best for the Russian peasant and the Russian peasant will go on bearing his burden, with his deep piety, his sense of kinship with Christ Our Saviour, who too had to endure, to help him in his extremity. . . ."

For the life of me I couldn't hold back: "Not only him. His oppressors too must find it helpful."

Z.N.'s face broke into an appreciative smile. As for Pushchin, he looked as startled as if the cat Vasska lying peacefully purring at my feet had got up on his hind legs and recited the Lord's Prayer. Presently he summoned up a vague social smile and to my indignation apologized for talking dull politics within a lady's hearing. Then, paying no more attention to me, turned back to Georges.

"You say, Prince, the Emperor doesn't know about these things. But a proposal to eliminate public whipping has been lying on his desk for the past few years. All it needs is his signature. . . . The knout is a barbarous instrument of punishment. It does dreadful things to the human body. And the execution is a slow business, twenty blows to the hour, according to the army regulations; it sometimes lasts for as long as three hours. . . . I've been in the army, I've seen it done. The knout rises and falls, one stroke every three minutes, up and down in a bloody spray. And you stand there at attention, watching, hearing those cries that are no longer human. . . ." His calm face was suddenly convulsed. "What about it, Prince? What of the Tsar's responsibility to his people? That holy duty handed down by God himself to an earthly ruler? Someone will have to answer for this one day!"

Plainly, I know very little about the man who is capable of such intense feelings about his oppressed country. But how should I know more? When have we ever had a rational conversation? Nothing but passionate murmurings in bed and inane compliments in the drawing room!

For the first time I wanted more. Oh, I don't mean love, I don't want love any more, that's all over. But I do want him to *see* me, as a person, an intelligence equal to his own. I want him to talk to me as he is now talking to Georges and Zahar Nikolaitch. Why not? Hermann Gambs finds conversations with me stimulating—values me in that way. Why not Ivan Ivanitch Pushchin?

Or does he think it might spoil things? Many men do. I remember John Polidori, silly young man that he was, asking Geordie solemnly: "Doesn't all that cerebration get in the way?" And Geordie with a laugh in his voice: "Devil a bit it does. . . ."

Georges, now quite pale, whispered: "But why—why hasn't he . . .?"

"Signed it, you mean? Well, as you know, the Emperor —and his brothers, too, for that matter—is obsessed with the idea of army efficiency. His ideal of military achievement is the sight of a regiment on parade moving as one man. If the fear of punishment were eliminated, and the soldier treated humanely, he might, God forbid, begin thinking that it isn't the greatest crime in the world to fall short of being a human automaton—and then who knows what might happen at a review?" The cold mockery in his voice was somehow even worse than the anger that had distorted his face a moment ago.

The discussion broke up soon after, my poor Georges

looking quite undone. In that respect he is very much like P.B., who too used to be *destroyed* by evidences of man's cruelty to man. I remember Geordie saying in one of his more cynical moments: "The difference between P.B. and me is that I can stand anything provided it is not being done to me and he cannot." (Not precisely true: after all, he did die for the Greeks, in Missolonghi—but he always had that perverse pleasure in traducing himself.)

I am considering giving Prince Georges *Islam* to read. It'll teach him as much as Pushchin's revelations.

Claire's Journal, August 20

To Moscow, with Zahar Nikolaitch. Plans: visits to my former employer, Countess Zotov, shopping in Kuznetzkii Most, tea with the Apraksins. However, added something else to that program.

Zahar Nikolaitch had his Monday, going-to-Moscow face on. Official, worried, formal—paisley waistcoat put away, correct garb of official green donned. While we were driving in, I asked him right out about the Secret Society (this is typically Russian: a Secret Society that everyone knows and talks about, a sort of a *secret du Polichinelle*.) Nothing all that revolutionary about it—in England such debating societies proliferate. He went out of his way to assure me that that's all it was, a debating society. Nevertheless I had a feeling that it isn't quite so, that Z.N. says that because he knows the people involved and likes them and hopes that they won't do anything rash. I am sure Pushchin is a member. . . .

I do love going to Moscow in summertime—the early start (we were up at five), the brisk clip-clop of the carriage horses, the fresh morning breeze; we pass groups of peasants, slowly proceeding Moscow-wards; we overtake a cart, loaded with potatoes, creaking over the ruts and potholes, driven by a peasant, with his *baba* next to him togged out in her best, a brightly colored kerchief drawn about her face against the dust.

Then Moscow itself, a dream city out of an Asiatic fairy

tale, springs up before you unexpectedly from behind the gauzy band of road dust that obscures the distance. I can imagine how Napoleon must have gasped at his first sight of it from Sparrow Hills: it's an extravagant conglomeration of hundreds of church domes, glittering with silver and gold snake scales, gleaming crosses conjoined by a metalic fretwork of bright chains, turrets piled on turrets of every form, onion shaped, pyramidal, orbed, pointed. . . . All this lies before you like a huge heap of jewels piled on a platter, sun rays bouncing off that mad splendor as solid as golden lances. You can't believe your eyes. Only when you drive in through the gates and yourself become part of the landscape does it all mute down into something nearer to commonplace.

In winter Moscow intimidates me. I don't even see it, I am too concerned with merely surviving in the implacable, piercing cold that shrinks the flesh on my bones. But summer Moscow is quite different. Summer Moscow is sun flashing on golden roofs, and green parks, and shuttling variegated crowds, and songs, gay and melancholy, coming from the side streets, backed by the jaunty twang of balalaikas.

I didn't even feel too downcast when a stop at Lenhold's music store brought me no letters from England—it was too pleasant to stroll through the streets, quite free and unobserved—I could almost fancy myself back in Florence, or, going back even further, in London. Something of those old times came back to me—the gayety, the audacity. On an impulse worthy of that old reckless all-or-nothing Claire, as Mary used to call me, I hailed a drozhky and was driven to Pushchin's address.

Pushchin lives near Arbat not too far from the Pomykovs' town residence. I knocked at the door, which was presently opened by a brisk young servant who looked at me questioningly but without surprise. Before I had a chance to get my sparse Russian together and ask for his master, he himself appeared at the door and ushered me inside, into a parlor, which was large but antiquated in style. I noticed with some amusement that he was not completely sure of my identity until I put up the heavy veil which I had taken the precaution of buying at Gualtier's before coming.

"*Ma chère* Miss." He kissed my hands swiftly, one after the other. "*Quel bonheur!*"

"Are you surprised to see me?"

"Well"—he gave me his sweet bland smile—"let me say, I had hoped. . . ."

The last time he had been at the Pomykovs', when I answered his usual questioning glint with a headshake, it hadn't been merely because of the asterisk in red ink that appears in my diary on certain days. Oh, he is quick on the uptake! He knows, I daresay, as a result of innumerable liaisons, that no matter how intoxicating those reckless moments of impersonal passion, there inevitably comes a time when the woman, incurable romantic that she is, begins to long for something more. Accordingly, that same evening a note was slipped adroitly into my book. "Am I never to see you anywhere but here? Is it totally impossible—or could one conceivably dream that—?" and so on. Oh, in the best romantic tradition. And his direction carefully written out under these civilities.

Well, here I was. Still holding my hands, he stood before me, swaying from heel to toe in a sort of humorous indecision, while his narrow slate-gray eyes smiled at me. "The devil of it, *mon ange*, is that I am expecting visitors almost any minute. No, no," he added quickly, "I have no intention of letting you go, now that you've bestowed this felicity on me. It's just some army friends on business, they won't stay long." He turned my hand over and kissed it. His warm tongue touched the center of my bare palm and I shuddered at the sensual contact. "Did you think it might be another woman?" he inquired playfully.

"Well, it could very well be, couldn't it?" I countered. "And most probably one with prior claims which I should be in honor bound to respect."

Here I got a look from him that was only too familiar to me. Almost every man I had ever known had given it to me at one time or another—Geordie, saying between his teeth, "pray don't be—unusual." Trelawny, clutching his dark locks in comical exasperation. Hermann, at our first talk mustering up a weak, she-can't-possibly-mean-it smile. . . . Only P.B. never looked at me so—but then he was another odd one like me.

His visitors arrived almost immediately after. A calèche drew up before the house and two officers got out. Before they even rang the bell I was whisked down the corridor into the next room. "I won't be long." With a swift, intimate smile, he shut the door on me, leaving me alone in what evidently was his bedroom. A small monastic cell, military neat, containing the minimum essentials of bed, armchair, and desk, with a neat stack of books on it. I picked up one of them and leafed through it as I waited: Rousseau's *Contrat Social.*

Presently the audacious impulse that brought me here began to ebb, the sense of gayety and adventure drained out of me. All at once I was back in 13 Piccadilly Terrace, that first time, waiting while Fletcher went to announce me. I had had to wait a long time before I was admitted, I remember, and at one point almost ran away. Ah, if I had . . .

I put on my bonnet and shawl and stole out into the corridor. The door to the room in which Pushchin was entertaining his guests stood open and I could hear snatches of low voiced conversation, the clink of glasses against a tray, and occasionally Pushchin's voice putting a quiet question. They spoke in Russian; but once a high boyish tenor soared up distractedly, saying: *"Mais je vous jure, je vous donne ma parole d'officier que ce n'est pas possible. . . ."*

Here I realized that my plans to leave were impractical: it would be impossible for me to get to the front door unobserved. Accordingly, I retraced my steps and resigned myself to waiting.

I didn't have to wait too long. Very soon, I heard them in the corridor. Immediately afterward, a cautious look out of my window showed the pair slowly going back to the carriage. Presently my host joined me, looking unwontedly serious. Murmuring a perfunctory apology he took the armchair, drawing me down on his lap.

His narrow eyes shuttled toward me sleepily. *"Dites-*

moi, mon ange, you don't understand Russian, do you? I don't believe I've ever heard you speak it."

"I understand it better than I speak it. Usually I learn languages very quickly but—" I broke off suddenly enlightened. "Did you see me in the corridor?"

He shook his head. Even though he hadn't seen me, his indulgent smile told me quite clearly, he had taken for granted that I had been there, eavesdropping: after all, isn't that part of a woman's nature, to satisfy her curiosity by any means, including spying? I said coldly: "I shall tell you exactly what I *accidentally* overheard. Item: a lot of incomprehensible Russian. Item: one emotional exclamation in French. And, oh yes," I added, bitterly scrupulous, "I believe an English forest was mentioned."

He frowned at me, evidently puzzled.

"Sherwood, you know. Sherwood Forest, I presume, where Robin Hood lived."

"Oh." He gave a short laugh. "This time it was not the name of a forest, but the surname of a man." His face darkened. A heavy crease knifed downward between his brows. "The first name could be Judas." Immediately he looked vexed with himself.

Judas. A betrayal of some sort, then. "Has anything gone wrong?" I asked genuinely concerned.

But he had gone impassive again. "Oh, no, nothing serious. My friends have an engaging way of doing stupid things first and then coming to me for advice." Shaking his head, he said to himself under his breath, *"Akh, dyeti, dyeti,"* with a sort of mournful exasperation and fell silent again.

We stayed for a while in not uncompanionable silence, busy with our thoughts. I don't know what his were about; mine were about him. Clearly, Pushchin is what is commonly known as a man's man. To him women are delightful creatures, charming to look at, lovely to sleep with; he enjoys them wholeheartedly—that's what makes him such a satisfactory lover. But his deeper loyalties are reserved for his own sex. Z.N. tells me that when Pushchin was in the army he was one of the most popular officers. That doesn't surprise me. I can see him worrying about his *dyeti,* his children; trying to ameliorate the soldier's hard lot; being fatherly with his subalterns. The way he was with Georges, sensitive and forthright.

"I admired the way you spoke with Prince Georges the other day," I told him. The slightest tinge of grievance coloring my voice: why couldn't he be as open with me?

"Oh, yes. Dull stuff, politics, isn't it?" His hand moved on me gently, in an absent-minded caress, such as a man busy with his thoughts might bestow on a cat in his lap; and like a cat I wanted to run my claws into him.

"Not to me," I said. "Any protest against tyranny will find me both interested and sympathetic. How could I be otherwise, with my background?"

"*Vraiment?*" His eyes twinkled. "Is it so dangerous, then, your background?"

Not taking me seriously at all, damn him. I said, driven to imprudence: "Enough so that if I told you something of it, and you chose to disclose it, you could probably ruin me."

"Oh, but I intend to," he said gaily. "Isn't that why you are here?" His attention was fully upon me now; his body had awakened to mine. I fended him off:

"No, wait, don't! Couldn't we talk? I want you to *know* me—there's so much I want to tell you—and to hear about you. . . ."

"Later, *dushenka.*"

He rose to his feet, swinging me up effortlessly in his arms—he is quite surprisingly strong—and laid me down on the narrow bed.

"No, wait, listen. . . ." My hands tangled with his futilely, as he expertly, smilingly, undressed me. I went on talking a little longer, struggling against the seduction of touch, subjugation of intellect, until the absurdity of trying to expound one's adherence to the Godwinian theory under these circumstances was borne in on me. An angry laugh broke from me. His white teeth flashed in answer. "*Ma folle petite* Miss, *anglichanochka moya.* . . ." His body invaded mine in the soft and ferocious onslaught I loved and yet was beginning to resent.

A marble reproduction of Thorwaldsen's bust of Alexander I stood outside Prince Volynski's library. Grisha would often stop and contemplate it with pleasure. The clearly carved eyelids, just a little weary, the merest ghost of the captivating smile he remembered on the subtly carved lips—altogether it was a beautiful face, half Roman emperor, half angel.

Today, as he paused before it, his contemplation was a troubled one. Was there cruelty in the thin lips, so ambiguously dented at the corners? As he often did, he imagined himself talking to Alexander in an intoxicating mixture of intimacy and daring, telling him everything. "Your Majesty, has anybody told you about the knout? About what goes on in the military colonies? I know that things like that are being kept from you by heartless scoundrels like Arakcheev, but you who are the epitome of what is best and kindest, who love your people. . . ."

The marble face gazed back at him with its mysterious smile, giving no answer. . . .

The door to the library was partly open. He now became aware of some sort of activity going on inside. A voice reached him, cooing as soft as a dove: "And what do you think you're doing now, dearie? What are you thinking of?"

A frightened gasp answered this soft query. Grisha pushed the door open and looked in. He saw Matryosha, her small face wizened with terror, crouching on the marble floor with her bucket and brush. Nikolavna loomed calmly over her, arms folded placidly across her breast, fingers drumming lightly on her plump upper arms. There was nothing especially intimidating in her aspect or in the reasonable voice with which she addressed the cowering girl. "Can't you see that spot there, dearie? Right there? I guess you just plain wore those big blue eyes of yours looking out for the men, or you'd see it easy enough." Her nostrils flared slightly in her serene face. "You little slut." With a totally unexpected movement her foot shot out. The girl sprawled on the floor, the bucket slopped over, soapy water went creeping over the floor.

"There now, look at that," the housekeeper cooed, "that's quite a mess you're making, dovey. Perhaps if I rubbed that pretty face in it, it would teach you to be careful." Her breath coming quicker now, she bent over and seized Matryosha by her untidy blond plait, her own eyes going round and flat, like a hawk's descending on a chick. Then she saw Grisha. Unhurriedly straightening up, she said in her honeyed singsong: "Why, your Excellency, I didn't see you. . . . See, I'm teaching this little girl here, you know how girls are. . . ."

And all at once Grisha was overcome by a loathing rage such as he had never felt before. The housekeeper's buxom figure wavered before him as though seen through frosted panes, an incandescent lightness seemed to lift up the top of his head. He said in a voice quite unlike his own: "Yes, I saw how you're teaching her."

"Why, Your Excellency, Grigorii Petrovich, I'm just doing what I'm supposed to," Nikolavna purred unabashed. "That's just what her ladyship your mother keeps me here for, to hold the girls in line, like . . ." As he moved toward them he put his bad foot down wrong and stumbled—this often happened to him when he was agitated—and she made a sympathetic clucking sound. "There now, no need to upset yourself," she said in a motherly fashion.

Grisha, being on his way to the stables, had his riding crop with him. He now brought it down with all his might on the back of the nearest armchair. The whistle and thump of it resounded satisfyingly in his ears—it would be even better when he lifted it again and brought it down on her plump shoulders and kept doing so until they were cut to ribbons. Nikolavna's face grew terrible with fear; she barely dodged the next blow and without another word scuttled around him and out of the door.

Slowly turning on his heel, Grisha watched her go. He felt cleansed, purified, a St. George destroying the evil. He caught sight of himself in the mirror and exchanged a pleased smile with his reflection, before he turned back to Matryosha who was slowly dragging herself upright from the floor. Rigid on her knees, her drenched shift clinging to her thin body, she fixed him with eyes opened to their utmost. Grisha said to her kindly: "If she touches you again, you come and tell me."

She gave a quick speechless nod. As he went limping out of the room, he was conscious of that blue incredulous gaze following him.

The mood of virtuous exhilaration stayed with Grisha all the rest of the morning. Riding to the Pomykovs', he kept remembering with pleasure how the bitch had run from him, how that plump face had disintegrated. Strangely, that was even more pleasant to think about than Matryosha's worshiping gaze. He was impelled to tell Miss Clairmont all about it in the middle of their lesson.

Miss Clairmont listened to him attentively. She had Vasska on her lap, combing out the snarls in his fur. The white cat submitted to her ministrations complacently, alternating his purr with an occasional pettish little cry.

"Yes, I can imagine," she said, her lips tightening, after Grisha was through. "Older women can be extremely cruel to younger prettier ones. And I am sure whatever cruelties had been visited on this Nikolavna in her lifetime of subjection would in turn be visited by her upon her inferiors—that's the way of serfdom, isn't it? Immoral, corrupting. . . ."

For once Grisha was conscious of being just a little impatient with her: when was she going to get around to praising him for his championship of Matryosha? But she went on: "I'm becoming more and more aware of this business of enslaving another human being. Only the other day, I heard Marya Ivanovna complaining how impossible it is getting to *buy* a good cook. . . . Could you really have beaten this woman without any consequences to yourself?"

It occurred to him, disagreeably, that perhaps he could not have. "Yes, *maman* might have been very annoyed with me, might she not? Nikolavna is her favorite." Would the old bitch complain? Well, let her, he would explain. . . . "But you mustn't think, Miss Clairmont, that *maman* knows about her behavior, she has no idea. . . ." No more, he thought bleakly, than Alexander about Arakcheev's iniquities.

"But if you'd beaten that awful woman, you'd be immune from the law, wouldn't you? Because she is yours, isn't she? Like a dog or a horse?"

What was she trying to get at? He said patiently: "No, I told you, she isn't mine, she is my mother's." The only serfs he owned were in Nikitino, a sizable country place left him by his uncle. "If she were mine, do you think I'd let her mis—mishandle?"

"Mistreat."

"Mistreat other servants. She wouldn't dare."

"I daresay she would perpetuate her cruelties a little more discreetly. . . . Sit still, you silly cat. You don't want lumps in your fur, do you?" But Vasska, after biting her hand gently, flowed off her lap and decamped. Absent-mindedly pulling puffs of white fleece out of the comb, she went on: "I myself find it hard to condemn anyone for whatever inhuman traits they have acquired through being a part of this inhuman institution. It's so easy—and so delicious—to enjoy one's power over another human being . . . and so corrupting. . . ."

There was a pall of some mysterious disapprobation hanging about this conversation. Trying to dispel it and to recall to her his own virtuous behavior, he said again: "If you had only seen the expression on her face . . ."

And now her troubled black eyes did lift to his. "What concerns me more, Georges, is the expression on *yours.*"

"My face . . .?"

"Yes, when you were preparing to beat a woman old enough to be your mother."

For a moment he couldn't believe his ears. Then, for the second time that day, fury swamped him.

"I'm sorry, Georges. We had decided, hadn't we, that I would always tell you the truth. . . ."

"I am obliged to you," said Grisha through his teeth. He bowed coldly and took his leave, although the lesson was far from being over. Miss Clairmont made no attempt to detain him.

He rode Nelly home at a breakneck gallop, taking her recklessly over several too-high fences on the way. With fury he reflected on Miss Clairmont's disagreeable ability to depress his spirits. How dared she do this to him? Not only fail to give him his due praise—had he not championed the weak, chastised the wicked?— but somehow to manage to turn it all around and, incomprehensibly, perversely, blame him. He hadn't done anything wrong; it was she who insisted on looking at things from some unnatural angle, seeing them all askew, quite differently from anyone else. . . .

It was much later, as he was combing his hair before going down to dinner, that the shielding anger slipped long enough for him to remember how he had smiled at himself in the mirror that time after the woman had run from him. Even then he had been obscurely aware of *something,* some odd familiarity about the smile. He now allowed himself to know exactly how it had been: his lips had been folded into the same relishing folds that Nikolavna's had, when she was stooping over the cringing girl.

Now, standing before the mirror, with a silver-backed brush clutched in either hand, he tested to the full that deep humiliation that comes when one finds in oneself a resemblance to that which one most despises.

Suddenly he was completely miserable. All the cruelties he had ever encountered or heard about seemed to crowd about him. The knout rose and fell, in a spray of blood, once every three minutes; the peasant woman dashed her child's head against the wall in a frenzy; Nikolavna smilingly terrorized Matryosha; and he—he too, with the same relishing smile . . . He flung himself down at his desk and began feverishly to write to Miss Clairmont.

"You were quite right. I understand everything now. I was proud of myself. I thought I was punishing the evil, but I wasn't, I was merely becoming a part of it, even enjoying it. . . ."

Another memory surfaced slyly—something else that was wholly vile, and that he could no longer hide from himself. Yes, it had been there at the very moment of his righteous anger, the familiar furtive stirring at his loins.

He sprang up from the desk as if stung and began limping about his room distractedly. Black self-hatred enveloped him. *So there you are,* an inner voice whispered, *deformed within as well as without.* Desperately his mind cast around for ways of canceling out the loathsomeness, expiating the dimly felt sin: fasting, prayers of contrition, difficult penance. He even found himself contemplating a hairshirt, or perhaps those rusty chains he had seen with pity and revulsion on the bodies of pilgrims stopping in the servants' quarters on their way to the Holy Virgin of Kazan. . . .

He forced himself to return to the desk and finish his letter. The pen sputtered, tiny inkspots hopping flealike around his agitated script, but he didn't take the time to mend it. He scribbled swiftly:

". . . I shall try to cleanse myself, by prayer and reflection and begging my Creator's pardon. But first I must beg yours for indulging in blind stupid anger at you while you were doing your best to awaken me to my sins. . . ."

He splashed hot wax on the folded note, pressed down the seal, and summoned Fomitch to whom he gave it to be delivered to Islavskoye. "Immediately, Fomitch, it's terribly important."

Something suspiciously like a grin indented the valet's face. "Right away, Excellency. I know how it is with the young folks' business."

"It's nothing like that, you old fool. Just take it and go," Grisha said, angrily. Immediately he caught himself up. "I am sorry, Fomitch. Please do as I ask."

Tomorrow morning, he told himself, he would get up at dawn and go to the church for the first services. The thought eased him. He visualized with grateful affection Father Condratii's meek pock-marked face with its scanty beard and faded eyes of indeterminate color peering timidly from under the worn miter.

He was able to get through dinner without his misery being apparent. Back in his room, he knelt down before the ikon in the corner and tried to pray. *Forgive, Holy Mother, the trespasses of my body, save me from the sin of anger. . . . Yes, and that other sin of carnal lust compounding the first. . . . Help me, a sinner. . . .* The dark byzantine visage of the Holy Virgin gazed at him, sad-eyed, from within the silver-crusted frame, the candles beneath the ikon burned, each circled by a small bright halo in that special touching way of the churchly candles. Murky, hypnotic peace began to descend on him, as he murmured and crossed himself and bowed. The world receded, leaving him safe in the sanctified corner. . . .

Presently the door opened and closed softly and he heard Fomitch uttering a respectful little cough behind him. Rising to his feet, he received from him a note and a small parcel.

"Dear Prince," Miss Clairmont wrote; and the sight of her handwriting brought back the sound of her voice, tender, melodious, just the tiniest bit acerbic, "you exaggerate your sins. I didn't wish you to sink into such a slough of despond. Your anger at the woman's cruelty was perfectly justified, but you must learn to look beyond the deed to the circumstances and recognize the horrors of the wicked system we live in. I hate seeing any traces of the serf owner in you. But I am sure your nature is strong and pure enough to resist the corruption. . . . Aff'ly your, C.C. P.S. I am less pleased with the form of your letter than with its contents. It was written in French. Whatever your state of mind is, I expect you to communicate with me in English."

Grisha drew a deep breath. He put down the letter and turned wonderingly to the parcel.

"That's from them, too," Fomitch told him. His utterance was irritatingly conspiratorial. "First they wrote the note and sealed it, then they said to wait and ran up to their room and came down with this wee package to give you. A book, feels like."

"And who asked you to feel?" Grisha asked, annoyed. Fomitch merely twitched his tufted eyebrows indulgently.

Grisha dismissed him and unwrapped the package, which indeed turned out to be a smallish book, bound in vellum. It looked familiar; he presently remembered seeing it several times in Miss Clairmont's loving hold. The *Revolt of Islam*, said the gilt letters on the cover.

He put it down reluctantly and returned to his prayers. But the feeling was gone. The devotional corner felt exposed to the world, and candle flames danced uneasily, as though some wind from outside were blowing on them. But he dutifully finished his prayers before coming back to Miss Clairmont's book.

Claire's Journal, September 6

Georges came for his lesson today, heavy-lidded but bright-eyed. I know that look, when you have stayed up the whole night reading a book you can't put down. He was somewhat surprised that *Islam* was written in verse: he hadn't realized that P.B. was a poet. Well, actually, it was a long time before P.B. started thinking of himself as one; he saw himself, rather, as a philosopher expressing himself in poetical terms. And yet in Geneva he *shaped* Geordie. Afterward, Geordie was different, wrote differently because of P.B.—and me.

I remember a letter came from Albé, acknowledging, although I must say, in rather offhand fashion, his debt to P.B. P.B. had been delighted: so humble he had been, seeing himself as just a star, a poor little star paling next to that mighty poetic luminary. And I—I was hurt; absurdly so. No mention of me at all. And yet I knew that I too had been important to him. Hadn't I helped too? Removed the unnecessary shackles he had chosen to burden himself with? It seemed to me the effects of this liberation could be seen in every line he wrote after Geneva.

I told my grievance to P.B. and was disagreeably surprised when he of all people did not acknowledge my claims as wholeheartedly as I would have expected him to. I was quite cross with him: "Even he," I thought, "even he is infected by that common disease, the conspiracy to discount women's worth. . . ." Oh, just a fleeting thought; an unjust one. He had always been overgenerous with me; he listened to me and made changes when I suggested them. Why then that silent withholding, that reservation when I made my just claim? I couldn't understand . . . I still don't.

We discussed some aspects of *Islam* until we were joined by Hermann and others, bound on a nut-gathering expedition in the woods. As we started going home we met one of the servants to tell us that there is scarlet fever in the village and we must come home by the garden. At home we found that Marya Ivanovna had already gone to Madame Zimmermann to ask for a lodging and presently she came home to tell us that it was all arranged and we would go there with the children for a week, until the danger is past. So now to pack.

Grisha knew Miss Clairmont's departure to be merely temporary. Nevertheless, it left him feeling strangely bereft. He consoled himself by diligently reading her friend's book. It didn't make for easy reading and many parts of it he understood only dimly. He was conscious of vast nebulous images crowding his mind, occasionally illuminated by a poignant passage that for a moment seemed to make all clear. Outsize figures roamed the cloudy landscape. A "hoary-haired youth," reluctant to shed blood, nevertheless performed impressive martial feats, decimating thousands; a spirited heroine defied a tyrant and was confined in an underwater prison, to be freed by a providential earthquake. It was a huge fairy tale, rather like *Ruslan and Ludmilla,* but replete with all kinds of somber meanings he couldn't quite fathom.

As he read, he found himself smiling in recognition—yes, beyond doubt, this was the mind that had devised the parable of Lilith: the same intriguing reversal of accepted values was to be seen there. In the very first canto there had been an electrifying description of a battle between an eagle and a serpent. The eagle won and flew away "with clang of wings and scream"; the snake writhed wounded on the ground. But—he had to read twice to make sure—this was not to be rejoiced at: it was the serpent that stood for good! And what was that about the Fiend God who

shall fade like shadow from his thousand fanes
While truth with joy enthroned o'er his lost empire reigns . . .?

By the time he had got to that, Miss Clairmont wasn't there to ask, but he suspected the worst.

Yes, a dangerous book—exhilaratingly so!—to be read in strict privacy, away from inquiring eyes. Thinking of his father's probable reaction to such a book, and remembering Monsieur Gambs's unspoken strictures about her confidences, Grisha was conscious of a surge of grateful pride: she trusted him!

He rode Nelly down to Islavskoye to make inquiries and found Zahar Nikolaitch with Pushchin in the billiard room. Pushchin, a pipe firmly clenched in his teeth, moved about the table in a cloud of smoke, with the sure spare movements of an expert player, spinning out a long run. The billiard balls rolled about the green field, as orderly as planets, white circling red.

Zahar Nikolaitch told him that they had just come back from the Zimmermans' villa, and that everyone there was well. "Monsieur Gambs and Miss Clairmont have incorporated the Zimmermann brats into their classes, and my spouse is congratulating herself on bringing culture to a backward household," he remarked with his ironic twinkle. "How charming of you to call, Prince. I shall certainly report your courtesy in the proper quarters. . . . Pavel, Timoshka!" He rang the bell. "Refreshments, quick." But he had to repeat his summons several times before the servants appeared wearing an even more unbuttoned look than usual. The whole house, within the short time that the family had been away, had acquired the half-desolate, half-rakish look of a bachelor establishment. Zahar Nikolaitch didn't seem to mind—he had been drinking a little: Grisha caught a faint whiff of blackberry cordial whenever he came close—and in fact to be unusually cheerful. "By the way," he added genially, teetering from heel to toe. "I gather there is an understanding between you and my daughter."

"Yes, we are betrothed, I believe," Grisha said smiling. The day before they had left Dunia had sidled up to him after the lesson in her twining secretive manner and whispered in his ear: "I have decided to marry you when I grow up."

"*A la bonne heure!* I shouldn't count on it, Prince. Young females of my daughter's age are notoriously fickle. . . . Incidentally, I believe Ivan Ivanitch has something for you."

[113]

"Indeed I have," said Pushchin, pausing to click up a score. He reached for his coat—they were playing in shirtsleeves—and drew a sizable letter from its inside breast pocket. "I was entrusted with some reading matter for you, Prince. It would have been sent to Andreyevo for you, but since you are so providentially here. . . ." He proffered the letter to Grisha, a friendly smile touching his flexible lips. "What a delightful blush! I have been told that this is a story copied out for your edification, but I can see it's much, much more than that."

"Ah, Ivan Ivanitch, Ivan Ivanitch," crooned the tipsy Zahar Nikolaitch with vast significance. "A go-between? Already?"

Grisha asked the two gentlemen to ride back to Andreyevo with him for dinner. A moment later, covertly fingering the letter (it crackled satisfyingly bulky in his pocket), he regretted the impulse: an afternoon's blissful reading would have to be postponed. The invitation was accepted by Pushchin alone, Zahar Nikolaitch preferring, as he put it, to "enjoy the nymph solitude while he could."

At Andreyevo Prince Pyotr gave Pushchin a brief examination through his lorgnette and extended two fingers in a courteous but absent-minded manner. The Princess bent her huge eyes on him with cautious graciousness. "My son told me so much about you," she said. "I am constantly hearing of his delight in meeting someone so closely connected with his favorite poet."

Pushchin bowed, with his calm smile.

"Maman, I beg of you. . . ."

"Well, what, *mon ami,* what have I done now?"

"You make it sound as if—I assure you, I am not happy in making Monsieur Pushchin's acquaintance only because he is Pushkin's friend. . . ."

"Quelle idée, Georges! I am sure Monsieur Pushchin knows I meant no such thing. . . . Do tell me more about yourself, Monsieur Pushchin. I hear you went to the Tsarskoye Syelo Lyceum. A charming spot—I remember accompanying Her Imperial Highness the Mother Empress there once for the graduation exercises. . . ."

She went on questioning him, sweetly and implacably, all through dinner. Pushchin took the examination with good grace. He ate with relish the superb fresh perch with its garniture of mushrooms and, as he answered the Princess's questions, bent upon her a respectful version of the amused and appreciative gaze with which he looked at all women. As the dinner progressed, one could see him rising higher and higher in her estimation. His French and his manners were faultless. In answer to the Prince's question he admitted casually that Admiral Pushchin, a well-known figure in the days of Catherine the Great, was indeed his grandfather. Then, it turned out, he knew the right people not only in Moscow but in St. Petersburg; and, when it came out that he had been transferred from St. Petersburg only two years ago to occupy his present position, the Princess, completely won over, gave him the mournfully comradely look of one exile greeting another. In the end it was in teasing and affectionate tones that she rallied him with: "I must tell you frankly, Monsieur Pushchin, that I consider your friend Pushkin a terrible young man."

"Yes, he is very naughty," Pushchin agreed, smiling.

"*Laissez-le tranquil, Irène,*" the Prince intervened. "Anyone who can brand Arakcheev as neatly as he has done deserves to be forgiven for his sins—at least, some of them! How does it go? 'Full of vengefulness and malice'—"

Pushchin obligingly quoted the whole of the waspish epigram that, many thought, had been directly responsible for the poet's exile. The Prince listened to it with a malicious and relishing smile. Later in the library where the men had repaired after dinner, he allowed himself to be amused by still another epigram—this one about Count Vorontzov under whom the poet had reluctantly served in Odessa.

> Half pundit and half ignoramus,
> Half a milord and half buffoon,
> Half scoundrel—but there is a hope now
> That he will be a whole one soon.

The Prince laughed.

"What a sharp tongue the fellow has—a truly impressive gift for an unforgettable phrase."

"Your Excellency has found the right word." A tiny flame flashed in Pushchin's gray eyes. "I venture to say Pushkin's name will live long after those of Arakcheev and Vorontzov are forgotten."

"Hmm, yes, I daresay." The Prince's large white hand groped for the lorgnette. "All the same, plenty of carbonarity in that whole crowd—your circle, I believe, Monsieur Pushchin? I can imagine the sort of discussions that went on in your Green Lamp Club."

Lifting the lorgnette he fixed the young man with a shrewd but not unkindly eye.

"Very true," Pushchin replied, unruffled. "There was no subject we didn't discuss—in between drinking bouts."

"Oh, you needn't tell me! Abolition of serfdom, constitution, revolution! All kinds of cataclysmic and unnecessary changes, *n'est-ce pas?*"

The Prince smiled, with considerable charm. His face was interested and alive without any trace of the usual well-bred ennui. He was obviously enjoying the conversation. "Why, he likes Pushchin," Grisha said to himself, agreeably surprised. Nevertheless, the tiniest admixture of envy colored his pleasure in his friend's success with his father: any stranger, it appeared, had more power of engaging his father's interest than any member of his family. "The truth is," he thought sadly, "we all bore him, and I more than the rest. . . ."

". . . I do recognize that the process of natural change must occur, *ça va sans dire.* Thus a human being passes through various stages, such as infancy, adolescence, and so forth. But"—he raised a finger, admonishingly—"throughout he stays a human being— he doesn't suddenly turn into an ape or a weasel. Equally, you can't hope—nor is it desirable—to turn Russians into Frenchmen or Germans, by the infusion of foreign ideas."

Pushchin bowed his neat head, courteously, a reasonable man yielding to the force of irrefutable argument. "You are perfectly right, your Excellency. Actually, I don't know that even in our most audacious discussions we had thought of altering the national character. . . . We thought, rather, in terms of allowing it to fulfill itself as completely as possible. Nevertheless, if I may enlarge upon your powerful analogy—there have been instances, have there not, of human nature being unnaturally distorted, stunted in its process of natural change? Thus, the Chinese have a custom of binding their female children's feet so that later they can only hobble. . . ."

Prince Pyotr's eyebrows rose. "And I daresay, in your view, law, authority, and so on are such unnatural restraints."

"What I had in mind, your Excellency, was excessive censorship, excessive police surveillance—these, indeed, I view as unnatural restraints that squeeze the human spirit into unnatural shapes."

"Yes, I can see how you would find these—inconvenient," said the Prince with a slight chilly smile. "On the other hand when I consider into what an *unnatural* shape, to use your expression, the Russian spirit would be distorted, should any of your Benthamite notions take root here—! No, sir, let us leave that godless rubbish to the godless and corrupt English, who cultivate it."

He pronounced these words with such unwonted venom that Grisha, surprised, blurted out: "But, Papa, I thought you approved of the English!"

His father's cold eyes dwelled on him briefly, with indulgent contempt. "Why? Because I insist on your learning the language? We didn't stop speaking French during the French Revolution, did we? Besides, I do approve of many English things. My riding boots are English made—and they export unexceptionable tobacco and soap and other excellent things. But the one English commodity I would definitely prohibit is the importation of their form of government. I know it is popular in your circles, Monsieur Pushchin. *Quant à moi*—there is an ungodly and frivolous contradiction in the very concept of constitutional monarchy. I reject it utterly."

"The Emperor doesn't," Pushchin observed. "At the opening of the Diet of Warsaw in 1818, he came out strongly in favor of the constitution."

"And he will never live it down, it seems." The Prince struck the top of his desk lightly. "Think back, *je vous en prie.* Constitution for whom? For the Poles. Not for his own people, not for Russia. Because in spite of the Swiss La Harpe, in spite of the *popovich* Speranski, he has always known, deeply, unquestioningly, right inside his bowels, the way a Russian sovereign has to feel about his people, that constitution is not the Russian way. You see, my dear sir, *mon très cher Monsieur Pushchin,* the Russian people are instinctively set against changes; *they will not be uprooted from their past.* That is what your band of suckling Jacobins has failed to realize. And don't mention Peter the Great to me, as you were no doubt about to do. He may have cut beards and introduced Western garb, but he did not tamper with the one inalterable trait in the nature of the Russian people: *they do not want to rule themselves.* With rare Christian humility they are content to lay their responsibilities in God's bosom: which means to give them entirely over to the Tsar in whom they recognize God's representative on earth. This is historically true. What other people have done what we have done? In the very dawn of history the ancient Slavs sent out messengers saying, 'Come and rule over us.' We are unique in that respect. That deep need to be ruled, to be ruled *absolutely*—that is and remains the truth the Russian people have lived by and will continue to live by forever and aye, amen. . . ."

As the Prince spoke, he gestured lightly with his lorgnette; each point he made emphasized by a tiny prismatic flash leaping from the diamond in its shaft.

Pushchin listened attentively. Halfway through the tirade, he began to grope absent-mindedly in his vest pocket, finally bringing out his pipe and tobacco pouch. To Grisha's horror, he began filling the pipe, but stopped just short of lighting it and apologized. "An evil smelly habit," he remarked. "I find myself instinctively resorting to it when I find myself faced by a redoubtable opponent."

The Prince's raised eyebrows and pinched nostrils relaxed simultaneously at this diplomatic remark. "You characterize the habit aptly." But his slight smile was indulgent. "It needn't be so, however. I myself have learned to appreciate good tobacco in England—from Lord Petersham, who used to mix his own. If you would care to try *some of my sort,*" he said switching into English, with a sort of nostalgic relish, "I shall not mind your *blowing a cloud.*" He opened a largish Wedgwood jar from which there emanated a fragrance so unlike the homely aroma of Pushchin's "sort" as to seem to belong to a totally different class of substance.

Pushchin showed himself worthy of this mark of condescension on the part of his host by the deeply appreciative silence with which he filled his pipe and lit it. Presently however he said with a mildly obstinate air, "If you draw your conclusion about the Russian character from the antiquity, Prince, what about the *vyeche?* In Novgorod? In Pskov? Surely the existence of that form of popular assembly indicates a willingness on the part of our ancestors to rule themselves. And it was an ancient custom, one that preceded Tsardom."

Again Grisha stirred uneasily. The argument had already gone on much longer than he could have thought possible. The Prince was, plainly, enjoying it; and indeed there was something in the younger man's air that took any offense out of his opposition: but Grisha, not certain how long his father could tolerate being contradicted, even in the most respectful fashion, couldn't hold back covert a sigh of relief when a footman came in to say that the bailiff had arrived and was waiting on his Grace's pleasure.

"Tell him to wait, I'll be with him presently. . . . I daresay you'll be staying to supper?"

Pushchin shook his head regretfully. "I believe Zahar Nikolaitch expects me back with the horse he so kindly lent me. We are planning to go back to Moscow together."

"That his horse? A neat little bay . . . You know something about horses, I take it?"

"I used to be with the mounted artillery."

"Yes, I thought I recognized the style when the two of you came pelting down the drive. My Grisha is a good horseman too, I must say, without boasting—light hands, good seat. Too reckless, though—break his neck one day, the way he takes his fences." Unexpectedly pride sounded in his voice. "What the English call 'a bruising rider.' " He laid his hand on Grisha's shoulder as he spoke and the combination of affectionate touch and unexpected praise brought sudden tears to Grisha's astonished eyes. He stood rigid and unblinking, his eyes stretched wide to keep the unmanly moisture from spilling over, while his father went on: "You might want to look over what we have in the stables. There's one horse in particular, a big black brute of a stallion—I just bought him. Probably paid too much . . . Well, my dear—Ivan Ivanitch, is it?—it has been most instructive to talk with you." Removing his hand from Grisha's shoulder he offered it to Pushchin with unwonted cordiality. "I am always glad to hear the other person's view, assuming that that other person can express himself rationally and not indulge in the *yurodivyi*-type raving that the so-called intellectuals of our time seem to prefer. . . . Glad to see you any time."

As they walked through the stables, Grisha reflected on Pushchin's enviable gift of making himself universally liked. Even Grisha's retriever Toozik, old and cranky, gave his carelessly outstretched hand a quick lick. Not that he went out of his way to get this response. Perhaps it was the way he had of looking at one with calm affectionate curiosity: "So that's what you're like," his attentive expression seemed to say. "Well, that interests me."

They stopped at Kestrel's stall. The oversized stallion, his huge body giving off a blackbird sheen, backed away as they came close, laying his ears back and thundering his hooves on the wood. "All right, you devil," said the groom in charge of him, half threatening, half admiring. The big horse trembled, snorted. When he grew still, getting used to their presence, Grisha became aware of another sound coming from the back of the stables: an odd, meaty, regular *thunk*.

"Now there's a sound I recognize," Pushchin said. His voice was as composed as ever; only his nostrils dilated faintly in revulsion. "Somebody is getting a whipping."

"Got it in one, your Honor," said the groom, approvingly.

Grisha hobbled hurriedly to the back of the stables and found Fedka lying stretched across a hurdle, his shirt off, his pants down to his ankles. Two stableboys held him down by wrists and ankles, while the head groom Matvey brought a bunch of birch rods whistling down on his bared back, stopping between strokes to push his rolled-up sleeves further back with a businesslike gesture. At each blow Fedka's body leaped convulsively like a landed trout.

"Stop it, stop it immediately!"

The head groom, arrested in mid-blow, stepped back and bowed. "His Excellency's orders, your Excellency."

"Let him up immediately," Grisha said, and found that his voice was trembling. He had always known, of course, that sometimes members of the household were punished by whipping—when his father, after listening to a report of someone's misdeed, would say tersely between his teeth, "Yes, well, see to it," he had known what was meant—but somehow none of it had any reality for him until now, when he actually saw it done.

Fedka, released, straightened himself painfully from his rack. Automatically his hands went down to cover his nudity. He stood dazed, head down, hands cradled together at the crotch, until Matvey said to him, "Get decent, boy, don't you see the young master is here?" He turned away then submissively—presenting back and buttocks latticed by crimson weals—and began easing his pants on gingerly, evidently in pain. Grisha caught a glimpse of his averted face, convulsed for a moment in a crying grimace.

"No need to upset yourself, your Excellency," said Matvey in a rumbling fatherly bass. Grisha gazed at him in childish horror. He had known Matvey all his life, had been taught to ride by him. A kindly steady man, with a deacon's face framed by a spade-shaped beard—only sometimes, as he handled the Prince's special matched team in informal race against a neighbor, a sort of calm deviltry would illumine it—and now suddenly an executioner!

Fedka, having restored himself to decency, had turned and was standing at attention. His face was pale and tear stained. His lips quivered involuntarily; a nervous sob escaped him and he angrily swallowed it, snuffling and wiping his nose on his sleeve.

"What did he do?" Pushchin's calm voice inquired behind Grisha.

"Sniffing around the housemaids, your Honor," Matvey answered. Grisha remembered the other day—"a girl comes around, like,"—and the artless, beaming smile. All that boastful young manhood he had envied now humiliated, diminished; a whipped boy stood before him trying not to cry.

"Well, let him go now," he said tersely, not looking at Fedka. "On my responsibility."

"If you say so, your Excellency." Matvey tucked the whip through his belt and, turning back into the kindly Matvey Grisha knew, added reassuringly: "If his Excellency your father asks, I'll tell him the lad had full measure. Go kiss the young master's hand, boy."

Fedka obediently stumbled over, head bent.

"Are you in pain?" Grisha asked softly and felt Fedka's lips quivering childishly against his hand.

"Let's hope so, your Excellency. Maybe it's taught him his lesson. Trouble is he's got a tough skin, same as a goat's. Take my eye off him and back he'll go to the maids' quarters, devil take him. Village stuff isn't good enough for him, lustful young Herod."

To Grisha's amazement, a shadow of the former swagger seemed to come back to Fedka's beaten body at these austere words. Glancing back as he walked away with Pushchin, he saw the others helping Fedka on with his shirt. Unfeeling snickers reached him. Nevertheless it was clear that in some mysterious way this callousness, like Matvey's unfeeling remarks, was more helpful to the punished man than his sympathy.

Pushchin's horse was waiting for him. Pushchin patted it absently, his eyes on Grisha. He said slowly, picking his words:

"If you are thinking, Prince, about the remarks I made the other day about the public whipping in the army—well, you must believe me this is nothing like it. Not even close." Pushchin's face went a little grim. "Not that I believe in any human being having to submit to the indignity of a beating—even when I was in school I hated to see my friends being birched. I shouldn't imagine this was much more. Frankly, I don't see your father spoiling a good groom for a little matter of tomcatting."

Grisha forced a smile. "No, my father isn't a strict moralist."

Still, there had been that bloody latticework on the healthy white flesh, and a hurt child's face.

"You don't like these things either, do you?" There was careful tenderness in Pushchin's quick look at him. "Well, you'll just have to toughen up, Prince. No," he added quickly, "no, not so, don't toughen up. The only hope of correcting the ugly system we live in is having young people like you staying sensitive to its horrors. . . ."

It was odd to hear him echoing Miss Clairmont's words. He gave Grisha's hand a swift friendly grip and the next moment was up in the saddle, gathering the reins in his hands.

As soon as Pushchin cantered out of sight, Grisha, accompanied by Toozik, went to his special reading spot. It was a pleasantly neglected recess in the outermost reaches of the garden, birdcherry bushes mingling with acacia allowed to grow wild; there was a dilapidated but comfortable bench and a statue of Apollo, his lyre broken, warning all intruders off by an upflung marble hand. Grisha would retire there to do whatever reading he wanted to do privately, out of the range of Monsieur Lachaine's inquisitive snuff-darkened nose. It was there that he struggled with the impassioned ambiguities of *Islam.* He now broke the seal on the envelope and pulled out the closely written pages. Her hurrying script leaped at him, drawing him into her Geneva summer.

Claire's Letter to Grisha, September 14

It is only fair to tell you the story of our farcical duel. I think it's the meanest trick in the world to start on something and break off in the middle: like Scheherazade clearing out on the five-hundredth night. The *commedia* started one lovely morning—a typical Geneva morning, all gentle sunlight and placid sparkle, cowbells tinkling in the distance. Mary and I were alone in our cottage, P.B. having gone off on one of his solitary rambles. I was copying a poem of Albé's. Little Wilmouse was on the floor at my feet cooing to himself, and sometimes I would tickle his chin with my quill and make him crow with laughter. He was such a delightful baby. . . .

And then Mary, who was mending P.B.'s jacket, found in one of its pockets a letter from Polidori challenging him to a duel.

I couldn't help laughing as I read this missive: such nonsense, copied out from a manual on writing fat-headed challenges, not a single banality missed. Nor was I altogether surprised. He had always made me uneasy: he was much too pretty and much too angry at us. It was disconcerting to see the ugly look of jealousy on a warmly Italianate, olive-hued face of a Perugino cherub, with its silken girl's eyelashes and melting brown eyes.

He would listen to Albé's conversation with P.B., those large windy arguments that took in the entire universe, and try to elbow himself in; there would be a deadly little pause—or Albé would murmur unkindly, "Down, Polly-dolly"—and the conversation would go on, over his head as before. What is that marvelously apt Russian expression?—*pyatoye colesso,* "the fifth wheel." Well, that's exactly what he was—an ungreased one, too, constantly squeaking and complaining at its lack of consequence.

He was a good doctor, that much I will say for him. He dealt quite capably with Albé's occasional bilious attacks; Mary sent for him once, when baby Wilmouse had convulsions, and thereafter the two of them established the cozy rapport that usually exists between Baby's Doctor and Baby's Mother. But oh, how he did hate Baby's Father and Baby's Aunt!

Mary laughed too, but half-heartedly, and then the next minute fell into a panic. She had to find either P.B. or Polidori, to make sure that the meeting wasn't actually taking place: early though it was, she would go to the Villa Diodati and talk to Albé.

Although I didn't share her fears, I was only too glad of an excuse to accompany her. The truth was, I was in trouble myself. For three days now I hadn't had a glimpse of Albé. The last time I saw him he had told me that he thought he was beginning to care for me. Adding ungraciously: "I don't know why—you're not at all what I like." But then he had smiled.

And now—silence, constraint, evasiveness, Fletcher delivering curt notes asking to be excused from seeing us. Was he angry at me? Was he trying to unlove me?

He received us in the drawing room, wearing a lavish dressing gown; above it, his beautiful face had a remote bleached look, like a fasting saint's. Literally so: the white transparency of his skin and the faint metallic odor that came from between his lips told me that he was back on his inhuman diet. He greeted us coldly. He hated intrusions: people had to be there when he wanted them and melt away like clouds when he didn't.

He read Polidori's challenge, murmuring incredulously over its inanities: "Not to be believed! —But surely, Mary, P.B. will disregard this twaddle."

I said eagerly: "Exactly what I've been telling Mary—I *know* P.B., he would *never*—" and stopped, chilled by the brilliant inimical look he sent me:

"Yes, I am well aware of your superior knowledge of P.B. and the human race in general. . . ." Still mysteriously angry with me, then! "Nevertheless, we might as well make sure. Ordinarily the good doctor sleeps 'til noon, but I believe I'll take the liberty of rousing him from his slumbers right now. . . ." He rang for Fletcher, who appeared and told us that Polidori wasn't there, having gone out early: to shoot some pigeons, he added. How came he by this information? Well, the doctor had his Lordship's guns with him and had told him why.

A sick whimper came from Mary. I still remember the sound: she had produced it once before, when she saw Wilmouse falling out of his crib and was too far to reach him in time.

As for Albé, his pallor turned sallow with rage: "The bloody-minded, vindictive little whelp . . . If he *dared* . . ." He went back to the letter to see if he could make out, amid all that bombast, any mention of where they were supposed to meet.

Just then Polidori himself made his appearance in the doorway, all beaming and triumphant for all the world like

Giovanni Davido after a virtuoso performance in Teatro Goldoni.

Albé said: "What have you done? Where is P.B.?"

Polidori strolled by us and placed Albé's pistol case on a table with an ostentatious little thump. Then he answered negligently: "How should I know?"

I suppose it was his Italian blood: they all have an instinct for histrionics. Albé, unconsciously falling into the style, said, "Cain's own answer, Doctor!" and then, more prosaically, "Well, what happened?"

And Mary gasping out, "Oh, God, have you killed him?"

"Nothing happened that you would disapprove of, my Lord." Oh, how he was enjoying himself, the pompous young ass! For once he had all our attention and meant to keep it. "I went to meet the gentleman at the time indicated—after taking the liberty of borrowing your pistols. Needless to say *I* at least was on time. . . ."

By this time the last of my fears had evaporated. "Oh, this is too stupid. P.B. wouldn't dream of meeting him!"

Polidori shot me a look of intense dislike and said, "She is right, you know. The intrepid philosopher never came." A long sigh went shuddering through Mary's rigid body beside me, leaving it limp with relief. "No possibility of mistake," he added complacently. "I waited."

"Waited to kill him? Ah, that's horrible." Finding her voice, Mary turned on him like a fury. "You came to our house—you took care of our baby—*played* with him—and all the time you were planning to murder us. You dreadful young man!" She burst into tears.

Polidori stared at her, horrified. I honestly believe this view of his activities just hadn't occurred to him. He was a very stupid young man, as devoid of imagination as of humor. "You don't understand! It was no part of my plan to kill—anyone. I merely wanted to teach him a"—here he reverted to bombast again—"a much-needed lesson. It's one thing to spread corruption under the guise of lofty philosophy, it's quite another to be called to account for it. Oh, it would have been a salutory experience for him."

Mary's tears abating gradually, she remarked with a

sniff: "It might have been a salutory one for *you*—P.B. happens to be a very good shot."

And so he was. He hated to kill birds, but I have seen him shoot the pips out of a three of clubs.

Polidori, not believing a word of this, gave Mary a little indulgent bow. "Perhaps then it was his conscience rather than cowardice that kept him from meeting me——"

"Nothing of the sort! P.B. would never shed anyone's blood, it's against his principles!"

"—as Shakespeare says in *Macbeth*, 'For conscience does make cowards of us all.'"

Of course it's not *Macbeth* at all but *Hamlet*, Act Three, scene one—

(Grisha could hear her crisp teacher's voice correcting a mistake only a dolt could make. . . .)

. . . And P.B., entering from the garden that same second, corrected him mildly to that effect. "But never mind that! My dear fellow, I am here to make my apologies to you. Would you believe it? I quite forgot our appointment." He sounded genuinely regretful.

Albé made a strangled noise and crammed both fists over his mouth, like a schoolboy.

As for Mary, she just went over to P.B. without saying a word and put her arms about his thin waist, laying her head on his breast. Unusual for her—she never was demonstrative in public. P.B., unsurprised, rubbed his cheek against the top of her head and proceeded to explain his remissness.

It seems that, on his way to their rendezvous, he had paused for a moment at his favorite spot on the upward path behind the vineyard to look at the miraculous view. Not unnaturally under the circumstances he began to think of death. They had had many discussions on that subject, he and Albé. "What is death?" P.B. would say. "What is it, after all? You awaken from the disorderly dream of life to an existence in which evil and pain cease and man becomes a part of the Eternal Benignant Principle."

A certain skeptical devil in me couldn't help wondering how these intellectual concepts would fare when the real thing happened. Would they help you hold back the cold terror, abate the body's frenzied revulsion? As you were drowning, would you remember that you were awakening to a better existence? I didn't really think so.

But what had happened to P.B. on this morning's walk transcended rational thought. He became a part of what surrounded him. He was the crystal lake and spectral mountains stooping to it; the light streaming down from the sky and the violet shadows in the valley.

"You see, once you accept—not just intellectually, but with all of you—your oneness with nature, then death becomes an easy thing, a merging of a drop of water with the mother ocean. . . . To come to it finally—to lay down the burden of self—to lose oneself utterly. . . ." There was a disturbing yearning in his voice. Mary stirred uneasily, tightening her arms about him. "A lovely, reassuring revelation it was . . . Its only drawback being," he added courteously, "that it put our appointment completely out of my mind."

Polidori's round face had screwed itself up into an expression of unbelieving sarcasm: "A most convenient lapse of memory."

"An unfortunate one," said P.B., with perfect amity.

Forgetting his mysterious annoyance with me, Albé shot me a look of intense enjoyment and settled down in his chair to hear the rest, as bright-eyed as though he was back in Drury Lane, watching a comedy.

Mary shifted her head from under P.B.'s chin to look up at him in disbelief. "You *were* going to meet this madman, then!" There was incredulous reproach in her voice, and P.B. answered it immediately:

"This is a very unhappy young man, Mary. I knew it, as soon as I read his silly note. I recognized immediately a spirit in torment—" His eyes went blindly bright with the look I knew. He was still, I could tell, in that exalted, one might say *oceanic* state, when boundaries between people seem to vanish and you can see clear inside. . . . "Where does one stop, dealing with such a one? Is there a limit to how far one must expose oneself? It's an audacious and mysterious thought. . . ."

(There is a particular species of holy men in Russia that is especially dear to the Russian heart. Beatifically unkempt, as guileless as lambs, they roam the face of Russia, stammering out their disjointed wisdom, and no home from the lowest izba *to a mansion is closed to them. Grisha had seen his fastidious mother dishing out a plate of soup for one of them with her own hands. The* yurodivyi *is what they are called, holy stammerers, God's little fools. Miss Clairmont's P.B. was the epitome of the rational man, the utmost in pure intellect; why then did he so irresistibly remind Grisha of those others?)*

Turning those disconcerting eyes on Polidori, who met them with a sort of horror, P.B. went on:

"There's a demon that torments you, the worst of the lot, the demon of insufficiency."

"Sir, you presume!"

"That's why you hit out and want to destroy, isn't it? Yes, I understand you. . . ."

"I *refuse* to be understood by you!" Polidori bellowed. There was anguished sincerity in the cry.

I burst out laughing. Albé joined me, with a heartfelt schoolboy crow of pure enjoyment: the pleasantest sound I had heard that whole week.

"Are you trying to make a fool of me?" Polidori demanded of P.B.

"Oh, no, no . . ."

"No, can't you see he is not?" Albé brought out still laughing heartily. "At that, it would be superfluous."

Polidori swung his head around. He was beginning to acquire the coarse blunted look of a baited bull. "But I did it all for you!"

Albé's laughter broke off. "For *me?*"

"I acted on your behalf."

And immediately the mysterious wrongness of things was back.

"You seem to be laboring under a misapprehension as to the nature of your employment," Albé said, very quietly. The angrier he was the softer his voice would go. Each word now fell as gentle and cold as a snowflake. "I have contracted for your services as doctor and secretary—but I certainly don't recall ever intimating that I also stood in need of," the soft voice dropped lower still, "of a Second Murderer."

And in an instant years fell away from Polidori. He became a stupid little boy who had blundered and would be punished for it: "I—I—you looked upon me as a friend—you confided in me. . . ."

Confided? My ears sharpened at the word. Exactly what was it that was being confided? I wondered.

A spasm of savage annoyance contracted Albé's face. "Yes," he said somberly. "I am prone to errors of judgment like that. And I talk too much—*that* is certain. . . . I think we had better part company, doctor, before your zeal—on my behalf—makes me look as ridiculous as yourself."

He bowed to the rest of us and saying with chilly courtesy, "Pray excuse me: I must go and change," left the room.

"Now what was all this in aid of?" Mary asked. But she didn't really care. All of her glowed with having P.B. safely back again. She tugged at his sleeve, looking at him with bright eyes, her ordinarily pale cheeks delicately flushed. "Come home with me, love."

I let them go home without me. I was determined to talk to Polidori, whom I could see outside in the garden, wandering around in a shocked aimless manner. And I was right. In the end, although he hated me heartily, he did me a great service. He told me what I wanted to know.

All the male principals of the absurd little drama are dead now. Yes, Polidori too. It seems he killed himself a few years later, poor confused wretch. I should never have expected it of him: to me he seemed merely a smug mediocre young man. Only P.B. with his clear eyes had been able to guess at the darkness within. . . .

By the time Grisha finished reading the brightness had drained out of the day, to be replaced by a pre-crepuscular pallor, sunless but clear. This phenomenon marks the coming of autumn, the balance insensibly shifting in its favor, night beginning to encroach

[129]

on the day instead of the other way around. Toozik, lying at his feet, lifted his head, gathered his dun forehead into a human frown, and bayed. Grisha looked around and saw Matryosha standing behind a tree, watching him fearfully. When she met his gaze, her hands went up to her face. Over them her eyes dilated in that blind spilling blueness he knew.

"What is it, Matryosha?"

Once over his passionate bout of self-revulsion, Grisha had put the incident in the library out of his head. The housekeeper had made no complaints to his mother, and indeed, whenever he came across her, treated him with special honeyed obsequiousness. Matryosha he had seen only fleetingly. Fomitch told him that she had been taken out of the scullery and put to work in the sewing room where a corps of needlewomen was kept busy working on infant clothes for his sister's coming baby. He had come upon her once in his mother's apartments, squatting on her heels, her narrow back turned to him, while she swiftly repaired a torn ruffle on the Princess' gown. A gracious remark from his mother indicated that she was back to being Marie again. It looked as though her fortunes had improved, possibly as a result of his intervention.

Why then was she hovering among the trees like an unshriven little ghost, big-eyed and wan in that false twilight?

He called to her again, and she drifted toward him obediently. For a while she stood before him silent, one small hand wringing the other; the fabric tightened and relaxed erratically about her little breasts, as if a frantic bird beat inside her blouse. And then without warning she fell headlong at his feet, her face pressed against his boots, her hands grappling desperately for his ankles.

Even in his confusion he noticed the tiny recoil as she touched his wasted leg. But she was beyond that: immediately he recognized it as not revulsion but purely tactile surprise, as if groping for a branch her hand had encountered a reed. The next moment she was hugging both his legs with equal frenzy. And oh, how she wept. A silent hemorrhage of tears, like life's blood pouring out.

"What is it? Tell me?" He tried to rise, was hampered by her frantic clutch and sat down again. At a loss, he touched her head awkwardly, and only then the silence was broken: sounds of anguish, piteous little squeaks and gasps, began to pulse out from the undone bundle at his feet, mixed with almost inaudible words. Bending down, he was barely able to make them out:

"They'll send me away—kill me, they will—take my life . . ."

"Who? Why?" He took hold of her shoulders—the bones felt as frail as a bird's between his palms—and pulled her upright. She stayed in his grasp obediently, her head hanging, so that he couldn't see her face. "Come now, you've got to tell me if you want me to help. Is it that old bitch? Has she been beating you again?"

The flaxen head at the level of his chest moved from side to side.

"What then?"

"She knows—she watches—get me sent away to Petrovka." (Petrovka was one of the Volynskis' outlying villages in Ryazan Province.) "She knows, she knows!"

Grisha gave her a little shake. "Knows what?"

Her voice dwindled away to a leaf stir. ". . . I'm with big belly."

In poems and romantic novels one read about the "fruit of passion," licit or illicit, as the case may be; his sister's condition was referred to, with delicacy, as being *enceinte*. Grisha found himself curiously moved by the explicit peasant term. Involuntarily his eyes ranged down Matryosha's inert body, searching for any sign of the "big belly" she so hopelessly mentioned; but she was as skinny as ever. Perhaps it was a mistake. "Are you sure?" She nodded several times, sorrowfully. "But—" Absurdly he wanted to know how and just in time stopped himself asking.

"They'll know," came the strangled little voice. "Shave my head and send me away, they will, and I'll die. . . ." She slid from between Grisha's palms and was again down at his feet. "Help me, help me, have mercy on me, I'll pray for you my whole entire life. . . ."

"But what? What do you want me to do?"

Matryosha sat back on her heels and turned up her tear-sodden face. A look, burning and direct, found Grisha's face. "Don't let them send me away from Fedka," she said. "Marry me to him, your Grace." She was now addressing him in the familiar second person singular; but the familiarity was one with which you address God in prayer; and wild despairing faith burned in her eyes.

"Oh," said Grisha blankly. "Fedka, is it?" Fedka, with his oily hair, his simple grin of satisfied sensuality—all this for him?

"They'll send me away to Petrovka, orphan that I am. . . . I'll never see him again, my love, my darling. . . ."

Fomitch appeared at the other end of the clearing. Seeing Matryosha, he flung up both hands in a gesture of disapproval and despair. Matryosha paid him no attention. She merely hitched herself closer to Grisha, like one seeking closer sanctuary at the foot of an altar, and kissing his hands—his skin crept at the dry passionate touch of her lips—she said: "Only give me my Fedka, give me my Fedyushka, your Grace, give him, give him to me or I'll die. . . ."

"Leave his Excellency alone, you daft wench," Fomitch said half-heartedly; but in his quick look, too, Grisha read an appeal for help. He was aware of a powerful responsive throb within himself; those were his people demanding help from him and something in him acknowledged the demand as rightful.

"Very well," he said. "Stop crying, Matryosha—I'll see what I can do about it."

The new note in his voice reached the girl. She rose slowly to her feet, her gaze fastening to his face, where it seemed to look for confirmation of what she had heard in his voice. Apparently she found it, because suddenly her whole body seemed to participate in a long shivering sigh.

"—pray for you all my life," she repeated and went away, stumbling a little as she went, and even yawning, like a child exhausted by a fit of crying.

Fomitch approached Grisha and silently kissed him on the shoulder. Then bending down he began to gather together the scattered pages of Miss Clairmont's manuscript.

"Well, so now you tell me about it, Fomitch," Grisha said, taking the pages back from him.

"What's to tell?" Fomitch smoothed his hair from the back forward, a sure sign of agitation with him. "My heart aches for the little one. Nothing but woe and sorrow in store for her, seems like. I took her to Tikhonovna, see if she could help. Nothing works, looks like. And there is that bitch watching out for her time of month to come around. . . ."

Grisha listened, wonderingly. The time of the month—there was that business of his sisters' coy withdrawal into something like vapors every month; they used to rest a lot and answer all his questions with trills of self-important laughter. Somehow he never thought of whatever it was happening to servants or peasant women; they certainly never took time off. The utter childishness of this reasoning now struck him forcibly.

". . . Comes the right time, she'll beat her right down, make her confess and straightaway to her Grace your mother. No putting her off with chicken blood on rags, the old bitch. . . ." Fomitch broke off. "May my tongue dry up, your Excellency, what am I doing, talking about women's dirty business to an innocent boy. . . ."

Grisha gulped. Dark business, mysterious business, with blood in it somehow, as some sort of a purely feminine, repellent common denominator between his pampered sisters and Matryosha—no, he didn't want to hear any more about it.

". . . Only I'm that worried about the little girl, I don't know anymore what I'm saying—after all, we're kin, my own sister's child. . . ."

"We'll just have to get her married off to Fedka as soon as possible. That should be simple. Cheer up, old man, don't look as if the world has come to an end. I said I'll see to it, didn't I?"

"God bless you, Grishenka, your Excellency." Fomitch again bobbed his gray head down to kiss his young master's shoulder. Grisha gave him a reassuring little hug. He was feeling full of tenderness and benevolent power.

Claire's Journal, September 18

Am happy to be back in Islavskoye. The green shade of the groves reflected in the calm water of the pond seems an old familiar face. Sad to see autumnal changes, the deep green turning yellow. The weather is still lovely. . . .

We had a minor tragedy today—a drama of honor sullied, faith betrayed! For a while now, Dunia has had a secret with Johnny, and gloried in it. The two of them would go off after lessons into the inner recesses of the lilac grove where they would play a mysterious game. How my Dunia gloried in this! "I have a secret with Johnny, nobody else knows!" Finally Johnny got tired of it—after all, he is all of five years older, quite a gap. Hermann asked him about it casually, and he said, "Oh, it's just a game she likes to play with some toy animals. One of them is supposed to be the tsar of them all—" My poor baby! How distractedly she shrilled, "Don't tell, don't tell!" Hermann said in a hurry, "Don't tell me, I don't want to know." But villainous Johnny went on implacably: "She calls him *tsar-sobaka* (tsar-dog)." Oh, dear, Dunia's tragic eyes, full of loss and disillusionment! I turned on the little criminal with such fury that he shrank: "No honorable man discloses secrets that he is trusted with!" But the harm had been done.

Later I saw my poor little darling sadly carrying her tiny idols out of the magic ring. She stopped to show them to me: as he had said, just a box of toy animals, a red carnelian pig, a carved wooden bear, a china borzoi . . . Dunia started drearily to enumerate them—apparently the game had consisted of assigning names and personalities to those knickknack animals: "That's Praskovya, the pig; that's Misha, the bear . . ." and then stopped. The magic had gone out of it all.

How very instructive: there they were playing lords of creation in their little lilac-circumscribed Eden, and of course it would be the destructive male who had to smash it all, take the magic out of it. Yes, indeed trust the male to smash and betray. . . .

At dinner the Princess said to her husband: "What's that I hear, *mon ami*, about one of your grooms being caught prowling around the maids' quarters? I must say, I should like to know whom he was honoring with his attentions." Her thin shoulders moved in a fastidious little shudder. "You must agree that the possibility of it being someone actually waiting on me . . ."

The Prince shrugged. "Exactly what do you expect me to do about this, *ma chère*? Make an investigation into chambermaid amours? I had the rascal whipped, that should be enough."

Encouraged by this interlude, Grisha resolved to talk to him about marrying Matryosha to Fedka at the earliest possible opportunity. He foresaw no difficulties: in his indifferent, indolent fashion, his father was usually disposed to grant his infrequent requests.

His mind kept reverting to the girl for the rest of the day. The feel of her lingered in his palms—the slippery floss of her hair, the frail cagework of her bones underneath the delicate flesh, her tears and kisses on his hands. All this aroused a protective, pitying tenderness in him. Falling into a reverie, he began picturing the pleasant task of organizing her happiness. Yes, he would see her married to Fedka (he visualized the two of them kneeling before him, hand in hand) and build them a little cottage to live in; and presently there would be a baby, looking like one of those cherubs that cavorted on the ceiling of his mother's apartments in Moscow, and he would be its godfather. The fantasy was becoming so sugary that he had to laugh at himself. But he went to bed, resolved to take the first steps about realizing it the very next day.

Before he had a chance to do so, however, his father left Andreyevo. An old friend, who had come to Moscow on official business and was staying at the house of Governor General Golitzin, had written him asking for the pleasure of his company.

As always, Grisha was amazed by the working of the domestic grapevine. Fomitch seemed to know all about it: what was in the letter from Moscow, and from whom it came, and even the fact that "the Governor himself enclosed a note to his Excellence your father, begging him to honor them with his presence, without you, your Excellency, he says, nothing will be accomplished. . . ." Fomitch recounted this with relish: his sense of family consequence was equal to the Prince's.

"All the same, Fomitch, it's too bad, I was going to talk to him about Matryosha. Now it'll have to wait till he comes back." The old valet inclined his head silently, his face clouding over. "Now don't look like that, old man. What is it? Do you think I'll forget about it? I won't, you know."

"No, Excellency, we know it and are forever grateful for your kindness. Only . . ." A sigh lifted his deep chest. "Seems to me, somehow the lass is doomed, like, no saving her . . . That's the feeling I have."

"Well, there is no reason for it, so cheer up."

Nevertheless, Fomitch's uneasiness infected him too. Later he was made even more uneasy by the glimpse of the girl herself. Fear emanated from her, made visible in the pulse beating wildly in her thin throat, in the way she glanced about her as if the house had become a huge cage in which she was trapped. He was made to think of a cat he had once, a pampered semi-Persian, who turned wild and took to skulking in the bushes. When brought inside she would refuse to eat and range the rooms meowing feebly with staring fur and widened sorrowful eyes.

He gave her an encouraging smile and a nod as she scuttled by him; the faintest possible responsive light glimmered back at him from her small strained face. It became clear to Grisha that keeping her uncertain of her fate was pure cruelty. If his father didn't return soon he would have to approach his mother about her.

He was conscious of a powerful reluctance to do so.

Every approach seemed wrong. Maman, *I promised your house-maid, Matryosha—I mean Marie—that I would marry her to the groom Fedka.* He could see his mother's eyes rising puzzled to him: *What have you to do with my maids?* —*Well,* maman, *she loves him, she came weeping to me.* . , . —*Why to you?* . . . It was exasperating that the very depth of his concern, his special desire to do the girl good, was precisely what got in his way. . . .

Later in the day a note came from Miss Clairmont, telling him that they were now back in Islavskoye, and she would be delighted to resume their English lessons the next day. Grisha, enormously cheered by this communication, immediately ordered Nelly to be saddled and rode down to Islavskoye.

Two pale blue spots moving at the edge of the unmown meadow near the Pomykovs' estate like two butterflies of unequal size became Miss Clairmont and Dunia as he drew closer. He called to them, dismounting, and Dunia came pelting toward him; she leaped at him and clung, screeching his name wildly: "Georges, *Georzhik!*"

The weather had turned hot again, as if the splendid summer, regretfully slipping away, had stopped for one more brilliant day to be remembered by. Miss Clairmont was carrying a rug on her arm. They spread it under a tree—the unmown grass sprang up tough and elastic under it—and settled down for a talk. Dunia curled up happily between them. Presently her familiar contented half-chant, half-murmur of "how-many-how-many" trailed off into silence; she had a way of going to sleep as precipitately as a puppy.

While riding down, all Grisha had been able to think about was Miss Clairmont's letter: so many enigmatic gaps, so much unfinished business in it, to be presently clarified by her. But instead of asking her about it he found himself telling her about Matryosha.

". . . I don't know—it seemed so simple when I promised her. And now—I know I ought to go and talk to *maman,* no matter how difficult. But something holds me back, it all seems so—I can't explain—awkward. Foolish of me, I know . . ."

But Miss Clairmont shook her head. "No, one has an instinct about those things. You can always sense how people close to you will respond even though you may not know their exact reasons. . . ."

"I may have to. My father may stay away longer than I expected. And I have this—forewarning—no, that's not the word . . ."

"Foreboding?"

"Yes, foreboding. That I should attend to this soon. Or something bad will happen. She is so frightened, so terribly frightened, you see."

"Mmm." Miss Clairmont was silent, nibbling at a blade of grass abstractedly with her even white teeth. The light leaf shadows dappled her attentive face. Her hair was now done differently from before, he noticed. It dipped along the side of her cheeks in black smooth loops, enhancing her Italian look. Finally she said: "Why not say that your groom—Fedka, is it?—has told you that he is in love with this girl, and you promised to help him? That would be more natural, wouldn't it?"

Grisha broke into a smile of delight and relief. "Yes, yes, that would be exactly right. I've been praising him for taking such good care of Nelly, so it would be perfectly natural for me to want to reward him. Why didn't I think of that myself?" He seized her hands. "Oh, Miss Clairmont, you are a wonder. You always know the right thing to do."

"I've been told that I am a manipulator by nature," she smiled. Her hands remained in his, thin, bony, pulsing with nervous life even as they stayed still.

"I shall talk to *maman* as soon as I get home."

"I suppose you have already spoken to the young man."

Grisha looked at her blankly. "To—? oh, you mean Fedka? No, why should I?"

"Why should you?" she repeated incredulously. "You don't propose to inform him that he is getting married?"

"Well, yes, of course, later, after it's all settled."

Her hands stiffened and slid out of his: "But—but that's medieval, isn't it? Those people are human beings, not animals to be mated at the master's will!"

Her incomprehensible anger communicating itself to him, he shot back at her: "You seem to forget that they have already— mated!" He was immediately horrified at himself. "Please forgive me. I was inexcusably rude."

"And I was unrealistic," she said quietly. "I forget where I am, the nature of the society of which you are a part. Yes, you are right, under the circumstances talking to the boy would be merely a gesture. . . . Friends again?"

"Yes, of course." But his answering smile was troubled. Was she disappointed in him? "You see, I was only thinking of Matryosha. . . . I want her to be safely married. . . . That's the first thing to think about, under the circumstances, isn't it?"

Her eyebrows twitched and lifted in sudden amusement, like a bee's antennae. Head tilted to one side, she looked at him mischievously. "You are saying this to the wrong person, Georges. I fear marriage was always the last thing I thought of—even 'under the circumstances.'" As he looked at her, the expression he knew—should I? shall I? of course, I will!—flickered across her face. With a little nod, as if to an unseen person who had impelled her to make the disclosure, she said matter of factly: "I mean, even when I knew that I was going to have Albé's baby."

"Oh." Grisha could find nothing to say after that blank monosyllable. Did she want to shock him? But her face was now merely grave. She was simply acquainting a friend with a previously unknown fact about herself.

"I don't mean to make a virtue of my attitude," she added with a slight smile. "In this instance the whole question of marriage was academic, since the father of my baby was already married."

"Yes, I remember. He used to have nightmares, with his wife in them. What was she like?"

"I don't know, I have never met her," Miss Clairmont said, still matter of fact. "I think of her as a vindictive little woman, rigid, *cold*. In love with her grievances. Of which, to do her justice, she had had many." After another weighted pause, she said: "He was going to return to her. If she let him."

The words bounced crisply, each one setting up a small electric shock. Taken aback, he stammered: "You mean, while he was still——"

"The decision was made in Geneva, yes. There were all kinds of negotiations in progress. He had gone as far as to send her, through a third person, assurances of his sincere contrition." Her voice was perfectly calm; no echo of perplexity or anger colored it.

"And he had just begun to care for you! Didn't you mind?"

"His wanting to go back to her? I did indeed. I thought it was quite dreadful. But not because of us. He made it clear that his renewed marriage would change nothing for us. He said—oh, I still remember how he said it: acid, resigned—'Once I'm firmly rematrionalized, things will go on as before. A decent period of mourning—and then I can call my nights my own again.' I must say this cynicism shocked me even though I knew that English society is built on marriages like that. He was amused at what he called my sudden outbreak of middle-class morality. But it wasn't that at all. I merely hated to see him conforming to the values of a society he said he despised. . . . It was all very simple. He didn't want to return to London to be socially ostracized. He wanted everything to be exactly as before, with all the doors open to him. If reconciliation with his wife was the answer he would be reconciled—even eating a plateful of crow in the process, if necessary. . . .

"I suppose he was growing homesick, minded not seeing his friends. They were always promising to look him up in Geneva, but somehow at the last minute the wind would change and blow them elsewhere. It gave him a troubling sense of unreality about himself. . . . And I—I too wanted him to go back to England; it seemed to me that protracted exile wouldn't be right for him. Some people can go on forever being expatriated—P.B. could, but not he, not Geordie." She had now that special look that both fascinated and intimidated him—blurred, unfocused, remote, as if all of her had gone back into the past with only the lovely voice left to tell him all about it. "He was too firmly rooted in England. Once out of it for good, no telling what might happen. Well, and I was right. Living an exile's life did corrupt him, make him unstable, discontented, self-hurting. The meaning of his life became blurred. For him the alternative to living in England was, in the end, dying in Greece. . . ." Eyes half-closed she paused to contemplate that end coldly. "I sensed all that, I suppose, and it made me afraid for him."

"And weren't you at all afraid for yourself?" Grisha asked curiously.

Miss Clairmont shook her head. "I was—oh, exalted at the thought of bearing his child, looking forward to it. . . . That was because, in spite of my superior wisdom, I was nothing but a green fool." Her lips curled in pitying contempt for the heedless young self-deceiver that she had been many years ago. "You see, I didn't expect to be punished or censured. After all, Mary had her first baby in London, and then Wilmouse, and no one we cared about

[139]

thought the worse of her because of it. We were a fairly self-enclosed group, seeing only the people who believed in the same things as we did, so that criticism reached us only at second hand. And there would be P.B. to take care of me—and Mary."

"P.B. would take care of you?" Grisha repeated. "Not—?"

"Albé couldn't. Nor did I want him to! He'd been through enough in England—reviled, lampooned, driven away—do you think I was going to let them use my baby against him? A bastard child to explain away just as he was trying to mend his marriage? No, I had it all worked out. It would be no danger to him. The baby would be born in December, so no one would connect it with him: no one knew about our London connection." She paused. "I have always wished that the baby had been conceived in Geneva and not in London." The lightest of sighs lifted her breast. Meeting his wondering eyes, she explained. "Because in London he didn't love me at all, and in Geneva—I told you, he was beginning to. . . . There were precautions I had planned to take. We had to go back to England in the fall: P.B. had some financial matters to take care of. But we would stay in Bath, until the baby was born. So that was all settled."

After a pause, Grisha asked: "What did he say to that?"

"Well—he was suspicious at first. Self-sacrificing women had always made him uneasy—and with reason: there is a certain unhealthy smell about self-immolation. But there was none of that in my plans: just enlightened self-interest and common sense. I didn't want to damage him and I didn't want to lose him. . . . And I was right, it was the right—the *only* thing to do. I was instantly rewarded. He trusted me then. Yes, we had that; nothing, *nothing*," she said with sudden fierceness, "can take that away; no matter what happened afterward, the treachery, the hatred, we had a time of perfect love and trust in Geneva. . . ."

They were both silent. A flock of starlings rose up out of the woods and wheeled across the sky. As if it was a signal, the quality of the day changed; the bright sky went glassy, a wind sprang up, lightly laced with chill. Miss Clairmont shivered and drew her shawl closer around her shoulders. "What are you thinking of, Georges?"

"Imagining how it all was. . . . But I cannot imagine you—*enceinte*."

Waddling, pear shaped, taut body gone ripe and soft—no, he couldn't see it at all.

To his amazement, she paled and her lips quivered. For the first time since he knew her he had a feeling that he had wounded her. "Yes, I see how it is. You feel I am not a maternal type." She spoke with sad disdain. "Unfeminine; more prone to be concerned with all humanity than one small scrap of it. My milk apt to curdle in my breast because of the fermenting ideas in my head. That's what *he* said, too." Her eyes flashed. "Well, he was wrong. I was the happiest expectant mother you ever saw. And when my little baby came, I loved her more than anything in the world."

"I am sorry, I didn't mean——"

But her anger was already over. She said, suddenly listless: "But she died, for all that."

"I am sorry," he said again, helplessly.

"Children do die, constantly," she said. "Mary's first baby died, and our sweet Wilmouse and his little sister Clara, named for me—and so many others. They die so easily, they are so fragile—you think they are safe, but all at once they wilt and die, like windflowers in the dry blast of summer heat—and then their ghosts come and torture you with remembered slights—their voices ask the same plaintive questions over and over—but they can't hear the answers, you no longer can explain to them . . ."

Her voice trickled away like a stream in the sand. With common accord they looked down at sleeping Dunia. The child lay quiet, her thin arms tossed overhead. Her dreams visibly chased each other like shadows across her face, making her eyelashes quiver, her lips move speechlessly. As it happens with children when they are not in motion, her flesh assumed an almost frightening aspect of fragility, as though a touch would leave a mark on it.

Miss Clairmont bent down to her, murmuring. The child awoke, smiled, and unhesitatingly threw her arms around her neck. "Time to go home, *petite.*" Gathering the child in her arms, she straightened up and, now quite in control, glanced at Grisha with a half-smile. "You had better pay your respects at the house, or Marya Ivanovna will regard this as a secret *assignation.*" She accented the word drolly. "Why don't you give this child a ride on your Nelly? I'll walk home. *Ça te plaira, n'est-ce pas, ma petite? Aller à cheval avec ton ami Georges?*"

She had gone into her past more intensely than was comfortable, Grisha guessed, and now wanted to be alone. Obediently he rode away, keeping Nelly at a gentle rocking-horse hand gallop, with Dunia bobbing weightlessly on the saddle in front of him. When he looked back he saw Miss Clairmont walking swiftly through the fields, head up, clothes streaming backward in the newly risen wind, making her determined way out of the entangling old memories.

Back in Andreyevo, Grisha stopped at the stables to look for Fedka, whom he found seated on an up-ended barrel cleaning some harness. Up above him the black stallion Kestrel had stretched his neck over the door of the stall to lip his hair gently. He came spryly to his feet, polished brass clinking in his hands, to greet the young master, and, on being asked whether he had recovered from the punishment, answered readily, with his usual pert grin: "As good as new, your Excellency. It did smart for a while, to be sure. Matvey Rodionitch has a heavy hand, lays it on like one's father, bless his soul. If not for your Excellency, I'd still be limping around like a three-legged cur." He bent his oily yellow head to kiss Grisha's shoulder.

Grisha was conscious of downright affection for the lively young groom; it was increased by the knowledge that he would presently bestow another benefaction upon him. He said, "And, now, what's to be done about the girl?"

Fedka's glance was perplexed to the point of idiocy.

"I mean Matryosha, she's the one you—" To his profound annoyance he blushed. Fedka answered him gravely, but with a lurking smile in his shallow blue eyes:

"Well, your Excellency, you'll have to believe that I'll never touch her again. So help me. I'm through with all that nonsense now."

"Why nonsense? You loved her, I suppose."

Fedka's full mouth spread wider in a smile: "Sure enough, your Excellency. A nice little girl, how not to love her? A little skinny, but there now, plumpness isn't everything." A sentimental look came over his ruddy face. "You get ahold of her, with those little bones of hers, she just melts in your hands, like . . ." He added hastily: "But never again, your Excellency, I've learned my lesson." Clowning he tenderly patted his buttocks. The black horse nickered as if laughing at his antics. His soft brown lips curved back from his big teeth giving him a comically rakish look. Fedka cuffed at him lovingly. "All right, you anathema!"

"She's going to have a baby, you know. Did she tell you?"

Fedka wriggled his shoulders. He muttered, "I don't know about that. . . . She talked some nonsense . . ." He flung both hands out in a gesture of resignation. "Well, your Excellency, I only have one back, and here it is. I was hoping maybe the thrashing made up for that too . . ."

"What about marrying her?" Grisha waited for the incredulity, the dawning delight, the gratitude.

But Fedka merely hung his head. A sleepy sullen mask settled over his face. Grisha looked at it in dismay. "Whatever your Excellency pleases." His voice was colorless. "We're not our own people, whatever you our masters command. . . ."

"Don't you care about her, Fedka? She loves you, ever so." ("Only give me my Fedya, give him to me," sounded again in his ears, and the girl's face looked up at him tear drenched, undone. . . .) "And she's so scared, so unhappy, poor little thing. Don't you have pity in you?" His voice held pleading, and Fedka's face unclenched.

"How not, your Excellency? What's a woman for if not to pity? It's a miserable business, being a woman, sure enough. All they've got to look forward to is a bit of love. . . . Only thing, a fellow's got to be careful like, keep it in its place, because you get carried away, you're the one to get clobbered. . . . As for marrying, well, that's not our business, we're lowly folk, do what we're told. . . ."

Grisha sighed. Fedka would do anything he was told; he would do nothing. He refused to fit into the idyllic little tableau in which Grisha, a benevolent *deus ex machina*, joined the hands of two pastoral lovers and watched them live happily ever after.

Somewhat dashed, Grisha said, "I'll talk to you again about this," and, answering Fedka's silent bow with a nod, left him.

Not a satisfactory interview; the one good thing about it was that, now that he had talked to Fedka, he felt able to make unhesitating use of Miss Clairmont's formula of "my groom Fedka asked me, etc." Unfortunately, when he went up to see his mother, he found her prostrated with one of her frequent attacks of migraine. She was lying on her bed, with the curtains lowered to shut out daylight and Nikolavna silently applying vinegar-soaked compresses to her forehead, and barely had strength to make the usual sign of the cross over him. Grisha kissed her hand—it felt cold and papery to his lips—and retired. Matryosha would have to wait.

His mind went back to Miss Clairmont, who, too, when she was Claire, had been visited with the twin affliction of a big belly and no husband. A grotesque parallel! But the differences were even more striking. No terror there or desperate pleas for help; no worry about disgrace, as would seem natural for a young girl of her class; instead, cool rational planning and a sense of adventure. The father of the child was, for certain high-minded reasons, unavailable; but she had her principles to fall back on and, more important, she had Mary and P.B. Whereas Matryosha had no one . . . Not true. With amazement he felt the denial rising heavily from the inmost depths of his being. "She has me. I'll take care of her."

Claire's Journal, September 20

The weather is rainy and cold; we are now irretrievably committed to autumn. Marya Ivanovna talks of going back to Moscow, and I am bracing myself for another Russian winter. Prince Georges came for his first English lesson since our return from the Zimmermans' (yesterday's walk *con conversazione* doesn't count). We stayed indoors and real aloud from Joseph Forsyth's *Remarks on Antiquities.* There was no opportunity to *talk.* A pity. For some reason, I wanted to. I should have liked to tell him the sequel to the non-duel.

How was it exactly? Mary and P.B. had gone home. Albé was in his bedroom, dressing. In the garden the wretched Polidori was agonizing over the results of his stupidity. I remember actually feeling sorry for him, as I stepped into the garden to accost him. I had always despised him as a vain shallow hanger-on. Well, so he was. But also he apparently really loved Albé.

"I am so sorry," I said, meaning it. And immediately he began to talk to me, simply, like a child in shock. He talked about the first time he had met Albé—there was a light about him, he said, he was special. You wanted to be useful to him. (Oh, disastrously true—to know him, to heal what hurts him—to give him anything of yourself that he wants or needs—how well I knew that unthrifty passion!) He talked about their travels through Belgium, and I listened avidly, eager to learn whatever I could. Albé's foot used to bother him after too much sightseeing, and he let Polidori massage it—not at first, at first he didn't even let him look at it, but later, when he got to know him better. He had even talked to him about it. He had said that if he—Albé—were a doctor, delivering a child with that kind of deformity, he would strangle it at birth. . . . And then there had been a chambermaid in Ostend whom both of them wanted and Albé had suggested that she should be allowed to make her choice without being told who he was; he was sure she'd choose Polidori, a sound man over a cripple. . . . Absurd Geordie! As if any woman would . . . Of course the chambermaid had chosen him, and he was so pleased—only he kept thinking that Polidori had tipped her a wink. . . .

It was odd to hear the usually stuffy doctor recounting that sort of an improper tale to me. But, blinded with pain as he was, he didn't really see me, he was just talking to a silent and sympathetic listener. And then inevitably he returned to the present. The strange moment of communication was over. He saw me looking sorry for him and he said with hatred: "Save your pity for yourself. I shouldn't think you'll survive me by long."

Thereupon, very coldly and deliberately, I began to bait him. I remember saying, among other things, that he was not very good in Shakespearean roles. And that reminder of Albé's gibe—"inept as the Second Murderer"—did it; out it came in a furious bellow: "You treacherous vixen, you're so damned sure of yourself, aren't you? You think you've gulled him, don't you? You and your so-called brother-in-law. Well, he knows everything, you whore. He knows whose child you're carrying."

I just looked at him, my face, I am sure, as stupid as his. "Not true," I finally brought out. "This is in your mean little mind. Not his."

"He told me himself."

At this point our conversation stops dead, he just melts away and disappears from my recollection, red face, furious scowl, and all. The next thing I remember is walking through the fields, my arms protectively crossed in front of my stomach, I suppose to shield my baby from the wickedness of the world.

I lingered there for a while, midway between Villa Diodati and our cottage. Placid sunshine was pouring down, crickets intoning their intense little noonday song. Then I went back, slowly, not wanting to. I had to ask him—I had to hear from his own lips that he had said that about our baby. But I knew he had. Unfortunately, I nearly always knew what he was thinking.

And indeed, confronted with this, he turned to me a face from which every trace of expression was erased—heavy, sleepy, as impenetrable as a fortress, not a chink for me to get through—and said: "I don't want to discuss it."

A slow answering anger rose up in me. He considered me capable of such sordid fraud, then. After having known me for four months—but of course, according to his calculations, I could already have been pregnant when we first met, four months ago! And not only pregnant but on the lookout for a victim whom I could maneuver into fathering my bastard child. Enterprising of me! Of us, rather, since presumably P.B. had sponsored this glorious scheme. I found that I minded even more for P.B. than for myself; how could he, how *dared* he suspect P.B.! "This is *ugly*, Geordie," I said, my throat raw with the acrid taste of disillusionment.

But apparently I had wronged him. He never thought that P.B. had anything to do with this. I did it all on my own, it seems—oh, he had no difficulty in believing *me* capable of a harlot's trick like that.

He couldn't see, what's more, why I took it so badly. It was only a woman's trick, after all. A typical bit of feminine opportunism. Wasn't it the most natural thing in the world for a woman having an affair with more than one man to persuade herself that she is pregnant by the one she prefers? Wasn't it being done every day?

"In your world perhaps." I thought of Lady Oxford, a former mistress of his, with a houseful of children, each one by a different father. And William Lamb—it was commonly known that he was not Lord Melbourne's son.

"But not in yours," he said with a barely concealed sneer, "it's quite different there."

Well, so it was, I told him. If he couldn't see the difference between indiscriminate lust—as casual as flies copulating on the wall, as furtive as stealing—and unions of free love between liberal-minded men and women living freely together, where physical union is only the natural conclusion of a spiritual one . . .

"Come off it, my love," he said baldly, interrupting my peroration. "Fucking is fucking, no matter how high minded."

Well—I must say that today, ten years older and centuries wiser, I tend to agree with him. My liaison with Pushchin—I could have tried to make it what it was not; to establish him as a liberal spirit worthy of my love and therefore privileged to make himself free of my body. What fustian! I don't love him—I only want him in my bed; and that, badly . . .

But I was young in these days, and I allowed myself to be diverted a little longer in defense of principles I lived by until the futility of it struck me.

"And it's not the point anyway. The point is that you consider us—me—capable of that sort of ignoble lie. Don't you know that if the baby were P.B.'s he would not hesitate to acknowledge it? And I wouldn't either—I would be proud and happy that my baby had such a father!"

His face contracted just a little: that hurt him, it seemed. Why? But before I had a chance to explore further, the expression changed. His lips curled deeper. It was a mean little smile. It said I was as alive to self-interest as anyone else.

"In the last count," he said in that sweet voice, that so gently, musically flayed you, "you are all alike—duchess or drab or arrogant little intellectual. What all of you want is to get a man between your legs and ride him, whip and spur!"

For the first time I could imagine myself not loving him any longer. There was comfort in the thought. When one is young, one is equal to anything. But even so there comes a time when you falter. There are some climates in which it is hard to live. The weather is treacherous, the winds shift too fast, blowing warm and balmy one minute, bitter chill the next—it's best to escape if you can.

One more moment, another bit of unattractive self-revelation would do it. That light about him would fade, he would stop being special. He would be merely a small man with a beautiful face spoiled by a sneer, and a taste for torturing those who loved him. . . .

Unaware of my withdrawal, he went on: "Hang it, be reasonable. At least admit the possibility of mistake." He was positively wheedling. I listened wearily, only wanting to go. "Very well, the child isn't P.B.'s. But there may have been others. How do I know with whom you've been sleeping between the time I left you in London and you came to Geneva? No reason for you to abstain, you know. I don't claim special fucking privileges. . . . But then to find that you're with child and insist that it's mine—poor little devil . . ."

There was a strange new note in those last words. Almost beyond his reach now, I turned back to consider its meaning. A tremor went through his face, opening it, making it vulnerable, young, bewildered, Geordie's night-time face, open to love as well as hurt. He went on, the words at variance with the face, "You can be perfectly open with me, you know. All this doesn't mean that I'm disclaiming my responsibilities. . . ."

"Only your paternity." I saw it now. Of course. And I should have seen it before. Corroborations came flooding in on me from all sides.

"If I were a doctor, delivering a child with such a deformity . . ." And before that talking to P.B. about arrangements: "I should be sorry for any woman who had to rely on me when her time came," he had said, his face dark and closed. "I wasn't much good to my wife when she was confined. Behaved like a brute, got drunk. The truth was, I was afraid. Those animal noises upstairs—and then I wasn't exactly sure what was being born . . . I shall do neither myself nor Claire any good by being around, that's quite clear."

"Claire will understand," P.B. had said.

But I hadn't, not until that moment. . . .

". . . So you needn't worry about the baby, Claire—whatever my doubts, I will take care of it. . . ."

"I am not worrying, Geordie." Hearing the different note in my voice, he stopped, looked at me uncertainly. Full of strength and certainty—enough for both of us—I went on: "I have never worried about our baby, Geordie. And you needn't either." I touched his cheek very gently, and said softly, talking directly to the wounded, uncertain self that looked at me dumbly through his eyes: "It'll be all right. You'll see, it will be all right."

I didn't know then, in the arrogant innocence of my youth, how dangerous it was to do this—to bypass the defenses and touch directly the vulnerable creature that lies beyond them, curling away from the revealing light, from the ruthless touch. But this time it was all right, I did no damage. His rigidity dissolved, a long long sigh, out of the very depths of him, came whistling out from between his beautiful lips. "Oh, God, darling . . ." he said, and taking my hand away from his cheek, kissed it.

We never spoke of it again, although I grew larger with my baby every day. He would smile and touch, but never say a word. And later—later—when he saw her, my beautiful little girl with his curls and his eyes and the same proud turn of the lips. . . .

(Added later that night.)

What an odd thing to have written: *this time I did no damage.* When have I ever done him damage, or touch him with anything but delicacy?

A domestic catastrophe colors the atmosphere of the entire house like a drop of ink spilled in clear water. Servants' eyes, meeting yours, turn opaque; their voices sound flat when they greet you; the air around you vibrates with unspoken anxiety. Grisha, returning from Islavskoye after his lesson, was immediately aware of something going wrong. Fomitch's gloomy face when he came into the dressing room to take off his riding boots confirmed his foreboding.

"What is it? What happened?"

Fomitch said, without looking up from Grisha's boots, "It's all up with the poor girl now."

Strangely Grisha felt no surprise. Only his heart gave a fatalistic little lurch: here it is, the anticipated disaster. "But why? How?"

Fomitch was silent, concentrating on slipping the soft leather past the lumpy instep. When that was done, he answered: "The bitch got it out of her, that's how, your Excellency. Just the way I figured she would. She knew it all along, it was just the matter of timing it right."

"What do you mean she knew? How could she?"

"They've got ways of knowing those things about each other, your Excellency. That's what they're women for."

"Couldn't Matryosha just deny it?" Despite himself, irritation colored his voice. To have this happen just as he had everything worked out, knew exactly what to say to his mother!

Fomitch's lips tightened. Starting on the other boot, he said with some asperity: "No doubt about it, your Excellency, another girl might have brazened it out, sure enough. Not my Matryosha. She's the timid sort. The minute that devil started on her, she just immediately fell down at her feet, 'I'm guilty, do with me what you will.' Well, that's just what Nikolavna wanted; right away, she's got her claws into her and is hauling her to the Princess, what else?"

Grisha's heart contracted with pity. Like a rabbit, with the dogs bearing down on it, frightened, done for. . . . He said unevenly: "How—how is she?"

"More dead than alive, that's how. Her Grace your mother was pleased to banish her from the house, so she is now in Afanassii's hut—that's my brother, her other uncle—sitting there, trembling for her life, poor orphan."

As he talked he went on mechanically helping Grisha change out of his riding clothes, Grisha submitted to his ministrations, equally mechanically, his heart in a turmoil of self-blame. His mother was still drooping from the effects of last night's bout of migraine when he had gone to see her this morning, and he had postponed talking to her until later and gone off to Islavskoye. With bitterness of hindsight he knew now that he should have stayed home, watching for his chance, until the thing was settled.

Fomitch, with a quick glance at his unhappy face, said gruffly: "No need to blame yourself, your Excellency. Even if you'd spoken to your mother and she had given her consent to that young good-for-nothing marrying Matryosha, it would have been the same in the end. She had it all planned, that blackhearted devil, may she writhe in eternal torment. And I, old fool that I am, I couldn't figure out how come she let the poor lass get into favor with her Grace your mother the way she did: recommended her for her sewing, had her handling her Grace's dresses, any time a *ryush* came loose"—Fomitch gave the word *"ruche"* the special comic flavor with which a Russian russifies a French word—"why, let Matryosha sew it up, she's neathanded. Well, it's very simple: who watches a scullery maid? If she gets into trouble, no big fuss is made. But if she's about her Grace's person, waiting on her— Oho! That's a different kettle of fish. Her Grace is then doubly angry: here she is bestowing her princely favor on the girl, letting her wait on her person and all, and the girl goes and repays her by whoring around, like she is some common village slut. . . . Out of sight with her, throw her out of the house like dirt, off to Petrovka with her, never mind that her uncle has been serving the family all his life, faithful body and soul. . . ." Fomitch's voice shook. He broke off, clamping his jaws together grimly, and again went down on his knees to help Grisha on with his shoes. He said in a colorless voice: "If I've said anything out of turn, your Excellency, don't take my words amiss. Certainly it's the girl's own fault for whoring around, the little fool, no two ways about that . . ."

Grisha, paying no attention to this humble recantation, gripped Fomitch's bowed shoulders. "To Petrovka? She's being sent to Petrovka? I thought you said she's at her uncle's."

"So she is, for the next ten days. The harvest'll be over then and they can send a man to take her."

"I see." Grisha got to his feet, pushing the chair away. Fomitch, still on his knees, craned his head up to look at him. Quick alarm flashed in his seamed face: "Your Excellency, what have you got in mind? Where are you . . .?"

"To talk to mother, of course. There's still time. . . ."

Fomitch caught at the skirt of his jacket. "No, no, your Excellency, don't you do it."

"What do you mean, don't do it? I promised, didn't I? My—my honor is involved in this!"

"It's no use, your Excellency, you'll just get her Grace your mother angry at you."

"Don't be silly, Fomitch. You know she never gets angry at me. . . . Besides, I know exactly what to say."

"No, sir, no, Grishenka, nothing will help now." Fomitch hesitated painfully, still clutching at Grisha's jacket. "No, you see, it's not just this business with Fedka that Nikolavna went to your mother with—all kinds of other things her Grace didn't know anything about—oh, she didn't stint the filth, trust her, the black-hearted bitch. . . ."

Grisha gently unclamped the valet's fingers and went to see the Princess.

He found her sitting at her desk writing a letter. Hearing Grisha come in she turned her head to give him a faint welcoming smile.

"Did you come to take me down to dinner, *chéri?* I must finish my letter to Sophie first. Shall I add a message from you?"

"Give her my love." Grisha turned to the ikons to cross himself, as he always did upon entering his mother's apartments, and sat down to wait. Anxiety gnawed at him. The sound of the quill scratching the paper scraped at his nerves. Finally she finished writing, folded her letter, sealed it with lilac-colored wax, and rang for a footman to take it away. . . .

"There now." She turned to him, smiling. He saw that she was still looking ill, her skin a parched yellow, the brownish shadows under her eyes darkened and spread. She was wearing one of his favorite dresses, green challis sprinkled with violets, but for once it didn't seem to mesh with her elegant person the way her clothes usually did: she might as well have been wearing Tikhonovna's old gray *kassaveika*.

"Do you still have your migraine, *maman?*"

"Only a dull after-ache." She touched a blue-veined temple, delicately. "This morning's *bagarre* made it worse."

Here was an opening. "Yes, I've heard." He cautioned himself to walk carefully. "Fomitch was almost in tears—what *is* all this about his niece?"

An expression of extreme distaste contracted her face like a tic. "The usual thing. She has proved to be—well, never mind, it has nothing to do with you."

"Well, actually it does, a little," Grisha said. To his own ears he sounded nauseatingly ingenuous. "My poor Fomitch was quite crushed about it; in fact, he——"

"In fact, he asked you to intervene? *Mon pauvre Georges*, I know exactly how it was, they really do tyrannize over you, those faithful old retainers. . . . Well, now you've done your duty, and you can tell him there's nothing you can do, the girl has disgraced herself and must go."

"Yes, but Fomitch says . . ." It was like a childhood game in which you had to have everything you said preceded by a set phrase or else pay a forfeit. "Fomitch says you're sending her to Petrovka."

"She can't stay here."

"But, *maman*—to Petrovka?"

Patches of red appeared on his mother's cheeks. "I don't want to discuss it, Georges—there are things you don't know."

"If you mean because she—because of her condition," Grisha persisted desperately, "well, there's my groom Fedka, he's in love with her, he wants to marry her. . . ."

"Is there any reason why I must be tormented?" the Princess interrupted him in a voice gone suddenly deep and vibrant. Another little spasm flickered across her drawn face. She picked up her lace handkerchief and pressed it to her mouth. Above it, her black eyes reproached him. But he could no longer stop.

"I am sorry, *maman*, I don't mean to. It's just that it seems to me—sending this poor girl to the end of the world, away from whatever family she has, when the man responsible for her condition is right here ready to marry her." It was going wrong, he could sense it. He blundered on: "Of course, she can no longer be in the house, I quite see that. . . ."

"But you feel that she should stay right here in the village, is that it?"

"Well, yes, and marry Fedka, so that——"

"Well, I don't think so." Snatching her handkerchief away, she showed him a face made unrecognizable by anger and cruelty, black eyes blazing, lines scything deeply downward from the nose to a mouth like a gash. Her voice grated. "I want the vile little creature miles away from me—and, if I were not mindful of our Saviour's teachings, I would have her whipped every step of the distance!"

"*Maman!*" Grisha recoiled. The face was so unfamiliar that it might have been a gorgon's; he couldn't have been more appalled if her smooth coiffure had been transformed into a nestful of hissing snakes.

"To think that you, Georges—that you, too . . ."

Hands clenched, neck cords standing out as rigid as bars on both sides of her thin neck, she burst into laughter, repeating wildly, "You too, you too." Presently the words became undistinguishable; mechanical cachinnating sounds issued from her squared mouth; her eyes turned up, showing white.

Nikolavna ran into the room. She flung up both hands, with a soft cry of dismay, and rushed over to her mistress.

"Your Grace, *matushka*, dear one! Oh, Lord save us, what is this? Nadka, Masha, Loukeria, look sharp!" she shouted to the maids crowding terrified in the doorway. The women surrounded the laughing Princess in a distracted bustle, bringing water, pillows, smelling salts, as the housekeeper called for them. Cradling the Princess's rigid body in her plump arms, Nikolavna said to Grisha: "And you, your Excellency, Grigorii Petrovich, even if I am nothing but a servant, I have to say this, it is a shame to worry your mother so . . ." Poisonous triumph lurked in her eyes.

Grisha left the room and stood outside the door, listening. A childhood memory surfaced: something very much like this, feminine bustle, doors slamming, snatches of that same terrible laughter from behind them, and his father, stony-faced, walking away from it all.

Presently the mechanical sounds altered, one human sob breaking through, then another. When he heard her begin to weep in an ordinary fashion, he went away.

That same night, Prince Pyotr came back from Moscow. It was too late for him to be told any of this, but the very fact of his being back was of great comfort to Grisha during the sleepless night.

The next morning Grisha went to wait upon his father in his dressing room. His valet, Maxim, was removing the lather from his face with delicate feathery strokes of the ivory-handled razor. The Prince's features as they emerged from the lather had a complacent, even pleased cast; a smiling crease dented each smooth cheek. "It's good to see old friends. Some interesting things Evgenii Mikhailovich told me. Poor man, he's not at all well. We're the same age but he looks ten years older, and worried. As I would, I daresay, if I had been living in St. Petersburg for the past few years." He was being unusually loquacious, a sign of a good mood. Maxim handed him his silver-backed English brushes with the ornate monogram on the back, and he began to brush his crop of curly graying hair.

"We might be going back there, all the same, one of these days. . . . I have a feeling the reptile"—Prince Pyotr's favorite name for Arakcheev—"is on his way down. . . . Just a few things Evgenii Mikhailovich has mentioned. Didn't play his cards right this time," he said with satisfaction.

"What did he do?"

"Only what you would expect him to do: be himself. It seems his whore had her throat cut so he's been staying on his estate sniveling about her and letting affairs of state go to the dogs. It's felt that the Emperor's eyes are being opened at last. Well, we shall see. . . . Another thing: possibly something will finally be done about the treasonable activities in the army. Evgenii Mikhailovich seems to think that the information they have been receiving can no longer be ignored. . . . Your friend isn't involved by any chance, is he? That Pushchin?"

Grisha felt a tiny lurch of the heart. "I don't think so," he said, looking at his father with scared eyes.

"I would shoot them all like mad dogs." The Prince's eyes went cold and implacable. "Every single one of them . . . Well, don't look so worried. In spite of his views, your Pushchin is not the conspiratorial type—looks you straight in the eye and says right out what he thinks." Putting his brushes down on the dressing table, he gave Grisha a brief reassuring smile. "Prince Golitzin has nothing but good to say about him."

Grisha smiled back shyly. His concern for Pushchin faded. What filled his heart with exultation, crowding out all cares, was the man-to-man confidential way his father was talking to him. "As though I were Sergey," he thought, with timid joy. It was a moment so precious, that he wanted nothing to obtrude on it: not even Matryosha. Impulsively be bent down and kissed his father's hand, inhaling the scent of the English soap. The Prince's eyebrows arched. "What's up?"

"I'm just so glad you're back, Papa," Grisha answered truthfully.

The Prince's cold face softened. "Well, so am I." He patted his son's cheek, carelessly. "You look a bit peaked. Have you been letting your mother coddle you again? I'd better take you riding later." The Prince got up, shrugging out of his dressing gown, as Maxim approached bearing a cambric shirt reverently between his carefully outspread fingers. Grisha looked with awe at his father's massive white torso, with the golden cross glimmering in the dark thatch of hair on his chest. "Or is it going to interfere with your English lesson? I understand they're back at Islavskoye now."

"I'm not going there today, *Papa*. Dunia is ill." He had received the note early this morning. Nothing serious, Miss Clairmont had written, but she is staying in bed and wants me near her to coddle her. . . .

"Very well, then. We'll go riding as soon as I've seen your mother. She's not well, I hear."

Grisha took a deep breath. "I'm afraid it's my fault. I angered her. But I don't know why."

The Prince grimaced. "Yes, sometimes that sort of thing passeth understanding, as the Bible says. . . ." The sense of masculine solidarity, built on the frailty and unreasonableness of women, flowed stronger between them. "You had better tell me about it, I don't want to put a foot wrong."

Grisha watched his father's face anxiously as he told him about it. Nothing unfavorable there, only rueful comprehension and amusement. Grisha's hope soared. It'll be all right, he thought, I'll save her yet.

"It was terrible," he said, shuddering as he remembered the gorgonlike mask and the laughter, "and I still don't understand why she should have been so upset, just because I was trying to make things right for the poor girl. That damned Nikolavna getting to her first—that was bad luck. And of course she wasn't quite over her migraine."

He remembered the painful tic that had contorted her face. His persistence must have seemed callous thoughtlessness, irritating her painfully stretched nerves. "You, too, Georges!" She had meant, he supposed, that he too, like his father, like all men, was being thoughtless and cruel. His timing, it seemed, had been unfortunate.

The memory of the gorgon face began to fade: when she got better, she would be herself again, kind and gentle, she would abjure that frightening alien cruelty. He sighed: it was always better when you confided your troubles; and there was a special sweetness about being able for the first time in his life to confide them to his father.

The lurking amusement on the Prince's face deepened. "That's how it is with women, my boy. Unpredictable, the best of them, and you might as well learn it here and now: the best possible training in diplomacy." He clapped him on the shoulder. "I'll see what I can do. Off with you now."

Later in the afternoon, Grisha ordered his racing drozhky and had Fedka drive him down to the village.

"Why do you suppose we are going there?" he asked, glancing with a smile at Fedka's snub profile beside him.

"I don't know, Your Excellency," Fedka answered abstractedly, his attention focused on the big highstepping roan who was going thundering down the road, tossing his mane and throwing his legs out in the angular showy manner of trotters. Fedka, driving a horse, became a person of authority; his large red hands were uncannily sensitive to the horse's mouth and knew how to exert the exact amount of control needed.

"Can't guess? We are stopping at *Afanasii's*—Fomitch's brother, you know." Again the feeling of expansive benevolence washed over him.

Their arrival in the village produced a commotion. Little boys stopped playing in the street and watched them, big-eyed, standing bolt upright, with their bellies stuck out and their thumbs in their mouths. Doors popped open, kerchiefed heads peering cautiously, and a peasant girl hurrying along with two buckets on a yoke across her shoulders came to so abrupt a stop that the water splashed.

An elderly man, bearing, in spite of a grizzled beard and lack of teeth, an unmistakable resemblance to Fomitch, opened the door and bowed low. Over his stooped back Grisha looked into the interior of the *izba*. It was low and sunless, with its walls and ceiling darkened by smoke; a heavy odor made his nostrils twitch: it was made up of tar, cooked cabbage, grease, and just plain frowst. A woman, barefoot, with a kerchief wound about her head, stood by the stove, stirring a pot, with children of all ages crowding about her. An old man lying on the shelf behind the stove stretched out a scrawny neck, like an old rooster. All of them gaped at him, frozen into a tableau. But Matryosha wasn't among them.

Grisha asked for her. "She's in the backyard; I'll go get her immediately for your Grace, your Excellency," said the peasant, backing away and bowing.

"No, I'll find her myself, don't bother. . . . I promised Fomitch," he added, finding it necessary to explain the visit. He stepped away from the door and started around to the back, aware of the usual shift of attention to his leg. "Come along, Fedka," he called over his shoulder.

Matryosha, wearing only her shift, was sitting on a log near the fence, her knees hugged close to her chest, her flaxen head drooping. A big sow chomped in a trough next to her; hens pecked away briskly, not a yard away. Oblivious of it all, she seemed to be in a sort of trance. Grisha had to call her twice before she raised her head and peered at him, vacant faced. Grisha had a disconcerting idea that she had been sitting like that ever since her banishment.

"Matryosha." Frowning painfully, shaking her head as if to rouse herself, she rose to her feet, and stood before him, passive, her hands dangling in the folds of her none-too-clean shift.

"Look who is here to see you," Grisha said, addressing her with the labored cheerfulness one uses in a sickroom. Obediently the girl's dull eyes shifted from him. In an instant her face was transformed; incredulous joy poured into it, lighting it up like a lamp. She was, all at once, a totally different girl. "Fedya," she stammered joyfully. "Fedyushka." Her voice was a little hoarse, as if from disuse.

Fedka remained standing where he was, a few paces behind his master. His whitish eyelashes lay stubbornly lowered on his ruddy cheeks. Presently, he lifted them, and looked at the girl from under his brows, saying nothing.

The girl was silent too, clasping her small red hands together. A look of love and yearning poured upon him from her widened eyes. The whole of her poor little face was swallowed up in their incredulous pale blue incandescence. Fedka moved restlessly and cleared this throat. "Well, Matryosha," he began and stopped, jerking his head in a hunted way.

Matryosha's lips parted silently. She continued to look at him with the same enveloping tenderness, and presently his sulky face changed, softened. "Well, Matryosha," he began again, "seems as though we've brought nothing but trouble to each other. A beating for me, and as for you—as for you . . ." His eyes darkened, as if for the first time he allowed himself to see what was in store for Matryosha. A watery glint came to them. His wide throat worked. "Forgive me, a sinner, Matryosha, forgive me for the trouble I brought you."

Matryosha answered him in a voice no louder than rustle of

grass. "Nothing to forgive, I gladly—I'm glad to suffer anything for you, Fedyushka . . ."

"Why, I don't think we need talk about suffering," Grisha began awkwardly. His voice sounded too stridently hearty in his own ears. "I've talked to my father and it really looks as if—I wouldn't be surprised if there were a wedding coming soon."

"As your Excellency wishes. We're your servants," Fedka muttered, hanging his head. There was another silence.

"We'd better go now," Grisha said.

"Yes, your Excellency," Fedka said on a relieved note. He hesitated, lifted a hand in an awkward gesture, and strode away. Matryosha too raised her hand and let it drop. Her lips trembled. Again Grisha's heart tightened with unbearable pity.

"All will be well, Matryosha. I'll see to it, I promise."

Her eyes turned to him, seeing him, it seemed to him, for the first time. All at once, she bowed down before him; not dropping the abrupt little curtsey she had been taught at the house, but bending low in the solemn deep deliberate Russian obeisance, her small hand touching in turn her brow, her breast, and finally the ground.

Claire's Journal, September 24

Dunia is more ill than we had thought. The doctor has been to see her and has ordered a mustard plaster. She has passed the morning uncomfortably, tossing and complaining, not letting me leave her for a minute, her hot little hands clinging to mine, asking me to sing for her, to tell her stories. She fell asleep listening to me; and is peacefully sleeping now with her old nurse keeping watch. . . .

The strange bittersweet pleasure of taking care of a sick child. . . . To be there when she asks for you, to feel that precious little body resting trustfully against you. . . .

Pushchin, on his way back to Moscow, stopped here for supper. He found occasion to stand close to me and murmur: "It has been such a long time . . ." True, much too long. At the Zimmermans' I would awaken at night, wanting him so that it sickened me. The memory must have shown on my face; he asked me in an altered voice:

"Shall I stay the night?" I shook my head. What would be the use? I shall be sleeping in Dunia's room tonight. But a blinding current of desire leaped between us. Without looking at him, I heard him draw his breath in sharply. His hand ringed my wrist so strongly for a moment that I gasped with pain. I am sure there will be a mark tomorrow. . . . He said something under his breath in Russian and turned away.

Now if this terrible physical attraction, this irresistible pull, were accompanied by loftier feelings; if there were love somewhere in this—oh, dear, what a disaster *that* would be, to be sure!

The nurse is calling me—I must go to Dunia. . . .

"You wanted me, Papa?" A timid hope sprang up in Grisha: perhaps he had been sent for to be told that all was well, his mother no longer angry at him, and Matryosha safe. The Prince turned from the window, where he was standing, and said: "Distressing news has just come from Islavskoye; the Pomykovs' little girl died suddenly last night."

"Dunia?" Grisha's eyes stretched wide with incredulity. He listened numbly. Pneumonia—rapidly fulminating complications —inflammation of the brain—the words came at him in jerky rushes and receded, making no impact: his father might as well have been talking of the dying out of some rare species of bird in Patagonia.

"But it can't be," burst from him finally, "it was nothing!"

"Well, it looks as though it had turned into something," said the Prince acidly. Any news of sickness or death irritated him. "Apparently they didn't notice the seriousness of the child's illness until the last minute—or some such stupidity. . . ."

Grisha's state of disbelief persisted even as he entered the Pomykov house. There was black crêpe on the door, the mirrors were shrouded, and old Pavel's face as he took his coat held the same expression of numb bewilderment that he felt on his own; but a hum of conversation came from the drawing room as though nothing had happened. The cat Vasska came slowly into the hallway. Looking up into Grisha's face, he meowed noiselessly once, and went on, plumy tail drooping.

Monsieur Gambs came hurrying out. Dressed in mourning

though he was, his clothes retained traces of the romantic disorder characteristic of his style. His black cravat, negligently tied, flowed as picturesquely as ever; his curly hair preserved its habitual Wertherian disarray. But his eyes were frankly red with weeping in a face gray and drawn with fatigue.

He wrung Grisha's hand. *"Schrecklich, nicht wahr?"* he said huskily. "A terrible misfortune, unforeseen, unexpected . . ." He went on to tell Grisha all about it: how Dunia had had a restless day, with steadily rising fever; how, after a doctor had seen her, she had fallen into what looked like sleep, which presently turned into unconsciousness; how with frightening rapidity her breathing had become so labored that they had to hold her up to prevent suffocation; how he had gone for the doctor in the middle of the night and couldn't find him; and when he had brought him back nothing they did was of any use, at five o'clock that morning all was over, she was gone. . . . The account had a certain weary glibness about it, as if it had been told many times. "Do you want to see her, Prince?" They went slowly down the corridor; the convivial sounds from the drawing room faded behind them and were replaced by a sonorous singsong of prayers from the schoolroom.

In the anteroom Zahar Nikolaitch, still wearing his green official's uniform (he had just come back from Moscow, Gambs whispered, where he had been told the terrible news), was walking back and forth with the aimless restlessness of a caged animal. He stopped when he saw Grisha; in his small sunken eyes, Grisha read the same stark unbelief. He embraced Grisha convulsively, uttering a harsh dry sob in his ear, and turning away resumed his feverish wall-to-wall pacing.

The classroom, emptied of all furniture, mirror and blackboard swathed in white net, had taken on the look of a chapel. A heavy smell of incense permeated it. The table at which he and Miss Clairmont used to sit was now a bier for the open coffin. Two large candelabra flanked it, candles growing from each branch; their small secretive flames wavered and swayed, asserting their scintillant claims against the waning daylight. A priest, black and columnar in his cassock, chanted psalms before a lectern.

A small shapeless presence huddled on its knees by the coffin; its cracked voice quaveringly kept pace with the chant, and a shrunken wrinkled hand crept in and out of the enveloping shawl, to make a sign of the cross. That was the Pomykovs' ancient nurse.

Dunia lay in the coffin, dressed in white. Grisha recognized the dress: the white muslin with pink ribbons she would wear on the special occasions when she was allowed to stay up late in the drawing room; the pink ribbons had been removed. Beneath a chaplet of flowers, her face was a composed small wedge of wax; her mouth was parted, her little white teeth bared in a tiny smirk. Grisha looked down at her, feeling nothing. It was all unreal, a senseless rite performed for some obscure reason over a wax effigy of a child; the original was hiding somewhere in the house indulging in an elaborate mystification at their expense.

The old nurse had stopped praying and was looking at him with an encouraging smile on her wrinkled apple of a face: "Kiss the little angel, Prince, say good-bye to her." As he bent down obediently to set his lips to the dead child's cheek (it felt inhumanly cold and soft, some artificial material rather than human flesh), an old memory from his childhood awakened in him: his own Tikhonovna taking him down to a little coffin and making him kiss the wax doll in it, telling him that it was his little brother who had died.

In the drawing room, people circulated about keeping up a subdued social hum; it was just like one of the usual Pomykov soirées, only executed in somber colors. Marya Ivanovna sat in the same chair as always. The pink nieces, now red-eyed and garbed in black, surrounded her. Miss Clairmont stood there too, silently, an attenuated black shadow, with a sallow wedge of a face like Dunia's back in the classroom.

Marya Ivanovna raised her splotched and swollen face to him. An incongruously social smile slid across it. "How kind of you to come, Prince. Did you see her? She looks lovely, doesn't she? Doesn't she really?" she inquired in grotesquely conversational tones. "Rested? At peace?"

"Yes, lovely," said Grisha, frightened by the queer eagerness on her face. Marya Ivanovna gave a triumphant little nod.

"There, what did I tell you?" she said, turning to Miss Clairmont. "She's not dead, she's just asleep. Resting from that terrible night we all had, my angel, my little treasure. Oh God!" she screamed and rising up from her chair cast herself down on the ground. Miss Clairmont bent down to her, saying nothing.

"*Schrecklich, schrecklich,*" said Gambs next to him, shuddering, as Marya Ivanovna, screaming and straining, was carried past them. "But it is *her* that I am most concerned about." He indicated with a movement of his head the thin black-gowned figure leaving the room without a backward look. "*She* hasn't shed a tear since this happened."

With common accord they moved to the dining room where the large table stood piled high with food. Grisha felt stirrings of ravenous hunger inside him. He accepted the plate that a footman handed him. Gambs quickly lifted' and emptied a small glass of vodka. He coughed and a little color came back to his face.

"The child died in her arms, you know," he said. "Everybody had given up, even the doctor, but not Claire, she went on fighting. Even when it was plain that everything was over, and I tried to take her away, she wouldn't go. 'I'll save her yet,' she said, 'I won't let this one die.'" Monsieur Gambs shook his head slowly with wonder. "For a moment, you know, I found myself believing her, I thought she'd somehow—she sounded so sure, you see. But the child was dead, she had—taken wing, even as Claire was holding her."

Grisha had a vision of Miss Clairmont, crouched over Dunia, blindly fighting off the ancient enemy. This one, in spite of everything, she would save . . .

"I suppose," he said, thinking aloud, "she was thinking of her own baby that died. . . ."

"You know about that, then." A shadow of his old circumspect disapproval darkened Monsieur Gambs's mobile face. Then he gave a tiny shrug, accepting the knowledge. "Yes, and imagine, Prince, what a terrible fatality, how it must have opened old wounds—Dunia was almost exactly the age of Claire's daughter when she died." His arched eyebrows came together at Grisha's look of amazement. "I thought you knew, Prince, from what you said, otherwise I would never have——"

"I knew about the child, but I thought that it died as a baby."

"Oh no, she grew up into a beautiful little girl—that's why it was such a peculiarly cruel twist of fate that Dunia should die too—she had taken the place of her daughter in Claire's heart, you see—it was like losing her child twice."

"I didn't know . . ."

Monsieur Gambs looked at him and suddenly reached for his hand. "We are both her friends, aren't we? We both love her, she has honored both of us with her confidence. . . ." He wrung Grisha's hand emotionally, his bright brown eyes moistening.

[163]

"Yes, I'll tell you. . . . It was a lovely little girl, they called her Allegra. . . ."

Allegra! A sweet, chiming name.

". . . And Claire loved her more than anything in the world. But she didn't die in Claire's arms. She was with her father when she fell sick. Or rather—that was the terrible tragedy of it, Prince—the poor child died all alone, in a convent where her father put her. . . . I can't bear to think of it—a little girl dying alone, without father or mother." He shook his head and went on speaking, rapidly and with agitation, tears pouring down his cheeks. "No, Prince, *he* may have been a great man, but he had no heart. I worship. his magnificent poetry, but I hate him as a man. . . ."

I hate him, Miss Clairmont had said, because he had murdered a being I loved. . . .

Johnny Pomykov came toward them, meandering disconsolately through the crowd, his fists rammed into the pockets of his black jacket. He leaned his head against Monsieur Gambs's sleeve and sighed. "I am feeling delicate," he said.

"*Ach du lieber Himmel,* only that is lacking," Monsieur Gambs muttered worriedly, taking in his pupil's unnaturally pink cheeks and dull eyes. He felt his forehead gently. "A little feverish, I think . . . I had better have you looked at." He led him away, pausing for a moment to say to Grisha over his shoulder, "I am sure I needn't tell you, Prince, that this must remain in strictest secrecy."

"No, you really needn't, Monsieur Gambs. . . ."

Claire's Journal, September 26

Last night, during my vigil, Geordie appeared to me. He looked the same as ever, except for the leeches at his temples. He limped over and peered into the coffin.

"Murderer!" I cried just as I had that other time. Hanging his head, he was silent.

I said to him: "How could you help loving her? Didn't you find it charming that she looked so much like you? Your hair, your eyes, your hands—it must have been like seeing oneself in a mirror. I would have expected you to keep her at your side forever, just for that reason alone. But you sent her away to die. . . . If I could only believe that her tiny life away from me made any sense! That she wasn't thrown away for nothing!"

Raising his head he tried to answer me. But when he opened his mouth it was crammed with worms. . . . And the next moment he wasn't there, only the priest intoning prayers, and candle flames shivering and dancing around the bier.

Candles ringed Dunia as she lay in church, stealthily turning into a yellow little mummy; candles, row on glimmering row, sprang upward toward the dark faces of the saints; a procession of penny tapers held in work-worn hands of peasants, come to pay last respects to the dead little *baryshnia,* wound flickering around her coffin.

There was a masque of black-gowned women going on among the candles; they all wore their mourning with the air of being committed to it forever, and in the presence of their massive grief the more restrained sorrow of the men seemed grudging, insufficient. They were not the main performers. Fitfully Grisha would catch a glimpse of Zahar Nikolaitch, his monkeyish face wrinkled into a grimace of grief; Pushchin was there too, attentive and saddened. Monsieur Gambs was absent. Grisha learned later that he had gone to Moscow with the ailing Johnny at Marya Ivanovna's frenzied behest "to take the child away from this accursed place before he too dies." Marya Ivanovna held the stage, sodden with tears, throwing anguished tantrums in the church ("Look at the mother, see how she throws herself about, poor soul," came sympathetically from the populace massed in the back). Miss Clairmont, however, remained tearless as before, standing in silent abstraction, her head bent, amid the flurry of genuflections and signs of the cross. She looked old and plain in her black dress. A deep furrow between her contracted brows gave her a darkly questioning look, as if she were holding an inward inquest into the causes of the disaster.

The Princess was always scrupulously mindful of her obligations to her neighbors. She might stay away from the Pomykovs' theatricals, speciously pleading ill health, but she rose up from her sick bed to attend the funeral of their daughter. Her manner to the bereaved parents was perfect, all friendship and compassion, and when Madame Pomykov, encouraged by it, so far forgot herself as to fall weeping on her breast, she bore the onslaught with equanimity, making the sign of the cross over her with her slender black-gloved hand and saying, "Put your trust in Our Saviour, *ma chère*, He alone will sustain and comfort you." Driving home from the funeral with her husband and son, she reassumed her air of gentle displeasure, saying little and occasionally touching her temples with a suffering look.

Outside the closed windows of the carriage, the landscape unrolled gray and secretive behind the slanting rain. Summer was over for good, buried with the dead child. Grisha felt his grief for Dunia dissolve into an all-embracing melancholy, that special Russian malaise that is described by a saying: "Black cats are scratching at my heart."

Later the weather cleared sufficiently to permit him to go horseback riding. As he waited on the front steps, Fomitch handed him a note from Miss Clairmont. It was a colorless little missive, merely telling him that the Pomykovs were leaving for Moscow the next day immediately after the Mass, since Marya Ivanovna understandably wanted to join Johnny as soon as possible.

"I suppose we'll be leaving soon too," Grisha murmured, folding the paper carefully and putting it away in his pocket.

"Yes, her Grace was saying something about it," Fomitch answered. Then casually, with an air of supplying a meaningless bit of gossip, he added, "Matryosha will be going off to Petrovka on Monday. Day after tomorrow."

Grisha stopped in midstep, appalled. "But I thought not for ten days!"

Fomitch looked back at him, wooden faced. "Monday, at dawn, that's what the orders are."

Whose orders? Grisha had no heart to ask. Glancing guiltily into his old servant's eyes, he found no reproach there. Fomitch had known from the first that the girl was doomed. He was venturing a last hopeless reminder, a slight unresentful nudge, but he expected nothing to come from it.

There was no need for the reminder: Grisha had never forgotten. The child's death may have obscured Matryosha for the moment; but she was there, in the back of his consciousness, inert, passive, depending on him alone to save her.

And he too was waiting. Just as he had promised salvation to Matryosha, so it had been promised to him—not in so many words, perhaps, but implicit in the look, the smile, the treasured man-to-man conversations in the dressing room and at the dinner table. It all will be made right, he told himself. It has to be.

Fedka brought Nelly to the door. Grisha looked at his cheerful ruddy face, shining with its ever-present smile, and anger pricked at him. How could he—? But perhaps he didn't know. He said abruptly:

"They're thinking of sending her to Petrovka day after tomorrow, you know."

"Is that so, Excellency?" Fedka dutifully tried to rebuild his smiling face into a more sober expression and failed.

Grisha swung up into the saddle. He looked with downright hatred at the yellow head of the groom, who in the meantime had begun shortening his stirrups. "Well, she won't be going. Don't worry, you'll be a bridegroom yet."

The young groom readjusted his stirrup, his expression carefully neutral. Grisha's lips tightened. The girl's face rose in his mind, irradiated with fearful tenderness as she looked at her lover. Had the fellow forgotten all that? He said, in a hard voice: "Don't you want to marry her? Don't you feel you owe it to her?"

Fedka's big shoulders moved in an almost imperceptible shrug. "It's what you our masters want us to do," he said, infuriatingly repeating the set formula. "All the same, your Excellency . . ." Grisha's barely repressed enmity had evidently communicated itself to him. Looking up from under his sandy eyebrows with a half-insolent expression, he blurted out, "It isn't as if I'm the first, others have been there too."

As soon as he had said that, his eyes went round with pure fright, even before Grisha, flushing with anger, bent down from his saddle and struck him. Fedka stepped back. The two of them looked at each other aghast. "What is this?" one disconcerted young face said to the other. Grisha straightened up and picked up his reins. "I am sorry," he said in a low voice. "You shouldn't have said that. You are never to say it again."

"No, your Excellency," Fedka said, covertly watching his hands. A small trickle of blood appeared at the corner of his mouth where Grisha's ring had cut it. He made no move to wipe it off, as he waited for his master to ride away.

After a moment's hesitation Grisha swung down from the saddle. "Take her back to the stables, I'm not riding today."

As he watched the young groom plodding away with Nelly, he wondered drearily at the growing wrongness of things. All those depressing reversals, always for the worse! Fedka saying to Matryosha so touchingly, "Forgive me for the harm I did," and then apparently forgetting all about her; his own pity and indignation when he had intervened in the whipping; and then, just now—he remembered with revulsion the warm elastic yielding of flesh under the impact of his fist and the smear of blood on his face. "A bad omen," he thought.

I hate to see any traces of the slave-owner in you. He saw Miss Clairmont's speaking eyes fixed upon him in sadness and disappointment. But that wasn't it at all, he assured her silently, it wasn't because he is a serf. It was as if someone had taken a cut at Nelly, I couldn't help hitting back, I couldn't have let anyone—

Earlier this summer he had wondered if he was in love with Miss Clairmont; he now incredulously asked himself the same question about Matryosha. Was that really possible? He, a Prince Volynski, in love with the frightened inarticulate serf girl who had once been offered him "for his health"? Who had serviced his father and his brother and was now with big belly by his groom? Ever since the episode with Nikolavna, when with a single look of incredulous gratitude she had somehow put herself in his hands, what he had increasingly felt for her was something akin to the proprietory tenderness he had always felt for animals, the mournful siskin, whistling in the cage in Tikhonovna's little room, the house cats, his ancient retriever Toozik, his darling Nelly. This was something more; with all of him, passionately and selflessly, he wanted that frightened child to have whatever she wanted: Fedka, her baby, safety from persecution.

But time was running out. Doggedly he limped back into the house to talk to his father.

"Well, *mon cher,* I don't know what to tell you," Prince Pyotr said. Grisha's heart sank at the expression of cold boredom on his face. "Your mother seems to have taken the bit between her teeth on this—couldn't wait 'til next week to get the girl out of Andreyevo before she corrupts us all. . . . I must say it wasn't very clever of you to go down to the village to see her: like throwing oil on the fire. . . . Oh, yes, that got back to your mother. Did you think it wouldn't? Very fine spy system your mother has, better than Benkendorff's," he added through his teeth.

"But—but I—what was the harm of taking Fedka to see her?" Grisha asked timidly; again, as before, he was sickened and horrified by his mother's mysterious vindictiveness.

The Prince gave a short vexed laugh. "Well, it won't do, my boy, just not good enough," he said puzzlingly. "At any rate there's nothing I can do now."

"Yes, you can, Papa. You can do anything!"

"*Merci du compliment.*" The Prince smiled in spite of himself at the fervor with which Grisha uttered this. His face softened. "I'd like nothing better than to oblige you, but hysterics defeat me. For certain reasons, which I won't go into, it is—inconvenient for me to insist on having my way. Not," he added with some acerbity, "that I wouldn't make a push to assert myself, hysterics or no, if it was something really important."

A sense of futility descended on Grisha: nothing in the world, he saw, could make Matryosha seem more important to his father than a blade of grass casually trampled down in passing. He said almost inaudibly: "But it's important to me, *papa.*"

"Yes, I gathered that," his father said dryly. He was silent for a moment, absent-mindedly picking up a paperweight that lay on the library table. The flesh-colored reflection grew and dwindled in the crystal globe as he turned it over and over in his hands. "I do understand, you see, I've been through all this myself at your age—and the girl is a tidbit. Your first one, too, isn't she? But messing with your mother's maids is sheer stupidity."

"Oh." Suddenly the meaning of his mother's hysterical outcries ("You, too, Georges!") caught up with Grisha. Blood rushed to his face. "But it wasn't—I didn't—I never. . . ."

His father gave him a quick look. "No?" The amused understanding slipped out of his face, to be replaced by boredom, and something else. "No, I suppose you didn't," he drawled. "In that case, you really puzzle me, *mon ami:* what *is* all the fuss about?"

Grisha swallowed. There was something profoundly insulting in that indifferent drawl; a contemptuous acknowledgment of a ludicrous inadequacy, always suspected and now known for certain, sounded in it. He answered in a low voice: "My honor is involved, *mon père.* I had promised the girl, and Fomitch, too—she is his niece . . ."

"Did you indeed?" said the Prince, looking somewhere past his left ear. "I should be most obliged to you if in the future you would think twice before giving awkward promises to my serfs. When I am dead and you and Sergey inherit my possessions, you can dispose of them as you will, marry them to each other, set up a village brothel, anything you please. Free them, for all I care, that seems to be in the air nowadays, all you callow cubs can't wait to disembarrass yourself of your possessions and the responsibilities that go with them. Just kindly restrain yourselves, while I am alive. . . . As for marrying Fedka off, that was out from the start. I don't like to see my stablemen marrying, not the good ones. And Fedka is one of the best. Look at the way he's been handling Kestrel. Everybody else is cagey with that brute, even Matvey, but not that little son-of-a-bitch, there's no fear in him. That's how I like 'em in the stables, with a bit of wildness in them, and there's nothing like marriage to dull the edge, take the spark out. . . . I'll tell you what I did, though." He sounded more friendly again, having apparently talked himself out of his bad humor. "That little wench of yours has got to go to Petrovka, no way out of that. Your mother is set on it. But in the interests of morality"—he gave a short dry laugh—"I've given orders to have her married to Klim there as soon as she arrives. That ought to give her some standing in the village, being married to the headman."

"To the—*mon père,* you can't mean the Petrovka headman!"

"Yes, the very one."

Grisha had seen the man once, when he had come to Andreyevo bringing his village's quit rent—a grim powerful man in his late fifties, blind in one eye, with a mouth like a gash in his reddish beard—and was repelled by the expression of gloomy savagery on his face. "But you can't!" he blurted out.

"What?" said the Prince frowning.

"He's a villain, you can see from the way he—and he's *old,* he's—" Is that what Matryosha was getting instead of the debonair young husband she had been promised? A bitter taste of failure clogging his throat, he said, with difficulty, "I beg of you not to, *mon père.*"

"I've already given orders. She'll get used to him. This is

beginning to be a bore, Grisha—I've done more or less what you asked me to do. . . ."

"I beg to disagree with you, *mon père*," Grisha said in a trembling voice. "I asked you to save that poor girl and you're making sure she's destroyed. . . ."

"That will do," the Prince said icily.

"I've never asked you for anything before . . ."

"Nor had you better again, if that's the way you propose to go about it. Have you gone mad? You may go now, and make sure that you never let me hear another word from you about that little whore."

"You should be the last one to call her that." The words had tumbled out unbidden; he heard them reverberating in his ears, as horrified as if he had spewed forth toads.

"What?" The Prince's rather prominent eyes widened and seemed to leap closer to his nose. He rose to his feet, overturning his chair, and came around the table swiftly.

Grisha shrank before this mask of anger. Before he had a chance to say anything, his father's heavy hand fell on his shoulder, spinning him around. He was seized by the collar, propelled across the room and out of the door. A blow sent him reeling down the corridor full tilt until he crashed into the opposite wall and went down.

"That'll teach you," said his father from the doorway in a voice of thunder, "you impudent lame whelp!" The door slammed shut. Grisha stayed on the floor motionless for a minute, the bust of Alexander seeming to contemplate his plight with a subtly contemptuous smile on its marble lips. Then he slowly struggled to his feet, just before Maxim came down the hall with a tray of wine.

Grisha came out of a nightmare in which he was back in the cemetery, standing by Dunia's grave with a candle in his hand, while they dug her up again. The spades went faster and faster, they thudded briskly against the coffin. An authoritative voice—his father's?—said: "Bury her again, she's dead," and abruptly he was awake. Did he oversleep? But as he lay there, he heard the clock, plaintively musical, strike four.

All at once he was staring stark awake. He lit a candle, got out of bed, and, shivering in the night chill, began dressing. A cold vicious excitement permeated him. He shrugged into his shirt, stepped into his elkskin riding breeches, thinking how strange it was to dress without the help of Fomitch, who had been sent away the day before and was now presumably sleeping in the serf quarters of their Moscow house. The boots gave him trouble even with the help of a bootjack. He considered calling Andrey, the young footman who lay fast asleep on the pallet outside the bedroom door, but his usual reluctance to expose his foot to anyone's eyes prevailed (he could just hear the young oaf telling the help afterward: "I saw the young *barin's* foot, brothers—just like a hoof it was!"), and he went on struggling with them on his own.

After he had finished dressing, he went inexpertly through the business of packing, which Fomitch would have done for him quickly and easily. Where did Fomitch keep his portmanteau? He finished by rolling up some clothes into a bundle and was ready to leave. At the door he took his last look at the room: it was already assuming that special look of vacuity with which a much-used room speeds a departing inhabitant, canceling him out; nothing left of his bodily presence except the impression of his body denting the unmade bed and the faintly steaming urine in the chamberpot.

The footman Andrey lay fast asleep by the threshold, his beardless young face turned upward; with a slight complaining wheeze, he turned it away, throwing an arm across his eyes against the candlelight, and slept on. Grisha walked through the quiet house without rousing anyone and let himself out through a side door.

He waited until the watchman's black bulk disappeared around the corner, the sound of his rattle receding with him, and went on to the stables. All around him night stirred secretively, preparing to take wing. A slight wind rose up, but the rain had stopped.

At the stables everything was quiet; horses drowsed in their stalls, occasionally stirring the straw or thumping a heavy hoof against the wood; variegated snores came from the darkness. A stableboy raised his tousled head out of the straw, starting sleepily at the sight of the young Prince appearing in the stables before dawn. Presently Nelly was led out of her stall, tossing her delicate head and nickering when she saw him. Grisha let the groom saddle her and then dismissed him. He himself folded a horse blanket and strapped it on to the saddle, together with the saddlebag into which he stuffed his belonging, tested the girth and adjusted the stirrups (doing all this much more deftly than he had performed his toilet). In a moment he had swung himself up in the saddle and was riding away.

Once out of the park, he let Nelly have her head. A shadow of accustomed exhilaration rose in him as he galloped along the deserted road, mists curling about the mare's pounding feet. For a moment he visualized himself, a romantic figure of a lonely horseman riding through the night to a mysterious assignation. Only he didn't feel romantic; he felt as mean and driven as a cutthroat hurrying to an ambush.

He reined Nelly in at a spot where, as he had worked out, a cart coming from the village would have to pass, pulled into a stand of birches glimmering white by the roadside, and, drawing his heavy cloak closer about him against the morning chill, prepared to wait. Nelly, excited by the gallop, snorted and danced under him, fidgeting on her slender legs. He dismounted and walked her back and forth until she cooled off: it would be the crowning catastrophe if she were to take a chill.

Dawn was creeping up now, a sparse glum lightening of the sky presaging a gray day. Dun-colored clouds crowded above him. A reddish glow infused a handspan of sky near the horizon like blood from a seeping wound. Somewhere a cock crowed—probably in the village. People were stirring there, a cart was being readied to take Matryosha to Petrovka, where she would be married to the gloomy one-eyed devil of a headman. He alone knew that she wouldn't be going there.

The entire scheme had sprung up in his head with icy clarity ten minutes after he had picked himself up from the floor—thus a worsted general, with nothing left to lose, dredges up from the depths of his humiliating defeat a desperate and audacious plan which, even if it won't save him, will at least inflict incalculable losses on the enemy. Immediately he addressed himself to it, all of him focused on the task, with no thought left for anything else; a door seemed to shut in his mind on what had happened before, with the same vicious finality with which his father had slammed the library door.

All Saturday night he had lain rigidly awake, eyes fixed on darkness, while rain scampered along the roofs like a squirrel.

Plans and possibilities revolved feverishly around each other in his mind like clockwork wheels. At last with a final dry click everything fell into place and he knew what he would do.

In a way it had all arisen from the fantasy he used to indulge in last summer: about keeping Matryosha in his own village of Nikitino, where his uncle, who had left it to him, used to keep his favorite mistress. A timid dream, half prurient, half sentimental, never meant to come to anything. The present plan was coldly, vengefully conceived, and no one could stop him from carrying it out.

Most of his quarterly allowance had not been spent and was lying, in a thick wad of banknotes, in a desk drawer. In another was a purse of gold coins his grandmother had sent him on his birthday. Together they made a good sum, enough to take care of everything.

Deciding on transportation was the most important thing. The best arrangement would have been hiring a carriage in Moscow. A hired troika of spirited horses with a skilled *yamshchik* would whisk him out of their ken without a trace. But there was no way to make these arrangements. He had only Sunday left; he would have to use whatever horseflesh was available in Andreyevo.

At first he thought of using a curricle, which he could drive himself. With Ovssyanik and Calembour harnessed to it, both of them good powerful goers with plenty of endurance, he could accomplish the journey in good time. He might not even need to change at the post station, if he drove carefully and rested the horses. Nikitino wasn't too far away, within thirty miles of Moscow, somewhere in the vicinity of the Troitza monastery; the Nikitino peasants supplied the monks with eggs and honey.

But in the end he decided to go on horseback, waylay the cart, and force its driver to take the road to Moscow instead of to Ryazan, with himself as a mounted escort. There were certain advantages to this plan. Getting the carriage readied before dawn would be bound to get too much attention from too many people, while taking Nelly out wouldn't do so. There would be no immediate pursuit. Even after he had failed to come for his lesson with Monsieur Lachaine, his absence would be construed as a tantrum: he was riding off his grievance and would come back when he was over it. Also there would be no reason to connect his disappearance with the cart presumably making its slow way to Petrovka. When they started to look for him in good earnest they would be looking for him alone.

Influencing this decision—probably more than it should—was the fact that he would have Nelly with him. "I couldn't possibly leave you behind, my darling," he said to her, laying his cheek against her soft warm muzzle.

After he had commandeered the cart, he would play things by ear. Send it back home if he could find a carriage for hire somewhere near Moscow; or take it all the way to Nikitino. In either case, somewhere along the road he would surely be able to find some seedy little village priest who for a consideration could be induced to perform a marriage ceremony.

The idea of marrying her had come to him last of all, a final touch to the battle plan, a desperate burst of killing gunfire to let loose when they finally caught up with him in Nikitino. Past that he didn't think.

His last bit of preparation was sending Fomitch to Moscow with enough errands to keep him there overnight. The old valet, who knew him better than anyone else in the world, might guess his intentions. He might interfere, raising an alarm—or, if not, be blamed later for not doing so. Failing to dissuade his master, he might even insist on coming along: Fomitch could be as obstinate as a mule. But Grisha wanted no partners in self-destruction.

With Fomitch out of the way all he had left to do was to get through Sunday. Somehow he had managed that.

He found himself getting hungry. Last night he had sent to the kitchen for his favorite sweet *boulochka*, which he didn't eat. He now got it out of the saddlebag with a slight self-congratulatory smile for his foresight.

The sunless sky grew lighter. All about him birds began to break into a sporadic morning clamor. A big white hare appeared on the other side of the road, sat there for a minute, waving his long ears, and then crossed the road with long deliberate leaps. A herd of sheep materialized out of the mist, driven by their shepherd, a thin shabby figure in a ragged sheepskin coat and bast shoes. The man cast an incurious look in his direction as he passed. Grisha wondered; what did he make out of the cloaked figure, muffled to the eyebrows, waiting at the crossroad? Probably nothing; the

[175]

ways of the gentry were incalculable and not particularly important to the peasant, until they impinged on his life.

Wheels rattled in the distance, he froze, his heartbeat thickening. There it was! A smallish cart drawn by a sturdy hook-nosed nag came into view. He limped to the middle of the road, holding up his hand, and the driver pulled back on the reins, bringing the cart to a stop.

For a moment Grisha, seeing only the driver there, thought he had stopped the wrong cart. Then something like a bundle of clothing stirred in the back. He let out his breath.

"Where are you off to, friend?"

The bearded face tilted up at him, obedient but perplexed. "Going Ryazan-way, your Worship. On business." With a backward jerk of the head he explained, "Taking a passenger along, a girl they want sent there—I've been given orders . . ."

"Yes, I know. Well, my friend, there has been a change in plans. . . ."

"How so, sir, your Excellency?"

"Do you know who I am?"

"How not, sir? You're our young master, his Lordship the young Prince Grigorii Petrovich," the peasant said with evident pleasure at getting everything right. "But what is that you were saying, your Excellency, about a change in plans?"

Without answering, Grisha went to the back of the cart. Matryosha lay there in the straw, huddled under a sheepskin coat, a kerchief around her head. She looked no bigger than a kitten.

"Matryosha," he said softly, bending down over the rail of the cart to peer into her muffled face. He saw that she was not asleep as he had thought at first. Her eyes were open, looking at him steadily with an expression he couldn't quite fathom, but she didn't move. He repeated her name, touching her hand. Her cold little fingers closed around his and obediently she allowed herself to be drawn upright, her kerchief slipping down to her shoulders.

His first thought was that it was not she, that they had substituted another girl. She sat in the straw as rigid as a doll, her little feet in bast slippers stuck out stiffly in front of her. Her hair, neatly plaited into two braids, lay on her shoulders, as lifeless as two ropes. All expression, all life, everything that added up to the special frail entity that was Matryosha, had drained out of her, leaving behind an inferior copy in grayish plaster, with blue pebbles for eyes.

Grisha dropped her hands—they slid limply to her lap—clutched her shoulders, and shook her. Her inert body gave no response; her head bobbed, the braids bounced on her shoulders, the face remained unchanged, without meaning or expression.

The driver twisted around in his seat. "That's how she's been for the last two days, they tell me, your Excellency. Not a sound, not a word out of her. Feed her, she'll eat. Give her water, she'll drink. Otherwise, nothing." He wagged his shaggy head, compassionately. "Somebody's spoiled that girl, no two ways about it, put a spell on her or something . . ."

The girl was quiet in his grasp, looking at him with vacant blue eyes. He noticed all at once that her shift was soiled; an unclean odor rose from her, unwashed body smell laced with the ammoniac tang of urine. With a shudder of revulsion he relinquished his hold on her, stepping back from the cart. And, as if that had been the signal he was waiting for, the driver leaned forward, clicked to his horse, snapping the whip: "Let's go, old lady!" The horse started with a lunge and a jerk, Matryosha fell stiffly backwards into the straw. The cart went clattering and bucking down the road and disappeared from view.

Dully Grisha watched it out of sight. A bitter lump, composed of tears and road dust and the unclean smell of her lingering in his nostrils, rose upward in his throat and he vomited where he stood, retching and straining in the middle of the road. The paroxysm passed, leaving him limp and strengthless, his legs trembling so that he could barely get back on Nelly. He let the reins drop on her neck and just sat her, with slack thighs, like a sack, letting her bring him back to the stables.

After he had handed Nelly back to a groom, he somehow made his way back to his bedroom, and falling across his bed, just as he was, boots and all, sank into an obliterating sleep. He roused briefly to see Monsieur Lachaine's wrinkled face bent over him, annoyance giving place to concern: "*Qu'avez-vous donc, Georges? Etes-vous malade?*"

"*Laissez-moi tranquil,*" he muttered, turning away. Other shapes beside Monsieur Lachaine's materialized around him, interfering with his sleeping. Fomitch was suddenly there, silently helping him out of his clothes, asking no questions. Then his mother; with loathing he endured the touch of her scented hand on his forehead. "I have a headache," he lied savagely in answer to her intrusive queries and burrowed back into sleep, annulling her together with the rest of the hideous morning.

He slept through the day and far into the night. Toward the end the quality of his obliviousness changed: dreams began to invade it. A rattling of cartwheels echoed through the emptied chambers of his mind, and a sturdy nag came trotting briskly toward him trundling a coffin, in which a childish shape reposed; a faint sour stench came from it; odor of dissolution or of a child soiling itself? it could be either. Strong tremors began to jerk his body; he was being ruthlessly hauled upward out of the depths like a hooked fish. Finally, despite all resistance, he broke the surface and was awake.

A candle blossomed by the bedside; its light illumined Fomitch's face, with its soft blunt wrinkles and the pigeon-tail back-tuft of gray hair. He put the candle down on the table and bent down anxiously.

"How do you feel, your Excellency?"

Meeting his eyes, Grisha saw that he knew everything.

Not answering Fomitch, he sat up slowly, dropping his head into his hands. His body felt cramped and his heart ached. Slowly, he allowed the memory to flood him, fully. Yes, it all happened, he had let it happen, he let them take her away. But already the horror was different: it was no longer seeing a living girl being bundled away into misery, they were taking a corpse away to be buried in a dungheap; and he was allowing them to perpetrate this indecency, not holding out for a decent funeral.

Only that wasn't true. The empty shell that was Matryosha was still alive, it had to be fed, taken care of, kept clean. With another throb of horror at himself, he recognized that he didn't want any part of that; all he wanted was to forget it all. Put it all away from him, bury her deep. . . . But he couldn't do that either.

"What to do, then?" he asked aloud.

"Everything is as God wills it, your Excellency, we are all his servants."

Simple resignation sounded in his voice. Lucky Fomitch, who had that utter unquestioning faith to help him. . . . *Not only him but his oppressors too,* sounded mockingly in his mind: Miss

Clairmont's irreverent voice, winging to him from the past. . . . He said to Fomitch abruptly: "I'm going to send you there."

"Where, your Excellency?"

"To Petrovka, of course, where else?" Grisha said angrily, rubbing at his inflamed eyes. "I want you to see how she—make sure that she isn't being hurt, that they are taking care of her. . . . I've got some money somewhere around . . ."

"Yes, your Excellency, I found it in your pockets and put it back where it's supposed to be. . . ."

Grisha shook his head impatiently: "Take it, take it all with you, and get there as fast as you can. Have them drive you to Moscow, and hire a *yamshchik* and . . ." He stopped, remembering his own feverish planning. Reflectively, with a sort of wonder, he said: "I was going to marry her, Fomitch."

Fomitch recoiled. "God forbid, Excellency!" He crossed himself rapidly several times. "That was just an idle thought sent by the devil. . . . That's his way, he raises up a rage in us so we don't know what to do with ourselves. . . . Why, his Excellency your father, he would have——"

"He's not my father," burst from Grisha.

"God help us, your Excellency, don't say so, Grishenka, don't sin. . . ."

"I have no father and no mother, Fomitch. Fomitch, I hate them!"

He laid his head on the valet's shoulder and burst into tears. Fomitch held him close, rocking him; a rusty sound struggled up through his throat: "Ekh, my child, my poor little child. . . ."

Presently Grisha stopped crying. He pushed Fomitch gently away and wiped his eyes on the monogrammed sheet: "Go today, please, Fomitch. And—and see to it for me—make sure she's taken care of. Take all the money I have and use it. . . ."

That made him feel a little better, but not very much.

By the time Fomitch returned, they had already left Andreyevo. One day Grisha woke up in his Moscow bedroom and there was his valet's stocky figure unobtrusively moving around the room as if he had never been away.

"Good morning, your Excellency."

Grisha looked at him with frightened eyes. "Well? Well?"

"I have just come in, your Excellency, forgive my lateness. I took the liberty of stopping on the way, at the Sretienka Monastery, to ask the fathers there to say a mass for my niece's soul."

Something jolted inside Grisha and went still. "She is dead, then." But this was no news. He had known it all along, from the moment she had toppled into the straw and had been driven away in the cart.

"Yes, your Excellency, God saw fit to take her unto himself." Visibly Fomitch braced himself for questions. But Grisha didn't ask any. He merely nodded and saw relief on the valet's face. "It was better that way, believe me, your Excellency," Fomitch said with a sort of sorrowful glibness.

"Yes, I know, Fomitch, thank you for everything."

He was conscious of a distinct disinclination to hear anything more about it. A hint of some hidden horror lurked in Fomitch's incommunicativeness, and his mind shrank from it, evading all conjectures. Better to turn back to the earliest memory of all, a naked girl smiling at her thoughts by the edge of the pond, as she drew circles in the water with the point of a reed. . . . Better to keep it that way, safe from terror or pain. . . .

In the end he learned all about it, however. One day, he had toiled up the stairs to Tikhonovna's little attic room and was about to knock on her door, when Fomitch's voice came from behind it, saying:

"Of course, he murdered her, the dirty swine. . . ."

Grisha's heart gave a huge guilty leap, as if some monstrous accusation had been directed at him. Everything in him clamored to run away from it, but he forced himself to stand and listen.

The story was simple. Matryosha had been duly delivered in Petrovka with the precise instructions that the headman, Klim Ivanov, was to marry her immediately upon her arrival. This was done, and two days later the bride was found lying by the stoop of the headman's *izba,* with a broken neck.

"She had gone wandering, in her lackwit way, like, and missed her step, he says to me, the one-eyed villain. Well, I know what's what, I keep my eyes open. I talked to the good people there, they told me she was doing no wandering, poor little soul, just sat there or went wherever she was taken. That black-hearted brute, he just took her to the top of the steps and gave her a push, how else? He wasn't going to be saddled with a feeble-minded wife."

"Lord save us, what sin, what wickedness, Fomitch!"

Fomitch fetched a gusty sigh which was echoed wheezily by the old nurse. "That's how it is, my dear old soul, plenty of black wickedness in this world."

Grisha turned around stiffly, and, hunched over like an old man, made his way downstairs.

MOSCOW

. . . Before them,
The white-walled Moscow they behold,
Its ancient turretry a-glow
With crosses of rubescent gold . . .

Alexander Pushkin, *Evgenii Onyegin*

Claire's Journal, September 30

Now that Johnny is recovering, I must say, Thank God for his illness. It has kept me mercifully busy. We arrived in Moscow on Sept. 28 and found the house in chaos and Johnny dreadfully ill with scarlet fever. Marya Ivanovna, faced with still another loss, went to pieces and I perforce had to take over. She produced such a noise with her lamentations that poor fever-racked Johnny finally turned his pinched little white face to her, and croaked, in French for some reason, *"Maman, je vous prie de me quitter, si vous ne voulez pas que je me batte la tête au mur."* I must say I rejoiced to hear these unfilial words: until then he had been too ill to utter anything.

Meanwhile nothing had been done about the house, even the covers not removed from the furniture, so that every day I find myself moving through rooms filled with squat white phantoms. Other ghosts surround me in the sickroom, ghosts of dead children. Sometimes I see Wilmouse's face on Johnny's pillow; sometimes, as I doze off, I feel a ghostly tug at my skirts; a querulous little voice complains, *"Vous ne m'aimez pas du tout, c'est Johnny que vous aimez mieux."* Ah, never, I loved you best, you were my little dear, my little mermaid. . . . all over now. . . .

Claire's Letter to Mary, October 2

. . . With Dunia gone, I probably ought to look for another situation, since she was my main charge. However, when I broached this subject, Marya Ivanovna began weeping immoderately: no, she would never part from me, I am all that is left to her of Dunia, she would adopt me as her daughter, etc. Zahar Nikolaitch added his pleas to hers, in a more rational manner. Finally we came to a temporary agreement: I would stay with them and continue to give Johnny and whatever niece is in residence English lessons, but also go out to give lessons in other houses. In one way it is extremely hard to be reminded every day of my loss; in another—well, I am not ready to go to another house, learn to accommodate myself to unfamiliar dispositions.

After hearing of Matryosha's death, Grisha went about for days, haunted by the exact sickening knowledge of how it was done. He could *see* the slight figure with its blanched face and matted braids taken to the top of the steps, carefully placed, given a push—whenever he thought of it, he would utter strangled sounds and beat his clenched hands against the wall. He felt literally ill with rage—the only way to be cured was by going down to Petrovka and dealing with Matryosha's murderer in person; have him flogged until he howls and then hang him, the one-eyed devil.

But after a while the evil figure began to lose its malevolence; it became, he himself didn't exactly know how, identified with others: his huntsman, efficiently getting rid of a maimed whippet bitch ("No use keeping her, Excellency, why let her suffer, a nuisance to herself and others?"), the head groom Matvey matter-of-factly shooting a lamed horse. Callous, homely acts, little murders performed with dispatch and a sort of grim mercy . . . No, the murderer was elsewhere.

This happened with Fedka too. Prince Pyotr had him brought to town and at first the very sight of his handsome figure, now tricked out in the extravagant style of a Moscow coachman, blue English cloth coat, gold lace, and all, aroused a dull hatred in Grisha: the betrayer, the heartless oaf! But one night, as he was driving Grisha home, Fedka slowed the horses down to a walk, swiveled around on his box, and said to him abruptly and without warning, "I keep seeing her, your Excellency."

"What?" said Grisha, startled. The groom's broad face, its ruddiness bleached out by the street lamp's light, had a wan pinched look.

"Her, your Excellency, Matryosha." His manner was queerly confiding, even familiar; he might have been talking to a comrade bound to him by a complicity in some unnamed crime. "She just comes and stands there, quiet like. 'Fedya,' she says to me, 'Fedyushka . . .' Such a soft little voice she's always had . . . 'My neck hurts,' she says, 'Fedyushka, rub it for me.' And she herself keeps rubbing it. . . ." They stared at each other, gripped by the uncanniness. Then Fedka, the white of his eyes showing briefly, turned back to his horses, clucking them into speed.

As for Nikolavna, with her venomed, honeyed ways—she was a petty tyrant and a bitch, but she wasn't responsible for the murder. . . . No, that was done before, with his mother saying, her haggard cheekbones spotted with red, "I would have her whipped all the way to Petrovka"; his father, drawling, "If it was something *important* . . ." Sometimes other lineaments would be adumbrated beside theirs; a marble face, beautiful and cold, unsoftened by its equivocal smile, would rise to present itself for its share of blood guilt.

A portrait of Alexander was hanging in the big reception chamber, facing that of Paul I: royal son facing royal father. Grisha was always struck by the contrast between the two. On one hand there was the dead Tsar's foreshortened froggish countenance with snub nose and popping eyes; on the other, the enchanting young monarch wooed you with his innocent and dreamy smile. But it was all wrong. While he smiled, ravishing your heart, soldiers staggered through punitive rows, their backs torn to the bone; mothers in military colonies dashed their babies' heads against the walls; peasants, crammed into tiny huts, copulated and multiplied indiscriminately, living and dying in hopeless squalor; Matryosha fell off the stoop, eyes wide open in an imbecile stare. When you began to think of those things, the charming smile became both fraudulent and sinister. In contrast Paul's unattractive face, popping eyes, maniac's wry mouth, and all, began to acquire the merit of honesty.

A deep secret dislike of his parents possessed him; he took to avoiding their company whenever he could. Making his prescribed morning visit, he would look covertly at his mother's face, which once had seemed wholly beautiful to him, and see it crumbling; little peevish lines appeared, like crackling, about its mouth and eyes; occassionally the great black eyes in their shadowed caverns would glance at him uneasily as if guessing his thoughts: with desolate vindictive pleasure, he wondered if she knew that he no longer loved her.

The Prince showed no awareness of the change in his son. Once he asked him carelessly, "Well, are you still sulking?" and Grisha's colorless "*Non, mon père*" seemed to satisfy him. His autocratic and indolent nature prevented him from probing deeper. Besides, this season the Prince was unwontedly busy. He had, for reasons of his own, decided to participate more actively in Moscow's social life, and spent a great deal of his time in the English Club, where, it was said, one went to find out what Moscow thinks and knows. In obedience to his wishes the Princess reluctantly began to receive on Tuesdays. On that day, upward of forty guests would sit down at the table for supper. Those functions in no way resembled the Pomykovs' untidy and indiscriminating hospitality. They were the product of careful selection; the cream of Moscow officialdom would gather there; the Governor General Dmitry Vladimirovich Golitzin himself was a frequent guest. After dinner, politics would be discussed in the Prince's favorite so-called English room, with wood-paneled walls and a huge English fireplace.

Grisha was expected to be present. "You'll learn more about diplomacy here, *mon ami,*" the Prince told him, "than can be found in Lachaine's history books." Once this concern for his career would have rendered Grisha inarticulate with pleasure. Now he merely replied formally, "As you wish, *mon père,*" and dutifully presented himself at those gatherings, perversely closing his ears to the discussions and excusing himself to get back to his studies as soon as he could.

With equal reluctance he accompanied his parents to the birthday reception at the Governor General's palace. This was a gala event. The great four-storied edifice on Tverskaya shone like a huge lantern through the slanting rain. The marble limbs of the statues flanking the entrance seemed to stir ponderously in the wavering glow of the flambeaus. An endless procession of carriages clattered up to the porte cochère, discharged their passengers, and went back into the rain-washed courtyard, where footmen and coachmen settled down for a long soggy wait, refreshed by donations of vodka and pickles from the vast Golitzin kitchens. Their masters meanwhile passed from the rainy darkness into the warm, brightly lit interior, and, divesting themselves of cloaks and capes in the vestibule, became themselves a part of the brilliant decorations. They mounted the grand staircase, lined with blooming orange trees in tubs on every step, and dispersed through the grand ballroom and the adjoining chambers where card tables and refreshments were set up.

By the time Volynskis were announced, the ball was in full swing. The grand polonaise which traditionally opened all balls was over and the orchestra was playing waltzes. Staid frockcoats and many-colored uniforms; white *jeune fille* tulles and rich velvets, feathers, ribbons, diamonds—all that twinkled and floated and

[187]

whirled underneath the blazing chandeliers. A gallery of mammas, grandmammas, and aunts, sitting in the gilt chairs against the walls, kept a watch on the dance floor, as keen-eyed and grim as generals surveying a battlefield.

The Volynskis stopped to pay their respects to the ancient Countess Golitzin, the Governor's redoubtable mother, who in spite of her advanced years still ruled Moscow society: a beady-eyed old dragon, parrot hued and parrot voiced. Old Prince Yusupov, at her side, another revenant from Catherine the Great's era, desiccated but still elegant in powdered wig and court dress, accosted Prince Pyotr speaking in the mannered drawl of his time. Grisha, having made his bow, leaned against a column and watched the dancers. *Like Albé*, he thought. Albé too would come to a ball where he couldn't dance, Miss Clairmont had told him, and stand leaning against a column, a solitary figure, stranger to gayety and vanity. "Childe Harold personified . . ." Laughter had entered her voice. "Such nonsense! Solitary, indeed—the minute he appeared, he would be mobbed by all the ladies who had renounced dancing for his sake. . . ."

"*Regardez donc,*" old Prince Yusupov's voice rose in outrage, shedding its Catherinian languors, "good gracious me, an examining magistrate dancing with the Governor General's daughter! How is that?"

The lorgnette quivered indignantly in the old courtier's bony hand; Grisha looked in the direction where it was pointing and was gladdened to see Pushchin gliding by with an elaborately dressed young lady in his arms. He danced correctly and sedately, but at the same time with a certain military crispness; there might have been spurs affixed to the heels of his dancing shoes, as he brought them together smartly and stood poised while his partner circled him.

"I'll tell you how that comes about, *batyushka,*" said the old Countess in her macaw's voice. "There aren't enough dancers, that's how. A young man comes to a ball, twirls a lady once or twice, in the goodness of his heart, and then you don't see him till supper. Talk, talk, talk is what they like best nowadays. . . . Meanwhile these sit and suffer." She flapped her fan toward the cluster of partnerless young women, talking together with excessive animation. "If that young man is willing to dance, many thanks to him, is what I say, and never mind who he is."

"Actually," Prince Pyotr remarked, "young Pushchin comes

from an excellent family. His Excellency Dmitry Vladimirovich values him highly as a competent and devoted official."

"Still, something highly irregular here," the old nobleman grumbled.

"*Autres temps, autres moeurs, mon cher Prince* . . . I must take my leave now, and pay my respects to his Excellency. Come, Grisha."

Governor General Dmitry Vladimirovich Golitzin, genial and glossy from his silvery topknot to his white kid court slippers, was receiving congratulations in the column-lined rotunda at the end of the ballroom. He was surrounded by a small group of officials and officers of the higher echelon, all heavily decorated. The talk swirling about him was the usual Moscow mixture of high politics and low gossip.

They talked of the Emperor, clearly enjoying his stay in Taganrog, in the company of the Empress: it seemed the townspeople had been referring to their Majesties as "the honeymooners"—a respectful rustle of laughter went about the circle. Also discussed was the significant absence of Arakcheev, who was still inactive on his estate, mourning his murdered mistress.

"Do you know what he is having put on her tombstone?" said Count Panchin, a tiny fidgety man, who prided himself on being Moscow's most competent "*nouvelliste*" or gossip. He gave an appreciative titter. "*Ici repose mon amie et la femme de mon cocher.*"

The Governor had been listening to this frankly anti-Arakcheev conversation with a noncommittal smile, an elbow cradled in one hand while the other stroked the beautifully tended sideburns: an older statesman pose he was fond of. He said now, thoughtfully, "Yes, it is quite possible that things might be different when the Emperor comes back from Taganrog."

Grisha, lingering in dutiful boredom on the periphery of the circle, felt a wave of excitement ripple through his indifference. Different? How? Did he mean that with that disfiguring influence removed things might again be what they once were? For a moment the cold image of the marble Tsar with its equivocal smile wavered and softened, became again the sunny vision that had smiled so kindly on two hero-worshipping boys.

"Do you really believe that we might go back to the postwar years, now that Arakcheev's in decline? Is that your opinion, honored Dmitry Vladimirovich?" The question—one that he himself was longing to ask—was posed in distinctly skeptical tones. Grisha looked around at the speaker. It was a handsome giant of a man in his thirties wearing a general's dress uniform. Among the decorations on his chest Grisha recognized the orders of St. Vladimir and St. Anne, the gold sword at his side proclaimed him to be a hero of 1812. An imposing yet oddly graceful presence: classical features, a cluster of youthful curls surmounting a high balding forehead, head held arrogantly high—but something faintly impertinent, a quick boyish spark, glinting in the dark eyes.

"If it's merely a question of the same measures that used to emanate from Arakcheev now coming directly from his Majesty— Arakcheevshina *sans* Arakcheev, as it were . . ." His superbly tailored shoulders moved in a slight shrug.

"We have no way of knowing what the Emperor's intentions are," said Prince Pyotr reprovingly. "In any case, it is not up to us to criticize any measures he may see fit to promulgate."

"No, that's just the devil of it," said the other, unabashed. Suddenly the classical features lighted up with mischief: an impertinent young lieutenant lightheartedly mocking authority peeped for a moment from behind the impressive façade of a high-ranking officer. "One could always curse out old Arakcheev, whereas if he is no longer available . . ."

Golitzin chuckled indulgently. "Now then, Misha," he said, shaking a white-gloved finger. His tone of voice was such as one would use to a scapegrace younger brother.

Plainly anxious to forestall any more provocative remarks, he turned to another member of the group, a colonel wearing the insignia of the Yegorovski Regiment, now stationed in Moscow, and expressed his pleasure at its return after the long absence. "The ladies have been after me, my dear Colonel—I have been urged over and over again to send a formal complaint to General Headquarters: why have the Imperial Guard forsaken Moscow? Is the air here not salubrious? Did we not feast you and cherish you?"

The Colonel, a typical army man, with a red face bisected laterally by a huge moustache and vertically by a livid saber cut from eye to lip, inclined his thick torso. "Why, your Excellency, we Yegorovtzi are only too happy to be sent here to mother Moscow out of the backwoods," he said in that special cracked army bass which is acquired by a lifetime of bawling commands. "We earned it, God knows. Not to boast, the Grand Duke Mikhail himself had a good word to say for us."

Golitzyn bestowed a stately twinkle on him. "Yes, we know, you're a great drillmaster, Andrey Semyonitch, your fame has spread far and wide."

Incongruously, the Colonel blushed, shyly and innocently, like an overage schoolboy. "Well, I am an old hand at it, your Excellency—know all the tricks of the trade. . . . An old colonel of mine told me when I was a mere lieutenant, wet behind the ears: 'If you want your men to look good at a parade, just have 'em contract the arse real tight, the rest will come by itself. . . .' Never forgot his advice, by God!"

A group of ladies standing close enough to overhear this remark uttered in paradeground tones shied away like startled geese. A small scandalized titter broke from them. Count Panchin, too, squeaked with delight, thrusting his foxy muzzle forward: "And that is all it is, honored Andrey Semyonitch? All you need to do—?"

The ladies moved out of earshot, as the infatuated Colonel, obliviously astride his hobbyhorse, repeated triumphantly, "Yes, that's it, just tighten the arse!" A patter of smalltalk rose up to cover his obsessive trumpeting.

Presently a name rising out of the flurry of regimental reminiscences pinned Grisha's wandering attention. "The Semyonovski Regiment—there was a regiment for you." The Semyonovski Regiment mutiny—unexpectedly flaring up, put down with murderous severity—had taken place five years ago, but it still festered in every one's mind, an uneasy canker, painful to all hands. The Colonel wagged his massive head sorrowfully. "Broke his Majesty's heart—his favorite regiment, he loved them like sons . . ."

"Whom he loveth, he chastiseth, with a vengeance," remarked the tall general with a slight grimace. "You should see the backs of the Semyonovski lads—the ones that survived the chastisement, that is . . ."

"Why, *mon Général*"—Prince Pyotr's voice was dry—"should they have been decorated for mutinying?"

"Everyone talks about it, as if it was a Pugachov-type mutiny.

Why, the poor fellows would have let themselves be cut to pieces for the Tsar. All they did was present a petition to remove Colonel Schwartz: they couldn't tolerate him. It was, with respect, a great mistake to put him in command."

"Couldn't—*tolerate*—him?" Prince Pyotr repeated in an exaggerated incredulous drawl.

The classical nose wrinkled in disgust. "He used to line up his men and make them spit at each other on command. If the moustaches were a millimeter beyond the prescribed length he would pull the hair out with his own hands. I really can't imagine any rational man approving this . . ." His tone said clearly, "Not even you," and with a mixture of dread and pleasure Grisha saw his father's face go stony. The Governor's genial face took on an expression of humorous alarm. There was a quick exchange of glances in the group. Count Panchin leaned forward panting like a poodle: a quarrel brewing!

"Some of the men were veterans of the Napoleonic War. Don't you find it rather disgusting, *mon Prince*, that men who fought at Borodino should have their whiskers pulled out by a creature like Schwartz?"

With loathing indignation, Grisha visualized a monkey in colonel's epaulets inflicting apish indignities on a soldierly figure that stood rocklike at attention suffering it all. Obscene, not to be tolerated! But the Emperor tolerated it. More than that, approved of it, punished those who resisted. His angelic guise notwithstanding, he was on the side of the madman Schwartz, the reptile Arakcheev. . . . No, he thought drearily, nothing will be changed . . .

"This is beside the point." The frigid politeness barely hid a rising temper. The Prince's slightly protuberant eyes performed their ominous trick of seeming to leap closer to the nose. "I will grant you that Colonel Schwartz overdid. But surely there are more important issues at stake. Is the common soldier to be allowed to pass on the qualities of the legitimately appointed commanders? Particularly in these times? If so we are very close to anarchy indeed, and reform in the army is badly needed . . ."

"Oh, I couldn't agree more with *that*," said the other, infuriatingly carefree.

Grisha, listening avidly to this exchange, was overcome by a desire to put himself on the side of this man who was so miraculously and beautifully unintimidated by his father. "It seems to me," broke from him, impetuously, "indeed, I feel sure that His Imperial Majesty can be induced to consider the abolition of corporal punishment in the army. Surely, as much can be done by kindness as by severity. . . ." He faltered to a stop. Oh, God, the preachy prissy inanity, he thought in despair. Just like a sappy schoolboy. What made me . . .? What'll he think? But the dark eyes of the General rested on him with an expression something like tenderness, the finely cut lips under the small moustache parted in a slight but charming smile.

The next moment the whole weight of his father's cold displeasure had shifted on to him. "You must excuse my son, your Excellence. Naturally, not being likely to join the army, he is bound to consider himself an authority on it." Prince Pyotr broke off, his lips tightening in annoyance at himself. Jerking at his lorgnette chain irritably, he turned away.

Grisha looked down on the ground, a thin cold smile playing on his own lips. *Good*, he thought, *good. The worse, the better. Now I can really hate him.*

The tall man gave him a quick look in which sympathy was mixed with friendly irony. "I am bound to say that I agree with the young gentleman. I myself abolished corporal punishment when I commanded the Kiev Division and I can't say that I noticed any grave harm as a result of this. Except"—again his handsome face was enlivened by the mischievous smile so inappropriate to his rank— "except of course to myself . . ."

Conversation swept on past the uncomfortable moment. After a while Grisha detached himself unobtrusively from the group and went back to the ballroom.

Pushchin, he saw, was still dancing. This time his partner was the young Countess Zalishina, known in society as Comtesse Poitrine. She was a small luxuriant brunette, with a tiny waist and full breasts, which she seemed to offer for her partner's delectation, within their sheath of wine-colored satin, like a brace of Persian melons. When music stopped, Pushchin brought her back to her seat and bent over her, murmuring, a faintly satyrlike look on his flat dark face. The Countess listened, humid lips parted. An aura of barely restrained sensuality hung over the pair. Grisha waited until another partner claimed the Countess before he approached his friend.

The satyr look on Pushchin's face gave way to one of friendly pleasure. "How delightful to see you here, Prince. Are you enjoying yourself?" All at once Grisha felt better.

The account of the conversation in the rotunda amused Pushchin. "It's so characteristic of us," he said, laughing. "Strains of music—cream of society present—serious discussion on the fate of Russia—and suddenly, overriding all this, there it comes, the paradeground rasp: 'Tighten the arse!' But he's not a bad chap, Colonel Efimov, cares for the men."

"And the other one, the general? Perhaps you know who he is—a tall, splendid man, very handsome—there he is, right over there," Grisha interrupted himself, spotting the towering figure of his father's erstwhile opponent on the other side of the ballroom. Pushchin's face lighted up. "Oh, yes, Orlov, Mikhail Orlov. I should have known him immediately from your description."

"You know him, then?"

"Yes, quite well. He was in the Arzamas." Pushchin was referring to the well-known literary society in St. Petersburg. "Rhine Orlov—that was his Arzamas sobriquet. All the members had sobriquets assigned to them. Some of them were very apt." His reminiscent smile broadened. "Pushkin was the Cricket."

"And what was yours?"

"Oh, I never was a member, I am not a literary person. In the Lyceum they used to call me Jeannot. Just plain old Vanya frenchified—that's me." Pushchin gave his tuneful laugh. "But it's true, Orlov is special. Reckless, outspoken, cares for no one: all the Orlovs are like that—outsize. It's not for nothing Catherine the Great picked his great-uncle for a lover out of the Grenadiers. . . . I didn't know he was in Moscow." His expression was mildly speculative.

Orlov turned his handsome head and saw them. Immediately his face lighted up, he left his group and came through the crowd toward them.

"Pushchin, you old devil," he said, seizing him in his powerful arms, and then pushing him back to take a better look at him. "Look at you, you scurvy civilian! What are you doing, collecting hemorrhoids at a desk?"

"Wish your health, your Excellency," said Pushchin, smiling. "What are *you* up to, Misha? Leading the good life?"

"Oh, the very best." His dark eyes gleamed. "Why not? You know how someone translated '*le bien général en Russie*?' 'It's good to be a general in Russia.'"

They laughed together cozily. They were, Grisha saw, members of an old club, talking its language, teasing each other with their mutual half-admiring, half-ironic knowledge.

"No, but really, what are you doing with yourself?"

"What should I be doing? An old married man and a retired soldier, in all senses of the word—what could be duller and more innocuous?"

"Oh, I'm sure there's some pepper in you still. . . ." There was an odd flavor to the friendly conversation, as if another one were taking place at the same time, just a little pejorative on one side, just a little defensive on the other. "How is the charming Ekaterina Nikolaevna?"

"Holding court, as usual. Will you come to see us? We're staying at my cousin Anna's, near the Donskoy. We'll talk of old times."

"Yes, I might come," said Pushchin reflectively. "But I'm being rude—allow me to present Prince Grigorii Petrovich Volynski."

"We've met," said Orlov with a slightly quizzical look. His large hand enveloped Grisha's in a warm hard clasp. "I hope you too will come to see us, Prince. I should be very pleased. . . . We are at home on Thursdays. . . ."

He nodded and left them, making his way through the crowds with his customary look of good-humored arrogance.

"What a splendid man," Grisha said awed, and listened eagerly while Pushchin told him more about Orlov.

Orlov had a brilliant record behind him; he had distinguished himself in 1812 as an officer and a diplomat. The Emperor had counted him among his close friends until he "betrayed his trust," by preparing, together with other important personages, a petition for abolishing serfdom. Thereupon, he was sent to the south of Russia where he was given an infantry division to command and disgraced himself again by inaugurating various liberal reforms. "So now he is a retired major general attached to the army but with no division to command and has been living quietly on his estate with his exceptionally charming wife. . . . Until now." Again that speculative look crossed his face.

"I'd love to call on him. Do you think he meant it?"

"Of course he did, why shouldn't he? You'll enjoy his company. And the house he lives in—it belongs to Anna Chesmenski-Orlova, the daughter of the original Orlov, Catherine the Great's lover. They tell me it's kept just as it was in his lifetime. . . . And his wife is a dear, one of the three beautiful Raevski girls. Both her father and brother are in disgrace now, it seems. For the usual reasons . . . I wonder how it is that just those people whom one is bound to respect and like always turn out to be in disgrace nowadays. . . . But look, here comes my little countess again." And indeed Countess Zalishina, having circled the floor, was now nearing them. Her backward glance as she floated on her partner's arm was both languid and provocative. Answering it with a bow, Pushchin underwent another of his disconcerting transformations, becoming, with an ease that never failed to astonish Grisha, a complete ladies' man. "You must let me introduce you, Prince. Not a brain in her head, but ah, those marvelous tits—those twin palpitant globes . . ." He kissed his fingers.

Grisha wondered sadly how it felt to be Pushchin, a cheerful sensualist, taking it gaily for granted that he would eventually without too much trouble possess the luscious wares so frankly offered him.

The musical phrase and the figure it defined came to an end, and the Countess, stepping away from her partner, sank into a low deep curtsey. A renewed surge of music raised and bore her lightly off.

Grisha looked after her unseeingly. The music faded, the chandeliers dimmed, he was in the backyard of a village hut, and Matryosha was bowing down before him, low and solemn, in her last passion of gratitude. For what? He didn't help her, he had merely helped to kill her. . . .

"*C'est un esprit dangereux, cet Orlov,*" said Prince Pyotr, on the way home from the Golitzin reception. "It wouldn't surprise me in the least if he was one of *them.*"

He was not talking to Grisha, to whom he hadn't uttered a word since his public rebuke before the Governor, but to the Princess.

"One of whom, *mon ami?*" the Princess asked in her exhausted voice. "What do you mean?"

"Quite plainly, *madame*, that he is a member of that same secret society whose existence is becoming more and more of a certainty."

And, as always when he heard the term "secret society," a slight but definite uneasiness rose up in Grisha. He thought of Pushchin and quickly dowsed the thought as though, even unspoken, it could in some mysterious way endanger his friend.

"They all take it much too lightly," the Prince said, acrimoniously. "And not only here but in St. Petersburg. There Miloradovich says: 'Let them read their bad poems to each other.'" The Prince's voice hardened; he disliked the flamboyant Governor of St. Petersburg almost as much as he did Arakcheev. "Here *notre cher* Dmitry Vladimirovich, whenever I bring up the subject, smiles and talks about the 'ferment of youthful minds.' Well, that youthful ferment is going to blow up in their faces one day, and serve them right. No one in a position of authority has any right to take treason lightly."

Despite himself, Grisha caught his breath. *Trahison.* Treason! A word with a taste of metal to it, a dangerous word. . . .

"From what I hear, there might even have been talk—horrible to say!—of assassinating the Emperor."

"*Quelle horreur,*" the Princess exclaimed faintly. The movement of her white-gloved hands in the darkness told Grisha that she was crossing herself.

There was a jolt at Grisha's heart like a small door flying open. He waited for horror to come flooding in, but instead there was again that same cold swell of dark satisfaction. *Why not? The worse, the better.*

There was a silence. Hooves clattered on the cobblestones, the wheels rattled, and above them the coach swayed on its excellent English springs like a boat on the waves. The light from the streetlamps shone sporadically into the dark interior, painting yellow splotches sometimes on a fold of the Prince's coat, sometimes on the Princess's hand, fidgeting with her folded fan. The faces remained in shadow.

Presently the Princess was heard to breathe her older son's name interrogatively.

"Sergey? No, he doesn't know anything—*he* at least is not one to talk about things he knows nothing about," the Prince said acidly. "Besides, Sergey is a simple loyal fellow, utterly devoted to his sovereign and his regiment—I doubt that any of these gentlemen would be foolish enough to approach him. They'd know what answer they would get. If a son of mine participated in that filth," said the Prince, deliberately spacing his words, like nails driven into a wall, "I would utterly disown him. I would see him shot against the wall and not raise a finger to prevent it. . . ."

I know you wouldn't, Grisha thought, coldly. Executioner . . . He stared out of the window at the rainy darkness. I must tell Pushchin, he thought. . . . But why do I think about him like that? Why am I so sure that he is involved? Why do I want him to be?

Claire's Journal, October 5

A bitter October, rainy, gloomy and cold, cold, *cold* . . . The servants came in to shut the windows for the winter. They hammer them up so that they can't be opened, leaving only one small pane of glass—a *fortochka*—removable. The Russian bear preparing for hibernation. Irrationally I had a sense of panic, as if I were being *immured*.

I find myself missing Georges and our conversations. When we started them, I had, I think, a certain almost mystic sense of parallel, an illusion of being able to nudge a young soul starting on its travels from one path to another, less thorny; it all seemed so strangely pertinent to him, something he *needed*. But actually I myself need it just as much. Talking to my lame little Russian Prince has become a necessity to me.

Hermann knows a great deal of my story. But the narrator is influenced by the listener. Hermann is romantic, idealistic, sentimental, like all Germans. When I tell him about myself, unconsciously I find myself weaving the Sorrows of Charlotte. But the boy's mind is like a newly tuned instrument, and a false note sounds painfully false to his ears—and mine. When I talk to him, I find I begin to know myself better.

Where *is* he, then? No word from him since we're in Moscow.

Claire's Journal, October 8

Pushchin here for dinner. He has been pressing me for an assignation. Now that I am expected to go out for lessons, my time is more my own, it would be easy to see him whenever I want. But I am convinced that if I were to sleep with him now, I would immediately become pregnant.

I have always felt that to conceive, something deep within you must consent, otherwise the seed is rejected. Well, that area in me had been sere and acrid for a long time now, a stony soil, unreceptive to tillage. But now—now that I have lost Dunia—

I remember how surprised I was at little Percy's being conceived so soon after P.B. and Mary had lost baby Clare. Mary is not the most passionate woman in the world and surely losing a child would not make her so. But later I understood. When the news of Allegra's death reached me, I was haunted for a long time by a compelling and shaming fantasy. I thought of going to *him*, even hating him as I did. "You have to sleep with me again, you must," I would say to him. 'You have deprived me of Allegra—give me another child, another Allegra." Madness . . . But I *was* mad, I believe, for a few days.

And now again . . . A thousand old wounds have opened and memories are bleeding through each one. I remember bearing her—out of the whirlwind of pain, out of all the uproar, a small curly-headed baby girl all mine . . . and my voice saying in drowsy happiness, "Let him know—tell him we have a perfect baby —flawless. . . ."

She was lovely. Such a merry baby, laughing with teeth like tiny pearls, lording it over everyone, captivating Wilmouse. Listening to my stories, marking the time with her little hand when I sang to her. Babbling ceaselessly— how I remember that cooing murmur of "how many how many." No, that was Dunia. I am mixing them up again. That had happened to me before, in Islavskoye—I was holding her convulsed little body in my arms and I thought, "Oh, how thin they have made her at the convent, but never mind, when she is well . . ."

The Pomykovs lived on Prichistenka, which, like most of Moscow streets after the fire of 1812, had that half-and-half look, a mixture of new and old, homely vegetable plots in front of squat middle-class cottages and manicured English gardens, half-ruined palaces of ancient nobility and newly built mansions. The Pomykovs' residence belonged to that last category. It was a large two-story house with a formal façade in the pseudo-classic style, one of the many that were rising up on that street.

Inside, however, Grisha found the informality he knew from before: a knot of domestics stood gossiping in the vestibule, old Pavel dozed on his bench, just as he did in Islavskoye.

The Pomykovs were out, but a sound of pianoforte and flute came faintly from the interior.

"Is Miss Clairmont at home?"

"Yes, your Excellency, that's them playing. They play a lot now, seems like," said Pavel, allowing himself this familiarity as an old servant talking to an intimate of the house. "Every time they have a moment, they sit down at the piano and trin-trin-trin . . ." He illustrated with his thick, splayed-out fingers. "Of course, now they have much more time for that," he added, his faded eyes filling with easy tears.

A footman Grisha didn't know conducted him through the rooms, which in spite of the formal arrangement of furniture and draperies still had the jumbled look, the homey cozy disorder; even the ivied *treillage* by the window, that *sine qua non* of every fashionable drawing room, had the disheveled look reminiscent of the Islavskoye arbors.

Miss Clairmont was playing with the disciplined passion that was as characteristic of her as her light step and singing voice; Gambs, gracefully disposed in the curve of the great Erard piano, accompanied her on the flute. He saw Grisha first and lowered the flute from his lips with a welcoming exclamation. Miss Clairmont turned to see who it was and, lighting up with pleasure, rose and came swiftly toward him.

"Georges!"

Monsieur Gambs laid his flute down and came over to shake hands, his handsome face beaming with smiles. Even Vasska emerged from under the piano to wreathe briefly about his legs. Only one presence was missing from the general welcome. He remembered the shrill "Georzhik!" the feathery weight lighting and clinging kittenlike on his chest; "how many, how many" sounded in his ears and he felt the ticklish prickle of tears in his eyes and nose. Miss Clairmont, watching him, nodded desolately and her pale mouth twisted.

"There, you see, he's back," Gambs was saying. "I told you Prince Georges would come back to see us." He laid his hand on Grisha's shoulder, an expansive gesture, reminiscent of benedictions so freely bestowed in romantic German novels; but the good will was genuine.

"One must always believe that friendship endures; that after a separation, friends meet, their souls interflowing, and it is as if nothing had changed. . . ."

"Oh, there's always bound to be change," Miss Clairmont remarked. Strolling back to the piano, she stood over it, pensive, her fingers butterflying soundless arpeggios down the keyboard. "For one, Georges will no longer be a pupil of mine. Our lessons were very well in the country, but imagine a young man being taught by a woman—in town!" The soundless arpeggios culminated in a faint discordant crash.

"Country or town," said Monsieur Gambs gallantly, "everything of importance has been taught us by women."

"Be that as it may," said Miss Clairmont, beginning on another subdued series of arpeggios, "from now on Georges will be learning his English from a man, *n'est-ce pas, Georges?*"

Grisha agreed: indeed the return of his Mr. Davies was imminent. He would join a battery of others, who under the jealous doyenship of Monsieur Lachaine, taught him drawing, piano, German, physics, and other prerequisites for entering the university.

Madame Pomykov entered the drawing room at her precipitate trot and, on seeing Grisha, greeted him with a brief burst of tears. In a short while, however, she recovered, wiped her eyes, and inquired about his family.

"*Votre mère—ah, la Princesse, c'est une sainte, alors.* Please assure her that I shall do myself the honor of calling on her soon. I don't believe I could have borne my loss without the comfort she gave me," she said, obviously believing every word of it. "And of course this one"—she nodded in Miss Clairmont's direction—"without her I would have been lost—I couldn't have survived—but where are you going, *ma chère?*"

"I thought I had better change," said Miss Clairmont. "I don't want to keep Gerassim waiting for me."

Marya Ivanovna abandoned her hand and clapped both of her own to her cheeks. "*Mon Dieu, comme je suis sotte*! Would you believe it? I completely forgot and sent him off to Kuznetski Bridge to pick up a parcel. Timoshka!" Apparently even in Moscow Marya Ivanovna, when in a hurry, screamed for her servants instead of ringing for them. "Don't worry, *mon amie*, I'll have the landau put to immediately. . . ."

"But that's not necessary—if you would have them call me a hack . . ."

"Ride in a drozhky in this rain? Are you mad, Claire?"

Grisha resolved the argument by announcing hastily that he was about to leave and would be happy to deliver Miss Clairmont in his carriage wherever she wanted to go.

"Charming of you, Prince, but I should have been only too happy to send her out in the landau," said Marya Ivanovna, after Miss Clairmont had left the room, "or indeed any carriage I have. Nothing is too good for her. You know, she has become like a daughter to me; there's no need for her to do anything but be here. But no, she insists on dragging herself all the way to the Sukharev Bashnya in this dreadful weather to give a lesson to the Jaenisch brats. . . . Well, if this is what she wants, if this makes her happy . . . By the way, Prince, we are at home on Wednesdays. Do come, we are expecting interesting people. . . ."

Outside the weather had worsened; the rain slanted down sharply, all-pervasive and cold.

Miss Clairmont subsided gratefully into the depths of the carriage. "This could be London, you know—terrible weather and a beautifully sprung English carriage." The footman, after having expertly arranged the rug about their knees, sprang up behind the carriage; it rolled off briskly along Prichistenka. Behind the glinting curtain of rain the old Potyomkin Palace swam by, grimly revealing itself in its ruined splendor through its leafless arbors.

"How pleasant to have you to myself like that, Georges! After not hearing from you for so long I did begin to fear that I would never see you again—that you had disappeared like—like *him*, you know," she said in an echo of her old, storytelling voice. And immediately it was as if no time had intervened; as if he had only seen her the day before and they were ready to take the conversation up from where they had left it. "People do go out of your life for no perceptible reason. One is never quite sure . . ."

"No, one can't ever be sure," Grisha agreed somberly. Not about anything.

Leaning her head back against the squabs, she regarded him with a small frown. "You look different somehow. As if—I don't know—Have you too been ill by any chance?"

She searched his face with the old intent look, and he thought that he must be careful or he would be whining that whole miserable story out to her. . . .

He had wanted her, agonizingly at first, after Matryosha had died. But she was unavailable then, mewed up in the sickroom with ailing Johnny. He had had to deal by himself with the twin wretchedness of mourning the dead girl and hating his parents: no help from her. Later he no longer wanted to be helped; by that time he had comfortably settled into his misery, he had begun to savor the desolate pleasures of hating. Miss Clairmont had an infuriating habit of never taking the expected stance. She might even, as she did that other time with Nikolavna, perform an irritating trick of shifting the point of view, making one see what one didn't want to see. She would show him that his parents too—but he didn't want that. The wickedness of what he felt about them made him stronger, and he wanted no interference with that.

"No, no, I am perfectly well," he said hastily and, to forestall further probing, added hurriedly: "What did you mean, that it has happened to you before? You mean him—Albé? Did he disappear?"

"Well, not precisely disappear, I knew where he was, of course," she said, obediently following his lead. "He went on to Venice as he had proposed from the beginning and we went back to England. I had my baby in Bath, and then we moved to the town of Marlow. The thing is he never wrote. He did write to P.B. after a while. But not to me, never to me. He cut himself off from me, totally. Well, after all I had expected it. I knew why he did so. One can bear anything, anything as long as one knows. . . . It's the not knowing that is not to be borne."

No, Grisha thought bleakly, knowing is also terrible. It occurred to him that pretty much everything was terrible, knowing, not knowing, everything. . . . "And you knew why he cut himself off from you, then?"

"Yes, it was because—" She paused and looked at him testingly. A slight uncertainty manifested itself on her face. Then she gave a tiny impatient headshake at herself and said baldly: "He was afraid that his presence would affect the baby I was carrying—that, if he were there during my confinement, it would be born lame like him. A stupid, self-hurting superstition. You must never feel like that, Georges. When you have fathered a child, try not to cultivate those unnecessary torments before it is born."

Grisha's face relaxed into a glum little grin. He experienced the illogical lifting of the spirit with which one greets the familiar phenomenon in a landscape grown strange. Miss Clairmont might show concern at his unhappy looks, but she could be depended on not to spare his feelings about his lameness. He said: "I don't think I'll ever—father a child."

"Of course you will," she countered crisply. "Just as he did. Twice that I know of. And tormented himself to no purpose each time. . . . Well, that couldn't be helped, I suppose. It's all very well to talk of being rational, but after a lifetime of yokel stares, after seeing pregnant countrywomen making a sign against evil eye when you come too near them——"

"Peasant women here don't make a sign against evil eye," Grisha said reflectively, "at least not in my presence, they wouldn't dare. They merely cross themselves—rather low down. Not only the peasants. Once a lady came to call who was *enceinte*. Oh, she was very uneasy indeed about me being there. She did the same thing on the sly." Here a singularly disagreeable thought ocurred to him. "It is quite possible," he said in an unnaturally judicious tone of voice, "that it is my presence that has been keeping my sister Sophie from coming to Moscow."

"Possibly," Miss Clairmont responded in the same crisp manner as before, "but much more likely it's your dreadful roads. Any pregnant woman who ventures on them is trying to lose the baby. . . . And, incidentally"—knowing exactly what was coming Grisha stiffened, bracing himself against the question—"what happened to—I don't remember her name any more—that little housemaid you were so concerned about? Is she safely married to your groom?"

"No, she is dead," Grisha said gratingly, not looking at her.

"Oh." A soft pitying exhalation of breath. Her gloved hand was laid on his sleeve. "Oh . . . I knew there was something. . . . Would you like to tell me?"

He shook his head, staring straight ahead at Akim's broad back on the box before them, its blue cloth steadily darkening under the rain. This was not a pain that he wanted eased, he didn't want to exorcise this ghost.

Miss Clairmont didn't persist. A little sigh sounded at his side, the hand was gently removed from his arm. They drove on in silence, the carriage splashing and rattling on Sretenka's rain-washed cobblestones. In the sodden distance the eccentric shape of the Sukharev Tower was adumbrated against the gray sky, like a child's sketch of a boat, its spire a thickened mast springing out of its squat octagonal body.

Grisha broke the silence. "It seems to me he should have stayed with you," he said with somber inconsequence. "I would have."

"Would you?" she said with a faint smile. "Yes, I think perhaps you would have. . . ." A sigh, deep and uneven, lifted her bosom. "Ah, if he had. . . . How wonderful if we could have stayed together . . . He couldn't, he couldn't. . . . But it was all right. I didn't mind, not then. In spite of everything I knew he loved me. I could wait—for the baby to come—for him to send for us. . . . All I needed to do was have faith and wait. . . ."

Her face glowed, all its haggardness smoothed out, the face of a young girl triumphantly in love. He thought of Matryosha, too, drinking in her fill of Fedka, that look of pure love, pure joy. . . . If that is how love made you feel and look—his heart was filled with wild yearning. To love someone, something! To catch that brightness no matter how briefly it burned!

But her look dimmed and Grisha remembered how it all turned out. He never did come, or send for them, the waiting was in vain, love turned to hatred. She hated him now. . . .

Claire's Journal, October 12

Can't sleep . . . Tossed in my bed, thinking, thinking, finally got up and walked around in my room. The hag that rides me has a mean little spur to trowel me with; it's a humiliating experience, to catch oneself in self-deception, particularly if one's creed has been truth, truth, truth, no matter what the cost. . . .

This afternoon, the rain stopping and a pale semblance of the sun peeping through the clouds, all of us, including Georges, who had dropped in, went to the Semyonov

Monastery and walked around the famous pond, where Karamzin's "poor Lisa" was supposed to have drowned herself. Trees and benches around the pond are covered with carved hearts and sentimental scribbles—this Russian version of *Clarissa Harlowe* is very popular. Some of them not so sentimental: Hermann translated one cynical inscription for me:

> Erastus's bride was drowned in this place,
> Jump in, *mesdames*, there's still a lot of space.

Georges and I wandered off by ourselves and he took the opportunity to resume our former conversation and ask me— His questions have a different flavor, now. He used to sound like a child listening to a fairy tale: "And then? What comes next?" Now it's otherwise: the questions are probing and judging. It's as if he had learned something new and bitter about the human race, and has to apply that knowledge to everybody—even me.

"After the baby came and you let him know that there was nothing wrong with its foot . . ." Casually, without wincing. I was so pleased—he couldn't have said this so easily a few months ago. He went on, "I understand why he wouldn't have written or sent for you before the baby came. But afterward? He never wrote afterward? Not even one letter?" He found it hard to credit.

I assured him that no, there had been no letters for me, not even one. Such charming letters he wrote to P.B.! Gay, witty, highly improper at times—and so much himself. I would scan them all looking for a message and occasionally find one. But none directly to me.

"Yet you had no doubts?"

"About his love, you mean?"

"Yes."

"None. None at all."

He however looked doubtful.

"But what made you so sure?" he asked baldly, and this time I couldn't help a touch of tartness: "Because he told me so, before we left. Yes, in so many words, I didn't deduce it from eloquent silences or soulful looks. 'I love you, Claire,' he said."

. . . So surprised he was. "Is that what love means? To be so safe with another human being that you can reveal yourself utterly? It seems I love you, then!" Whenever a doubt plagued me afterward I would remember his beautiful face made simple by wonder: is this love then? yes, yes, it's love, I have won, it's no use, you love me . . .

As we walked among the leafless birches, I tried to explain to Georges how it had been. He himself had warned me, I said. There was a perverse demon in him that made him torment precisely those he loved, he told me. It was a way of testing them because he was so unsure of them—and of himself.

". . . Do you think you can stand it, little Claire? Read between the lines, interpret sullen silences, forgive neglect—always remember that I love you?"

"Always," I told him, "always."

"Never stop loving me?" His eyes blazing into mine questioningly, his small white hands crushing mine.

"Never," I told him, "never." And then they came in to tell me that the carriage was waiting. I lifted the hands that were clenched on mine to my lips and kissed them. If he had kept that desperate clenched hold on me—I would have stayed with him, no matter what. But he loosed it, and let me go, and I went away. . . .

". . . So you see, Georges," I said, "I was prepared. I had known all during our Geneva summer that there would come a time when I would be tried. . . . I merely had to be equal to the ordeal."

"I see," Georges said. But the doubtful look persisted. He even gave a slight involuntary headshake, quickly checked. I insisted on his telling me what it was, and at last he did.

"You see," he said reluctantly, his excellent English going hesitant and stiff with embarrassment, "it's just— you were being tried, you say. Well—so was he, wasn't he? I mean, if he loved you, not to be with you would be an ordeal for him too. . . . And I don't see—" He broke off, in evident embarrassment.

I finished for him: "You don't see him imposing such a hardship on himself."

His abashed silence was an answer in itself. We walked on, around the pond that peered at us from between its banks like a disillusioned gray eye. All at once I began laughing—a laugh of reluctant malicious enjoyment that overcomes you when you are faced with an incontrovertible proof of your idiocy.

"You are, of course, perfectly right."

"But then," he said puzzled, "I don't think I understand . . ."

"Oh, it's very simple, Georges. It was a theory I built up to protect myself. People do that a lot, you know. When they can't bear the truth. But how extraordinary that until now—until just a minute ago when you . . ." Another spasm of laughter seized me, as I again went over that unimpeachable piece of deduction. Albé was not the man to deprive himself of anything; ergo, if he deprived himself of me, it was because he didn't want me. *Quod erat demonstratum.* How exquisitely funny that a piece of schoolboy logic should so irretrievably upset a conviction that for years had helped me to keep some vestige of self-respect . . . But of course that's why I had clung to it so jealously.

"No," I said, wiping my eyes, "no, I fear we'll just have to jettison that particular theory. Nobody was testing anybody. Albé simply stayed away because he didn't want me with him." I looked full on his troubled face. "Does this bother you, Georges? That your teacher was so fatuous? That the infallible Miss Clairmont was so limed in self-deception?"

He thought about it. His hazel eyes rose to mine solemnly and I saw that at least some part of the trouble that had shadowed them had cleared. All at once I had a feeling that something important would be said. . . .

He answered slowly, "No, I value that you tell me this, even if it makes you—not infallible. That you tell me the truth—as you promised you would."

It seemed that I had at least this time passed some sort of test.

A mysterious fact remains, however, all logic notwithstanding, not to be explained away by self-delusion. He may not have wanted me with him, but—and this I still know within myself, uncontrovertibly—but he loved me. Oh, he stopped eventually, but he did *then*, he *did*. When we were in Marlow and he was in Venice; when the stories about his excesses started trickling back to us; *he still loved me then*.

I had known it with the same certainty with which a woman knows that she is carrying a living baby in her womb. Through the silence, through the seeming desertion, I still had felt myself to be a part of his life—of him. Yes, even after I had sent Allegra to him. And when that mystic connection between us was severed, I had known that too, beyond a doubt.

It was as though I had cracked apart and the certainty had flowed out of me and I was empty, empty. Robbed of the two things that had meant everything to me: he no longer loved me and Allegra was lost. . . .

So here I am. Old facts have reestablished themselves into a new riddle and I am sleeplessly pegging away at it. Why? Why? Why, if he loved me, stay away, if not to test me? If he wasn't testing me, why, loving me, did he yet not want me with him? Round and round I go.

A protesting meow from the bed. Vasska, deprived of his faithful source of warmth in the cold room, is summoning me back.

I will no longer chew the flavorless bone of the past. What, after all, does it matter?

Claire's Journal, October 13

Strange, how hard everybody has always found it to believe that he had really loved me. They all thought it was fantasy, self-delusion. Trelawny, with his thundering laugh: "Oh Claire, eternal myth-maker! Love you? He was incapable of loving anyone except himself." And Mary—she would listen to me, with her mouth screwed up in disbelief; she thought I'd gone mad in white linen like Ophelia. Watching me as I moved about our house in

Bath, my belly prowlike, she would shake her head at my folly. And later too—I overheard her once discussing me with P.B.

"I shouldn't have believed it—waiting here patiently, comforting herself with fairy tales, while he disports himself like an Eastern pasha in Venice . . . Sometimes I think it's pure obstinacy." There had been true sisterly irritation in her voice.

After Geordie died, I remember the wonder with which she recounted to me Fletcher's story—that he had spoken of me on his deathbed, tried to form a message. I don't know what it might have been and I don't care, it came much too late. The man whom the doctors killed in Missolonghi was a stranger to me. But Mary, as she told me the story, had looked at me with respectful surmise— perhaps I wasn't a romantic liar, perhaps he *had* loved me after all. . . .

P.B. alone had never doubted me. It was all perfectly clear to him—he understood all about those subterranean, invisible lines of communications that transcend distances and silences, those unconscious messages sent in letters written to someone else.

Yet there had been letters from Geordie that P.B. wouldn't let me see. How angry that made me! When it had been agreed between us that it was my only way of keeping in touch. I even saw in his reluctance another sign of the masculine solidarity, the implicit closing of ranks against a woman. Even P.B.! Of course I know why now: it had been something *he* had said about me—against me, something too outrageous, too painful for me to be allowed to see. Yes, even as early as then . . . For some reason I can admit it to myself today. I couldn't then. . . .

Sergey came to visit and stayed in Moscow nearly a week before going on to Kiev, where he had been sent with a group of other officers from his regiment. With his arrival a liveliness sprang up in the palace on Nikitskaya, which, in spite of its host of well-trained servants and illustrious guests on Tuesday, had seemed to reverberate as empty as a granite box.

Grisha, hitherto steeped doggedly in his studies, was pleased to take a brief leave of them and tag along while his brother did all the things a lively young officer does in Moscow. Sergey visited his parents' loge in the Bolshoi to see Ivanova perform; acquired a battery of nailbrushes and scissors at Rosenstrauch's on Tverskaya and shopped at Loubianka for a Persian shawl for some mysteriously unspecified female back in St. Petersburg. He went to the Carriage Row to look at a curricle and to the English Club for a flutter at faro in the famous Infernal Room where the notorious Turgenev "the American" used to fleece inexperienced players. He also dutifully stopped in at the assemblies given by their Moscow cousins to dance a quadrille or an écossaise. To those Grisha usually declined to accompany him, nor did Sergey invite him to other less respectable haunts where the young officers went afterward.

However, even while engaging in these frivolities, Sergey did not forget his mission in Kiev, where he hoped to prove himself as good a judge of horseflesh as any. For this reason he also spent some time in his father's extensive stables. The grooms might be serfs, but they were also experts in their field. The brothers would listen respectfully to Matvey's deep voice as he instructed Sergey in the pitfalls awaiting an unwary horse buyer: "Especially watch out if a horse looks too fat, Excellency. That's all air. Those son-of-a-bitch dealers, they feed them up with bran and salt to make them look good so they puff up like toads. What you want to look for are those nice little nags from across the Don River; fresh like peeled chestnuts, they are. . . ." Around them the air was full of familiar smells and sounds, steamy-sweet aroma of chewed oats and manure; stirrings and rustlings of straw, thumping and whinnying of horses in their stalls.

Afterward they would have the horses saddled and regardless of weather go for a ride along the Moscow River, sometimes going out to the Chistyi Ponds where it was still more country than city and they could enjoy a good gallop.

The heartwarming thing about all this was that Sergey so clearly wanted him around. His merry older brother, with his guileless air of being pleased with the entire world—Grisha wouldn't have dreamed of confiding in him, but he felt nourished by his uncomplicated affection. He would get up in the morning with an unwonted sense of pleasant anticipation, a feeling that there was some change for the better in the weather. Was it snowing at last? No, that wasn't it. But Sergey was here.

"I wish you weren't going away" burst from him once when they were coming back from a ride.

Sergey couldn't share the wish. Moscow was well enough, but there were more exciting things in the offing. "What I wish is that you could come along with us," he told Grisha. "Wouldn't that be fine, traveling together, looking at horses? I bet you'd be as good as anyone at picking them. . . . I've never been to a horse fair before. . . ." He looked at Grisha with affection. "Would do you good, that's certain. Look at you, all peaked, like a miserable little hermit, always with your nose in the book. You shouldn't let old Lachaine drive you the way he does. Where's all this studying going to get you? Hmmm?"

"Into Moscow University, presumably, where else?"

Sergey laughed. "Listen to you. Talking as if you were one of those provincial grinds studying for a scholarship, and not a Prince Volynski. The trouble with you," he said accusingly, "is that you like studying. You find it fun boning up!"

Grisha didn't deny it. Actually, he looked forward to the examination, a pompous but not frightening ritual that would take place in the stately building on the Mokhovaya, in the great domed hall brooded over benignly by the busts of two Empresses. He would pass it brilliantly and put on with pleasure the student's uniform.

"The only place you go is to the Pomykovs'." Sergey's rosy face took on an expression of indulgent scorn. "Too much talk going on there. I'm just a simple army man"—his voice slid downward into a martial basso—"it's all way over my head. . . ."

Grisha smiled. "You managed to have a fine time with the young ladies, all the same, when I took you there."

All the pink nieces had fluttered and cooed, Sergey had preened. He shrugged his shoulders now, loftily disavowing all that. "I have no use for *les petites filles*. A woman of the world is more my style." His hand went up to smooth his little moustache.

Woman of the world indeed! Grisha remembered with some relish his brother's heedless eyes sliding indifferently over Miss Clairmont's slender gray-clad figure, dismissing her as nothing but a plain Miss, no different from all the governesses one encountered by dozens in one's friends' houses. If he were to tell Sergey just how different she was!—but he never would. He felt the same half-guilty pleasure as when, in their childhood, the two of them ranging the gardens, he would deliberately skirt some secret magic corner of his own, keeping it to himself.

"No, really, Grisha, you ought to go out more, enjoy yourself. . . ."

"In exactly what way is it you want me to enjoy myself?" Grisha inquired, with sudden anger. At the involuntary touch of his heel, Nelly broke into a gallop. He immediately brought her back to a canter, and she obeyed, signaling her bewilderment at conflicting orders by a flicker of her finely cut ears. "Sorry, my darling," Grisha said, patting her brown-satin neck. The only sweet, predictable, unreservedly loving female of his acquaintance; certainly the only one, he thought, perversely pressing on a sore spot, that he had any hope of getting between his legs. . . .

Sergey opened his mouth, closed it, and flushed, his clear brow furrowing; angry pity, resentment at the unfairness of it all passed across his all too readable face. They rode on in silence.

After a while Sergey's face cleared. He said: "Why don't you come with me tonight? Some of the Yegorovski officers are giving a supper at Lopashov's on Varvarka—that's a damned good place, nothing stuffy about it, I like it much better than Europa. . . . Yes, I know, we're supposed to have supper at the Golitzins', but I mean afterward, it'll go on all night. There'll be gypsies there." Sergey's eyes brightened. "I'm mad for gypsy singing, I've been going to hear them every night. . . . There's one in particular. . . . Anyhow, you come along with me."

Grisha demurred and was overridden. "Nonsense, of course they won't mind. Fine chaps, all of them. You're my brother, aren't you? And I want you with me—this is my last day here, God knows when we'll see each other again."

With timid pleasure at his brother's insistence, Grisha consented.

They could hear the gypsies singing as they entered Lopashov's: harsh voices mixing with voices of piercing sweetness, their shivery dissonances flowing together into a precarious cross-grained harmony.

The owner himself, as sedate and bearded as a deacon, bowed them into the private room where about twenty officers sat at a long table covered by a Russian embroidered tablecloth. Some of the uniforms were off, others unbuttoned; an atmosphere of easy gayety prevailed. Supper was still being served. Platters of *kulebiyaka*, *pelmeni*, suckling pig in horseradish loaded the table; the best Achuev caviar twinkled grainily in silver bowls. Waiters swooped and circled busily around the table, with bottles of champagne.

Hilarious cries greeted Sergey. He was evidently popular. With wistfulness Grisha saw him imbedded in the comfortable entity of a regiment, entirely at home, wanting nothing better. He was cordially greeted as Sergey's brother, the host himself, a tall ruddy officer somewhat older than the rest, with long drooping mustaches *à la cossaque*, rising from his seat at the head of the table to bid him welcome.

Grisha acknowledged those courtesies shyly and squeezed himself into a corner. After a while he began to feel almost at home sitting there next to Sergey's protective presence, his leg out of sight under the table and a glass of champagne standing before him. "Just like anyone," he thought vaguely, sipping the cold tingling drink and looking about him curiously.

The gypsy chorus was seated in their traditional formation at the other end of the room. A row of dark women glowing in their brilliant shawls sat decorously in front; the men, gay-shirted and swarthy, stood in the back. An accordion wailed; two guitarists strummed away cleverly and passionately. The choir warbled, with barbaric little cries of excitement punctuating the melody, clapping their hands and subsiding to a hum whenever a soloist would rise from her seat to do her special song.

"God, how I love the gypsies," said a young officer next to Sergey. "Sometimes I listen and listen and then I think, if you could just give everything up, follow them, hear them sing wherever they go . . ."

"This one is mine," Sergey said to Grisha as one of the girls rose to sing. "She's something special—draws the soul out of you when she sings. Burns you to ashes in bed, too." Sergey's eyes, slightly prominent like his father's, glistened with a familiar blind patina.

The gypsy's amber eyes fell on Sergey with a look of devouring possessiveness. Grisha examined her with curiosity: a passionate face, with no trace of softness, thin hawklike nose and thin curved lips. She was a tall willowy creature, with black braids flowing like serpents down to a long supple waist; above it her deep breasts blossomed and stirred as she sang. Her voice flowed dark and powerful into the silenced room.

Looking at her long throat vibrating with the song Grisha suddenly remembered Miss Clairmont in the field early this summer, singing: *Plaisir d'amour ne dure qu'un instant.*

As soon as she finished, she came to the table and leaned her supple body against Sergey, winding her dark arms around his neck.

"Ah, Prince, darling one, and I waited, waited, thought you'd never come," she said in a guttural singsong, rounding and narrowing her amber eyes at him. As Sergey pulled her into his lap, Grisha had a sense of trepidation for him, as if he were playing with an imperfectly tamed tigress.

"That's my little brother, Styosha, you be nice to him too," said Sergey, laughing.

Styosha gave him her yellow-eyed stare and bared her white teeth in a quick smile. Then, removing herself from his brother's arms with a pliant movement, she went back to her chair to resume singing.

"Look, *rastegay*, my favorite," said Sergey greeting the great round meat pie with the same look of childish greed with which he had been looking at the gypsy. Smiling with pleasure, he helped himself to several thin slices, artfully carved *à la rose*, from the middle outward, a special trick of the tavern.

Voices rose, more uniforms were shed; the choir went on singing, faster and wilder. The girls began to dance: first one then another rose from her seat and swam across the room, bright shawl trailing, breasts and shoulders in a quake. The host leaped to his feet and went down the room with a plump brown little partridge of a girl, his fingers snapping over her demurely bowed head, his long booted legs performing the most outlandish steps, while the guitars wailed high in a frenzy and the other officers laughed and applauded. "Bravo, *barin*, well done" came approvingly from the gypsies. He finished his turn by flinging the girl across his shoulder and starting out of the room. But at the last minute he put her down, grinning and smoothing his long moustaches, and she returned decorously to her chair.

Later, however, Grisha saw that her seat was empty, as was their host's. There were other such disappearances. A girl would vanish with an officer and after a while reappear and take her place, unruffled.

Sergey's Styosha sang on. Her voice rang out, sweet and strange, with a seductive dissonance in it, like a cracked glass bell, rising easily above the others, while the musicians bent toward her offering their madly twanging guitars, tambourines pulsed, and the chorus shouted out desperate melodic refrains. She too danced once, briefly, making a swift gliding round of the room. For a moment she froze before Sergey, eyes half closed, offering her subtly stirring bosom, and then glided on, lithe as a snake.

"Good, eh?" Sergey turned his flushed and laughing face to Grisha. "That's how she is in bed too, enough to melt a rock. Makes all those Aspasias and Omphales on Zaharovka look like a bunch of nuns. . . . You're still a virgin, aren't you?" He caught Grisha by the arm, his slightly bloodshot gray eyes owlish with affection. "No, no, don't get angry at me, I don't mean anything— Damn it all, I love you, my little brother, my quiet little sobersides of a brother. There isn't anything I wouldn't do for you. . . ." Obviously he was in a state of euphoric self-satisfaction that sometimes overcomes young men, particularly simple young men, uncomplicated life enjoyers, in which they are fond of everyone connected with them, and yearn to see others as happy as they are. "You're not drinking enough, that's your trouble."

Grisha smiled waveringly and drank. A subtle warmth rose up in him, dispersing all malaise and gloom. He surveyed the merriment boiling up around him in a detached unenvious way, perfectly comfortable with it all. He could sit like this forever, he thought, exchanging friendly smiles with men he didn't know but nevertheless liked heartily—fine simple friendly fellows all of them—cozy in his corner, listening to those songs, that now muted down to passionate sadness, now blazed up as reckless as fire, and be perfectly happy; an observer, a listener, nothing more expected of him. . . .

He became aware of an argument going on at another table between Styosha and his brother. He was whispering in her ear, smiling, and she listened, stormy faced, her thick eyebrows meeting over her eyes in a black bar. Occasionally her eyes flashed and the corners of her thin mouth drew down bitterly. Sergey's hand moved to her breast and a handful of coins poured chinking down her blouse. She gave him a sudden dark look and nodded. The next minute she was away and back with the chorus. Her troubling voice rose hauntingly: "Ah, say, burn away . . ." and the guitars thrilled about it. Grisha emptied another glass of champagne and the whole jumble, voices, colors, songs, spun about him deliriously.

The next thing he knew, he was stumbling along a corridor, his brother's arm around him. "Where——?"

"You'll see," said Sergey tenderly. Keeping an arm around Grisha, he opened a door and pulled him inside a small room. "There now, he is all yours."

These words were addressed to Styosha, who stood in the middle of the room, her face impassive, her dark arms crossed on her breast.

The world rotating carousel-like around Grisha came to a sudden stop. "What is this?" His eyes traveled past the motionless girl to the bed standing against the wall, with its cover drawn back, and he understood. "Wait now, Sergey. . . . You can't . . ."

"Why not?" said Sergey jubilantly and gave him a hug. "You're my brother, I'll do anything for you. . . . She'll give you a good time, won't you, Styosha?"

"But—but if she's the one you—if she's yours . . ."

"There won't be any less of her afterwards," Sergey laughed. "She doesn't mind, do you, Styosha?"

The girl shook her head slowly. Her eyes flashed at him for a moment, a quick feral gleam immediately obscured by her thick dark lashes and then her face was impassive again.

Sergey gave him another encouraging hug and retired from the room closing the door softly behind him.

"Now what," Grisha thought, absurdly, "what do I—?" He was cold sober and frightened.

The girl undressed impatiently without a look at him, petticoat after bright petticoat dropping down to the ground. Spurning them out of the way with a narrow foot, she lay back on the bed, her arms over her head, watching him with her wild amber eyes.

This was the first time Grisha had seen a woman so flauntingly naked; the dark exciting body looked threatening. A half unwound braid twisted black between her breasts; the nipples were dark brown, a stark black triangle flared between her strong brown thighs, black tufts curled in her armpits—somehow there was an angry look about it all. A memory of Matryosha's immature nudity

[217]

as he had seen it first came to him: soft, vulnerable, easily penetrable . . . *But she didn't want me either.*

"Well, my falcon?" The guttural voice honed down to a false sweetness, underneath which Grisha sensed an undercurrent of anger and mockery.

An answering anger sprang up in Grisha; he could see himself winding that coarse black braid in his fist, entering that insolent body in violence and anger. Watching him she gave an abrupt knowledgeable laugh and leaning out of the bed drew him toward her.

Grisha elbowed himself awkwardly out of his coat, while her quick fingers unbuttoned his shirt. He took that off too, obediently. Rearing herself upright on the bed, she wound an arm around his neck: her other hand had stolen into his trousers and was prodding and fondling him busily. Her thin lips closed on his in a harsh sucking kiss. Grisha felt his member stirring in her warm rough hand.

"Ah," she said, and releasing him lay back again, stretching. "Come on then, little Prince, Styosha is waiting. . . ."

And here suddenly Grisha was faced with the logistics of further undressing: his shoes would have to come off before his trousers. He hesitated, a heavy reluctance liming his movements: to expose his foot to that inimical yellow gaze . . . ?

"No, don't you bother with that," she said much too quickly, apparently guessing his dilemma. "Just come as you are, come quickly, my falcon. . . ."

The revulsion in her voice was unmistakable: as little as he wanted to expose his foot did she want to see it. And immediately, disastrously, he felt his manhood go flaccid, the readiness draining away. A cold terror seized him. It would be, he knew, no good, no good at all. Setting his teeth against a sudden desire to cry, he stepped back from the bed.

"What is it, my falcon? Don't you like Styosha? Come now, don't give up so easy. Styosha'll take care of you, never fear. . . ."

But the amber eyes, alight with secret contemptuous laughter, contradicted the wheedling voice. His lips quivering childishly, Grisha picked up his shirt, fumbled it on, and with unsteady fingers began to button it. The voice behind him went on cajoling, falsely sweet:

"Ah, no, don't you go away, don't you shame me now, young

sir. Your brother'll be so disappointed, here he told me especially, you take care of my little brother . . ."

"Yes, and paid you too, didn't he?" said Grisha in a trembling voice. With a shock he realized that those were the first words he had addressed to her. He dug into his pockets, pulled out a couple of banknotes, and without looking threw them at her. "Here's for your time."

"Oh, what kindness, what goodness," the girl said in a honeyed drawl, picking them up, smoothing them out on the bed before her and then swiftly folding them small. "Thank you, thank you, kind young Prince." She swung her long brown legs over the side of the bed and began to dress, putting on one petticoat after the other as casually as she had shed them.

"How do I get out of here?" Grisha asked with loathing, not looking at her.

She cocked her head, glancing at him mockingly; "Why, it's a simple thing, *barin*, just open the door, it's not locked."

"I mean out of the building. Is there a back door?"

"So there is, my dear, right next to this one. . . . Wait, I'll get your coat for you," she said with a quick look of complicity. Brushing past him, she opened the door a crack and called one of the servants. Grisha waited numbly until his coat was brought to him. There was something insulting in the briskness with which she helped him into it, like a nursemaid bundling an unwelcome charge out of the way.

"I'll just wait here a bit and then slip down after a while and tell Prince Sergey that you've gone home," she said, unhurriedly fastening the last petticoat and beginning to plait her hair with her deft long fingers. "And don't you worry—I'll tell him it was ever so," she added with another look of complicity and a sudden flash of white teeth.

The corridor was deserted and Grisha was able to make his way to the back door and leave without a word to anyone.

Toward the dawn Sergey came bumbling into Grisha's bedroom, awakening Fomitch, but not Grisha, who had been lying there sleepless.

"Don't fuss, Fomitch, I'm just here for a minute. . . ." He leaned close, sending a puff of liquor-laden breath into Grisha's face. "Well? Well? What did I tell you?" a gleeful whisper, blurred by drink. "Wasn't it marvelous? Nothing like it, you're half a man—

less!—until you've done it. . . . Never mind, go back to sleep, you've earned it." A hearty moustached smack landed near his ear. Sergey's dim figure blundered out of the room, followed by Fomitch's sleepy grumble. A chair fell, the door closed, all was still again.

Almost the worst thing about it, Grisha thought, staring dry-eyed into the dark, was being glad that Sergey was leaving.

Pushchin, who worked in the criminal division of the court, could be found during the day at the great new judicial building near the Voskressenski Gates right outside the Kitai-Gorod. It was one of the new buildings that went up in 1821, and its assertively neoclassic look contrasted strangely with the archaic contours of the Church of All Saints next to it. However, Moscow's softening influence was beginning to work on it already dulling the cold official glint of the Imperial eagles surmounting its fronton, diluting the prescribed official yellow of the walls into something more honey than dung. Even the Doric columns—give them time, one felt, and by dint of that same peculiarly Moscow magic they would begin to acquire the same cozy Russian look as the squat Byzantine pillars of the neighbor church.

Two distinct currents could be perceived in the sluggish sea of humanity moving across the cobbled square, one directing itself to the church, the other to the courthouse. Vehicles of all descriptions, ranging from a strong-smelling peasant cart to a dandified curricle, beat their way through it slowly. Akim the coachman stopped in front of the courthouse steps, and Grisha was about to dispatch the footman Mitka into the building with a note when with delight he saw Pushchin himself standing on the steps next to a column. A small ragged peasant, swaddled in earth-colored wrappings, was addressing him earnestly, making one jerky little obeisance after another as he talked. Pushchin listened attentively, his military erectness a contrast to that cringing semicrouch; presently he gave a nod and patted the bowed shoulders. The little peasant sagged at the knees gratefully, ready to prostrate himself altogether; Pushchin's hand on his shoulder kept him vertical. He gave him another encouraging pat and started down with his crisp military tread.

"Pushchin! Ivan Ivanitch!" Grisha called, impatiently pulling the rug away from his knees and rising up in his carriage. Pushchin saw him and came over with a cordial but somewhat preoccupied look. "And what brings you to these parts, Prince?"

"I was looking for you," Grisha said in a low voice. "I wanted to ask your permission to call on you this evening—if you would give me a little of your time—there's something I—"

"Delighted," Pushchin answered promptly. Cutting into Grisha's embarrassed stammering, he gave him a reassuring pat, not unlike that bestowed on the petitioner on the steps. "Unfortunately, I am obliged to go out to supper this evening—but perhaps if it isn't out of your way to take me home in this superb carriage of yours . . . I was going to walk. I don't keep a carriage," he added, making this confession of what seemed to Grisha an inconceivable privation in a perfectly natural manner. "I do not need to leave for the next two hours, so we will have time to talk."

He swung himself briskly into the carriage and leaning forward gave directions to Akim, who began to turn the horses around, shouting threateningly at the passersby and laying about him with his whip. Like all coachmen, Akim had nothing but contempt for the pedestrian.

"Watch it, brother," Pushchin remarked mildly. "Some of those are my clients."

"Yes, you are a judge, aren't you?" Grisha asked respectfully.

"Examining magistrate, Prince. I hold preliminary hearings for out of town criminal cases. Not an exalted job but not without its compensations. I must confess I feel at home dealing with the little people."

"The Governor was most complimentary about you the other day," Grisha offered.

"Charming of him . . . You see, those preliminary hearings do actually determine the future course of the court action. It's rather a satisfactory feeling when you are able to disentangle and dismiss a complaint before some poor devil gets so entangled there's no saving him. Most of them are frightened to death anyhow, not being residents here and not knowing what their rights are. . . . And then the fees, the bribery—you know the saying: those who can, rob, those who can't, steal. . . . One has to make a push to be useful to one's fellow men. . . ."

Grisha remembered that Pushchin at one time considered being a common policeman.

"And sometimes I'm downright glad that I'm merely an examining magistrate and not a trial judge. . . . Like the other day—a case came in, a young peasant—originally from Ryazan, but he had run away from his village and was hiding in Moscow, that's how he came under our jurisdiction. He was being held on a charge of parricide. It seems he came home after being away a year—he was working in Moscow, helping to make up the quit rent—and found his wife pregnant by his father . . ."

Grisha gasped and looked at his friend with an expression of utmost horror.

"Oh, this happens all the time," Pushchin said, his lips flattening as if he had bitten into a rotten apple. "Not the murder, the other thing. The so-called *snokhach*—'seducer of daughter-in-law'—is a well-known phenomenon in the peasant family life. It's as common as incest. It's the way they live, all herded together in small huts, everybody sleeping in the same room—the devil is strong, as my old aunt used to say. . . . One way to help would be to build them larger huts, so there is a little more privacy. But you know what, Prince? Not even the most enlightened landowner thinks of doing that."

"But perhaps nobody realizes. . ."

"I suspect that the practice is blinked at for very practical reasons. A son is recruited into the army or is sent to the city to work for quit rent; just before he goes he gets married. Since he won't be there to propagate the family, why shouldn't his father take over his conjugal duties?"

Grisha swallowed. "But that's—that's——"

"Immoral, you would say? Well, there you are. Morality is morality, but the stock has to be kept up. After all a man's wealth depends on the number of souls he possesses. And these aren't humans—they're just livestock."

His father pointing to a group of peasants and saying, offhand, "A good fertile stock. . . ."

"Well, apparently this wretched boy had a different view of himself, even perhaps a rudimentary sense of honor—just as though he was one of us," said Pushchin, with a tight smile. "Granted he exercised it in a regrettably savage manner . . . But I must say I am just as glad that I wasn't called upon to sit on this particular case."

"What'll they do to him?"

"Send him to Siberia after an appropriate amount of lashes.

Death penalty has been abolished in Russia—if you happen to die under the lash, that's your hard luck. . . ."

Grisha, sickened, was silent. Into his mind there came a memory of riding through the meadows and coming upon a company of peasants mowing hay. The mowers had taken time off to rest among the haystakes: women's kerchiefs gleamed like poppies, the men's brown bodies glistered with sweat. An intensely blue sky arched over the pastoral scene. . . . Now in his fancy a shadow ran across the innocent sky, a cloud of vile brown and gray blotted out the blue. From the huddled crowd in the field there came hideous stirrings and animal groans, a stench rose, bloody and fecal. A young man emerged from the huddle, pale as death, his hands twisted behind his back, a bloody mark on his brow. . . . Grisha shuddered and swallowed dryly, feeling a hideous qualm rise up in his throat.

"You've turned quite pale, Prince. I am sorry, I didn't mean to distress you." Pushchin sounded remorseful. "It seems to me I'm always bringing ugly things to your attention."

"No, it's all right, Puschin. I want to know. Everything."

They drove the rest of the way in silence.

Briefly left by himself in Pushchin's parlor, Grisha looked about him with curiosity: so that's where he lives, that's the habitat of that mysterious singular being, my friend Pushchin. Few clues to the riddle to be found here: impersonal surroundings, nondescript furniture. In his own home, where ordinarily a man's personality lies thick and palpable on the objects with which he chooses to surround himself, there was less of Pushchin than by the Doric column of the courthouse.

"Can I offer you anything, Prince?" Pushchin inquired, coming back into the room. He had taken off his official bottle-green uniform, replacing it with a smoking jacket, gaudier than expected.

Grisha shook his head. The agitation that had possessed him ever since he had decided on a visit to Pushchin now boiled up higher, well nigh choking him, so that he couldn't speak. He bowed his head, contemplating with unusual attention the faded arabesques of the worn-out carpet. The next words he uttered seemed to come not from him but from a friend standing next to him and talking for him, while he himself directed all his attention to tracing the permutations of the design: "I'd like to join your society, Ivan Ivanitch. The secret society."

There, it was out! Silence thundered in his ears. Then Pushchin's calm everyday voice said, "Exactly what do you think it is, this secret society that everybody seems to know about?"

"It's there to change things, isn't it? That's what I want, to change everything, to smash this rotten system. The way it was done in France!" Suddenly he wanted it: the violence of oncoming change, everything toppling down, himself obliterated with the rest. . . . He said with an unconscious smile: "I wouldn't mind dying on the barricades. It would be such a nice death."

"Bless my soul," said Pushchin, mildly startled, but still cautious. "Do you believe that the French Revolution would be practical in Russia?"

"But that's what you are preparing for, isn't it? That's what your society is about. My father thinks so. . . . You *are* a member of such a society, aren't you, Ivan Ivanitch?" He looked up at last.

Pushchin answered slowly, "I belong, together with some of my friends, to an organization called the Practical Union. But it's not a secret organization. Its aim is to strive to accomplish the abolition of serfdom with all the legitimate means in our power. All of us, for example, have sworn to free our own serfs and influence others to do so. Anyone who shares these views is certainly welcome to join us. You, Prince, would be far more valuable than I." He gave a little laugh. "I own no serfs and don't expect to inherit many from my father."

A huge sickening disappointment descended on Grisha. After a moment of stricken silence, he brought out:

"And—and that is all?"

"You don't feel that it's a useful effort, Prince?"

"Yes, of course," Grisha answered mechanically. He peered with painful attention into that composed friendly face which yet was as closed as a fortress, giving away nothing. A sense of injury, of being hardly dealt with flooded him. He had spent the last day coming to this resolve, girding himself to approach Pushchin. Now it was as if he had absurdly mustered all his strength to move an empty barrel.

He said: "You don't trust me, then."

"My dear Prince, why do you . . .?"

"You don't trust me. If there's something—anything I can do to show you that I can be trusted . . . Any test . . ."

The courteous mask before him barely stirred. "My dear boy, I assure you that is totally unnecessary. . . ."

"Then, . . ." Grisha licked his dry lips. He said with difficulty: "Is it because I am lame? Even a cripple can give his life for a cause, you know."

A blackmailing whine, a shameful bid for pity—he was aware even as he spoke how theatrical it sounded. But the desperation was real. He said, constricted, "If you don't want me, Ivan Ivanitch, I don't know what to do," and turned away, his lips trembling.

"Ah . . ." A compassionate sound. A strong embrace held him for a moment, his undone face tucked into a sheltering shoulder; then, with a bracing little shake he was released. A different face, open and fatherly, looked at him; there was tenderness in the gray eyes. "My dear boy, don't—of course, it's nothing like that, how could you think that it could be so? You're precisely what we want—young, idealistic, wanting change. . . . But too young— much too young."

Grisha kept his head turned away in shame. To add to his troubles, he was snuffling shamefully, and no handkerchief to be found. *A snotty schoolboy*, he said to himself with hatred, *no wonder no one*— Shakily, he managed to utter: "In eighteen-twelve thirteen-year-old boys went to fight for the fatherland. And Russia is being destroyed—you have said so yourself."

"That's true enough." With a sigh Pushchin went over to the sideboard and poured vodka out of a small carafe for both of them. Grisha, finally locating his handkerchief, blew his nose surreptitiously and felt better. A shy hope rose in him. Taking a glass of vodka from Pushchin, he looked at him with painful anxiety. "Will you accept me then?"

"I suppose I'll have to," said Pushchin with a half-smile. "But I think I ought to tell you first exactly what it is you are joining. Alexey!" he called and was answered by the manservant who had earlier taken Grisha's coat: a young fellow, thin faced, russet haired, white lashed, who glanced at him with sharp knowledge-able eyes. "Bring in the samovar and get us something to eat."

After the food was brought and the servant had retired, Pushchin slowly filled and lit his pipe—every movement he made seemed to Grisha to be imbued with indescribable ritual significance—and, puffing at it abstractedly, launched into his discourse. Grisha

[225]

listened, respectfully rapt, unconsciously devouring slice after slice of the black bread and herring that Alexey had brought in: he was all at once ravenously hungry.

October dusk began to fill the room, steadily darkening it, until Pushchin's compact figure, marching back and forth in its aura of bluish tobacco smoke, seemed to dissolve in the transparent darkness. His calm voice chimed on. Lucid and impersonal, ticking off fact after fact, not unlike M. Gambs delivering a beautifully organized lecture on the Hanseatic League. He touched, schoolmasterishly, on the history of the society ("started in 1817, by a group consisting mainly of the Army officers; based, in its original inception, on the German *Tugendbund*"); its organization: two main branches, northern and southern, one based in St. Petersburg, the other in the south, in Tulchino and Kamenka, where the bulk of the Army was concentrated; its aims—change from the present form of government, to one less autocratic and more responsive to the good of Russia, such as limited or constitutional monarchy, or the republic ("We of the northern branch prefer the former; the southern branch wants the latter"). All this to be arrived at by whatever methods were necessary. . . .

Grisha said slowly, "My father said there may be a plot afoot to assassinate the Tsar." His throat suddenly went dry. He cleared it and went on: "Is it—is that the—necessary step?"

Pushchin came to a stop before him, a dark faceless figure, with smoke swirling about him. "It might be," he said with a calmness that sounded terrible in Grisha's ears. "There are different opinions on the matter. Do you have any, Prince?"

Grisha gulped. The walls of the dark room seemed to close in on him, waiting. "Well?" said Pushchin gently.

"Whatever the Society decides on," he said and fell silent as out of breath as if it had been knocked out of him.

"It has not been decided on," said the calm voice. "Eventually as a member you will be one of those to decide. If you still want to be a member."

The walls swam backward, it was suddenly possible to breathe. "Yes, yes, I do," he said in a rush, in an agony of relief. It had only been a test; the bitter cup removed from one's lips, the dark alternative indefinitely postponed. He eased his clenched hands. "Are you accepting me?"

"Oh, yes," said Pushchin, "I am. Well," he added, and his voice was now totally ordinary, "no use sitting here in the dark. Alexey." He raised his voice. "Bring in the lamps."

Lamps were lit, abolishing the darkness and the mystery together. Grisha blinked against the light, looking about him with wonder. Was this the same room? And Pushchin, emerging from the shadows as his former friendly simple self—was that the stern catechizing presence of only a few minutes back?

He said again—but so differently from before—eagerly, happily: "Is this all?"

"Yes, that's it. We did once have a very elaborate ceremony, the sort that they used to have in the Masonic lodges, before they were abolished; swearing an oath over bared swords and a Bible, all that sort of thing. But of course that's a lot of nonsense. A word of honor should be enough among gentlemen. . . . But there's a lot of childishness in every movement, no matter how serious. There are still members who like to make an awesome ritual of being accepted into this society. . . ." Grisha blushed. Shamefaced, he confessed to himself that he too would have liked only too well those romantic trappings attendant upon a cabal: chained hands, masks, a sword pressed against his bared chest, solemn vows intoned by the flickering torchlight.

"Some members," Pushchin went on, "are childish in more dangerous ways. This summer, one of the young officers in the southern division met an officer of English extraction called Sherwood, whom he sized up—on four hours' acquaintance—as a useful addition to the society. So Captain Sherwood was inducted with all due ceremony, and given the list of the members in the southern army so that he could add his own prospects to it. We have reason to believe that this list is now in the hands of the authorities. . . . I am telling you this, Prince, not only to warn you against that sort of easy zeal in recruiting, but because it is only right to let you know that you might be joining an organization that is both proscribed and doomed."

"That's all right," said Grisha, in a daze. "I don't mind—no, I don't mean that," he added, flushing, as Pushchin's eyes rested on him reflectively. "What I meant to say was that I am ready . . . for whatever happens."

"That's good." Pushchin smiled. "Luckily the Emperor moves slowly. He has had another list of names on his desk since eighteen-twenty and he hasn't done anything about that. . . . Possibly because it had occurred to him that the names on that list are those of people who believe in what he himself had said ten years ago . . . So perhaps he will ignore this list too—or else move when it is too late. . . . At any rate, your name is on neither, that's certain," Pushchin said cheerfully. "We just must make certain that it won't appear on any later ones. . . ."

He glanced at the clock on the mantelpiece. "It's getting on, isn't it? Time for me to start dressing, I fear. Well, Prince . . ."

Encountering Grisha's serious and expectant gaze, he stopped midway in what was going to be a courteous dismissal. "As I have said before, it is customary to demand from a new member his word of honor that he will be faithful to the society and not disclose any of its actions. Do you swear this, Prince?"

"I do."

"Then, as the president of the Moscow branch of the northern division of the Secret Benevolent Society, I accept you as a member. Shall we drink to that?"

They touched glasses solemnly . . .

He stood for a while outside Pushchin's house, smiling to himself with joyous incredulity. It happened, he did it. There was a feeling of change in the air. Something damp and soft touched his cheek timidly; a microscopic white star blossomed on the dark cloth of his sleeve and melted, another, then another. It was beginning to snow.

Claire's Journal, October 20

How lovely, after the two horrible rainy months, to see the muddy streets covered over by the fluffy white blanket of the first snow. I was so entranced by this spectacle that I forgot what it presaged: that which I fear most, the killing inhuman cold of a Moscow winter. At least, this time, having spent 300 rubles on a fox-fur lining for my coat, I am somewhat prepared for it.

Georges came today. I was struck by a special look he had: as if—I don't know—uplifted, glorified. I asked him, laughing, whether he had taken communion out of season, and he gave me a startled look. "Are you a witch, Miss Clairmont?" I was reminded of Geordie saying to me resentfully: "You walk in and out of my mind as if it were a room with an unlocked door. . . ."

Later, when we were alone, he told me about it. He had become a member of a secret society, the purpose of which is to change the nature of the present government. *The* secret society.

At the time I was only pleased because he, so clearly, was. Now I am worried. How dangerous is such an adventure? Imprisonment here would not be the pleasant social incarceration of Leigh Hunt, with prison walls papered over in trellised roses and a daily reception for his admirers. . . .

Is it another one of the games men play to make themselves feel better about their inadequacies? Geordie's game? Trelawny wrote to us about it; his ordering the uniforms, trying on feathered helmets—a spoiled little boy playing soldiers. He was tired of the love game, he was going to try the other one. . . .

I hear them talking about his glorious death, his life given for a glorious cause. What nonsense! He went to Greece because he was bored, because he was tired of vegetating in Italy, tired probably of his Contessa. And he died in the middle of a stupid adventure because there was no woman to take care of him, to stand between him and the bloodsucking doctors.

Claire's Journal, October 21

A visit to Pushchin. He fell upon me with a savagery that would have frightened me if I weren't sharing it. We didn't even get as far as the bed. Our clothes flew off like leaves in a gale, our bodies ignited and disappeared and so did the room, the house, the world. One deep groan like a roar in my ear, and then I lost consciousness even of him and myself.

Afterward I slipped out of his relaxed grip and finding a needle and thread—he keeps everything as neat as a woman, army style—began to repair my torn dress so that I could go home without a scandal. He watched me sleepily out of narrowed smiling eyes.

"How demure you look, *mon ange.*" There was amiable mockery in his lazy voice. "Nothing is more pleasing than a show of domesticity in a woman—afterward."

But when I reached for my warm flannel petticoats—now that the lovemaking was over, I was cold, *cold* in this spartan room—he prevented me. "*Pas encore, ma petite anglaise.*" He twitched apart the blanket I had wrapped around me and buried his face briefly between my breasts. When he lifted it, his eyes had gone slitted and dark again. But he got up and padded off to the corner of the room where a small stove languidly dispensed insufficient warmth and began to stoke it—"*All* the fires," he said, smiling at me over his shoulder, "must be kept going in this weather."

He has a lovely straight back with flat shoulderblades and a shading of hair going down into the cleft between the neat muscular globes of buttocks. He is lightly furred all over—so unlike Geordie's smooth polished body—There is something agreeably primitive, animal, sylvan about that faintly furry contact—it brings to mind Arcadian dallyings, nymphs coupling with satyrs. . . .

Now I am romanticizing what Geordie used to call "a pleasant bout of fluffery." . . . But he *is* an appetizing man.

I said, watching him, "There's a new conscript to your society, I understand."

His back stiffened. He turned around slowly and fixed me with an expressionless look. "I quite fail to understand you, *mon ange.*"

"Georges told me, you see."

His expression now was totally unloverlike, even unfriendly. "I really can't imagine what Prince Volynski could have told you to make you think . . ." His lips tightened. "There is nothing more garrulous than a boy in love."

"In love? You mean with me?" I laughed, genuinely amused. "Be sure, if he were, he would have told me nothing. . . . No, I am—I suppose I am just the person to whom he tells everything. That is my place in his life." The slightest flicker of an incredulous smile passed across that impassive face: quite obviously he couldn't see a woman being important to a man except in one way. "So you see he had to tell me the most important thing that had happened to him. Just the barest fact. Nothing about the nature of the society, and your name wasn't mentioned—I just guessed at it."

"Then, *ma petite Miss*, as sometimes happens even to the wisest of your sex," he said pleasantly, "you have guessed wrong. . . . I daresay the boy has joined the Lyubomudri and is making much ado about it."

I shook my head impatiently. I know about the Lyubomudri Club—Hermann told me all about them. A perfectly open club, a coterie of would-be young Fausts that meets quite openly to discuss German metaphysics. "This—secret society—what are its aims? Revolution? Seventeen-eighty-nine all over again?"

"French Revolution in Holy Russia?" Quite openly laughing at me he mimed horror. "Is such a thing possible?"

"I shouldn't think so," I said bluntly. "The Russian masses are too inert, too reconciled to their fate. . . . I should hate to see Georges drawn into a hopeless venture that can only end in his destruction. What's more, I'll do my best to keep him out of it. . . ."

"And you think you can?" he asked, mildly curious. "That is, assuming he is involved?"

"I will find a way." I leaned forward and said with all the earnestness I could muster. "I will tell you something about me, Pushchin. Not to make myself interesting, but as a way of presenting my credentials, so that you too will tell me what I want to know." And I did so, in as few words as I could—brisk, dispassionate, like an official reading a dossier. "So you see you can trust me, if only because I have given you something to hold over me."

He stared at me and roared with laughter. "Oh, women, women! Anything rather than be overlooked."

Ignoring this I repeated: "Will Georges be in danger if he joins your organization?"

Perhaps in my voice there sounded the anxious authority of a mother inquiring about her child; finally, unwillingly, he responded to it. He said shortly: "Prince Volynski is in no danger."

"That *will* be a disappointment for him," I remarked. "I am sure he'd like nothing better than to die on the barricades."

And that got me a startled look of respect.

"There is no point in wasting valuable lives, is there?" he said slowly, for once abandoning his expression of good-natured mockery. I think he was answering himself as well as me. Like a good officer, he must hate exposing his men to unnecessary danger. He went on, carefully preserving the look of talking to himself, with nobody but the house cat to overhear him. "Boys like Prince Grisha are far too important to Russia. They are the ones who will eventually reach high places and be able to influence events; they are the ones who will bring about the abolition of serfdom and set limits to the autocracy. It would serve no purpose for them to die on the barricades. . . . You are an extraordinary woman, you know, *chérie.* However did you manage to make yourself so important to a boy like Grisha without sleeping with him?"

I began dressing, and this time he made no objections. With a slight stab of regret, I saw that there would be no more lovemaking: the readiness had left his body. I said: "He knows that I will always tell him the truth."

At that he burst into laughter again. "No, no, you mustn't do that. Don't tell us the truth—that's for God and his angels and even He doesn't reveal everything. Why should you, then? Oh, but I forget. Your antecedents being what they are, you don't believe in God, do you?"

He bent on me a sweetly pitying smile. Atheism is so unwomanly, it seemed to say. . . . Nevertheless, there had been, as we talked, the slightest change, a minuscule difference in his attitude toward me. For a short while he experienced, I believe, the pleasure of being able to talk to a woman capable of understanding him about what was nearest to his heart. Oh, we shall talk again, I am sure. . . .

Claire's Journal, October 23

Tonight Hermann read us the introduction to his *Moïse*: lines breathing with revolutionary fervor, which I all at once begin to find just a little too facile.

> *Je chante le mortel, qui de la tyrannie*
> *Osa briser le sceptre, et dont heureux genie*
> *Près d'un peuple jouet d'un despote irrité*
> *Le premier ramena la douce liberté.*

But he read very well, looked very handsome while doing so, and was much applauded. Thereupon a lively discussion ensued about whether the French Revolution could ever take place in Russia—a subject of more than academic interest to me now.

I was happy to see Zahar Nikolaitch showing some of his old zest. Sorrow takes people differently. Marya Ivanovna, mourning Dunia, had gone swollen and blowsy with her grief; he had shrunk, dried up, retired into himself, that lively ironic spark in his eyes quite extinguished. Tonight was the first time since Dunia's death that he seemed like himself.

Z.N. thinks that a cataclysm like the French Revolution can only happen if it arises directly and spontaneously from the common people. But the Russian people are too deeply entrenched in their condition to rise against a Tsar no matter how oppressive. It seems that all the revolts in Russian history have taken place during the time of—the word he used was a Russian one, untranslatable. It is amazing how many untranslatable words there are in the Russian language, words that describe special Russian conditions unduplicated anywhere else. This one was *smoota*. It means, Z.N. explained, a troubled time, a time of uncertainty and confusion when the identity of the ruler is in doubt. As an example he gave the Pugachov uprising which took place during the reign of Catherine the Great. Her best generals were sent out against this simple Cossack; he was, it seems, a brilliant tactician. "The interesting part of this," Z.N. said, "is that Pugachov claimed to be Peter III, Catherine's deceased husband. Now everybody knew that that couldn't be so. Pugachov was merely an illiterate middle-aged Cossack, quite unlike in appearance to the late Tsar. But such is the people's need for an absolute ruler that even when they revolt they must be headed by a semblance of the Tsar."

"I see," I said, "the Russian people will bear anything as long as it is inflicted on them by the rightful sovereign."

Z.N. gave me an appreciative smile. "How else? After all, the Emperor even now possesses a very real spiritual power. He is, you know, the visible head of the Church."

Well, so are the British monarchs heads of the Church of England ever since Henry the VIII. But in Russia it's something much more basic and mystic; to them the Tsar is the visible emanation of God on earth, which is certainly more than any member of our royalty has ever laid claim to being. A nation with that sort of mystic adoration of its sovereign offers but a poor soil for a libertarian revolt.

Georges' visits here are taken for granted. Everybody is so used to his being my pupil, that even though that is no longer the case no comment is made about our quiet conversations together, not even by Marya Ivanovna. It's still only Prince Georges practicing his English with Miss Clairmont.

Tonight, before leaving, he asked (his voice discreetly lowered) to borrow *Political Justice*; also *Islam* which he wanted to reread. He felt, he said, with a speaking glance, that he would understand it better now. I joyfully gave it to him, together with some other writings of P.B.

Grisha did much of his reading in Tikhonovna's attic room. There, in that tiny refuge, a great sense of peace and safety would descend on him. The old lady sat rocking in her chair, humming to herself quaveringly, a constant stream of sewing flowing through her crooked old fingers. The tiny stove glowed peacefully, rustling its embers; all about him was the complicated, not unpleasant smell of incense and old tallow and harmless old-age frowst. It was strange how untrammeled his mind felt in this constricted little cell.

A library began to accumulate there, on top of Tikhonovna's

brassbound old trunk. Grisha brought up the copies of *Islam* and Godwin's *Political Justice* that Miss Clairmont had given him. To them he added Radishchev's *Journey from St. Petersburg to Moscow*, that incredible indictment of serfdom written as early as the eighteenth century, and Pushchin's copy of Professor Kunitzyn's *The Natural Rights of Man.* (The author, Pushchin's erstwhile teacher in the Lyceum, had, as a result of this book, been barred from all teaching positions.) Pushchin's pencil underscored certain passages: "A monarch's power is limited by natural rights of personal freedom, freedom of conscience and speech," and "no one has a right to own another human being, either without or with the latter's consent." Benjamin Constant's *Adolphe* stayed downstairs in his study, to be sure, but *Cours de Politique Constitutionelle* by the same author went up to the attic, as did his father's special *bête noire*, "accursed Jeremiah" Bentham. All this was probably unnecessary—nobody supervised Grisha's unbridled reading or checked up on the books he bought at Glazounov's Bookshop on Gostinnyi Yar—but highly enjoyable.

These were good days for Grisha. His incapacities were absolved, he was saved from despair and no longer alone. Like Sergey, he finally belonged—perhaps to an even larger regiment than his brother:

>   . . . a mighty brotherhood,

he said to himself, quoting rapturously from *Islam*,

>   Linked by a jealous interchange of good.

True, he met comparatively few of them in Moscow, but he was told about others and knew that he would meet them someday— "perhaps on a battlefield," he thought, not without a pleasurable quiver. He was entrusted with their names, he was privy to their activities. Thus he knew that a new fire and urgency had been brought to the meetings of the northern branch in St. Petersburg by a rising young poet named Kondratyi Ryleev. There was Nikita Muraviov—"a truly ministerial brain, our Speransky"—writing a constitution in St. Petersburg. In the south there was Sergey Muraviov-Apostol—no relation—who preached and practiced brotherhood between soldier and officer. Colonel Pavel Pestel, in Tulchino, was hard at work on an impressive project called "*The*

Russian Truth"; his powerful brain had reviewed all possible political and historical possibilities and finally emerged with the republic as the best form of government.

"But the northern branch prefers constitutional monarchy," Grisha said. "I am sorry about that—it's so splendid, the idea of the republic. . . . What about you personally, Pushchin? Wouldn't you rather have a republic?"

Pushchin didn't answer immediately. It was a mannerism of his that Grisha found singularly lovable—that slight meditative pause before answering, as though to make sure that a serious question was being properly answered. Miss Clairmont too would pause like that before answering. "That's because both of them are careful to tell me the truth," he thought and found a secret enjoyment in thus linking together the two people who were most important to him.

Pushchin said at last, puffing musingly on his pipe: "What Pestel envisions is the downfall of monarchy and a transition from total slavery to total liberty, including reapportioning of property and abolition of rank."

"Eldest of things—divine Equality," Grisha murmured irresistibly. One of his great pleasures nowadays was the miraculous aptness of so many lofty quotations. This one too came from *Islam*.

". . . Well—how is all this to be accomplished? According to him, through an autocratic rule of the provisional government set up for ten to fifteen years, complete with secret police, censorship, whatever is necessary to enforce the totality of equality and freedom."

"Enforce—freedom?"

Pushchin's eyebrows rose. Mildly ironic he asked: "How else do you suppose a handful of idealists is going to see the realization of their ideals? In a vast country like Russia?"

Grisha was about to mention *Islam's* mild and highminded revolutionaries who proceeded on quite different principles when he remembered that, as a result, they had been wiped out to a man.

"No, Pestel is nothing if not logical, and I see his point and admire the grandeur of his aspirations. But I have a very limited and literal mind, I am afraid. When I hear of censorship, even though it may be imposed for the loftiest possible reasons, I can't help thinking about my poor Cricket who under Pestel's provisional government might have to be kept out of circulation—for the good of the Republic—just as he is now. And that consideration, I'll admit, gives me pause."

Somewhat deflated, Grisha inquired: "Then you don't believe the republican form of government is best?"

"No, I wouldn't say that. It is the most desirable form of government, actually: certainly its most natural form. I just am not sure that Pestel's version of it appeals to me—the will of a few chosen elitists imposed upon a population that knows very little about it."

"What then?" Grisha demanded, baffled. "What are you for?"

"I am, I suppose, for whatever could be achieved without those immoderate convulsions that usually end up by warping precisely the goals you are after. . . . It's a question of personality, I daresay," he added, almost apologetically, "I am a slow-moving man by nature."

"And yet—forgive me, Ivan Ivanitch, but aren't there some questions that should be resolved fast? As, for example, the abolition of serfdom?"

"Yes, a fateful issue. Yet here too one cannot move as fast as one wants to: there are several important aspects to be considered." Again he took his time, considering them, as he refilled his pipe. As so often, Grisha, looking at his contemplative profile, was struck by the intriguing contrast between the stern thinker's forehead and the faintly pursed sensualist's lips. "For one, freeing the serf would be meaningless unless you also let him have land. The Russian peasant is closely tied to the land he cultivates: if he is separated from it, he will have to migrate to the city. There are too many as it is flooding the cities, looking for work, with their owners' consent, in order to pay their quit rent. And they hate it—I know, I constantly come in touch with them in my line of work. What they want is land. Even more than freedom. . . . An acquaintance of mine tried to free his serfs once. Well, he had trouble with the government, that was to be expected—but also with his peasants. They immediately asked him, what about the land? Well, he says, you'll be free people, you can rent it from me, and tried to explain how it would work. They listen to him, the little peasants, they scratch their heads; finally they say: 'Tell you what, *barin*, let's go on being yours and let the land be ours.' And that's about what I get from the beaten-up little countrymen that come up to Moscow.

[237]

They wouldn't know about the republic nor care, really: 'anything your Honor pleases, just so I can breathe easier.'" Pushchin paused; then he said with the faint surprise of a man who following doggedly a circuitous road unexpectedly comes up head on to his objective: "That's what the republic means to me, I suppose: the public thing—making life easier for the little people—letting them have what they legitimately want."

Claire's Journal, October 25

I wish it were possible for me to share—even though only vicariously—in Georges' new subterranean activity. But, alas, it is out of the question.

Even telling me as much as he has, apparently, was wrong. It seems a member is prohibited from disclosing his activities even to his wife—such absurdity! With some asperity, I inquired: "I daresay there are no women members?"

Georges opened his eyes wide: such a possibility had not even occurred to him. Of course not! All women are allowed to do is to stand by, smiling bravely, while their men go about their disastrously managed business. Only later, when everything goes to rack and ruin—ah, yes, *then* their services are indeed called upon, to share the misery, to mourn.

When Albé sailed away to Greece, I couldn't have cared less what happened to him. But my heart went out to his poor little Countess, poor wretch. The last great love—but only good enough to share his bed, not his fate.

Meanwhile, poor Georges is terribly contrite about having to keep a secret from me. "I have taken an oath of secrecy, you see. . . . Are you angry?"

He scanned my face anxiously. Well, so I was, but not at him, as I hurried to tell him. Not even at Pushchin, who, I am sure, is having his bit of quiet fun at thus balking my curiosity. Just at the situation. These glib complications *à la* Marivaux: he doesn't know that she knows that he knows. . . . Sordid and ridiculous.

I should like nothing better than to be quite open with

Georges. But that would mean having to disclose my affair with Pushchin; and *that* has nothing to do with him.

An uncomfortable thought: suppose he were to ask me outright about Pushchin? Would I tell him? I think I would have to. Everything between us is based on the premise that I always tell him the truth.

A purely academic speculation. Fortunately, that is not a question he is ever likely to ask me.

Clare's Journal, October 26

One really does learn better with age. Even I do, it seems. Whatever is told me now is told freely, without inner reservations. I haven't pressed Georges about his secret society. Nor about the little housemaid, mysteriously dead.

Not that he would hold such confidences against me the way Albé did. Georges' is a naturally generous soul, free of suspicions. Some people have such a bad opinion of themselves, are so eaten up with self-hatred that they see any revelation of themselves as something that can be used against them later. . . . I think if not for that things might have been different. He might have been kinder, he might have been able to give me the half-contemptuous affection that men show women after they had fallen out of love with them. He might have let me see my baby. . . . But no, once he stopped loving me, he had to hate me, because he had let me see too deeply into him. I became a danger to him, he saw me as a sort of malevolent witch in possession of a lock of his hair or a piece of his clothing to use in some deadly brew for his destruction. As if I would ever want to hurt him with what I knew! All I had ever wanted was to do him good—to be of use to him. . . .

One wouldn't have expected joining a secret society to enlarge one's social life: nevertheless Grisha found it to be so.

"*Il faut circuler, mon cher*," Pushchin told him. "After all, we are a very small portion of yeast working in a very large and inert body. Recruiting is one of our most important tasks."

Grisha had already been made aware of the extreme paucity of the Moscow membership. The society had its best strength in St. Petersburg and in the southern provinces where most of the army was stationed. Moscow, on the other hand, had never been a military center. With exasperation Grisha thought of his brother, strategically placed right in the middle of things. All of it wasted on Sergey, going with simple zest about his regimental duties and revels, in total ignorance of the momentous stirrings around him! Now, if he, Grisha, were in his place, enviably, an officer in the Preobrazhensky Regiment—he envisioned himself engaging in all sorts of profitable revolutionary activities, proselytizing brother officers, earning his men's devotion, doing all he could to improve their minds as well as their lot. As Orlov did once.

"Orlov *is* one of us, isn't he?" A question he asked whenever he met any of Pushchin's friends, who like Pushchin served in Moscow's administrative and judicial departments. Some of them indeed were members. The greater part, however, were merely sympathizers who knew a great deal about the society and could be trusted.

"Misha Orlov was one of the original founders," Pushchin answered. "But he got out a few years ago: he was getting married and his wife's family made him promise to do so. We shall have to try to bring him back to the fold while he is still in Moscow."

"And Pushkin? Is he too—is he one of us?"

But Pushchin shook his head. "No, it's enough for him to be what he is, Russia's greatest poet." As always when he spoke of his friend, his calm voice was colored with special tenderness.

"Oh, yes, oh, yes, of course. I only thought he would want to be . . ."

"So he did. We had a devil of a time keeping him out. No, he is far too precious to risk. Besides, the dear fellow can't keep anything to himself: he would immediately land himself and all of us in trouble. . . . But when I read him, Grisha, I know he is what it's all about. . . . You don't mind my calling you by your first name, do you? I must confess I've rather taken to regarding you as a younger brother."

Grisha, blushing with pleasure, assured him that he was only too delighted.

That same evening Grisha accompanied Pushchin to one of Princess Zinaide Volkonski's celebrated soirées. Her magnificent house on Tverskaya was famous. Moscow's foremost intellectuals frequented it, and there was always some choice entertainment, a concert or a play and, very often, a reading of some controversial piece of literature unavailable to the general public. That night there was to be a reading of *Woe by Wit*, that brilliant and acerbic comedy by Griboyedov, which censorship kept from appearing on the stage but which was nevertheless well known to everyone in Moscow and St. Petersburg: handwritten copies of it had been in circulation ever since it had been written.

Grisha, who ordinarily abominated crowded affairs, found that he quite enjoyed himself. For one, the Princess preferred *routs*, social functions that dispense with dancing, so that there was no need for him to take his usual Byronic stance on the sidelines while everybody else danced. And then the company that filled the salon was of a quite different caliber from the kind encountered either in the snug private assemblies or the stiff official receptions. Here conversations sparkled, witty and uninhibited. You constantly found yourself on the perimeter of some lively discussion. Ancestral portraits, tucked away in between lush Italian oils and marble statuary, seemed to stare with sour displeasure at the irreverent talkers beneath them. "What you need, good sirs, is an old-fashioned whipping," those darkened bilious faces seemed to say.

Among these groups, the hostess moved, shedding on all her languorous smile. Princess Zinaide was known all over Moscow as the Tenth Muse, and deliberately dressed up to the flattering sobriquet. As was her custom on these occasions, she wore a simple white robe, falling in classical folds about her opulent body. Her crisp dark hair was dressed *à la grecque* and her genius of a coiffeur had even managed to impart to it a certain look of "divine dishevelment," as though it were blown upon by the breath of inspiration: an exquisitely wrought emerald and gold laurel wreath rested on it. But for all her poetic languors, she was a superb hostess; she greeted every guest with graciousness, saw to it that her liveried footmen never stopped circulating among the company with refreshments and wine, and in the end quite efficiently got everybody seated to hear the reading.

The Princess had engaged the famous actor Mochalov to do the reading. He was primarily a tragedian; but he read with fine sardonic verve the role of the hero, young Chatski, who, returning from abroad, comes up against the impenetrable reaction of the society and is defeated by it. Grisha was charmed by the protean skill with which the great actor managed to evoke a crowd of well-known Moscow characters. Occasionally, as the laughter of recognition interrupted him, a small relishing smile slipped over Mochalov's flexible lips: as much as anyone he enjoyed this witty flagellation of the Moscow society. But the *clou* of the performance was the bitter monologue attacking its special representatives, the heartless and corrupt official, the brutal landowner lording it over hordes of serf attendants:

> Both life and honor oft they saved for him
> Among his drunken brawls—

Mochalov read in his magnificently modulated voice,

>   —now at a whim
> They're traded out of hand for three borzoys . . .

"One of us, he must be one of us," Grisha whispered, kindling.

> And here's another, avid for ballet,
> By hundreds brings for Moscow's delectation
> Young children from their parents torn away;
> But creditors will not allow delay;
> And so, to give them gold,
> Cupids and zephyrs, one by one, are sold.

Grisha fancied that there was a special tremor in Mochalov's voice as he read those lines: he had been born a serf.

After the reading was over, Grisha met the playwright's cousin, Prince Alexander Odoevski, a young officer in the Mounted Life Guards.

"A new admirer of your relative, Sasha," said Pushchin, introducing him. He addressed the young man familiarly, having known him well in St. Petersburg.

"Yes, he has made me understand for the first time why satire is a much more effective weapon than a sermon," Grisha said. Ordinarily he was too shy to talk at length in front of a stranger; but there was a reassuring friendliness about the slim elegant youth. "When he talks about serfdom, for example . . . It's easy enough to say serfdom is morally wrong—but when it's shown beyond a doubt that to own human beings is not just wrong, but disgusting, ignoble—downright *mean*, you know "—momentarily shifting into English he used Miss Clairmont's special word of disapprobation—"now, that gets under one's skin, don't you think?"

The young officer listened attentively. A shining young man—he had a way of slowly brightening when he listened to something that pleased him, as if the wick of a lamp inside him were being gradually turned up. He suddenly stretched his hand to Grisha. "I can see that you think about these matters as I do. As all people concerned for Russia must. You must be ours." There was an archaic, quaint, knightly flavor about this impulsive utterance. Grisha, flushing with pleasure, took his outstretched hand and returned its quick warm pressure.

"Good boys, dear boys," said Pushchin paternally, patting them both on the shoulder. "But don't bother to convert him, Sasha, *c'est déjà fait.*"

He walked off, leaving them handfast and embarrassed. Odoevski shed his embarrassment first. "He's making fun of me, *ce bon Jeannot,*" he said smiling. "That's exactly what I've been doing ever since I came to Moscow: trying to convert my cousin Vladimir. Do you know him? No? Well, his views are very liberal, he thinks basically just as we do. He's the editor of *Mnemosyne*, you know, and he's always meeting with the Lyubomudri to talk about freedom, and discussing Schelling and Montesquieu and all that. But I said to him straight away, that's just talk, if you mean what you say, if you're for freedom, you join, otherwise it doesn't mean a thing. . . ." His clear eyes rested on Grisha with smiling trust. "That's what *I* did, as soon as I knew how I felt."

"Yes, I too—and it feels so much better, quite different from before. . . ."

Odoevski looked about him smiling with pleasure. "This is a terribly nice place. And Zinaide is a darling, I am so fond of her. Do you know what she told me just now?" He paused impressively. A revelation, terribly important, something that would forever seal this budding friendship, seemed to tremble on his smiling lips. "They have a cook that makes the most marvelous *pirozhnoye*. My favorite desert. Well, I happened to mention it the other day, and that's what they are serving tonight. . . . I am afraid I love sweets. I even keep lemon drops in my pockets when I am standing guard," he confided seriously.

Grisha kept a lookout for Orlov whenever he came to a soirée, but it wasn't until his third visit in early November, that he saw his handsome arrogant head towering above the crowd. He accompanied Pushchin, who went over to speak with Orlov, and was surprised to find that he too was remembered. The original invitation was repeated: "Do visit us. We don't go out much nowadays, my wife is expecting, but we are always delighted to have company. . . . By the way," he said to Pushchin, "another old Arzamasian has paid me a visit—to wit, Adelstan." Orlov pronounced this romantically improbable name with a half-humorous, half-nostalgic air. Pushchin bent his brows over it for a moment.

"Oh, Nikita Muraviov," he said, "I'd forgotten that old nickname. Yes, he told me you were one of the people he especially wanted to see during his stay in Moscow."

Muraviov—that was the creator of the constitution, the new Speranski. Grisha felt a stir of excitement. Something was up!

"Well," Orlov said carelessly, "he had some interesting news—or rumors—to impart. The Emperor, it seems, is thinking of making the Guard part of the military colonies. . . . I suppose that's not impossible. The Emperor has distrusted the Guard ever since the Semyonovski affair. That sort of thing upsets him. He is on the timorous side, you know." Orlov was speaking of the Tsar with slightly contemptuous regret, as though he were an acquaintance who had turned out otherwise than expected. "What was it the Cricket wrote recently?

At Austerlitz he fain would flee,
In year 12 fairly shivered he . . .

And of course he's terrified of the lot of you."

All this was said in a clear loud voice. Pushchin listened with the shadow of the same expression that Grisha had seen on Governor Golitzin's face that first time he saw Orlov. Apparently now as then the tall General didn't care who listened to him.

"At any rate, as I told Muraviov, my times are gone—let the younger folk take over. Like this one. Now confess, Prince, old Pushchin here has caught you in his illicit net, hasn't he?" Orlov demanded, smiling.

"It would be more accurate to say," Grisha answered, flushing, "that I sought the honor myself."

"Bravo! Bravo!" Orlov struck his white-gloved hands together lightly. "So you're recruiting fledglings now, Jeannot? Well, why not? One must have childish faith to think of making revolution in Russia, God knows."

"About Muraviov," Pushchin said, "that bit about the Guard is nonsense, of course, just exploratory talk. . . ."

"Yes, I rather thought he told all this to me to set me pawing the ground, like a retired warhorse . . ."

"But he does intend to call a meeting as soon as Fonvizin comes in from the country. You ought to attend it, Misha."

"Ah!" A slight smile stirred between the little moustaches that framed Orlov's well-shaped mouth like two elegant apostrophes. "Another draft of the famous constitution to be discussed in detail? That was the main reason I left, you know. Nobody was more earnest than I in those days, until I perceived that all that was wanted was talk and more talk."

Pushchin sighed. "Yes, a national failing. To quote from *Woe by Wit*, 'We make noise, brother, just make noise . . .' But much less now, things are too serious. I think I can safely assure you that Nikita Muraviov hasn't come all the way from St. Petersburg to Moscow to lecture on his constitution."

Orlov listened, curly head thrown back as he contemplated the ceiling painted in the Italian style by Princess Zinaide's painting tutor. "I'll tell you what, my friend Jeannot," he said finally, "I am really not interested in any more discussions. But when you—and only you, my dear friend, because I trust your good sense and honesty implicitly—tell me that the time has come to act, then I shall consider it seriously. . . .I'm leaving now, before I am required to take our hostess in to supper. I am getting fatter than an Arzamasian gander, as it is, from those damned Moscow suppers. . . . *Au revoir, mes amis.*" With a friendly nod, he departed.

Although Mikhail Alexandrovich Fonvizin, retired Major General, was a married man, his house on Starokonyushnaya Street retained the appearance of a luxurious bachelor establishment. His study was full of the souvenirs of his Caucasian days when he served under the famous General Ermolov: Persian carpets, brightly arabesqued, covering floor and walls; a sizable collection of pistols and swords ornamented with that special blackened Cauca-

[245]

sian silver that is dear to the heart of the romantic young. Grisha, looking at them, at once thought of the Terek boiling down steep mountainsides and barbaric chieftains riding away with the heroines draped over their saddles. But in the middle of all that military nostalgia a large "Voltairean" armchair of green Moroccan leather, with piles of books balanced on both wide armrests, spoke of its owner's sedentary book-loving tastes. Fonvizin himself, although he smoked a long oriental *chubuk*, lacked the romantic look. He was a soft-spoken, ponderously moving man in his middle thirties, whose military bearing had relaxed into a comfortable slouch. He greeted Grisha with gentle, almost sorrowful cordiality.

Grisha retired quietly into a corner from which he respectfully watched other guests as they wandered up and down the large room, lighting their pipes, drinking tea, talking in quiet although not necessarily conspiratorial tones. His first meeting! He was full of suppressed excitement; his eyes roamed unfocused from face to face, and only after a while was he able to attach names to faces. Some of them he already knew as Pushchin's colleagues in the judicial department; others were army men, among whom he recognized Colonel Mitkov of the Finlandski Regiment, also a friend of Pushchin's. They were all much older than he; after a while his youth began to embarrass him, making him feel as though he was there on false pretenses. He was greatly cheered when young Prince Odoevski came in, glittering and smiling in his bright uniform, and after making the round of the room noticed him and took the seat next to him. Bye-and-bye he took out a paper cornet full of lemon drops and offered Grisha one. Grisha declined, inwardly shocked: a lemon drop at a meeting of the secret society!

Nikita Muraviov arrived last. Grisha looked at him with wondering respect, as he took his place behind Fonvizin's big cluttered desk. He saw a slightly built man, neither handsome nor imposing: a yellowish face, strongly marked lips, near-sighted eyes in brownish hollows. In spite of the captain's uniform he wore, he had a half-professorial, half-bureaucratic air.

He began by listing new members conscripted in St. Petersburg. He had a way of pausing after each name, sending a portentous glance into his audience—every time he did so, Grisha would involuntarily follow this look to its destination and find only polite attention there: evidently it was a mere mannerism. He had another, less attractive one of cleaning his ear with a rapidly vibrating index finger at which he then looked attentively.

". . . In May of last year, as you know, Ryleev recruited Captain Vladimir Yakubovich of the Caucasian Division." The pause, the steady stare. "Yakubovich has made an offer to the St. Petersburg duma. He would, he said, attempt the Tsar's life during the maneuvers."

It was the same monotonous utterance with which he had listed the other business, and for a moment Grisha did not take it in. In the front row Pushchin sat up straighter, his pipe arrested halfway to his mouth.

". . . and I am here, gentlemen, to ask the opinion of the Moscow chapter on this proposal." Sitting down at the desk, a well-sharpened pencil in his hand, he turned himself into a scribe.

Pushchin's voice said calmly: "We should like to hear St. Petersburg's reaction to this proposal."

The neat head above its stiff red-piped collar swung in his direction. "It was deemed judicious to postpone the attempt. Yakubovich, most reluctantly, agreed to hold off for another six months. His feelings *envers* Alexander are quite bitter. He thinks himself unjustly overlooked in the matter of decorations for what were his undoubtedly heroic exploits in the Caucasus. He was wounded in the head, you know, chasing the local chieftains."

A chuckle came from the burly Mitkov. "That black silk bandage he wears made a great sensation while he was here. The Moscow ladies succumbed by the dozens."

Grisha, listening with stunned attention, suddenly realized that he actually knew the potential regicide: Sergey had pointed him out at an assembly. The mention of the black silk bandage did it: the whole man leaped into his memory—black kerchief, black drooping moustaches, consciously "fatal" eyes, a sudden savage smile disclosing a white snarl, all the trappings of a Byronic hero so assiduously cultivated as to be suspect. Yet Sergey too had assured him that Yakubovich was the real thing: "They say Pushkin wanted to use him as model for *The Caucasian Prisoner*." And the wound under the theatrical bandage was real enough.

"Incidentally," Muraviov added, "he's a crack shot. That's why he was exiled to Caucasus in the first place: too many duels."

There was a pause. Grisha looked fearfully at Pushchin. But he seemed unprepared to say anything else. Sucking contemplatively at his pipe, he settled back in his chair, waiting for others to speak. Presently Fonvizin did so. "Apropos of that whole business of assassination," he said, his somewhat sheeplike face drawn up into a grimace of distaste, "do you seriously think, my dear Nikita Mikhailitch, that the fact of Alexander being treacherously shot from ambush would bring the troops rallying to our colors?"

"It's a problem. And yet . . ." Muraviov thoughtfully took out a pocketknife and began sharpening still another pencil. "One must begin somewhere, mustn't one?"

"It isn't so much the question of where to begin as where to stop. Alexander has heirs—Constantine, Nikolai, Mikhail . . ."

"Yes—well, presumably Alexander's death would be the signal for, first, the uprising, second, the takeover by the provisional government," said Muraviov, counting off on his thin fingers, "third, the proclamation that would render this a constitutional monarchy under whichever ruler we find fit. . . ."

"Which one of the Grand Dukes would treat with an organization that had executed their brother?"

"Alexander treated with his father's murderers," said a voice from the back.

"There is still another alternative," Muraviov again, didactic. "Pestel says, '*il faut avoir la maison nette.*' According to him the entire Imperial family should be eradicated."

There was unreal feeling about all this: they were just a group of acquaintances gathered together to talk politics, to discuss the abstract possibilities of revolutionary change. Something quite different from the furtive bloody trappings of unholy conspiracy that his father had intimated. And yet, upon reflection, perhaps that was the very inwardness of conspiracy. For, sitting here in the cozy drift of pipe smoke, with samovar glowing at a table nearby and servants discreetly bringing in refreshments, the unbelievable became an everyday thing, banal and domestic: you found yourself calmly listening to people you knew calmly discussing the advisability of killing the Tsar. Was it only a few months ago that he had looked at Pushchin's darkened face and asked, with indignant wonder: "Don't you love the Tsar?"

"Does Colonel Pestel suppose that that sort of wholesale massacre would be accepted by the people with equanimity?" Fonvizin asked incredulously.

Muraviov's thin shoulders rose in a shrug: "I was merely listing the possibilities for the members. . . . As for me, I am inclined to agree with you. It would indeed be an embarrassment to the Provisional Government."

Fonvizin got up and began to pace the room with his bearish tread, ponderous and soft at once. "About seven years ago, in this very room, another young man offered to kill the Tsar to preserve Russia. He would take two guns along with him: the second one to be used on himself—this would be a deed, he said, that couldn't—mustn't—be survived by its perpetrator. . . ."

Grisha's eyes dilated. Yes, he could see *that*, that would be how he himself. . . . He muttered disjointedly, unconscious of speaking: "Yes—a holy sacrifice—a sacrifice to God . . ." Odoevski's voice echoed him, low and trembling, "Give your life as well—who would want to live afterward?"

"Yakubovich is utterly unlike that selfless and dedicated young man," Fonvizin pursued. "*His* motives are questionable. We are not agreed on the very advisability of regicide. But, if we do decide on it, it would have to be a holy sacrifice, as our young friend put it, and it would have to be done with a clean weapon. Yakubovich is not that."

"Again I agree," said Muraviov. "Such an action must be performed as part of a plan, not at the convenience of an individual. And the instrument used"—again he performed the unattractive mannerism of cleaning his ear and glancing at the finger—"should be kept distinct from the society. The attitude of the young man you mentioned, Mikhail Alexandrovich, was the correct one: ideally speaking, after its function is completed, the instrument should eliminate itself."

"Ah," said Pushchin gravely, "you mustn't expect Yakubovich to oblige the society in that way." There was a distinct undertone of amusement in his sober voice.

Fonvizin's good-natured face was stony. "I am almost tempted to send an anonymous warning to the authorities around the Tsar. Without mentioning names, naturally."

"I don't think that's necessary," Pushchin said. He rocked back and forth on his chair, reflectively. "It's not all that hard to kill the Tsar, you know. He goes riding all by himself every day at a certain time, followed by one aide. . . . Yakubovich could have done so any time these past three years—ever since he came back from Caucasus with that handsome black scarf wrapped around his head. But"—he brought the chair legs down with an emphatic little thump—"he didn't. He's a vain man and a violent one, I agree. Still, the flattering attention paid him by the society should be enough to satisfy his vanity. . . . But he must be restrained rather than inflamed, as I am sure Ryleev knows. . . ."

"I told you he promised to hold off for the next six months."

"But his services were not altogether refused?"

Muraviov glanced at his nails. "Well . . . The St. Petersburg duma feels that no possibilities should be overlooked. Look at the southern branch: I hear they have a *cohorte perdue*, a dozen men, ready and willing. All we have is Yakubovich. . . . We regard him in the nature of a weapon, safely put away——"

"Just make sure the safety is on," Pushchin said quietly. "We really mustn't play games, you know. . . ."

His tone was like a splash of cool water on Grisha's flushed face.

Muraviov, scribbling busily, said in his pedantic voice, "Then the sense of the meeting is that the Moscow branch is categorically against such an attempt on the Tsar's life?" An acquiescent murmur answered him.

The meeting was at an end.

"You are perfectly right, of course," Odoevski said to Pushchin afterward, as they drove home in Grisha's carriage. "It's probably the easiest thing in the world to kill the Emperor. Why, take me—I myself have often been assigned to stand guard in the Winter Palace, I've come face to face with him. . . . He always has something nice to say when he comes out—and then that smile. . . ." Odoevski sighed. "But he looked sad in September before he left for Taganrog. . . . As if he knew. . . ."

"Knew what, Sasha?" Pushchin asked.

"Oh, all manner of sad things—about all of us—about Yakubovich. . . . I know it's all nonsense—it's just that way he has of looking right at you, into your soul, it makes something happen inside of you. Like falling in love. . . ."

"Yes, the royal seducer. . . ." Pushchin murmured.

Grisha remembered that joyous involuntary uplift of the enchanted soul, on seeing Alexander: "Anything, anything for him. . . ." And now?

". . . That's why I am not really worrying: Yakubovich couldn't do it, no one could. He'd simply look at you and your hand wouldn't rise. Would yours, Grisha?"

Grisha shook his head. "No, I remember reading about Brutus, and thinking, *I* couldn't. . . . But then I'm not a soldier by profession, just a squeamish civilian."

"That has nothing to do with it. No, it's him, it's the love that springs up in your heart when he looks at you. . . ."

"But if that's how you feel—" Grisha began and stopped.

"Why am I a member? What else can an honorable man be nowadays? *Je veux vivre comme un être sensible, pas comme un pauvre vegeteur.* . . . Yes, I know he's responsible for what is happening today. . . . And yet there's always that feeling that he doesn't know, that if he knew about us, what we want, he'd be with us. . . ."

"I shouldn't count on that," Pushchin remarked dryly.

They all fell silent. The sledge skimmed silently over the well-packed snow, that seemed to glimmer with its own suppressed radiance. The streets were deserted; occasionally other sledges passed them or came swiftly toward them in the same ghostly snow-muted silence. Above them, night sky was bathed in curious pink luminescence, reflecting the glow of the streetlamps.

Claire's Journal, November 24

Last night I stood by the window watching the snow whirling down and listening to the tuneful clamor of the church bells. Georges asked me what I was thinking. I hesitated to answer: I didn't really want to talk about it. But the immediate change of expression on his face told me that I must. Not to would have seemed a petty retaliation; you won't tell me your secrets so I shan't tell you mine. Despite everything he still feels guilty about his enforced silence concerning the secret society.

So I told him what the bells made me think of: the time P.B. came back from visiting my little Allegra in the convent at Bagnacavallo where she was immured. Bless him, he did that for me as soon as he knew about this arrangement, to be ready with whatever bit of comfort he could distill out of the wretchedness. My poor imprisoned bird—I saw her thin, pale, her spirit broken. She used to be such a gay little girl. . . . P.B. did reassure me. He told me how the two of them played during his visit, romping all over that sleepy old convent. Finally she hid in the belfry and rang all the bells out of tune, "anticlerical imp that she was," P.B. had said, laughing his special laugh, whose shrillness never drowned out the sweetness.

"It doesn't sound as though she was mistreated," Georges remarked, relief showing in his kind young face.

"Oh, no, the nuns were simple, not too clever women, fond of children; and then too they were impressed by her parentage. . . ." I caught my breath as the old grievance swept back, full force. "So that was to be the superior education for a daughter of a great English poet—to be taught pious dogma, to have her bright little mind blunted and tamed. But then of course she was only his bastard—it was quite different for little Miss Legitimacy back in London with her mother." All my hatred hissed out in these words, and Georges looked at me troubled.

He said to me the other day, "You speak of him differently from the way you did during the summer." Ah, but it was different then!

Such a good summer—beguiled by its genial warmth, I had actually begun to live and feel again, to remember the happy things, love as yet unsullied, hopes unbetrayed. . . . Yes, I had been happy then, with the illusion of my child returned to me, day blending into idyllic day, each accompanied by its shadowy counterpart, a ghost of another happy summer, my Geneva summer, keeping pace with it. All over now, both of them—Dunia and Allegra both dead. . . . *His* fault, his . . .

Claire's Journal, November 25

One can't be selective about memories: open the door a crack for one privileged prisoner and the whole disreputable crew comes jostling out. *He* wrote that once: "The thought goes through—yes, through . . ."

And now—no help for it—protesting, reluctant, I am

drawn backward in time, I am back again in the garden of our Marlow house, with my little girl. Mary's neat figure is framed in the window she has thrown open to call me, her bright brown curls blown back. I can see it all, like a painting of something caught at a portentous moment: *Mary Calling Claire to Come and Read the Letter.*

Oh, that letter . . . Once a poem fell out of the pages of a manuscript he had sent to P.B., a poem that could only be meant for me. Something about a voice *like music o'er the waters.* I don't remember any more. I used to repeat that poem like a spell, and abruptly, vindictively forgot every word of it when I began to hate him.

But I still remember every word of that letter.

All night long I pored over it in the little room I shared with my sweet little love. What was he really saying to me? Once I would have known immediately. Words would have been mere husks out of which I would have picked unerringly the kernel of meaning. But it had been so long—almost too long—a little more and I couldn't have read beyond the surface. . . . Even now I wonder if I . . . That nightmarelike doubt to be kept off at any price. . . .

No, I couldn't have read it wrong. So I kept my promise and he—liar! murderer!—he repudiated his.

"You and Hermann were talking about me yesterday, weren't you?" Miss Clairmont asked and immediately tempered the question by a disarming smile, deceptively artless. "I don't know how it is but one always unerringly *knows.* . . ." She was embroidering; her quick fingers raced over the hoop with the same impatient yet controlled energy with which they struck music from the keys. "No, it's really quite all right, Georges, so you needn't look ill at ease. I've told you before, I don't mind my friends discussing me." Her dark eyebrows gave their comic twitch. "The thing is eventually I like to join in the discussion."

Grisha laughed with her and conceded that that had indeed been the case. "Something I wanted to know and couldn't ask you, for fear of giving you pain. . . ."

The subject had been Allegra.

"You are perfectly right," Gambs had said with gravity, "it would be unkind to talk to Claire about the circumstances under which her daughter was given to that heartless man. . . . Particularly after a similar loss has awakened all the painful memories."

He had meant Dunia. But Dunia had been snatched away by an enemy there was no gainsaying. The other little girl—nobody had torn her out of Miss Clairmont's vainly resisting arms; it seemed she had been given away freely, no attempt to withhold her had been made.

". . . I don't think you quite understand Claire's position," Gambs had said, tucking his handsome square chin into his snowy neckcloth. "There were so many considerations. Claire couldn't withhold the child from the father who obviously could do her so much more good than she could herself. She was young and poor, you know, and so were her relatives. And there were other weighty reasons why it was important for the child's father to acknowledge her—why Claire actually owed it to those whose life she shared to make this sacrifice. . . ."

Grisha found it irritating that Monsieur Gambs, whose lectures were so lucid and lively, who with one cut of his ferrule across the map could show so clearly why certain trade routes were logical results of certain geographic conditions—why that same Monsieur Gambs would lapse into a special style, strangled and gnomic, whenever he talked about Miss Clairmont. He had waited for elucidation but in vain. Monsieur Gambs had had his say on the subject of Miss Clairmont and her child.

"Dearest Hermann is a bit pompous at times," Miss Clairmont remarked after Grisha had finished repeating that conversation. "To put it plainly, Georges, what he meant was that, since there was no legitimate father in the offing, it was only reasonable for the world to assume that P.B. was the father of my Allegra. That was one of the things Albé saw fit to mention in that famous letter." She pattered it off with bitter glibness: "'I am perfectly aware that a child of dubious parentage living with her unmarried mother in a household as vulnerable to attack as yours presents a very ambiguous situation, unfair to everybody concerned.' . . . Hypocrite," she added scornfully.

"Oh, I see. How terrible for all of you. . . ."

Miss Clairmont's shoulders performed a small shrug under her warm but unbecoming dove-colored shawl. It occurred to Grisha that she did not dress becomingly. Her colors should have been brilliantly gypsyish, but because of her profession she was constrained to wear respectably subdued colors that emphasized the sallowness of her skin.

"We were used to calumnies. P.B. certainly didn't mind, bless him. 'I do feel as though she were mine,' he would say. 'So absurd to apportion children like property. . . .' Mary minded. She had taken the necessary steps toward respectability, she had gone through the ritual of marriage with P.B.—to the great delight of that famous freethinker, her father. No matter how much she tried to discount it, this sort of slander was a thorn in her flesh. And, besides, another indigent relative for P.B. to support, another mouth to feed . . . But she was good about it—yes, Mary was always good. She said to me, 'You mustn't, if you don't want to, we'll manage.' Nevertheless, after saying this, and with utmost sincerity, she couldn't help but be relieved when I recounted to her all the reasons why it would be best for Allegra to be brought up by her father—yes, and found it only too easy to believe them. . . ."

Grisha considered this.

"Then they weren't the true reasons?"

Miss Clairmont's eyelids went down slowly, the long eyelashes throwing fanlike shadows on her sallow cheeks. Unsmilingly she shook her head.

Grisha was aware of a small glow of gratification. Miss Clairmont did not fail him: the reasonable, workaday explanation was there only to mislead an ordinary mind; inside it there would be another, something totally original, slightly canted, completely suitable to the special, not-to-be-duplicated circumstances that usually surrounded Miss Clairmont. This true reason for it all would be yielded to him alone, to no one else, not even Monsieur Gambs who called her Claire and thought he knew all about her.

She said: "That letter asking for Allegra . . . I had been waiting for something like that. A part of me recoiled in dismay; another part was triumphant: at last, at last the time had come—he was asking me for a sign of affirmation, an act of faith."

"And—you gave it to him?"

"It had always been understood that I would," she said austerely. "I had promised to do so."

"Promised to give him your baby?"

"To give him whatever he wanted; any time, no matter how precious to me. 'Only try me, Geordie, you'll see . . .' A wild audacious promise made by an eighteen-year-old romantic wholly intent on what she wanted . . . But he had needed it, you see. He was ten years older but he was a romantic too. It made all the difference in the world to him to know that there was one person in the world who would do anything for him. That's why he could love me in Geneva; he knew, finally, that it was safe to trust me and that I would give him a visible proof of it when he needed it. . . ."

This was exactly like the tales Tikhonovna used to tell him. Apparently Miss Clairmont too had been a citizen of that country where extravagant promises were made and punctiliously kept, and firstborn children of credulous queens given away in return for their heart's desire. . . . Which upon being granted invariably turned to dust.

Misunderstanding, for once, his involuntary smile, she said: "You think this was self-deception again. I don't blame you. But it wasn't, not this time. That was made perfectly clear in his letter. He had said"—again she lapsed into a glib patter—"'If Claire will send the child to me in Italy, I shall do my part. I believe that we had an understanding to that effect. . . .' There it was! Even P.B. knew what that meant. 'He is putting you to the test, isn't he?' he said. So, you see . . ."

Grisha nodded, convinced. Not until later did it occur to him how strange it was that he should accept so unquestioningly the judgment of a man he had never met. "And he—P.B.—thought you should do this? Send him Allegra?"

And for the first time he was aware of a reserve, a withholding, so uncharacteristic of her that its very presence made him watchful. He persisted: "What *did* he say about it?"

She said, "I don't quite remember . . ."—sounding all at once almost sulky and even sly like a child questioned by its elders about something it doesn't want to discuss. "You know," she said with a little laugh, "you probably have a somewhat unrealistic picture of our relationship, mine and P.B.'s: two perfectly attuned souls floating together in syrupy ambiance, like those insipid angels in Raphael's *Transfiguration*. Not so. We disagreed, we even fought; I would storm at him, and he replied in kind, his voice going shrill with anger. Needless to say he was more often angry in my behalf than at me: how he would rage when Albé . . ."

"Then he disapproved?"

She gave him a trapped look. "Approved! Disapproved! Those

[256]

are meaningless words. They don't enter into the situation at all. He knew that I had to—that with everything that had happened before . . ." The clever hands faltered and the needle flashed out of the embroidery plunging like a tiny serpent's fang into her finger. A bright crimson globule welled up and stained the silk. "'Take care of what you are about, Claire,' he said. Oh, I knew what I was about, none better. But what was I to do?" she said in a wail. "Don't you see, that awful letter said plainly, 'Send me Allegra, as a sign, and I'll do my part.' What could be plainer? It was the moment I had been waiting for. Was I—were we, my baby and I—to lose him altogether? Through cowardice? Through lack of faith? Well, I kept my promise, I sent her to him." Her voice withered. "And he never, never let me see her again. He sent her to Bagnacavallo. Where she died."

She was silent, her finger at her lips. Grisha was silent too. He saw a child cradled salamanderlike in flame, flitting over the convent walls, flickering feebler, finally quenched. The hooded nuns drew closer, lamenting . . .

Claire's Journal, November 29 (written in the afternoon, after talking to Grisha)

He sent her away to Bagnacavallo rather than let me come to see her. I have been told how he had raged at my impudence in asserting my right to come and see my child, even in his Ravenna palazzo.

P.B. asked me one day, "If he did send Allegra to you, Claire, once you had her with you, would you let her go back to him?"

We both knew that I wouldn't. Never, never, never, never . . .

"There you are then." P.B. turned his narrow palms out and smiled at me sadly. "He doesn't want to run the risk of losing her."

And there had been a fugitive flicker of pleasure in the midst of my anger. He loved her then, he was taking no chances of losing her. *I have lost many things I valued, but this little windfall I intend to keep*—he had said that to P.B.

Trying to hide the painful pleasure I wanted to know why he wouldn't let me see her on his grounds, on his terms, under his supervision. But P.B. had looked distressed. There he was irrational, he absolutely refused to do so. Even a hint of my presence within a mile of him was intolerable, it seemed.

Why? Was he afraid of a scene? Was he so guilty that he couldn't bear to see his victim? So craven that he feared to face an enemy? But I wasn't his enemy! I only became so when he kept my child from me.

An ascending spiral of senseless malice with nothing to stem it until death stepped in. . . .

When Grisha stopped in his mother's apartments for his ritual visit (they went on unchanged, morning and afternoon, the kiss on the brow, the sign of the cross, the gentle detailed inquiry about his health), he found the Princess unusually perturbed: she had just received a letter from his sister Sophie who was awaiting her first baby in St. Petersburg. "She is frightened, Georges. She is putting a brave face on it, but she wants her mother, I can read it between the lines." Her slender dark brows canted at an anxious angle, she scrutinized the letter carefully, as if indeed she could perceive between the closely written lines the invisible underpinning repudiating the cheerfulness of the visible communication, speaking silently of fear and pain. "*Écoutes donc ce qu'elle dit là. . . .*"

Grisha listened obediently for a while, and then his thoughts reverted back to Miss Clairmont, remembering how she had looked: the finger across her lips, the tiny smear of blood just above her mouth had given her for a moment a wild and pitiable aspect . . .

"It might be all over even now," said the lamenting voice, and he started galvanically, jolted out of his thoughts, death on his mind. "This was written five days ago, after all, the baby might have been born, and I not there with her, *mon Dieu* . . ."

"Don't you worry, your Grace, she is not due for another two weeks at least," came Nikolavna's honeyed voice from the other room. She came out and stood in the doorway. Nikolavna was always there, a comfortable bustling presence from which he averted his eyes, learning not to see what he had not the power to remove. Whenever she stood in her usual posture, her arms comfortably crossed on her breast, exuding comeliness and health, he still saw a slight pale ghost groveling at her feet. "And it'll be a good birth, nothing to worry about. Marfa and me, we were pouring out the wax yesterday; it all came out just lovely; no doubt about it, a healthy baby boy . . ."

"Oh, don't talk such nonsense, Nikolavna. And you know I don't like you to tell fortunes. These ridiculous superstitions, no curing them no matter how you try," she said to him in French. Nevertheless she sounded comforted.

"Yes, your Grace, and I also lighted a candle for the new baby, with a prayer to the Holy Mother, and the light flared right up, just as if She heard my prayers. . . ."

"That's better. You're a good soul, Nikolavna. . . . Well, this letter settles it, I must go to her at all costs. Better a week of jouncing and bumping on the roads than this constant agony of mind. . . . There's your father now."

The Prince came in slowly and stopped in the middle of the room, squinting at them with a strangely astonished look.

"*Ah, c'est vous, mon ami, regardez donc ce que Sophie nous écrit,*" the Princess said holding out the scented rectangle of paper to him.

The Prince disregarded it. Turning toward the ikons, he crossed himself. It was not his usual courteously moderate salutation to his Maker, but a wide fumbling gesture; he might have been a peasant in a church, about to prostrate himself. He said: "The Emperor is dead," and sat down heavily on the nearest chair.

The words made no sense. Grisha listened to them stupidly, not taking them in, until his mother's soft wail echoed them: "Dead? Dead? *Il est mort? Notre ange est mort?*"

The Prince passed his hand across his face as if to rub away the expression of senseless astonishment from it and replace it by something more suitable. "I was with Golitzin when Count Manteufel arrived from St. Petersburg to give him the news. Unbelievable—*une catastrophe!* He was ailing, we knew that, but it was nothing serious, the last dispatch from Taganrog was most encouraging—and then apparently, two days later, his illness took a turn for the worse and now . . ." His voice broke. "I can't believe it, I still can't . . ."

The Princess wept silently, her handkerchief pressed to her face. Nikolavna echoed her from the doorway, rocking her stout body from side to side, her apron thrown over her head. A warm tide rose up in Grisha, prickled in his nose and eyes. Dead!

"Yes, boy," said the Prince, putting his hand on his shoulder.

[259]

The hand trembled. "That's how it is with death. Spares no one, not the lowest nor the highest, not even the monarch on his throne; comes suddenly like a thief in the night. You must be ready for it at all times, wherever you are, whatever you're doing, and you're never ready . . ."

All at once he looked old, the crisp modeling of his stern handsome face melting like softened wax.

"Papa," said Grisha, in a trembling voice and turned his head to kiss his father's hand. Not noticing, the Prince left the room, still walking with those uncharacteristically shambling steps.

After a minute Grisha followed him, leaving his mother prostrate in a silken heap in front of the ikons. As he went down the stairs, there was all about him an indefinable sound of mourning, as if the very walls of the mansion were reverberating with lamentations.

"What is Grand Duke Constantine like?" Grisha asked Prince Pyotr at breakfast the next morning.

"You mean Emperor Constantine," his mother corrected him. Now that Alexander was dead, the oldest of his brothers became Emperor even before the oath of allegiance or the coronation, eventually to take place in Moscow.

His father didn't answer; but this morning it was not the cold punishing silence of displeasure with which Grisha was only too familiar, it was just inattention. The night before a messenger had come to ask his presence at the Governor General's house. On returning, Prince Pyotr had not disclosed what had taken place there. But if the news of Alexander's death had aged him, whatever he had heard on Tverskaya seemed to have the opposite effect. His grief was shunted aside, his hard gray eyes sparkled with suppressed excitement; occasionally he would burst into exclamations expressive of agitation and anger but not otherwise explanatory.

Now again, as Grisha repeated his question, he gave vent to another of these mystifying outbursts. "The fools, the wretched incompetents."

"Who, *mon ami*?" the Princess inquired languidly. Unlike her husband she was still weighed down by grief and looked more frail than ever after a night spent in prayer.

"I mean all those asses that the late Emperor had surrounded himself with. . . . They have indeed botched up things thoroughly between them."

A footman entered and silently delivered to him a note on a salver. He picked it up angrily, broke the seal—the envelope, Grisha noticed, bore the Golitzin crest—and swiftly read the message. Uttering a brief furious sound like a snort, he crumpled it up and threw it down on the table.

"In answer to your question," he said to Grisha, resting his fulminating gaze upon him, "Constantine is a prince who wants nothing better than to go on being a viceroy in Poland. Nevertheless he shall be proclaimed Emperor of All The Russias today at the Uspenski Cathedral. So it has been decreed in the Moscow senate."

"A reluctant Emperor?" Grisha said.

"Exactly so." The Prince seemed grimly pleased at the description. "Moscow, following the example of St. Petersburg, will be taking the oath of allegiance to a reluctant Emperor."

The Princess bowed her head. "*Remettons-nous à Dieu. Il saura mieux ordonner les choses que nous autres feubles mortels.* . . . You are not finishing your breakfast, *mon ami*?"

"No, I have lost my appetite." The Prince rose from the table, leaving the deviled kidneys uneaten on his plate—he preferred and usually enjoyed elaborate English breakfasts—and stalked out of the room. The Princess raised her eyebrows and picked up the crumpled missive he had left behind. She read it aloud:

"Oath to Constantine to be sworn at the Uspenski this morning at eleven. The casket will remain unopened until further notice."

"What casket?" Grisha wondered.

The Princess merely shrugged her shoulders. "Men are so fond of their little mysteries," she said indulgently.

Outside the bells began to ring in solemn funereal chimes, informing the clear winter air with the sound of mourning.

Zahar Nikolaitch was more forthcoming on the character of the new Emperor than the Prince had been. "Not a charmer like Alexander. In looks he resembles Paul—has his temper too, I hear, though not to the point of madness, or so one fondly hopes. . . . At any rate, somewhat of an eccentric. Once he said that he didn't like to go to war because it damages the uniforms. . . . I don't know, there's something human about him, he's not a cold fish like Nikolai."

Grisha visualized Nikolai as he was when he appeared at a ball in St. Petersburg that his parents gave to celebrate his sister's wedding: a tall slender figure, holding himself unnaturally erect as if on parade, with classically handsome features somewhat marred by a petulant expression. "Apollo with a toothache," a court wag had called him.

"And what about Constantine's marriage to Countess Lovich?" Marya Ivanovna asked. "The most romantic thing in the world! They say his marriage has improved him beyond recognition."

"That, my dear, holds true of all of us," said Zahar Nikolaitch politely.

Pushchin, on being asked how Alexander's death and Constantine's accession "would affect us," merely shrugged his shoulders. "They certainly weren't prepared for this in St. Petersburg. Well, who could have expected this? A man in the fullness of his years, perfectly healthy—he could have lived on for years . . ."

"Or at least until someone like Yakubovich cut him down," Grisha said and was surprised to hear the accusation in his voice.

At least he is safe from that, he thought, and together with his unexpected sorrow felt a queer lightheartedness, as if a great burden had rolled off his shoulders. By dying the Emperor had regained his angelic aspect. Grisha no longer saw traces of duplicity or cruelty in his portrait; the enchanting smile shone back at him, clear and lovely. It was possible to feel at one with the crowds that filled the churches, raising the mournful outcry of "Where have you gone, our savior, our father? To whom have you left us poor orphans?" He himself, going to a mass in the nearby church of St. Nikita, had been swept up in the tide of sorrow. Next to him a gray little peasant had wept aloud, touching his dusty forehead to the floor over and over again, and he, Grisha, too had felt orphaned, with great tearing sobs rising to his throat, as the deacon's voice filled the dark vault, throbbing with sorrow.

But what next?

"What will happen, Ivan Ivanitch? Are they still thinking of—do they suppose that now may be a good time—" He paused, with that little loss of breath that always overcame him when about to pronounce the sinister, the fateful word. . . . But Pushchin had no such compunction.

"For a revolution? Well, you see, the trouble is we were all caught unawares; the armies have already sworn allegiance to the new Emperor; and, once they did so, it's difficult to make them go back on their oath the next day. The Russian soldier takes his sacraments very seriously. . . . Besides, you heard what Naryshkin said yesterday."

Naryshkin, a colonel in the Tarutinski Infantry, had talked of the way the soldiers had taken their oath. "Real enthusiasm there, you could hear their hearts were in it. That hurrah rang loud and clear, not a false note anywhere—I am an expert in that sound."

"And my brother Mikhail writes the same thing from St. Petersburg. His artillery division took the oath quite happily." He picked up the letter from his desk and read aloud: "'For some reason all sorts of benefits are expected. The soldiers think that their term of service will be shortened, that all kinds of new liberties will be inaugurated; there is even a persistent rumor that the military colonies will be disbanded. . . .'" He folded the letter methodically and put it away. "That should give pause even to the southern branch, fire eaters as they are."

Grisha looked at him quickly. "You don't go along with them, do you? The southerners?"

Pushchin gave his little considering pause. "I have reservations, yes. Sergey Muraviov in the south keeps saying that his men are ready, they will follow him anywhere. Well, so they would. They love him, and justly so; he has looked out for them, made their lot bearable, so they'll follow him, as they would into any attack. Blindly. Because they won't know where they are going. He does not feel it necessary to enlighten them, you see. . . ."

"But why? Does he think they are incapable of understanding?"

"If he does so, he is wrong. When the Russian soldier fought Bonaparte in 1812 he knew exactly what he was about: he was protecting Holy Russia from the onslaught of the Antichrist. He went into every battle ready to die for his country. Well, that's the kind of a spirit I should like to see before I commit men for whom I am responsible to an undertaking which is likely to cost them their lives. And that, Grisha, is why I don't mind the delay provided by Constantine's accession."

"And there will be no revolt? It's all off?" Despite himself disappointment crept into Grisha's voice.

But Pushchin shook his head. "I didn't say that. You can't prepare for an event, live it, eat and drink it, without its happening eventually. Perhaps when all illusions about Constantine will have evaporated. . . . You see, Grisha, Constantine's great advantage is that he had been away for twelve years. He hasn't been around playing soldiers, making men's lives unbearable for them, like Nikolai and Mikhail. The men know all about *them*—but Constantine? Nobody knows what he is like, so there is room for hope. . . . Later, when it is seen that he is exactly like his brothers, which I am certain he is . . . Meanwhile, one good thing is sure to happen." Pushchin's thoughtful forehead smoothed out, his smile shone out as delighted as a boy's. "They'll surely let the Cricket out. Alexander had a personal grudge against him, which is not the case with Constantine. . . . So there you are, we all of us have our hopes, in spite of ourselves . . ."

Nevertheless, in spite of the country's complacent acceptance of its new monarch, oaths of allegiance and hopes notwithstanding, after a while it began to seem as though there were some enigmatic hitch about it all. Mysterious confabulations took place in Prince Pyotr's study. Grisha, passing by, caught the names of Moscow's Archbishop Philaret, St. Peterburg's Governor Miloradovich, Grand Duke Mikhail.

Some strange ambiguity seemed to cling to the whole business of Constantine's accession to the throne; undeclared, mysterious, it crept underground, occasionally putting out an eccentric leaf. Thus Fomitch remarked one night, in a casual fashion, as he helped Grisha with his toilette: "Looks like we'll have no Tsar to rule over us, for our sins."

"Why do you say that, Fomitch?"

"Well, where is he?"

Grisha could see what he meant. Still it was understandable that, after having been Poland's viceroy for twelve years, Constantine would want to make arrangements for his adopted country before he left it. Grisha tried to explain that to the valet.

But Fomitch shook his grizzled head. "No, that's not what the people say."

"What do they say?"

"Well . . ." Locking his hands behind him, and swaying, he acquired the storyteller's voice, plangent and mysterious. "They say there's a golden casket in the Uspensky Sobor . . ."

Grisha started: that casket again!

". . . buried deep underground, and in it the late blessed Tsar has left a will, telling his brothers what to do, giving them a special task: whichever of you, he says, does this task best, that's the one to rule Russia. . . ."

Grisha listened to this interpretation, fascinated by its folklore flavor. A familiar theme, right out of Tikhonovna's fairy tales, three Tsar's sons riding out on a fabulous quest to prove their worth by—what? Subduing Koshchei the deathless? Snaring the firebird? Constantine seemed like the best bet, he reflected, abandoning himself to fantasy. According to the stories told about him, he had a certain eccentricity, a simplemindedness, sure to enlist magical aid. A simpleton was always dear to the Russian heart: in the end it was Ivan the Fool who usually won out over the smart and arrogant brothers. Perhaps therein lay the reason for the uplifted spirits, the enlivened hopes, which Constantine's succession seemed to arouse among the common people: the foolish prince would be the one to bring them the firebird. Did that perhaps stand for freedom? Inarticulate, humbly hopeful, did the Russian people in this way voice their secret yearnings for a better life, garbing them in the oblique language of the fairy tale?

He asked Fomitch curiously: "Do you believe that story, Fomitch?"

Fomitch smoothed down his uprising cowlick and grinned. "Nonsense, of course, Excellency, that's what the uneducated folks say. . . . Still and all, something must be behind it."

As it turned out, Fomitch was not far off, as Grisha discovered when more letters from St. Petersburg disclosed the true state of affairs.

Claire's letter to Mary, December 1

. . . A most unusual situation has arisen here: something, I think, that can only happen in Russia. On November 29 we got news of Emperor Alexander's death in the city of Taganrog. His brother Constantine was proclaimed Tsar and all the officials and the army duly swore an oath of allegiance to him, as is the custom. Now it turns out that Constantine had abdicated all claims to the throne several years ago, and the act of abdication is laid up in the Uspenski Cathedral in Moscow in care of Archbishop Philaret. But Grand Duke Nicholas, next in line of succession, had never been told this during Alexander's lifetime and he too has sworn allegiance to his elder brother. Constantine in Poland is furious at having been proclaimed Tsar *malgré lui* and refuses to come to Russia. Couriers are flying back and forth between St. Petersburg and Warsaw. This spectacle of two putative monarchs playing at battledore and shuttlecock with the fate of their country would be ludicrous if it weren't so disgusting. As always the desire of the people is the last thing to be considered. . . .

Zahar Nikolaitch relished the situation thoroughly.

"Just consider the legal aspects," he would say, sniffing joyously as though a good bowl of borshcht, sent up hot and fragrant from the kitchen, had been set before him. One could almost be annoyed with him for enjoying so openly what could become a national peril and was certainly a national inconvenience, Grisha thought, except that you could see that it helped him forget about Dunia. "There's Nikolai, who, after having taken an oath, is nothing more than a honorary colonel of the Finland Regiment. His only recourse is Constantine's formal abdication. But!"—his forefinger went up, his intelligent little eyes gleamed—"Constantine who had already abdicated all claims to the throne in 1823 is now merely a viceroy of Poland; therefore why should he be put to the trouble of abdicating, either personally or by manifesto, from a throne that was never legitimately his? Oh, yes, a very promising impasse—played right, it could go on for months!"

"Really, Zahar Nikolaitch, there is nothing to laugh about," Marya Ivanovna would say rebukingly.

"I know, I know, my love, most reprehensible of me, but still . . ." An internal chuckle would shake his skinny body.

On Nikitskaya Street, the reactions were not as lighthearted. Prince Pyotr, who knew and liked Nikolai, resented every moment of ambiguity on his behalf.

"No question about it, they jumped the gun, taking the oath," he would say heavily to Grisha, with whom he talked unreservedly now. "The Grand Duke Nikolai had bad advice. That upstart Miloradovich was the one who prevailed on him to take the oath. I hear he's actually going around saying: '*Quand on a soixante-mille bayonettes dans sa poche, on peut parler courageusement.*'"

"Yes, I've heard that the Guard isn't overly fond of Nikolai," Grisha said incautiously. His father regarded him long and coldly. When he spoke it was again in the measured and clipped tones of displeasure.

"I have no idea where you got that information, but it is of course purest nonsense." He turned away brusquely. The confidences were over.

The whole household, meanwhile, was bustling with preparations for departure. The Princess's plans for visiting her daughter, momentarily submerged in the shock of Alexander's death, had revived; nothing could keep her now from the journey at the end of which not only her daughter but possibly a grandchild would await her. As for the Prince, it had been quite clear, as soon as the news of Nikolai's possible succession had come to Moscow, that he would leave it for St. Petersburg at the earliest opportunity. In fact, he was late: he should have been there already to give his royal candidate the benefit of his advice and sympathy. Letters from St. Petersburg had hinted that he was remembered, wanted, asked for. His wife's traveling pace would be far too slow for him. *"Non, ma chère,* I have no intention of dragging along like a snail when I can be in St. Petersburg in less than three days."

"You would let me travel alone?" the Princess demanded, plaintively.

"Alone? Why, you are traveling with a retinue unequaled by royalty. You have no need of me in your cortège. I shall go ahead and be your herald."

After uttering her familiar plaint of *"tous les hommes sont les mêmes,"* the Princess resigned herself to his contumacy. Lying back on the chaise longue, while the invaluable Nikolavna, together with the majordomo Ilya, packed and planned the minutiae of the travel, she gave herself over to pleasant dreams, dealing not only with the reunion with her daughter, but also with the city she loved. With a scornful glance about her and a curl of the lip, she saw herself finally removed from the cozy, homy, totally inferior surroundings that she had always innerly despised. In common with the playwright Griboyedov, though for different reasons, the Princess saw Moscow as a city of Hottentots.

"I wonder," she said, a girlish smile of anticipation lighting up her haggard face, "I wonder how I will find the conservatory. Not that I don't have the utmost faith in Trofim Ivanitch, he's an excellent gardener, but still without my eye on him . . . Isn't it odd, my dear, how I never would have a conservatory here, it's as if I knew. The only thing . . ." Lighting on Grisha, her dreamy gaze became imbued with the familiar anxiety. "Oh, if I could only close up this house altogether! I wouldn't dream of letting you stay here alone, examinations or no, if we didn't have to come back. I don't know how I will survive two such journeys. But your father insists on being here for the coronation."

"Whose coronation, *maman?*"

"You really mustn't joke about this, Georges, it's very serious. Catiche writes me that Her Imperial Majesty the Empress Mother had known all about Constantine's abdication, and when the Grand Duke told her about his personally taking the oath to his brother, *elle était totalement bouleversée!* If he had only asked her! You see, you men never think we know anything, you don't bother to consult us. . . . Oh, *mon petit,* when I think of you spending Christmas here by yourself . . .! But of course there are the Pomykovs, and I am sure they will be only too happy . . . In fact, quite possibly you may not even miss us at all. . . ."

Grisha dutifully denied this. Nevertheless, it was true, he did look forward to being left to himself. It was with a downright feeling of relief that he saw his father departing on a sleigh drawn by a troika of his favorite matched bays. Fedka drove them; he sat on the box, his whole figure imbued with gay self-importance, all set to beat the late Emperor's record of covering the distance between the two cities in forty-two hours. Akim, an older and steadier man, was entrusted with the Princess's ponderous coach-dormeuse; which left two days later together with three more coaches carrying bedding and other baggage, and the small contingent of household staff needed to make the trip bearable.

Their departure had a curiously exhilarating effect on Grisha. It was as if suddenly the atmosphere in the old palace had cleared, purged of anxieties, antagonisms, and guilts. Left alone in it, he was at last able to breathe easier.

But he was far less complacent at learning that Pushchin too was planning to go to St. Petersburg. "I had applied for leave some time ago," Pushchin told him. "The permission has just come through, and I shall leave on the fifth."

"How long will you be gone?"

"About a month. Semyonov will be the acting president of the chapter while I am gone."

"Not Fonvizin? I do like Fonvizin, he's so very kind."

"Well, Fonvizin will probably be going back to his country place in Kryukovo. I don't know how he managed to stay away as long as he did, with a young wife waiting for him there. . . . a delicious morsel," Pushchin said with a gleam of his rakishness. "Take a good look at her, if you go to visit Fonvizin. Unfortunately, I don't think you'll be allowed any more than a look."

Grisha let this go by without comment. All at once his pleasure at being left on his own in Moscow was dissipated. A familiar anxiety, the fear of being left out of things, began to take its place.

"Is something going to happen? Is that why you are going?"

"Not at all," Pushchin responded calmly. "I go to St. Petersburg every year—I did so last January. All my family is there, you know, and my father is an old man. Naturally while I am there I expect to see the duma and acquaint myself with their views on the present situation."

Grisha was silent. The duma in St. Petersburg—that *gouvernement occulte* from which all the decisions came—there would be meetings, consultations, one would have a chance to meet the poet Ryleev, whose *Voinarovski* he had just finished reading . . .

"I want to go with you too," burst from him suddenly in a schoolboy's voice, and he blushed.

Pushchin smiled at him. "No, you stay here, Grisha. No point in your leaving. You've got your February examinations to pass."

"Yes, but . . ." Grisha refused to be diverted. "Ivan Ivanitch, suppose something happens? Yes, suppose something does happen and I'm not there," Grisha said with something like a groan.

"Why should anything happen?"

"Well, the situation is changing, isn't it? With Nikolai and all . . ."

"I don't know. . . . That's what I'll find out in St. Petersburg. I'll come back with instructions for the members."

"Yes, but . . ."

"I'll be more likely to miss things than you. If anything starts, it will be in the south, you know. They are the ones who are fretting for action. And if any action breaks out there . . ."

"Yes, what then?"

"Any military movement starting in the south," Pushchin said in a clipped didactic tone of a veteran soldier planning a campaign, "must move north and pass through Moscow. In which case there'll be plenty to do here. After all, the Yegorovski Regiment is stationed in Moscow: it will have to be dealt with. That's why I'm glad that Orlov is here."

It sounded logical enough; yet in Pushchin's tone, as he mentioned Orlov, there was a conciliating, slightly artificial note one hears in the voice of an adult fobbing off a child that he finds inconvenient to take with him. As though conscious of this, Pushchin added: "If there is anything in the wind, you will hear from me. I'll be writing to Moscow, you know."

"And you'll let me know if anything . . ."

"Yes."

"Promise, Ivan Ivanitch?"

"Yes."

With that monosyllable and a solemn gaze from his friend's narrow gray eyes, Grisha had to be content.

Claire's Journal, December 4

Saw Pushchin this afternoon. The servant Alexey let me in with his quick foxy smile, respectful but knowledgeable. He knows all about me by now, I daresay. And I know about him. Pushchin has freed him and taught him how to read: Georges tells me that now he is even able to read poems by Pushkin.

When I came, Pushchin was looking through papers and burning some of them in his stove. This activity gave me a slight shock, reminding me disagreeably of Vienna, where my brother and I were told about the police surveillance and were thrown into a panic. . . . There were other signs of imminent departure: a battered trunk half full of his clothes and books. For some reason a thought flashed through my head: "He is going away for good."

The question spilled out before I could stop: "Do you intend to come back?"

His look at me was unwontedly grave, but he didn't answer. In fact, he didn't touch on the subject he really wanted to discuss with me until after we had made love.

Bless the man! I truly believe that if he were facing the gallows, he would try to prevail on his executioners to have a woman brought in instead of the traditional last supper.

Now whatever brought gallows into my head? —A grisly thought . . .

Afterward he asked me, "Do you remember, *mon ange*, telling me last month that you had enough influence with Grisha to stop his joining the secret society you believed he had joined?"

And instantly I was on the qui vive. "Yes? Why?"

"Well, do you suppose you could keep him in Moscow?"

"Why, is he thinking of going away?"

His look was grave. "He might follow me to St. Petersburg. I don't want him to."

Again I wanted to know why. He found it difficult to tell me: to disclose to a woman, "a casual piece of his"— Geordie's charming expression!—any part of his man's business. But he knew I had to be told, no help for it. . . . He did so, finally, with as good a grace as he could.

"Well, you see, *ma belle*, there might be some disturbance in St. Petersburg."

I was aware of a slight chill. "You mean, an insurrection?"

"Perhaps . . . I don't know. . . . It's a good idea to be prepared. For anything."

"But you had said there would be nothing like that." It was a stupid remark, and I think its stupidity cheered him up.

"I am sorry, *dushenka*," he said meekly. His gray eyes were full of laughter. "I didn't mean for it to happen." Very delicately he trailed a finger down the length of me, shoulder to haunch. Then the laughter went out of his eyes.

"Alexander's death has changed everything, you see, together with the mess his *louche* brothers have got themselves into."

"Yes, I understand. It's the *smoota*, isn't it?" He stared at me, thrown off by my use of the Russian word. I explained Z.N.'s thesis: that it is that sort of confusion, when the people don't know who is ruling them, that is most propitious for an insurrection. "And this is true now, isn't it? With two monarchs or none?"

He nodded, looking a little dazed. "Precisely. I must say, sometimes you— At any rate, yes, this is the time, now, if ever. If we don't take advantage of it, and at least make an attempt, I don't think we could live with ourselves afterward. . . ." Reverting to caution, he added, "At least one has to go to St. Petersburg and see what the situation is."

"And if you do—make an attempt, what are the chances of success?"

"Minimal." After a moment. "None."

"And yet you . . ."

"Yes, and yet we. . . ." His lips pulled back from his white teeth in a set and rigid smile. "We are not ready, the people aren't ready for us. . . . But one has to try, doesn't one? And it will not be completely useless. Sometimes even an unsuccessful attempt advances the cause. . . . But I don't want Grisha there. No reason for him to be destroyed. Can you stop his going?" His eyes were steady on mine, questioning, commanding. "Any way at all."

I answered him with his own words: "One has to try, doesn't one?"

We were silent together in that narrow little bed. Suddenly a terrible, terrible sadness engulfed me. I embraced him with a convulsive shielding movement, as if throwing my body between him and the sword, the bullet, the cannon shot heading his way. All at once his solid vital body seemed so frail, so vulnerable. As he drew me close, aroused again, I mourned its terrible mortality. A few drops fell from my foolishly welling eyes on to his shoulder.

"What's this, now?" An embarrassed tenderness shone in his face. He buried his face in my hair, and I heard, muffled, "*Akh ty, anglichanochka moya . . .*"

This was a different sort of lovemaking from before, gentle and sorrowful. Even as he moved within me, bringing me and himself to the soaring melting resolution I knew and loved, there was good-bye in it all.

[272]

When I left, he said again, "Don't let Grisha go."
I am sure I'll never see him again.

Pushchin went away on December 5 in one of those new diligences that had recently been set up to shuttle between St. Petersburg and Moscow departing from the latter every Tuesday, Friday, and Saturday. Grisha saw him off, his spirits sinking lower every moment. They embraced each other for the last time before Pushchin climbed into the diligence.

"Good-bye, Grisha. Take care of yourself."

"Remember what you promised, Ivan Ivanitch. You'll write to me?"

"Of course I will." Soothing, fraternal.

"And send for me if anything . . ."

"Of course. God bless you, my dear boy." His smiling lips brushed Grisha's cheek. Was there anything portentous in that brotherly hug? Was it protracted longer than expected? But Pushchin's face, pinkened by the cold air, was as cheerfully calm as ever. Grisha had to struggle with himself to hold back the contemptible childish bleat of "Please take me with you."

At home a great melancholy descended on Grisha. All the emotions he might reasonably have been expected to feel when his parents went away, loneliness, a sense of being deserted, now surged in on him. He exercised Nelly in the manège, going round and round, and his dejection went around with him, an uninvited stranger perched on her satiny crupper. Back at the house, he leafed his books over languidly, not taking any of it in, or wandered restlessly from room to room, catching an occasional glimpse of himself, pale and disconsolate, in the shadowy mirrors. Time stretched before him like an interminable dry desert, unenlivened by any mirage, each day canting implacable toward the suppertime, with Monsieur Lachaine and himself facing each other across the mirror-polished table. Yet when Monsieur Lachaine went away to spend a week with an old friend, a tutor in a family that lived in a country place on the outskirts of Moscow, Grisha's sense of grievance increased as though he was really deserted by everyone.

With Pushchin gone he found himself isolated from the activities of the society. He shrank from approaching the acting President Semyonov, a curt-spoken, somewhat abrasive man, whom he didn't know very well. Fonvizin, in whose avuncular presence he was much more at ease, was unavailable having gone to his country place, presumably to taste anew the connubial pleasures Pushchin had praised.

Even Miss Clairmont failed him; she was in an uncharacteristically uncommunicative mood. Something was on her mind, evidently. When he came to the Pomykovs, as often as not she would be in the music room, practicing; interminable triolets of a Beethoven sonata flowed out without a stammer from behind the closed door, like a brook to whose source she returned over and over again. On emerging she would retire to a corner with her embroidery frame, intent on her thoughts, and so remote that one no longer could venture on the familiar gambit of asking what they were.

Zahar Nikolaitch, sensing his displaced state, would talk to him with his customary kindness asking him about the February examinations.

"If I were you, Prince, no matter what your parents' plans are, I would think twice before going to any university but ours. I don't know how it happened, but the Moscow University is the only one in the country that has retained at least a semblance of academic liberty. Messrs. Magnitzky and Golitzin (I don't mean our own dear Dmitry Vladimirovich, but the former Minister of Education) have done for the rest."

Grisha had already audited several lectures on literature and philosophy. The huge old auditorium had been filled to overflowing both by the undergraduates in their scarlet-collared uniforms and outsiders of all ages, fashionable surtouts of officials next to the frieze greatcoats of army officers. There was a ferment and a liveliness about the variegated crowd that appealed to Grisha; more and more he looked forward to being part of it.

"Really, Zahar Nikolaitch," Marya Ivanovna said crossly. "How can you talk such nonsense? Of course, Prince Georges will be joining his parents in St. Petersburg, that goes without saying. They can no more spare him than I could our Johnny. . . . I can't tell you, Prince, how vexed I am at the thought of losing your parents: it is so sad to part with friends." Marya Ivanovna still acted as though his parents were her closest friends.

She cheered up when Grisha assured her that they would be coming back for the coronation. "Yes, that can't be much later than April, can it, Zahar Nikolaitch? Whoever it is that will be crowned?"

"Oh, I don't think there's any doubt about that," her husband returned. "We shall be crowning Nikolai here, one of these days. I hear Grand Duke Mikhail, who has come back from Warsaw with letters, has not yet taken the oath of allegiance to Constantine. In fact, he is being sent back to Warsaw again, for final instructions, I should imagine . . . Yes," Zahar Nikolaitch drawled reflectively, "interesting things are going on in St. Petersburg."

And *I* am here, Grisha thought bitterly.

But his bitterest moment came when Prince Alexander Odoevski came to see him. He had been away from Moscow visiting with his old father and had just returned. Grisha, who was in the midst of his German lesson when he was announced, hastened down to greet him. The young officer had brought in with him the frosty radiance of the winter morning. His smiling face burned rosy with the cold, a powdering of snow glittered on the beaver collar of his military *shinel*, which however he declined to take off.

"No, no, my dear, I really have no time, I'm just here for a minute. I simply had to stop and see you. . . . I have been thinking of you a great deal." Stripping off his gloves, he seized Grisha's hands, irradiating him with his joyous candid smile, which presently grew misty as he went on: "Remember how we talked? That night coming back from Fonvizin's? Well, when we heard about *his* death—I thought, I am glad, I am so glad he didn't get to know. About us, I mean. About Yakubovich and all that. . . ."

"Yes, yes, and so did I. I said to myself he's safe now. . . ."

"I too. I wept like a child about him, didn't you? But now, now it's all different, we can forgive him and he can forgive us. . . . I am sure he sees us, you know. . . . I think he's with us, blessing us. . . ." Releasing Grisha's hand he made the sign of the cross.

"And Nikolai?"

"Nikolai? Nikolai is a—an army colonel. He's not dangerous—he is merely repression and injustice. One can't possibly love him. It's much easier to oppose someone you don't love. . . . Oh, I'd like so much to sit down and talk to you about all this, I have thought about it so much. . . . But I have no time, I must be off."

"But where are you . . . ?" But he knew the answer already.

"To St. Petersburg, where else? My father hated to see me go. I hated to leave him too, he's the dearest old man and I love him. . . . I lied to him, said my leave was up. Well, it wasn't. But"—his radiant face grew serious, his voice went low—"it's understood among us, you know, when something extraordinary happens one should immediately go to one's post. . . . Good-bye, Grisha, my dear old man, I'll write. I've gotten to like you so much, you don't know. . . ." His smack on Grisha's cheek was fresh and brotherly. He wrung his hand again and, clapping his shako more securely on his head, clattered gayly down the steps.

"Sasha, wait!"

But he was already gone. Grisha limped hastily down the stairs. Standing by the door, which the footman had hastily flung open for him, he saw Odoevski leaping lightly into his sleigh. It was drawn by a lively troika of matched roans; there seemed to be a gayety about them too, as they pranced and fretted, ready to go. Sasha settled himself in the sleigh; he reached into his pocket; a tiny morsel appeared in his fingers and was popped into his mouth. The coachman snapped the whip and the sleigh moved off briskly.

Grisha stood in the doorway looking after him. In his imagination he could see a general movement all over Russia, all of it bound for the same destination. The couriers out of Warsaw galloped north in frantic haste; his mother's huge coach swayed languidly in the same direction, moving steadily along the snow-covered roads; his father sped furiously along them; so did Odoevski, nibbling at his lemon drops, his rosy face alight with anticipation, Pushchin, too . . . Only he stayed behind mired in inactivity.

"Georges! Prince Georges!"

Turning Grisha saw Miss Clairmont beckoning to him from a hackney drozhky. Without being told to, his coachman pulled up, and the matched pair of grays came to a prancing stop next to the hackney's apathetic nag.

"A marvelous winter day, Georges. I am enjoying all of its beauty even as I shrivel in the cold." Her face looked small and pinched above the fur of her pelisse.

"Where are you going? May I take you there?"

"I am just going home after a lesson, and yes, you may."

Grisha dismissed Miss Clairmont's *izvoshchik*. It gave him a moment's pleasure to see her installed comfortably in his own carriage, with the fur rug tucked about her. She smiled at him, and looked less pinched.

They drove slowly along the quay. Below them the Moscow River glinted like a silver serpent. It was now solidly frozen. Small fires glimmered along the banks where rows of stalls were beginning to rise built directly on ice. Further down, across the way from the Foundling Hospital, there would be skating: another one of the soaring activities out of his power.

Grisha said suddenly, without meaning to: "I am planning to go away. I don't think I can bear to stay here any longer when everybody . . . " He stopped short; she wasn't supposed to know anything about this. But, when she looked at him swiftly, he had a feeling that somehow she did.

She said carefully: "I thought the plan was for you to study here until the February examinations came up."

"Yes, that was the plan." Resentment flared up in him. He was a puppet, it seemed, subservient to other people's wills. But it didn't have to be like that. At any moment he could assert himself and leave. There was nothing here to keep him, except vague injunctions by people who were absent and probably not even thinking of him. "But not necessarily mine."

"I see. . . . Are you going to St. Petersburg?"

"Perhaps. St. Petersburg is not the only place where . . . I might go south," he said.

If he wasn't wanted in St. Petersburg, there were other places to go to. South was where it all might start, Pushchin had told him. Suppose he were to go there, introduce himself, use Pushchin's name. "Here I am, use me for anything you wish, I am ready to give my life. . . ."

"Anything is better than staying here. You don't know," he told her angrily, "what it's like for me here."

"No," Miss Clairmont agreed quietly, "it's perfectly true. I don't even know *how* you live." She was silent lifting her muff to her lips. Her breath stirred the lustrous guard hairs of the fur. "May I ask you to do something for me, Georges? I have a fancy to have tea with you in your house. So I can see you in your own setting; see how you go on by yourself, what you do. . . . I want to, terribly. I have been doing so many dull things today, and somehow I just don't especially want to see Marya Ivanovna. . . . Are you worrying about my reputation?" she asked, amused, as he hesitated. "A superannuated governess long past her prayers? Of course, if you have other plans, if you'd rather not . . ."

Grisha assured her that he would like nothing better than to entertain her at tea and told the coachman to drive to Nikitskaya.

Extraordinary how natural it seemed to have Miss Clairmont drinking tea in his study. She had let him show her through the palace, exclaiming courteously at its magnificence; in the music room the twin Erard pianos, scrolled over with marquetry, engaged her attention: she had run her fingers over the satiny keys and told him, with some asperity, that they were not perfectly tuned. But it was in his study that she had settled down before the fire in the small English fireplace as thoroughly at home as a cat in a basket. Fomitch bustled about with the samovar and presently retired, evidently at a loss at this unexpected feminine incursion. She sipped the tea from a Sèvres cup, enjoying the texture of it as much as the beverage it contained, the ruddy warmth of the fire lying peaceful on her face and breast.

"How comfortable you are here, Georges!"

Comfortable! His bitterness mounted. What could she know of the special cruelties life could inflict, the worst of them perhaps the bitter disappointment, the galling sense of powers unused, untried, trammeled by a miserable handicap, while your friends went on without you . . .? He burst out resentfully:

"When I joined the secret society, I thought something important would come of it for me—that I would be allowed to participate. Well, it's not like that at all. When there's a possibility of something happening—" It was quite against the rule to speak to her like that, but he couldn't help it, he had to. "—I'm out of it, it seems! Just as always. I suppose I can't blame them for thinking that I'm useless, that I can't do anything because of, because—" This time he couldn't say it, not even to her. He set his jaws rigidly and said in a tight voice, not looking at her, "It would seem to me that anyone has a right to be allowed the opportunity of dying for his beliefs," and was again angrily aware of sounding theatrical.

Miss Clairmont listened to him attentively. She said: "Has it occurred to you that perhaps you are being kept out of whatever it is you feel you are being kept out of, not because you are considered useless, but because you are valued?"

[278]

"I? Valued?" he asked with genuine astonishment. "For what?"

He remembered Pushchin saying tenderly about Pushkin: "—much too precious to be put in danger." But he knew very well that he did not belong in that category.

"I have always known, Georges, that you set very little value on yourself."

An extraneous remark having nothing to do with his grievance. Grisha hunched his shoulder impatiently. "I shouldn't have spoken to you of any of this."

With disheartening alacrity she agreed. "Very well, Georges. We shall talk of something else." She finished her tea unhurriedly, put her cup down, and patted the Moroccan leather ottoman next to her chair, inviting him into her circle of firelight. "I think I'd like to tell you about one of our Geneva evenings—the most important evening, I think, in my life."

"Pray do, Miss Clairmont." But inwardly he bristled: just like Tikhonovna's "Don't fret, Grishenka, I'll tell you a fairy tale . . ." Did she think he could be wooed out of his misery by one of her stories? But he seated himself obediently by her side.

If any of this showed on his face, she chose to disregard it. "It happened," she said, "about a week before we left Geneva, he to go to Italy and we to England. That day a letter had come to him. . . . I told you, I think, that he had written to his wife, asking for reconciliation." A tiny spasm of pain fluttered across her face; but it wasn't that memory that had stung her; what she was remembering, he knew, was the time of telling him about it, a sunny September day, and Dunia lying on the rug between them, in living breathing sleep. "He had sent that letter through an intermediary, and he had been perfectly persuaded that it would bring the desired results. . . . I hadn't read his missive to his wife, but I was quite willing to believe that it was a masterpiece. 'Such a good wheedling contrite epistle,' he told me, 'brimful of *mea culpas,* and oh, so damnably heartfelt. I promise you I shed gallons of tears over my wickedness.' And he wore the mischievous grin of an urchin gulling his elders. . . ."

Grisha too, listening ever more attentively, couldn't withstand a sour little grin. She had done it again; his rightful misery was not proof against the enticement; even as he resented, he would still step into her Geneva summer, her Italian winters, whenever she beckoned.

"Well, on that day that I am speaking of he had got his answer—a total flat uncompromising refusal. Oh, he was quite undone. He had always minded being rebuffed—even by someone he didn't want. His vanity was smashed, his pride shattered; besides, he now saw himself truly exiled from England with no hope of return on his terms. . . . There was one expression in that letter that was peculiarly damaging: she had found his proposal that she should take him back to her bosom 'quite monstrous.'" Miss Clairmont's face went stony. "When he was a child, his mother, a lady of uncertain temper, would call him 'lame little monster,' whenever he displeased her. . . ."

"*Impudent lame whelp*," *his father said, looming enraged in the doorway.*

". . . All that converged on him. He floundered near to drowning. I was the only slender plank in that bitter sea. So he clung to me," she said with an eloquent ingathering motion. "It hurt too much, you see. He wanted to stop hurting, to be healed, to know peace. So he had finally to show me that secret, that festering wound that had hurt him all his life, infecting all his being. And so—and so he spoke to me about his nightmare. . . . Remember, Georges? I told you about his nightmare? When we were first acquainted?"

First acquainted? But he had known her all his life. There was no time when she hadn't been there. . . . "Yes," he said, "about his being in a large room with a crowd of people who laughed at him. . . ." He remembered more. "Cavorting before them."

"Yes." She was silent for a while. "You know," she said thoughtfully, "I have a theory—oh, completely unscientific—that all of us have a special nightmare into which we channel all our fears, all our angers, which we fear and hate because it tells us more about ourselves than we want to know. It's like coming face to face with your *Doppelgänger*—a presage of disaster.

"That happened to P.B. by the way—he told me he saw himself once walking about the terrace in Lerici. 'Was it very frightening?' I asked. No, he said, he hadn't minded, 'it was merely meeting someone I have always known.'

"Well, Geordie minded. His was truly the ghastly twin Goethe talks about, someone to be avoided at all costs. 'The worst of it,' he said, 'is that deep in my bowels, I feel it to be true, I really am that posturing montebank, that cringing limping clown mouthing verses to avoid being laughed at. . . .'

"Pitiable and terrible, isn't it, Georges? Even his great gift was tainted, you see: he saw it as posturings of a clown to keep attention from his deformity. . . . Yes, he told me that, he trusted me that much. Finally. He let me into the fastnesses of his heart—that inner place he had never opened to anyone before. So we were safe, both of us. Do you see now, Georges? It was a true act of faith on his part. Well, one act of faith deserves another— that's why I had to trust him with Allegra. Because he had trusted me with himself. Not in vain." She lifted her chin. "At last I was able to be of use to him. Even though later he forgot how it had been and grew to hate me for being allowed to see so much, I did help him then, to get shut of that ugly twin that obliterated his true image in the mirror. That night, finally, he saw the true reflection of himself. In *my* eyes."

Grisha looked at her uneasily. Again, as that first time she had told him about the nightmare, he felt the impact of her mysterious particularity. What was she driving at? What parallel was she hinting at?

She did nothing to explain further, having, it seemed, come to the end of whatever it was she had to say. Chin on hand, the smooth oval of her face unreadable, she was staring into the fireplace, as though watching a troup of salamanders reenacting an old play in the heart of the fire.

"It would be impertinent in me," he said uncertainly, "to see any similarity. Except of course the obvious one," he couldn't help adding, self-flagellating.

"Yes," said Miss Clairmont into the fire, "the obvious one of needless suffering. . . ."

Needless in *his* case, perhaps, Grisha thought. After all, *he* had everything, he was someone, a great poet, universally famed; when he chose to put himself in the way of a heroic death nobody dared to prevent him. And women loved him. That true image of himself that Miss Clairmont helped him see—surely he must have seen it reflected in other women's eyes beside hers. *His* wretched handicap didn't keep him out of any beds, it was too tempered by fame, greatness, extraordinary personal beauty. . . . It was only when one lacked those perquisites, when one was nothing—ah, yes, Miss

Clairmont, in her fondness for her favorite pupil, had overlooked that. He too had seen himself reflected—he remembered Matryosha's cornflower-blue eyes squinting downward in horrified curiosity; the gypsy's amber stare, alight with mockery—and there would be others, it would always be so. . . . An exclamation of misery broke from him.

"Sometimes I think there's nothing left for me but the monastery. . . ."

And that took her abstracted gaze away from the fire. Her eyebrows rose in gentle mockery. "Are you so very tired of worldly pleasures, Georges? Have you sampled so many?"

"You don't understand," he blazed at her. "You couldn't, not possibly . . ."

"But I do. Oh, Georges, almost every young man feels that way for a time—young girls too!—that the world is closed to them and the key thrown away. But it's not true: the door is open." Leaning forward, she took hold of his chin and turned his wretched face toward her. "This is not a monk's face, I assure you."

"You can't understand," he said again, hopeless, "you can't know . . ."

"Ah, yes, that limp, that bit of ugliness, that cancels everything—brains, appearance, character! Makes you unfit for the world! Yes indeed, I know all about it. From him. All the acclaim—all the women in his bed—and still he was nothing, unwanted child, posturing clown, lame monster. *Damaged beyond repair, from birth*, that's what he said to me. And I said, I said to him"—her voice went low, with a lulling, wooing sweetness—"my child, my love, my lame angel, can't you see how wrong you are? It's only an imperfection—it only makes one love you more. . . . I said that to him. . . . A woman will say this to you one day, Georges. I promise you. . . ."

But promises are easy to make.

"And I always keep my promises. . . . Don't look away from me, my dear. . . ."

Both her hands held his face. She had never done this before. It had always been a swift, light touch, quickly withdrawn. This time it lasted, and so did the extraordinarily sweet look in her dark eyes. Grisha trembled beneath it. His hands moved without his volition; blindly reaching out, he laid them on her breast; so, two summers ago, he had cupped the cool breasts of the marble goddess in the

[282]

garden, willing the marble to turn into living flesh. Now, terror stricken, he awaited a miracle in reverse: the living flesh beneath his palms would turn to stone; a cold marble facsimile of Miss Clairmont, his friend and mentor, would presently face him in petrified outrage.

But that didn't happen. She merely looked deeper into his frightened eyes and, with one of her little nods, incisive, reassuring, leaned toward him. Her lips touched his mouth. Styosha's kiss had been avid and impersonal. This was merely tender. His hand was withdrawn from her breast but not relinquished. Holding it in her own, she rose, and, her face gone smooth and drowsy, drew him along with her, retracing the way he had shown her earlier, going back through the narrow corridor to his bedroom. He stumbled after her, dumbly; it was all a dream.

He watched her voiceless in his bedroom as she moved about with dreamy purposiveness. A key clicked gently, turning in the door; curtains rustled together at the windows now filled with violet dusk and the room drowned in transparent darkness, lit only by the candles flickering under the ikons. She came back to him and, still saying nothing, began to help him off with his clothes; her cool fingers touched his bare breast and he shivered. Just before the uncomfortable logistics of undressing interfered, she sank down to the floor and began to ease the ugly shoe from his foot, as practiced and lighthanded as his own Fomitch. He looked down on her bowed shoulders and his heart froze with dread: now, now, as the wizened horror appeared, there will be the stiffening, the fumbling, the minute recoil quickly controlled but telling him everything he needed to know . . . But no such thing happened: instead, unbelievably, as he rocked awkwardly above her, standing cranelike on one foot, there came from the floor a small comfortable chuckle at his awkwardness. Weak with relief, he gave himself entirely over to her, letting himself be undressed, drawn toward the bed, gently pushed into it. . . .

With the incurious passivity of a muddled child, he watched her undressing swiftly. The ormolu clock on the marble mantelpiece struck the half-hour, arresting her for a moment in the classical pose of a startled nymph, head lifted, long throat stretched, one hand restraining at the hip the downward slither of the petticoats; candlelight slipped along her sloping shoulders and small breasts. The sheer beauty of it almost sufficed. . . . But he waited for more.

She came into his bed. Oh, he knew it well, he recognized it; early in the morning, floating in the watery world of submerged consciousness, this was the delicious body he would create out of the dawn-imbued darkness. A smooth shoulder slid under his cheek, cold toes touched his, and moved up and down his wasted leg, caressing; cool-warm flesh flowed along the length of his body. He held it, hardly breathing. The warm slender body turned beneath him, welcoming him, silken thighs clipped him, kindly fingers guided him where he most wanted to be.

Claire's Journal, December 9

Afterwards. Dazed hazel eyes watching me gravely as I dressed by the bedside. A long boyish arm reaching for the hem of my skirt. "Don't go." "I'll come back whenever you want me," I said and kissed his eyes closed. The boy sighed and slept.

I went out of the room quietly leaving him so, just as I used to do in Diodati, and was immediately faced with the unenviable prospect of quitting this gloomy old mansion by myself, running the gauntlet of servants' stares. Something I hadn't thought of. . . . Just then, however, I became aware, with a nervous start, of another person in the room with me. But it was only Fomitch, Georges's old valet. It became evident that he had been waiting for me in the study; approaching me, he bowed down low, kissing my hands and murmuring. *Matushka*, I recognized, and *golubushka*, soft Russian syllables full of gratitude and good will.

He urged upon me a small glass of wine, which was apparently standing in wait for my appearance, he helped me tenderly into my coat and boots. It was strange and touching to have an elderly servant fussing over me with such fatherly solicitude. I was led through empty rooms from which all signs of human presence had been cleared, as though by magic, down a deserted staircase in the back, and out through a side door.

In the courtyard a sleigh waited for me behind the intermittent curtain of snowfall. My guide helped me into it, tucked the bear rug tenderly around me, and uttered a few imperious words to the coachman. Then he stepped back with the last low bow to me. The horses soared soundlessly; harness bells rang out with a sprightly brassy sweetness, thick white bees circled about me, gently stinging my cheeks, as I was borne off right into the middle of a Russian fairy tale.

When, upon awakening, Grisha found himself alone, his first thought was that he had been cozened by an especially vivid dream. But his naked body seemed to remember with its skin certain contacts and sensations, reassuring him that it was all true. He got out of bed and limped briskly to the window, to draw open the curtains. The daylight was gone too, the windows lined with the deep violet velvet of a winter evening.

A sense of giddy displacement, of blissful topsy-turviness invaded him. Strange to wake up in the evening with a surfeit of energy and well-being that belonged to morning awakenings! He hadn't felt so lighthearted since childhood when he and Sergey would get up in such good spirits for no reason at all that Tikhonovna would find it necessary to dampen them with the morose little saw of

> Early birdie singing pretty
> Don't get gobbled up by kitty.

Presently Fomitch came to light the lamps and dress him. No comments from him; but every wrinkle in his face seemed to exude discreet, congratulatory, I-told-you-so joy. Grisha avoided his eyes, but it seemed that he couldn't keep a huge, incredulous smile from his lips. Refusing dinner, he ordered a sleigh and, inevitably, was driven to the Pomykovs'. No other course of action seemed reasonable.

He heard the piano from the entrance hall and remembered that this was the night the Pomykovs had their musicale. He entered the music room unobtrusively and stopped at the door, looking for her in a kind of blissful panic. But she was not in the audience, she was at the piano with Monsieur Genichsta and the two of them were playing Beethoven's piano concerto for four hands. Neither of them had any thought for anything but that. Their faces, wholly at variance with the sprightly melodious conversation which flowed from under their hands and filled the room, wore identically stern and impassioned looks. Sometimes they smiled at each other, gravely.

All at once his happiness was tarnished, treacherous cracks ran across its shining surface. It was a fragile thing after all. His thoughts whirled black; to think that she could—only a few hours after—he was nothing to her, she had forgotten all about him.

The piece was brought to a sparkling conclusion. She stood up bowing to the friendly applause, sinking to the floor in a curtsey to Genichsta, who, with incredible effrontery, carried her narrow hand to his lips and kissed it. Then, still unconscious of his, Grisha's, presence, she took her place in the audience next to Monsieur Gambs. Genichsta went on playing, and she listened to him with attention which precluded her seeing anyone else. Once she turned her head, smiling, to whisper something to Gambs, whose answering smile to her was odiously familiar.

It was all very simple, Grisha thought. She had found him wanting, she had forgotten him, she had decided to expunge him totally from her life. Of course, as a gentleman, he was bound to bow to this decision. He would never trouble her again: he would go away, as unnoticed as he came.

At this moment she turned her head and saw him sullen and distraught in the doorway.

And suddenly that special look that never failed to dismay and thrill him at the same time came over her face—the look that meant that she had again stepped inside of his mind and knew exactly what he was thinking. Her lips gave a complicated little twitch of a smile, tender, ironic, reassuring, and she shook her finger at him lightly. A playful intimate gesture, meant for him alone, annulling the crowd of intrusive strangers about them. Immediately he was happy again.

After the music was over he found her standing at a window by herself. She had rubbed a spot clear of the frost, and was looking out at the snow that was beginning to fall thick and dreamy into the violet void. Her favorite shawl now shielded her unfashionably from the cold, covering her evening gown. She looked extinguished in it, little and plain. But Grisha was only too enchanted by the plainness, he much preferred it to the near-prettiness of the last summer or the grave beauty of her face when she played with

Genichsta. He alone was to know what was inside that sheltering plainness.

He had composed a speech for when they would be alone; graceful and subtle, hinting at much; but all that deserted him. All he could say in a gasping croak was: "When—? When—?"

The misty circle on the frosted window pane darkened and lightened with her unhurried breath. She said, "If it should be convenient for you to call for me after my lesson at the Jaenisches' tomorrow, Georges . . ." in such a simple and matter-of-fact manner that Grisha was almost plunged into gloom again.

The next day he took his racing sleigh out himself. He waited for more than an hour across the way from the Jaenisches' house on Sretenka. Eventually her slender figure appeared in the doorway. She lingered there, saying good-bye to someone inside (a misgiving flickered up in him: who was it? whom was she so reluctant to leave?). Then the door closed behind her and she started down the street, walking at her usual wind-blown pace, the snow squeaking under her fur-topped little boots. He called her name and she went hurrying toward him, stretching her gloved hands to him, looking young and gay.

This time it was different. With calm exhilaration he hung over her, knowing what he was about, not hurrying, like a rider bound for a sure destination, who yet can take time to look about him at the delicious countryside he is traversing. The lamp had stayed lit—she wanted it so—and he could see as well as feel. The great eyes gazed up at him steadily and lovingly, the lips smiled. But suddenly there was a change; a spasm ran over that calm and affectionate face, the mouth slackened, the black eyes clouded over and closed. Her body moved differently, lifting him like a wave. The steed that the happy rider bestrode soared up like Pegasus, taking him to his journey's end.

His breath steadied. A voice said sweetly in his ear: "Thank you, my darling."

Thank you? He lifted his head from her breast and looked at her.

"You've made me happy too, you see."

"You mean—the same way as I . . .?"

"Yes."

"You mean, women too . . .?"

"Yes, my dear. The ones that have considerate charming lovers." Her hand lazily pushed the strand of hair off his moist forehead. "Like you, dear Greesha."

It was the first time she had called him that—strange to hear his name on her lips with that slight foreign turn to it.

He lay beside her, utterly content, no part of him that wasn't comfortable. His sleepy gaze slid down his body, seeing it as another—a lover—might see it. Long, skinny, but not too bad, even in spite—his gaze encompassed it unflinchingly—of the ugly club-like extremity. There is nothing that puts one more in charity with one's body, he thought, drifting off to sleep, than the knowledge that it is capable of giving pleasure.

Claire's Journal, December 12

Grisha said to me the other day: "I like to hear you calling me Grisha," he smiled, mimicking my imperfect pronunciation, "and not Georges."

"I suppose," I told him, "you stopped being Georges when I stopped being Miss Clairmont."

"Yes," he said delighted, "yes, that's it."

But not quite. Reasons beneath reasons, beneath layered reasons . . . I call him Grisha for the same reason that I keep the light on when I am in his bed. To remind myself of who he is. Because unseen in the night with my foot encountering the familiar contours of a wasted leg, he could so easily be someone else—I could so easily pretend that this was another boy, one I had never known, but had always wanted to have had. And when the senses darken, I know it is he, his name rises to my lips. *Geordie*, I cry silently.

So I make myself focus on the face above me, clenched in the intent grimace of lovemaking. Canted cheekbones, soft ridges over the winged eyebrows, lips full but meeting each other in that long, sinuous Slavic line. I say to myself, "I am sleeping with a Russian boy; with Grisha."

Grisha knew vaguely that the Constantine–Nikolai confusion

was slowly beginning to resolve itself. True, Gualtier's and Rosenstrauch's busts of Constantine, reproducing with unflattering accuracy his pop-eyed and disordered countenance, were still being sold, while the classically handsome facsimiles of his brother stayed unbought on the shelves. But news from St. Petersburg pointed in the other direction; final instructions from Warsaw were expected any day now; Nikolai had moved into the Winter Palace and was said to be working on a manifesto, with the help of Speranski. This same manifesto was being brought to Moscow by Count Komarovski and given to Governor General Golitzin; it would be read in the Uspenski Cathedral any day now.

But the untidy politics of the interregnum had lost reality for him; the secret society too had receded from the forefront of his consciousness. He still got vague intimations of meetings and discussions going on somewhere without him, but it was no longer essential for him to be part of them. He was completely and joyfully committed to another occupation. Another country had opened to him: he explored it with an absorption that left no room for anything else. . . .

It seemed there were surprising things to be learned about a woman's body, once her clothes were off. Unclothed, Claire no longer gave that impression of extravagant slenderness. Her long narrow waist, that could be spanned by his two hands, flared into the unexpected sweep of hip; her legs were sturdy, her ankles didn't match her slender wrists; it was as though two different styles of body were capriciously joined together, and in some curious way that very imperfection made her body charming and exciting.

It was permissible now to notice the small black mole over the corner of her mouth, punctuating her smile. How charming that its counterpart could be found on the swell of her small breast, right above the nipple.

Lovely imperfections, delightful inadequacies: they laughed at them together. There was an essential Englishness in her that resisted the Russianness around her. Perfectly at home in four languages, she couldn't master Russian; she stumbled and mispronounced, and was comically vexed with herself. And Russian humor was alien to her; thus she just couldn't see the fun in Pushkin's rhymed official report on locusts in Bessarabia:

. . . Prilityeli,
Vsye syeli,
I opyat ulityeli!

"'They came, ate everything, and flew away again'—well, yes, but what of it?"

"Oh, you are so very English," he cried with loving exasperation. "Probably that's exactly the sort of reports they write in England. But we Russians are so verbose that for us it's excruciatingly funny to report things as they are. . . . *Anglichanochka moya* . . . Don't you like me to call you that, Claire? Why do you look so serious?"

"You can call me anything you like, Greesha. . . ."

A note came from Monsieur Lachaine, his script shaken out of its pearl-like alignment, as though by ague, to say that he had fallen ill in his friend's house and would have to stay there till he recovered. Heartlessly Grisha saw this as a special dispensation arranged by a benevolent deity for his benefit.

He did not hear from Pushchin, a remissness that would have hurt him much more before his present blissful preoccupation. But then he began to get intimations that a letter from his friend did arrive in Moscow. He heard about it from Colonel Naryshkin, whom he happened to meet on the street. It seemed that Pushchin had written to Semyonov; that the letter had passed through several hands and was now in Orlov's possession. A week ago, this evidence of being bypassed would have undone him; he would have seen in it the unmistakable evidence of how little he meant. Today he accepted it philosophically—it was natural, he said to himself, that he as the youngest and least-known member should be overlooked—merely deciding to pay a visit to Orlov.

Accordingly, in mid-morning of December 19 he had himself driven to the huge house near the Donskoy Monastery, that Mikhail Orlov and his family were occupying during their visit to Moscow. It was a cold frosty sundrenched morning, precisely the kind that he had always loved. New snow had fallen. It was pleasant to glide noiselessly in his racing sleigh through a white and brilliant Moscow. He crossed the Kamennyi Bridge, which arched over a frozen river, and passing out through the Donski Gates found himself in open country where he could let the horses out. They sped gayly over the snow, snorting in the cold air, their haunches moving rhythmically, their hooves flinging back sparkling sprays, and presently brought up in front of the Orlov mansion, an awesome stone pile, with columned fronton and lines of flying sphinxes and griffins plastered extravagantly across its circular façade.

There was another carriage waiting beneath the porte-cochère. Dappled gray coursers, of the famous strain evolved by Orlov's uncle, pranced and fretted splendidly before it. A gigantic coachman sat as motionless as an idol on his box, reins streaming taut through his huge fists.

Presently Orlov himself came striding out. As he paused on the steps, drawing on his gauntlets, his fur cloak flung carelessly across his great shoulders, his tall figure had a brooding and picturesque air; he looked like a monument to himself, a portrait of a hero delineated for posterity after some legendary exploit. Grisha, overawed by his magnificence, barely dared to accost him.

He was, however, greeted as cordially as ever. Orlov clapped him genially on the shoulder and expressed his regret at not being able to receive him; he was going to the Uspenski Cathedral to hear Nikolai proclaimed Emperor.

Grisha mentioned Pushchin's letter. "Yes, indeed I have it. Semyonov brought it yesterday." He looked at Grisha steadily, a frowning wrinkle searing deeply between his finely drawn eyebrows, and seemed about to say more but thought better of it. "Would you like to go to the Uspenski with me? After all it is a historical occasion—all sorts of revelations will be vouchsafed to us." An indefinable mockery colored his voice. "I don't particularly want to go, but there are certain ominous rumors floating around that I should like to verify. . . . I'll give you Pushchin's letter after we come back."

Grisha agreed with alacrity. As he got into Orlov's sleigh, he speculated with some uneasiness about the nature of the ominous rumors. But he didn't dare to ask Orlov, who, preoccupied with his own thoughts, had fallen naturally into another classical pose of a brooding hero: a booted leg gracefully advanced forward, one gloved hand resting on the jeweled handle of his court sword, the other smoothing his dark moustache.

Passing by the Hunters' Row, they were startled by a shocking hubbub of piteous shrieks; a bloody stain spread from behind the stalls reddening the snow: pigs were being butchered there. "A bad omen," Orlov said, with an uneasy movement of his handsome head, as though his collar, with its line of gold-embroidered laurel leaves, had suddenly grown tight. Mechanically his gauntleted hand sketched a sign of the cross over his broad medal-covered chest.

The Uspenski Cathedral reared its five golden heads serenely against the flawless blue sky. On the square a great crowd hummed and shifted, without trying to enter the church: this was not an occasion for the common people. They stayed outside patiently, stamping their feet against the cold and craning for a better look while carriage after carriage discharged officials and officers who mounted the steps and entered the cathedral. Instinctively, way was made for Orlov's confidently striding figure. Grisha, following him inside, suddenly became aware of a sound behind him, just a breath louder than the subdued murmur of the crowd; a ghost of a whistle, secretive and sly, sketched a tune which although familiar was so out of place that Grisha did not immediately identify it. He listened again, incredulous. No doubt about it, someone was whistling the Marseillaise.

The whistling broke off as he looked around. Curiously he scanned the faces in the group behind him. Which one of them was it? The young officer of the Life Guard, stony faced, his shako held stiffly before him? The "archive youth" in a beaver-collared olive-green greatcoat, his pale impertinent face wearing a slight smile?

Entering the cathedral was like plunging into a dark incense-perfumed cave. As the eyes became accustomed to the darkness, great painted saints began to emerge out of it; their elongated Byzantine figures untethered from the pillars, they seemed to swim slowly upward to the vaulted ceiling. The great gilded *ikonostas* gleamed, thrumming like a harp to the hymning choir. Presently a procession of clergy came from behind it, proceeding solemnly to the altar, with censer and candles. Last of all came the Metropolitan Philaret himself, reverently bearing in his hands a silver casket ("There it is, at last," went through Grisha's mind) which he put down on the lectern. He began speaking: "Russians, twenty-five years ago, we found our happiness in fulfilling the sovereign will of Alexander the Blessed. You will hear it once more, and find your happiness anew in fulfilling it again."

He beckoned hieratically and was joined by two officials: one of them was Governor Golitzin, the other his father's old friend Count Komarovski, whom Grisha remembered from St. Petersburg. The

two courtiers stood, actorishly solemn, lit by that special transfigur-
ing light that separates performers from the audience, while the
ceremony proceeded. The silver casket was opened, documents
taken out of it, verified, read aloud by the Metropolitan, in a voice
that little by little became casual, even perfunctory, as though an
ordinary business transaction were taking place. Snatches of
phrases reached Grisha's straining ears: "We by the grace of God
Alexander First . . . our beloved brother Grand Duke Constantine . . . of his own will . . . passed on to him who follows him
in the order of inheritance . . ." Then, slower, stronger: "Our heir
to be our second brother Grand Duke Nikolai . . ." A great
concerted sigh rose from the crowd. "I permit and bless," said
Philaret, sweeping a sign of the cross generally over the documents.

Outside the crowd still moved restlessly, waiting for the end of
the service. Bells clamored joyously. Cold air splashed into Grisha's
face like a handful of icy water. Blinking in the fierce sunlight he
momentarily lost sight of Orlov's tall figure; then it rose again
ahead of him on the steps, in a circle of people surrounding the
Governor General. None of those faces showed any sign of the
festivity that could have been expected on such an occasion; on
the contrary, they all wore a furtive and anxious look. Their heads
together, their voices inaudible, they had the appearance of conspirators. Presently the circle broke up; Golitzin nodded dismis-
sively and moved off, his pink barbered face grave. Orlov, grimmer
than ever, strode by Grisha, evidently forgetting all about him.

"Mikhail Alexandrovich, what is it?" Grisha asked breaking into
a limping run beside him.

Orlov glanced at him unseeingly. "The devil's in it, that's what."
He said nothing further until they were in the sleigh, making their
way back home. Then he broke out into a bout of swearing. Grisha,
uncomprehending and frightened, looked at his chiseled lips, from
which there issued a stream of army obscenities, soft spoken but
heartfelt. "Well," he said, finally, "they fucked it up, just as I knew
they would."

"Who? What happened?" Alarm stabbed him like an icy dagger.

"It seems, *mon ami*, that an insurrection has taken place in St.
Petersburg on the fourteenth. Several battalions refused to take the
oath of loyalty to Nikolai and marched out on the Senate Square,
out of their barracks, led by some of our acquaintances, who else?"

[293]

Orlov smiled icily. "Nothing came of this, however. The larger part of the army didn't join them, and they were eventually dispersed by cannon fire."

Grisha was silent, looking at his companion with childish terror.

"Needless to say," Orlov rapped out bitterly, "the insurgents were all handily rounded up and are now being questioned. It's all over."

"Pushchin?" Grisha brought out.

"His name wasn't specifically mentioned. But since he is one of the acknowledged leaders . . ."

"But perhaps he wasn't there."

Orlov looked at him with surprise. "But of course he was there. Pushchin is not the man to hang back when his friends are endangering their lives for a cause, no matter how idiotically . . . Ah, the bunglers, the stupid bastards, damned theoreticians. . . . Now they have really done for themselves, damn them." Again he began swearing, savagely, grossly; his dark eyes glittered with tears.

"Two gentlemen to see your Honor," said the footman, as he caught the fur cloak Orlov threw at him. "They are waiting in your Honor's study."

Grisha followed his host across a reception hall that seemed larger than the Dyevichye Meadow. It was dominated by a huge canvas, from which a comely woman of uncertain age looked down at them with a faint sensual smirk, coquettishly rearing her plump shoulders and breast out of the imperial ermine. Her beautiful white hands casually held a scepter and orb. On the opposite wall a handsome officer of grenadierlike proportions flashed back at her the conquering smile equally suitable to a victorious general or a triumphant lover.

Two men were in Orlov's study, warming themselves at the great Delft-tiled stove. One of them was a thin dark man with a sharp profile and short cropped hair that gave his head a look of a soft-quilled hedgehog. Although dressed in civilian clothes, there was about him certain military crispness that reminded Grisha of Pushchin. The other, in the uniform of the Izmailovski Regiment, was a rawboned redhead, with the gloomy hangdog look of a brigand. It was apparent that neither of them knew the other, and Orlov impatiently made the introductions, including Grisha in them: "Captain Mukhanov . . ." That was the red-headed bandit. "Ivan Dmitrich Yakushkin . . . Prince Volynski . . . Well, gentlemen, I suppose you know about December fourteenth in St. Petersburg. . . ."

Grisha listened, heartsick, while host and visitors exchanged disasters. They sounded like army comrades comparing heavy losses after a catastrophic defeat. They mentioned regiments— "Moskovtzi—Grenadier Life Guard—Finlandtzi"—and people "Ryleev—Odoevski—Pushchin—Yakubovich—Obolenski. . . ." The names fell heavy as hammer strokes, like names called out at an execution. "Everything lost, the best people, the best comrades," Mukhanov bellowed mournfully. He had a loud hoarse voice that went with his brigandlike appearance. As he spoke his arms whirled in large uncouth gestures. "Something has to be done, Mikhail Alexandrovich, we can't just sit here and let it happen!"

Orlov gave him a trenchant look. "Can't we?" he said with bitter mockery. "What would you suggest?"

"It's quite clear that more bad news will be coming by and by," said the other man. "Possibly from the south." His pleasant tenor came as a relief after Mukhanov's hoarse tones. "I shall say good-bye to you, Mikhail Alexandrovich. Under the circumstances, I had better stay away from your house; it might endanger you, without doing any good." He rose to his feet making a spare and graceful inclination of his cropped head. "A few of our common acquaintances are gathering at Colonel Mitkov's to discuss the situation. I am going there myself as soon as I leave you."

A meeting at Mitkov's? "I must go there too," Grisha thought. He turned to the speaker eagerly to ask permission to accompany him—he didn't know Mitkov's address. But before he had a chance to say anything Orlov's powerful hand fell on his shoulder, restraining him. "Don't leave for a bit, Prince, I want to talk to you," Orlov said pleasantly. His eye rested reflectively on Mukhanov's disordered countenance. "Why don't you take Captain Mukhanov along with you," he said to Yakushkin. "I am sure he will be interested in the discussion at Mitkov's, won't you, *mon cher?*"

Yakushkin murmured courteously. However, Grisha saw, the look he flicked toward the other man, as Orlov ushered both of them out of the study, was not totally expressive of pleasure. Grisha staying behind watched the group as they paused in the reception hall, waiting for their coats to be brought to them. And again Mukhanov burst into immoderate speech, inaudible to Grisha, but accompanied by the same set of awkward whirling gestures.

Having seen his guests off, Orlov returned to the study, looking angrily amused. "That madman Mukhanov. His idea for retrieving the situation is to go to St. Petersburg and assassinate Nikolai. All you need to do is attach a small revolver to the hilt of a court sword and let fly during a dress parade. What a buffoon! I am sorry I had to foist him off on poor Yakushkin, but it was the only way I could get rid of him. So off they go, the two potential regicides." Meeting Grisha's astonished look, he explained. "Yakushkin offered to kill Alexander once, for the good of Russia, and then to kill himself. He was very young then, and easily inflammable." Grisha remembered the meeting at Fonvizin's and his story of the young man who offered himself for the double sacrifice. And that had been this soft-spoken controlled man! Speechless, he shook his head over the unpredictability of the human beings. "Hard to believe, isn't it? The kindest gentlest man, soul of honor . . ." Orlov said. Breaking off, he looked at Grisha blankly, his brows knitted in weary bewilderment as if he had forgotten why he was there. "Ah yes," he said, remembering. "Pushchin's letter . . ."

He began to look through his desk impatiently, pulling open drawer after drawer. "Here it is," he said at last, handing the letter to Grisha.

Grisha stared blindly at the crumpled page criss-crossed with the familiar clear script. He saw again the calm dark face, with tenderness and amusement beaming at him out of the narrow gray eyes. For a few moments the sentences swam before him, making no sense. He focused on them doggedly. "By the time you get this letter everything will have been decided. . . . We can count on a few thousand soldiers. . . . The opportunity is here before us, and we must take it or be counted scoundrels forever. . . . Show this to Orlov."

"Somewhat outdated, in the view of later events, don't you think?" Orlov remarked with a grim chuckle.

He took the letter out of Grisha's reluctant hands and, opening the stove, tossed it inside. With a fiery yawn the stove ingested the letter; for a moment it trembled in the updraft, the script glowing lighter than flame, then, dwindling to a mere ardent particle, rushed upward and disappeared. Involuntarily Grisha uttered a protesting cry, as though it were Pushchin himself who was consumed in the fire.

"There'll be a lot of papers burned all over Moscow in the next few days," Orlov remarked. "No point keeping ammunition against oneself, is there?" With a sigh of weariness he threw his huge frame into a chair.

Grisha didn't answer. Pushchin's last letter! Gone, consumed. And Pushchin himself? A sense of loss filled his chest, as heavy as stone. He remembered that there was a meeting at Colonel Mitkov's and felt a yearning to be there too, to be a part of the orphaned band. But when he asked Orlov for Mitkov's address the tall man shook his head.

"I don't think you ought to go there, my dear. No point to it, and it really isn't safe."

How mean and cowardly to think of being safe! He flashed out, in revulsion: "But if *they* aren't thinking of their safety . . ."

"At Mitkov's, you mean?" Orlov was unoffended. "Well, actually they have nothing to lose. All of them—Fonvizin, Mitkov, Yakushkin—are on the lists already in the possession of the government. Oh, we've had our Judases, never fear. . . . Alexander was slow about those lists. I assure you, Nikolai won't be." Unexpectedly a chuckle of genuine amusement escaped him. "How frightened he must have been. And how angry at being frightened! That is a family given to panics, you know. *And* to punishing heavily anyone who causes the panic. I *know* them, you see." Again as that other time at Zinaide's he sounded regretful, even deprecating, as though apologizing for a ramshackle acquaintance, not quite up to scratch.

Well, Grisha thought, after all he had been a close personal friend of Alexander's; while in the army, he outranked both Constantine and Nikolai. Yes, he probably did know all about them.

"Golitzin told me something about that *dépêche* that Komarovski brought him, along with the manifesto. One of the things said there was: 'We've put the fire out in St. Petersburg, see to it that it doesn't break out in Moscow.' That means they're really going to crack down. Youngsters like you, unsuspected but committed, will be Russia's only hope from now on. That's why it's more important for you to stay uncaught than to go to a wake at Mitkov's."

"But you are going, aren't you?"

Orlov shook his head. "I prefer to spend my last few days with my wife."

"Your last few days . . ?" Grisha stared, at a loss.

"Oh, yes, I expect them to get to me pretty soon."

"But you're not a member!"

"But I was once—and not without importance in my day. I should be most surprised to be overlooked." Again he looked genuinely entertained. "They're probably laying bets, in the English Club, on who will be arrested first. I don't suppose you're a betting man, *mon cher*, or I'd suggest your betting heavily on your humble servant."

As it turned out he was right. Two days later Grisha went to see Golitzin. He was shown into the study where the Governor General was working, a pile of official papers on the desk before him. He greeted Grisha with his customary affability and asked whether he had heard from his father. "Any news from St. Petersburg— anything that can supplement the official dispatches—is welcome, and of course your father is in the best position to— Not that one expects anything but trouble." His bland diplomat's face was scored by worry.

Grisha shook his head. No, the only letter so far came from his mother; it mentioned the "dreadful events of December 14" only in passing and was more concerned with the more pleasant event of December 15, when his sister was safely delivered of a child. It was a handsome robust boy, his mother wrote exultantly, and they would call him Nikolai.

He said, "I am making bold to come to you for information, Your Excellency. I wonder if you have heard anything further about Ivan Ivanitch Pushchin. He is a friend of mine—" His voice trembled and he had to stop for a minute. "The dearest friend I have," he finished, pronouncing each word with defiant clarity.

He immediately perceived that his avowal of friendship for Pushchin would not place him in jeopardy. The Governor's face melted into genuine distress. "Yes, poor fellow, I was fond of him myself. . . . You know, something must have told me—for some reason I found myself reluctant to give him his leave, I kept postponing . . . *Ah, c'est affreux, incroyable . . .*" He pounded softly with his white fist against a half-filled sheet of paper lying on the desk before him. "Do you know what this is? A report I have been requested to send to St. Petersburg dealing with Misha Orlov, who, even as we are talking here, is on his way there, under guard. Misha Orlov, *figurez-vous!* Oh, I know about his past, but ever since his retirement there hasn't been a hint of anything. . . . I am sure that our new young Emperor will consider that in his mercy. As for poor Pushchin, there's no doubt about him, I am afraid. He was there in the Senate Square, one of the acknowledged leaders. They arrested him the next day. God forgive me, I still can't help feeling that there must be some mistake—a more level-headed trustworthy public servant never existed. I shall miss him."

Claire's Journal, December 21

All the conversation here is about December 14. Z.N.'s analysis was astonishingly accurate. The soldiers in St. Petersburg would never have stirred from their barracks to go to the Senate Square for any of the revolutionary slogans that had aroused the French in 1789. What finally made them do so was the assurance that they were being forced to take a false oath, that their true sovereign—i.e., Constantine—was in danger. There is a story going the rounds that the soldiers cheering for *"Constantin i Constitutzia"* (Constantine and Constitution) thought that *"Constitutzia"* was Constantine's wife. I don't know how true that is. But I am appalled at those poor men following the officers they trusted to a fate they didn't understand. They should at least have known what they were fighting for. Grisha says, "Yes, that's exactly what he said," meaning Pushchin.

We know that Pushchin was arrested the next day after the uprising. He was at the Senate Square, leading the men. I am sure that his cheerful commonsense was far more reassuring to the men than the heroics of the more flamboyant leaders. Commonsense? How silly of me to say that: he was doing the most quixotic thing one could think of—staking his life on an enterprise he knew would fail!

Needless to say, these bad news have cast a pall over the Pomykov household. Pushchin was a general favorite. Even my maid Pelageya said regretfully: *"Takoy dobry barin."* A good-hearted gentleman, indeed. There was a reminiscent giggle as she said it, and then her round face darkened with genuine regret. Exactly the way Pushchin would like to be remembered, it seemed to me: light regret, a pleasant memory, and no Cheltenham tragedies enacted. One was, however, and in grand style, by Marya Ivanovna, who, upon hearing the news, erupted into hysterics, and had to be restored with sal volatile. Zahar Nikolaitch gave her a helpless look and retired into his cabinet. She went on, wringing her hands and keening.

"Oh, what a man he was! What a heart he had! I alone knew what he was like. . . ." And then unexpectedly rounding on me, "You didn't. But what do you know of love? You—you cold-hearted English miss with icewater in your veins—you're incapable of understanding how lucky you were! Look at you—not a tear to spare, nothing. Are you a woman? Where is your heart?"

Explicit enough. Still I was beginning to say in a cravenly cautious manner, "Of course, I didn't really *know* Monsieur Pushchin . . .," when she bent upon me a look that was at once venomous, triumphant, and sorry, a look a woman might give a rival, saying unmistakably, "I know all about you."

How did she find out, I wonder? A little underhand surveillance? Or just pure instinct? Pushchin is a man of appetite but also of discretion and good taste. I am sure he keeps his mistresses very neatly in different compartments. He could never commit the untidy *gaffe* of discussing me with her—he certainly didn't discuss her with me. . . . Luckily Grisha missed all this.

Claire's Journal, December 23

Grisha is completely heart-broken over Pushchin. He is suffering the tortures of remorse because he hadn't been there with his friend. And yet there is too, inevitably, a sense of relief because he had been spared. And that, I think, he finds even harder to forgive himself for.

I told him: "You mustn't mind surviving. Not only because it wasn't your fault but because someone must be left to keep the ideas alive. I am sure Pushchin meant that for you."

I can't say that cheered him particularly. "But he's gone, I'll never see him again. And you mustn't tell me not to mind *that*," he told me fiercely. "You can't understand, it's not your loss . . ."

At least not like the other losses I've suffered. This is a man who didn't love me and whom I didn't love. We've come together merely to share pleasure: the first time I've ever done so, the first time I deliberately withheld myself.

Ah, but I remember the lively eyes undressing me, the artful hands, the sense of turbulent animal life unleashed within me. . . . The lazy murmur afterward of *"Anglichanochka moya* . . ." As for mourning him, I did that the last time we were together when I knew I would never see him again.

And I've done what he asked me to.

Claire's Journal, December 24

We spent the evening talking about the only subject that has any meaning for us nowadays: the fate of the participants of December 14. Inevitably Pushchin's name came up. Hermann was sitting next to me: his hand found mine and gave it a slight meaningful pressure. I looked at him, startled; and yes, every line of his expressive face held understanding; his fine eyes were suffused by sympathetic moisture. Presently a smile came to his lips: an undertaker's smile, determinedly full of commiseration in the face of bereavement. He even nodded at me, as if to say, Yes, I understand it all.

Dearest Hermann, the kindest of men. How often I long to shake him!

Later I taxed him with it, bluntly, "Why did you look at me *so*? What did it mean?"

He didn't answer directly. What followed was a gentle homily, dealing very flatteringly with my instinct for greatness. "I for one had never guessed that, beneath this commonplace and worldly exterior, there beat a hero's heart; that here was a man who would give his all for freedom. But trust *you*, Claire . . ." And taking my hands in his he again produced that resolutely understanding, generously forgiving smile. "I must pity as much as I admire any woman generous enough to give her heart to such a man in such times as these."

Plainly, Marya Ivanovna has talked to him.

Oh, dear me, how easy to chart every step in his response. Shocking discovery—anger, jealousy, disgust—Claire tottering precariously on her pedestal. Then, with a heroic effort, all is retrieved. Pushchin (the disclosure having been made *after* his arrest!) is not a worldly rake but a martyr to the cause of freedom; therefore, it's not a vulgar intrigue but a lofty romance; both participants equally noble; Claire's effigy stops tottering and is safe again on its pedestal.

Why is it so important for him, I wonder, to keep me there?

Claire's Journal, December 29

Arrests on a large scale are taking place in Moscow. The victims are picked up by *feldjägers* on orders from St. Petersburg and taken away posthaste. Most of them come from the ranks of the officials serving in various branches of the government. Grisha knows many of them: he has listed their names to me with growing dismay—Fonvizin, Mitkov, Naryshkin, Semyonov, Kaloshin. . . . The Governor General Golitzin, a kindly man, horrified at losing the flower of his official family, has provided some of the poorer men with furs and boots to keep them from freezing during the frenzied ride across the winter countryside.

I can't help feeling apprehensive about Grisha, even though I know that these fears are groundless. All those who have been arrested are old members, in the movement long enough to get their names on the lists compended by the secret police. Grisha is much too recent a member for that. Also, from what he tells me—rather resentfully—I suspect that he has been deliberately kept out of their recent meetings, probably on Pushchin's instructions. So to all intents and purposes he is safe.

"Well, *mon cher*, things seem to have simmered down here." Prince Pyotr's first letter to Grisha arrived after New Year. It was unwontedly long, and seemed to breathe forth a genial complacence: plainly the letter of a man who knew himself to be at last vindicated by the events. "All that is left to do is to sift out the ashes so that not the smallest ember is left live. What a legacy to leave a young monarch! All this should have been attended to during the lifetime of Alexander, and so I have said over and over again, only to have my predictions scoffed at by blind and irresponsible officials, like the late Governor Miloradovich. It is ironic that he should have fallen victim to his irresponsibility; one of the first casualties of the fourteenth, he foolishly went to expostulate with the rebels and was shot down for his pains. . . .

"Some of the faces that have appeared in the ranks of this half-baked Frondist rabble are not unexpected. I have always thought that Mikhail Orlov was a member. However, the complicity of your friend Pushchin comes, I must say, as a surprise to me. . . . It's almost as though some sort of madness had seized on all those individuals. . . .

"Our plans have been changed by all this. There is no point now in your staying in Moscow waiting for us to come back. God only knows when we will do so. The Emperor is unwilling to be crowned until every trace of subversion had been rooted out. Accordingly the date of the coronation has been indefinitely postponed. Your mother misses you greatly, and is especially distressed at the prospect of spending the New Year away from you. I have promised at least to deliver you to her for Easter. I suggest therefore that you join us here as soon as possible. Among other things, I am beginning to have serious reservations about the University of Moscow. It has turned out to be a breeding ground for radicalism: an astonishing number of the miscreants of December 14 are its graduates. The university of St. Petersburg is a much better-managed institution. You will not lose by the change, I assure you. His Imperial Majesty has been most gracious to us, offering to stand godfather to my new grandson, who has been named after him, and recommending Sergey for promotion. I am sure his kindness to our family will extend to you too, if you show yourself worthy of it. . . ."

Leave Moscow? Leave Claire? And yet, after the first surge of dismay, Grisha was aware of a sorrowful acceptance, as though a punishment, long eluded, had finally overtaken him. It was wrong, surely, to know perfect happiness, even if only in snatches, when people far superior to you, to whom you were tied by unbreakable though invisible bonds, were being hunted down, questioned, imprisoned. He had been spared their fate, through sheer insignificance, but at least he should have posted himself closer to the place of their martyrdom. It would have been more fitting, he thought with self-blame, to have started out for St. Petersburg on his own instead of waiting for his father to send for him. After the news of the fourteenth first came out, he had wanted to do so. But Claire, upon being confided his intention, had shaken her head.

"Don't you think that your arrival in St. Petersburg, unsummoned and in an obvious state of distress, would be far too revealing?"

But surely self-betrayal was, under certain circumstances, more admirable than a talent for staying safe. "But I want to share their fate!" and amended unhappily, "at least I ought to want to." He gave her a reproachful glance. She was the cause of it all. Without her, he would have been miserable enough to act properly.

"Ought to? Why? Self-immolation, Greesha, benefits only the wrong people. And if you are thinking about Pushchin—"

Of course he was, he had never ceased to do so!

"—I don't believe for a minute that he is the sort of man who likes seeing his friends share in his misfortunes."

He had to agree to that.

"On the contrary, I should imagine that whatever satisfaction he *can* find in his situation is precisely in the number of his friends who do *not* share it."

And that was undeniably true. Pushchin's face rose before him faintly irradiated by secret satisfaction, as looking out of his prison he saw his friends walking about free. Yes, that was Pushchin, who had such a tender, fatherly sense of responsibility toward his friends, found it so natural to protect them, that Schiller's philosophical gibe at Kant was clearly applicable to him:

Gladly I serve my friends, but alas, out of inclination,
Thus, though this pains me oft, virtuous I am not . . .

He felt a throb of admiration. His unique Claire! How unerringly
she had been able to sum up Pushchin, whom, after all, she knew
only superficially!

"And I too—like him—I prefer you to be safe."

When she smiled at him, everything came into focus, everything
seemed clear, there was no need for self-blame or heroics. She
wanted, she needed him; he was important to her. It was becoming
easier and easier to believe that.

The last time they had been together . . . Usually he was the one
who drifted off to sleep. It had always been a special delight to wake
up and find himself greeted by her contemplative and tender gaze.
But this time, he had been the first to awaken, roused by a frail
doleful sound. Immediately Matryosha had come to his mind.
"Crying somewhere . . . Where? Must find her . . ." Then his
consciousness had righted itself and he had looked at Claire's
sleeping face. It had mirrored a profound sorrow, tears crawling
slowly from under the closed eyelids. He had shaken her gently.
For a moment she had struggled, entrapped in a dream, and then
her eyes had opened on him, huge and mournful. She had said to
him, like a child: "I've had a bad dream."

"What was it?"

"Allegra," she had said, piteously, "I dreamed about Allegra."
Twisting away from him, she had buried her face in the pillow and
wept. With her black hair tumbled sideways, the nape of her neck,
with its light veiling of silky down, had looked terribly vulnerable;
her shoulderblades rose quivering, like truncated wings. His heart
had turned over. How young she looked suddenly, his good angel,
his instructress in love; no older than he, no older than Matryosha,
who too had wept to him.

"Don't cry, don't cry, Claire." Near to tears himself, he had
nuzzled his face next to hers.

"I did it, I did it," came muffledly from the pillow.

"What? What did you do?"

"I did it, I sent my little girl to him. . . . I *used* her. . . . I was so
sure. Oh, P.B. knew, he knew what I was doing, he told me so.
'Giving implies renunciation,' he said. 'Otherwise it's a bargain or a

gamble and the results uncertain. . . .' So stern he looked . . . And he was right, it was just like that. . . . I gambled with her." Her voice died in heartbroken weeping.

"Don't cry," he had said again, helpless.

"But I was so sure, you see. It wasn't even a gamble, I was so sure. . . . All I had to do was remember my old promise and trust him with the dearest thing I had and he would remember too and come back to me. . . . And I sent her, and she died. . . . All my fault . . . I am a murderess, too. . . . If I had kept her, she would be alive, I wouldn't have let her die. I would have saved her." Her slender body moved against him, not seductively, in a restless writhing of pain; and he couldn't bear it.

He had said, roughly, "How do you know you would have saved her? You were with Dunia and *she* died." Her body had frozen. For a moment he had been terrified: had he dealt her an irretrievable wound in reminding her of that other loss?

But after a minute she had said in a wondering voice: "That's true, isn't it? I was there with her, and I couldn't . . ." She had fallen silent, her breath on his shoulder cooling the spot that her tears had wet. Presently her lips had touched it. "Thank you, Greesha." Her body was shaken by the last deep sigh; it had steadied, solidified in his arms. With amazement, he had realized that somehow he had comforted her. . . .

To leave her? To make his life where she was not? He stared rebelliously at his father's letter. If he left Moscow, it would be for purposes of his own, certainly having nothing to do with the new Emperor's graciousness to his family. He didn't care to have his career furthered by the hand that would deal hardly with his friends. His mouth firmed. He would go to St. Petersburg, but only to be near to, available to, his friend Pushchin; to learn all he could about him, to hold himself in readiness for whatever he could do. Once he did that, or satisfied himself that there was nothing to be done, nothing could keep him from coming back to Moscow. . . .

He became aware of a footman standing in the doorway: "There's a person asking for you downstairs, your Excellency."

"A person?"

"An officer, your Excellency. He is waiting your pleasure in the reception room."

Who could it be? The thought that it might be someone from

Golitzin's office bringing news about Pushchin quickened his steps as he went downstairs.

"Prince Grigorii Petrovich Volynski?" A spare youngish man in an underofficer's uniform made two short steps toward him, came to attention, saluted stiffly. "Feldjäger Krueger, in His Imperial Majesty's service. I am authorized to present to you these orders." He twitched a document smartly out of the white leather belt that encircled his waist and handed it to Grisha.

In bewilderment, Grisha opened and read it. It said simply in laconic official terms that Prince Grigorii Petrovich Volynski was required at the instance of the Imperial command to go to St. Petersburg, under the surveillance of the *feldjäger* bearing this order.

Shocked into stupidity, Grisha read and reread this document. The meaning of the words seemed to hover somewhere above the handsome calligraphy, refusing to alight. He fixed on the signature, trying to disentangle it from the stately flourishes and arabesques that filled the lower part of the paper. General something—Chernyshev, he thought languidly, who is Chernyshev, have I heard this name before? No, I don't think so.

Abandoning the incomprehensible, he raised his eyes to the emissary, studying him intently, with the same dreamlike curiosity, as though the meaning that had eluded him in the paper might possibly be found in his face. Not an ill-featured countenance, but not a promising one: light lashless eyes, a lipless mouth, flaxen hair. Something Teutonic about it all—probably he hailed from the Baltic provinces, like so many functionaries in Alexander's administration. His name indicated that. "Yes, and there was something German in the way he said my name—'Folynski,' instead of 'Volynski,'" Grisha thought with the queer detachment one feels in a nightmare, unconsciously turning the document over and over in his hands. The *feldjäger* leaned toward him and, deftly tweaking the paper out of his grasp, with the slight condescending smile of an adult taking a book from a child who is merely pretending he can read, put it back carefully into his *sabretache*. He said: "The carriage is waiting outside. I suggest that you dress as warmly as possible."

Still in a state of numbness, Grisha asked conversationally, "Oh, you want to start immediately, then?"

"If your Excellency pleases." But, though he was courteous enough, he seemed, now that he had delivered his orders, to have in some subtle way taken the possession of Grisha's person. It was apparent in the way he followed him upstairs, without asking permission, in the way he placed himself square in the middle of Grisha's study, taking a quick censorious look around it. "I have been instructed," he said, "to take along any incriminating papers I find." His flat light eyes rested on Grisha peremptorily, as though he expected to be directed to these incriminating papers. Grisha obligingly pointed toward his desk. Without further ado, the *feldjäger* proceeded to search it.

Leaving him to it, Grisha said to Fomitch, who stood in the doorway watching these proceedings with his eyes stretched to their outermost: "You had better pack a portmanteau for me, Fomitch. I am going to St. Petersburg."

Amazingly Fomitch caught on faster than he had. Horror replacing indignation in his face, he caught at the lintel with both hands: "With—with him?"

The *feldjäger* slammed the last drawer shut. "We are leaving in twenty minutes."

"Go on, Fomitch. I count on you to pack the proper clothes," Grisha said, "the important thing is to pack warm, isn't that right, Officer—Officer—?"

"Feldjäger Krueger, at your service," said the man, automatically coming to attention. "If your clothes are not packed in twenty minutes, we must leave without them, your Excellency."

This threat worked. Muttering, "Mother of Christ, Our Gracious Lady, save us," Fomitch let go of the lintel and staggered away to pack. By the time Grisha rejoined him in the bedroom he had the portmanteau ready and was busy stuffing some gear into a shabby little bag of his own.

"What's that for?"

Fomitch gave him a quick look. "For me, of course, Excellency. You don't think I'll let you go alone with that accursed German?"

"I have no instructions to allow that," said the accursed German appearing in the doorway. "I am to take your Excellency to St. Petersburg under my sole surveillance."

Fomitch's face purpled. "No," he said hoarsely. "That's a lie, that is. You think I'll let my *barin* go by himself? There's no law that says such can happen!" He darted nimbly in front of Grisha, spreading his arms out protectively, his wrinkled face awry with fear and fury. "I know your kind, the master's not here, so you just walk in and take over. Well, you better think twice."

"Fomitch, my dear old soul . . ."

"There's no law," Fomitch went on, not attending to him, and glaring at his enemy, "that allows the likes of you to take an innocent child out of his home. Hey, people," he shouted suddenly, wildly, "here, everyone, come help, they're taking our Prince away . . ."

Grisha seized his defender's shoulders and swung him around. Looking at the undone old face before him, he was conscious of a tide of fierce pity and love rising up in him, not unmixed with anger: the old man was making him ridiculous. "Fomitch, stop it." He shook him roughly. "This officer is merely doing his duty, you are not to show him any disrespect. Now you just help me on with my coat and boots and stop carrying on . . ."

But Fomitch was not quite through. Suddenly changing tactics, he wrenched himself out of his master's hold and fell down on his knees before the *feldjäger*. "Your Excellency, Mr. Officer," he said wheedlingly, banging his forehead on the floor before his enemy, "forgive me, old blockhead that I am, for acting so, just let me come along, your Excellency, and take care of my Prince. The child has never traveled alone, he's not a well child, you can see for yourself . . ."

"Damn you, you old fool . . .!" Grisha stopped short, biting his lips. He stooped down to his old valet, and drew him to his feet. He said gently: "Look, there's no need for this. It's all a mistake, you see, and I have to go and clear it up. There's nothing to worry about, I'll be back soon."

The stalwart old arms closed about him convulsively, the thick body shook with sobs. Grisha buried his face for a moment on his valet's shoulder and inhaled the familiar smell of old tobacco and soap and the cheap pomade with which Fomitch tried to keep his unruly grizzly cowlick in place. "Take care of everything for me. Make sure that Nelly gets exercised and—and let everybody know what happened," Grisha said unevenly. "*Everybody*, you know?"

He felt the bowed head nodding rapidly at his shoulder.

Outside in the hallway all the servants had gathered in an oddly formal array, as they would do on the occasion of their masters' birthdays or arrival from the country. Even now, they arranged themselves in their customary hierarchy, with the undermaids and scullery boys in the back. But they muttered among themselves in bewilderment.

"Lordy, what is it? God save us! Where are they taking him?" came subduedly from the back. A woman's voice rose in a suppressed wail and was joined by another.

"Grishenka, Grishenka!" a quavering voice besought him. Tikhonovna had come out of her attic room. She was tottering toward him down the stairs keeping up a thin wordless wail until she reached him. She buried her old face on his breast. Her kerchief had slipped down from her head, and the sparse hair showed as thin as white floss on a babyishly pink scalp.

Grisha held her awkwardly, terrified by the fragility of the extreme old age. After a moment, she pushed herself away from him. She fumbled off the tiny ikon she always wore (he knew it well, an embroidered image of the Holy Virgin framed in a bronze hoop, doubly precious for having been blessed by the bishop of the Strastnoi Monastery) and straining upward weakly put it around his neck—"May she keep you! May she shield you!"—and clung again.

Finally he put her away from him, a disembodied husk of an old body, as weightless as a fly. Thin piteous weeping followed him outside where a sledge was waiting for him.

Claire's Journal, January 4, 1826

Terrible news. Grisha's valet came to the Pomykovs' house in despair to say that Grisha has been arrested and taken to St. Petersburg.

The poor old man contrived to see me alone. He went through a despairing pantomine for my benefit, miming the arrest, the arrogant *feldjäger*, the wrenching of something precious out of his, Fomitch's, arms; he wrung his hands, he looked upward for help, and, all that failing, hurled the shapeless cap he was holding on the ground, and burst into tears.

And I—I could no more shed tears than Lot's wife. I was seized with such despair that everything froze in me. I was back in Lerici, listening to the news from Bagnacavallo;

hearing about a lost boat; thinking, "No, *no.*" All of me one huge denial.

I must go somewhere, do something, .change it all somehow—I can do nothing, nothing except wait. . . .

Claire's Journal, January 5

The same cold horror of incredulity—this can't be done to me!—as before, when it became clear to me that I would not be allowed to see Allegra again. I couldn't believe it: "There is some misunderstanding; all I need to do is write a letter; P.B. will go and explain to him . . ." After all, it was my child, mine. I bore it, in pain and joy, while *he* wallowed about with Venetian courtesans. Oh, I knew it was all up with him. For some mysterious reason, he stopped loving me. Well, one can bear losing a lover. But one's child?

Something of the same feeling informs my agony about Grisha—I agonize over my lost child, not my lost lover; they have taken my child away, what are they doing to him?

Claire's Journal, January 6

There's a public notice today in the back pages of *The Moscow News.* Hermann translated it for me:

"Unexpected events of the fourteenth have disclosed the existence of a vicious, hitherto unsuspected conspiracy. . . . Such an attempt, even though unsuccessful, can have serious consequences. To prevent those, severe and immediate measures were needed and are being taken."

The Holy Week has begun. I saw a procession going on its prescribed route from the Church of Assumption to the Moscow River, bearing ikons and singing hymns. The raiments of the priests sparkled palely bright against the snow. To my eyes it had the air of a funeral procession. The solemn harmony of the hymns they intoned fell bodingly on my ears.

Claire's Letter to Mary, January 6

Our political horizon has been very stormy. Arrests and imprisonments innumerable and all among the flower of the Russian youth; all that there was of talent and rising merit has been mown down. For what reason, I cannot tell . . .

The weather has been precisely such as to foster the utmost melancholy. Clouds hang overhead looking pregnant with snow or storm, or any of these seasonal eruptions that ordinarily I shrink from but now would welcome as a change from this sullen grayness. And cold, *cold*!

Sometimes I think I might die of this dreadful cold. No, it isn't impossible, it happens here; sparrows fall frozen off branches and coachmen have been known to be found dead on their boxes. Poor wretches.

How to describe it, the blackness that descends on the soul—no, not blackness, because that mercifully obliterates everything, but the brownness, the vile dun fog, through which you dimly see the miserable world and the corrupt things moving in it. We knew it, all of us, didn't we, Mary? Each of us dealt with it differently. You locked yourself up, away from us; P.B. bore it patiently—"I bear what I can and suffer what I must." Albé *wallowed* in it; and I—I fought it with self-disgust and resentment, clutching at anything, coming up to the surface with the sheer violence of my anguished struggle. . . . But now, now I find myself sinking, with no desire to come up for air. . . .

Claire's Journal, January 9

Z.N. has called me tonight into his study to show me the letter he had written to Prince Volynski inquiring about Grisha's fate. As he was reading it to me, the door flew open and in sailed Marya Ivanovna *furiosa*.

Dunia's death had softened and subdued her. I had got so used to the altered, reasonable Marya Ivanovna, that this recurrence of her dreadful temper caught me unaware.

The loud voice spewing forth accusations, the scarlet-faced rage, the violence emanating from her—yes, I flinched nervously.

And such accusations! I was a professional seductress, a woman of ill-repute, destroyer of happy households; no one was safe from my excessive appetites, my shameless wiles. The proof of it all: here I am, shamelessly closeted with her husband!

Poor Z.N. He tried gentle humor ("My dear, I am so flattered by your jealousy that I almost find myself loath to disabuse you. . . ."); appeal to reason (showing her his letter to Prince Volynski, which she immediately struck out of his hand); finally, in desperation: "Marie, how can you talk so to Miss Clairmont? Our own dear Miss Clairmont? Whom Dunia loved?"

"Yes, she even stole Dunia's affections from me, she made my own child love her better than her own mother!"

I left the study, getting away from the ugliness.

Later she sought me out in my room; another scene ensued. She fell on her knees, begged my pardon, abused herself as immoderately as she had me, and with rivers of tears besought me not to abandon her. It would have been much less taxing if she had done this in a dignified and moderate manner but moderation has never been a virtue to the Russians.

I can see that I shall not be able to stay here much longer!

Claire's Journal, January 12

Zahar Nikolaitch has a highly placed correspondent in St. Petersburg who writes to him cautiously describing the situation. Whenever such a letter comes, Z.N. looks grim. "The proclaimed intention of the government," he told me, "is to decimate the liberal movement, root and branch—including, I daresay, branchlets like our dear young friend." And he uttered the Russian plaint of *"Uvy!"* so drawn out and mournful that it makes the English "alas" sound brisk in comparison.

The Emperor himself is taking a personal part in the

questioning. Very fitting: didn't his ancestor Peter the Great participate with relish in such inquisitions, even handling the rack himself on occasion? Apparently this monarch too is excellently suited for the part. The results have been spectacular. Many of the "criminals" have broken down under the impact of the royal presence and are so stricken with remorse that they are telling everything, supplementing the lists of names that the authorities already have. Probably that's how Grisha's name was obtained. So much for those precious vows of secrecy!

It's so very Russian: a tsar that acts as an inquisitor and conspirators that disintegrate into remorseful schoolboys as soon as their conspiracy is discovered.

But I know—I *know*—that Pushchin didn't. I invoke that calm dark face with its quiet glimmer of a smile and secretive gray eyes giving nothing away and I don't see him distintegrating, destroying his friends, parting with names. Never!

But Grisha, oh, my child, my poor little lover. What are they doing to him? My agonized imagination sees him in a cell, and I can't bear the thought of it!

I must try not to despair. After all he hadn't *done* anything; he wasn't even there—*that* at least we accomplished, Pushchin and I! He couldn't be punished just for thinking, could he? Yes, he could in this country.

ST. PETERSBURG

I love thee, Peter's fair creation,
I love thy looks, austere and grand,
Neva's majestic divagation
Along the granite-bound strand.

Alexander Pushkin, *The Bronze Horseman*

St. Petersburg! He had forgotten what it was like: a city armored in granite and ice, floating on spectral mists, under skies streaked with opalescent green. As they drove into the Palace Square, the last pallid reflection of daylight went slipping down the Petropavlovski Cathedral's long spire. Dusk muted the square Rastrellian pile of the Winter Palace, turning it into a gray block pierced by tall windows blazing forth lemon-yellow light. It all looked phantasmagoric, solid yet unsubstantial, a structure erected by a sorcerer's whim, out of ice and fog, to topple noiselessly when its purpose was accomplished.

A sense of unreality had held Grisha captive all through his journey. Cocooned in his fur coat, he slept and drowsed, stumbled out for the change of horses, fell asleep again, always in the same state of bewilderment. The three days of travel had spun off as smoothly as a dream: urgent forward motion, snowy countryside reeling away on both sides of the speeding sledge, bells jingling; in front of him the solid silhouette of the driver, and further forward a glimpse of a horse's head tossing sideways. A few episodes clearer than the rest: the buxom hostess of an inn where they stopped, shaking her kerchiefed head at him in pity, her cheek on her hand: "And where are they taking you, such a young one?" The stationmaster, saying under his breath with a dark look at the *feldjäger's* green ramrod-straight back: "Yes, many of the likes of him flying all over the countryside, like buzzards to a feeding . . ."

A convoy of four grenadiers came marching out of the Winter Palace's side entrance, where the sledge had stopped, and took him over from the *feldjäger*. He went limping through countless corridors, his escort tramping clankingly on both sides of him. Once he slowed up, out of breath, and was immediately prodded on by a rifle butt. And that ungentle prod was like the violent jolt in the middle of a dream that preludes awakening. It all solidified into reality.

After a long tramp through the basement corridors he was finally deposited in a long low-vaulted room—guard room by the looks of it. It was sparsely furnished, with a long deal table bisecting it. A grenadier stationed himself inside the glass door, white-pantalooned legs a-straddle, gigantic and motionless, an oversize specimen out of Sergey's toy soldier regiment. Grisha looked about him, every detail of the room registering with unnatural brightness on his retina—scratches on the table, discolored floor, several officers' swords propped up in a sheaf in the corner. He took off his coat and sat down at the table. Beyond it, he saw now, was a green leather couch; an officer lay on it fast asleep, his greatcoat rolled up under his head.

Grisha's arrival awakened him; he sat up and stretched, his face babyishly creased from his improvised pillow; a wide yawn split it. He sat on the couch, shaking his tousled head and scratching himself vigorously. His eyes stopped on Grisha and widened. "*Voyons*, a new guest!" Grisha returned the look, with equal curiosity. Barrel-chested, round-faced, blue-eyed, a gap-toothed smile dawning under a small fair moustache—he reminded Grisha of Sergey's regimental friends. "I don't believe we've met, have we? Allow me to introduce myself, I'm Lieutenant——"

A hollow bark came from under the sentinel's bucketlike shako: "Prisoners are not allowed to talk to each other."

The Lieutenant gave him a comic scowl. "Come on now, Potapenko, I've known you a long time. We're not going to discuss any political matters, just introduce ourselves. I don't believe I've seen you anywhere around here, have I?" he said to Grisha.

"I've just been brought up from Moscow."

"Moscow? Oh, then you . . ."

The rifle came down with a thud. "No talking among prisoners."

The blue eyes blazed suddenly. "To the devil's mother with you, you son-of-a-bitch. And suppose I do go on talking, what is it going to be—rifle butt in the teeth? That's more than you and yours ever got from me in the twelfth!"

The toy grenadier unexpectedly turned human. "Your Honor Dmitry Vassilitch, what am I to do? Those are my orders. And no, sir, you'll get no rifle butt in the teeth from me—I'll be the one to be given the rods if they find out I let you talk. . . ."

"All right, all right, don't cry." The Lieutenant made a contrite grimace. "I know the regulations. I was just taken aback to see this boy—this young man—couldn't imagine that he was mixed up in our business." There was an interrogative lilt to his voice and Grisha answered it by nodding silently.

Silence ensued. There was a brief thunder of clattering footsteps outside, and Grisha saw through the glass door a squad of four dragoons in bronze helmets and cuirasses go marching by. He glanced back at his fellow prisoner. The Lieutenant seemed to have lost interest in him now. He was lolling back on the couch, staring at the ceiling and humming to himself. The tune teased with its familiarity. Presently Grisha recognized it as *Veillons au Salut de l'Empire*, a well-known air to which the members of the society, he knew, used Ryleev's words:

> Our native land languishes, sinking,
> Oppresséd, oh, despot, by thee . . .

After this introduction, however, he switched to a jauntier Béranger tune. In a little while words joined it. He sang them casually, not quite under his breath, carefully not looking at Grisha:

> *On a pris, on a pris*
> *Petit Serge, le fourmi . . .*

Listening to these senseless words with growing attention, Grisha understood that he was being given information. He bent his mind to the interpretation. *Le fourmi*—an ant—*muravey* in Russian—Mouraviov! It stood to reason that *"petit Serge, le fourmi"* was that same Sergey Mouraviov whose regiment in Kamenka would, according to Pushchin, follow him anywhere. . . . Taken! The southern branch had done as poorly as the northern, then. . . . But he wasn't all that interested in that dimly known legendary figure. What he wanted more than anything else was information about Pushchin. Perhaps . . .? He cleared his throat, and, his voice wobbling huskily with nervousness, sang in his turn, equally careful not to look at his listener.

> *Connaissez-vous mon ami,*
> *Mon ami Jeannot?*

The Lieutenant wrinkled his forehead over this for a moment. Then, intelligence flashing from his blue eyes, sang back:

> *On a mis, on a mis*
> *On a mis Jeannot Pushchin.*
> (So the sobriquet was a familiar one!)
> *Dans la Pierre et Paul forteresse.*

Pierre et Paul? That could only mean the dreaded Petropavlosk citadel, built on the island in the middle of Neva, and used as a prison for political offenders.

The grenadier at the door shifted uneasily, gave them a hunted look, but this time didn't call them to order. Involuntarily the two young men exchanged pleased smiles like two schoolboys in a classroom gulling the teacher, and Grisha was aware of an incongruous flash of triumph, quite irrelevant to the bad news he was given. A cozy sense of camaraderie pervaded the bleak guardroom.

The Lieutenant reached into the pocket of his *shinel* and pulled out a largish piece of black bread. He broke it in two and gave half to Grisha. "Better have it, it doesn't look as if we'll get any dinner. . . ." They chewed away in silent amity. The Lieutenant said, between swallows, in a low voice nicely calculated not to reach beyond Grisha's ears: "Not deliberately starving us, just disorganized. The Palace is chock full of prisoners. . . . A little soldier from my regiment slipped this to me on the sly. . . . I've always got on well with my men. . . . But they wouldn't follow me to the Senate Square," he said, even lower. His stocky chest rose and fell in a sigh.

They didn't talk after this. The Lieutenant made no further attempts to communicate with Grisha. He sat quietly on his couch, his cheerful young face slowly darkening and sharpening with some unhappy thoughts of his own. Time wore on, palpably. The candles on the table guttered, shadows flowed and ebbed, filling the corners as the sparse light foundered. Outside there was a sense of constant vigilant activity going on; squads passed and repassed, silhouetted in the glass door; commands rang out, rifle butts crashed against the floor, marching steps neared and receded. It was strange and melancholy to sit here idle, in the midst of all that suppressed activity. Grisha listened to it, propping his head on his hand, his eyes on the guttering candle, which began to grow gigantic before his eyes, its wavering flame burning a hole in the ceiling. . . . A hand shook him awake again. He looked wildly into the young officer's face and for a moment couldn't quite take in what he was saying. "Why don't you take the couch? You'll be more comfortable there."

Grisha rubbed his gummy eyes. "Oh, thank you. But you?"

"I'll sleep right here on the floor next to the stove. No, don't worry, I'm an old campaigner, I can sleep anywhere. . . ."

Staggering with sleepiness, Grisha was taken to the couch. He fell on it and hurtled into a black hole where room, couch, roommate were immediately and totally extinguished.

In the middle of the night he woke, with the sensation of being eaten alive. He stumbled off the couch and stood there, scratching himself frantically. The candles had grown squat. In their enfeebled light he saw the Lieutenant, lying by the stove, wrapped up in his greatcoat, his round face gone remote and stern, like a medieval knight's on a catafalque. His eyes flew open and he looked up at Grisha, immediately and thoroughly awake. "Ah, the bedbugs got you," he said, grinning, and throwing off the greatcoat, got to his feet. "Let's see what else we can arrange."

Not listening to Grisha's apologies, he got three chairs together into a semblance of a bed. "If you scrounge yourself up a little, and then I'll tuck you in . . ."

"Thank you, I am so sorry, I didn't mean to . . ."

Still like schoolboys in a dormitory, they whispered together.

"What do you think will happen?" Grisha asked, getting up on his improvised bed. "How long will we stay here . . .?"

"God only knows. The important ones don't stay around too long, they get hustled off for questioning immediately. . . . But little unimportant ones like us—well, I've been here three days . . ."

The doors flew open. Two sentries stepped into the room, their muskets at the ready, their gigantic shadows fluttering black and ragged behind them.

"It's all right, men," said the Lieutenant. "I'm helping my friend here to find a place to sleep. That couch is a fucking bedbug hotel. There you are," he said to Grisha, tenderly spreading his fur coat over him, "all neat and comfortable, like in Christ's bosom . . ."

The next morning a detail of soldiers came in to take the Lieutenant away; it was accompnaied by an elderly colonel in full uniform, with plumed tricorn, grizzled, erect, full of regimental probity. But not without bowels: he looked at the young lieutenant with grudging pity. "Ekh, Dmitry Vassilitch, so here you are. So that's where all the accursed *chphilosophy* brought you," he said, venomously corrupting the word, his hard eyes fixed angrily beyond the wayward Lieutenant on those others, who had muddled the stalwart lad with their theories, leading him hopelessly astray. "Well, can't be helped. 'Tenshun!" The squad stamped obediently into place.

[320]

"Just one thing, Colonel," said the Lieutenant, taking his place in the middle of the detail, "if orders could be given to feed this young man. . . ."

"What's this?"

"Well, we had nothing to eat the whole day yesterday. I'm an army man, I can get along, but this boy—he's not used to it . . ."

"They didn't feed you? Idiots, asses, I'll skin them alive," the Colonel thundered, making terrible eyes. The Lieutenant winked at Grisha encouragingly—a long look, fraught with an astonished sort of brotherliness, passed between them—and, stepping smartly in cadence, marched out of Grisha's life. The Colonel followed, grumbling angrily to himself. His solicitude, however, must have been confined to the military, because no food arrived until later in the afternoon, when a soldier brought in a pewter tea kettle containing pale tea. Grisha was drinking it thirstily, together with the remnant of the bread his erstwhile roommate had given him, when his father was ushered in.

Grisha stumbled to his feet, smiling awkwardly, aware of a vast relief filling him. At last! The heavy-hearted loneliness that had engulfed him since the Lieutenant was taken away was rolled back. The sheer relief of seeing that all-powerful arrogant figure, in this ghastly room! A little laugh escaped him at the sight of the incredulous look his father cast about him, not believing the surroundings in which he found his son; the next thing to do would be to get him out.

"So," said Prince Pyotr slowly. His lorgnetted look of cold disgust encompassed the room and finally stopped on Grisha. "This is indeed the right and proper spot for a member of an old and honorable family. Hauled here from Moscow like a common criminal, held under arrest in a guard room, due to be questioned about conspiring against his lord and sovereign. . . . I congratulate you, Prince Grigorii Petrovich Volynski."

Grisha hung his head. Yes, there was that, of course, he had forgotten. . . . There would have to be anger, there would have to be a tongue lashing, before he was forgiven and saved. He said, almost inaudibly: "I am sorry."

"Sorry!" The word fell from his father's lips as cold as an icicle. Grisha looked down at the cup of tea he was still holding. The comforting heat was going out of it; he would have to drink this pale repellent liquid cold. . . . But he didn't dare to lift the cup to his mouth. Unable to bear the silence, he asked timidly: "How—how is *maman?*"

"Prostrated ever since she was told of your exploits. Oh, it was a fine moment indeed for all of us: wonderful for your mother and sisters; wonderful for Sergey, having to hear that his brother had been plotting with the very rabble he had helped to disperse. Not to mention myself, having to see that upstart Chernyshev smirking with pleasure while he commiserated with me on my misfortune . . ."

With a weak flare of curiosity Grisha wondered again who Chernyshev was.

"Now listen well to what I have to say. His Majesty is lenient enough to take into consideration your youth and foolishness and the deleterious influence of the man Pushchin. In his heavenly kindness, he took the time to assure me personally of his mercy to you if you show your contrition by answering all the questions that will be put to you and give the authorities whatever information you have on that scum that you have become involved with. I felt it was safe to assure him that you would do so."

Grisha was silent; his head beginning to ache under the impact of the pitilessly clanging voice.

". . . Well?" it said, implacably. Grisha started.

"What—what is it you want me to . . .?" Some deed of contrition, something to atone, before he would be forgiven, taken away from here . . . A childish grievance began to scratch at his heart: no inquiries about whether he was being fed, how he had slept; only anger because this Chernyshev, whoever he was, had humiliated him. . . . All at once, he remembered Fomitch, babbling with fright, absurdly shielding him from the *feldjäger*.

He didn't look up; but he saw his father's hands balling themselves into fists; the voice rasped: "Didn't you understand? Give them all the information they need. Whatever you know about the *canaille* Pushchin, and whatever others . . ."

"Tell on Pushchin?" Lifting his head he stared incredulous at the portly stranger standing coldly incensed on the other side of the table.

"Are you under the misapprehension, you unutterable little booby, that by speaking up you would be breaking faith with the treacherous renegades who have somehow involved you in their filth? But they are falling all over themselves informing on each other! Yes, including the arch-conspirators. Ryleev, Trubetskoy, Obolenski. . . . That young pup Odoevski is writing the Tsar from his cell every day, like a love-sick girl, promising to disclose to him *the very root of things*—I've seen those letters myself! How do you suppose your name was obtained? Who do you suppose gave it to them but that triple-damned Pushchin?"

"No," said Grisha, "no, not Pushchin." His legs gave way under him and he fell down on the chair.

"Why not? Do you think they have principles, any of them? If they have no loyalty to the Emperor, why should they to themselves? You owe them nothing, I tell you. But you do owe something to your sovereign and mine. And to me. Do you know what I told His Imperial Majesty?" Putting his large white hands flat down on the table he leaned forward. "I said to him, 'Sire, unless my misguided son shows all proper contrition and redeems himself, I will adjure him, he will be no son of mine.' And I assure you I meant every word of this."

"Oh, yes," Grisha said, "yes, I know you did." He dropped his head down between his arms. There was a silence.

"From your birth," said his father's voice clearly, "I knew you would be a disappointment and a curse to me."

His footsteps retreated toward the door, it opened, closed. Panic overtook Grisha. He wanted to run after his father: *anything, anything, only don't leave me*. But his hands, gripping the edge of the table so hard that the nails ached, held him where he was. Only in thought a small boy ran limping after his father begging not to be left behind. And then the child was gone, as was the father. There was no one left but himself . . .

Later in the afternoon a detail of soldiers headed by a sergeant came for him. Again he was marched along ill-lit subterranean corridors and, finally, taken to the floor above and delivered into what he incuriously recognized as one of the great halls of the Hermitage. It was brightly lit as though for a state occasion but empty except for a brace of guards at the doorway and an officer at the further end. A row of card tables stood there covered by green baize against which neat white piles of documents showed up with special clarity. The businesslike look of this arrangement contrasted strangely with the festive radiance of several large candelabra stationed around the tables.

An officer was sitting at one of those official tables directly under the painting of Pope Clement IX. He wore the uniform of the Izmailovski Regiment with the general's oakleaves on the collar. It occurred to Grisha that, if the grenadiers standing stiffly by the door looked like oversize toy soldiers, this officer looked like a fit commander for them. His coloring came from a toymaker's paintbox. His hair and moustache were too black, his lips and cheeks too pink, his eyes were two shiny Greek olives. Some unidentifiable part of him creaked as he leaned forward to motion Grisha courteously to the chair in front of his table. In a pleasant tenor he identified himself as Adjutant General Chernyshev.

"I have the honor of knowing your father, Prince. In fact I had the pleasure of talking to him only the other day. Very distressing for a father, particularly with his record of unimpeached fidelity to the Emperor, to find his son in this situation." His voice was gravely sympathetic; but Grisha thought he saw a glint of malice in the shiny black eyes.

Grisha was silent, waiting.

"Well, now to business, my dear sir," said Chernyshev. "I understand your father has been to see you. I hope from my heart that you intend to follow the sound advice he has doubtless given you." He waited for a moment as though giving Grisha a chance to do so. "Of course, at your age—you are how old? Eighteen?—it is easy to be misled. The question is, by whom?" He waited again.

"Nobody," said Grisha. His voice was hoarse and he cleared his throat, before repeating, "Nobody misled me."

"I see. It was your own idea." There was gentle railery in his voice. He leaned toward Grisha across the table, and again that indefinable tiny sound came from him. This time Grisha was able to place it: he had heard it before, emanating from old Prince Yusupov. Adjutant General Chernyshev, it appeared, also wore stays. He went on, persuasively, "Look here, Prince, let us understand each other. *Je ne vous parle pas comme votre juge, mais comme un gentilhomme votre égal.* His Imperial Majesty isn't interested primarily in dispensing punishment to young scapegraces like you who at best are merely dupes of the instigators. Much more is at stake: a conspiracy that threatens the monarchy, the stability of Holy Russia itself. It is much more important to uncover the roots of such a conspiracy than to snap off insignificant little twigs—if you'll forgive me"— he smiled winningly—"like yourself. What is wanted is information. The Emperor is inclined to be merciful to a contrite sinner. Do you understand me, Prince?"

"But I have nothing to disclose."

"Really? Nothing? No information about any persons involved in a heinous conspiracy against the Emperor?"

"I don't know anything about any conspiracy."

"To be more specific, nothing about a meeting in which the members met to discuss ways and means of assassinating the Emperor?"

Grisha opened his mouth and found that no sound came from it; his throat had dried up. He stared with childish terror into his interrogator's eyes, which had lost their friendly Greek-olive shininess and were now as hard as agates. Mechanically he said, "I don't know what you mean," and heard his own voice, wavering, weak, the voice of an inept culprit making the last unconvincing denial before being punished.

"We know all about it, you see," said Chernyshev, smiling and nodding at him confidentially.

The door at the furthest end of the room crashed open and another detail of four soldiers and a sergeant came in. They moved at a deliberate pace, accommodating themselves to the man who walked between them, blindfolded and chain-bound hand and foot. They came to a stop. The blindfolded prisoner stumbled and righted himself, clanking in his chains.

"What the devil," said Chernyshev angrily, rising to his feet. Grisha too rose, staring: there was a frightening familiarity in the bearing of that hooded, chained figure.

The sergeant drew himself up, inflating his pouter pigeon chest even more, and saluted: "If it please your Honor, bringing in prisoner Ivan Pushchin for questioning, according to orders."

"Pushchin," Grisha whispered.

Chernyshev was saying angrily, "He was not due here until an hour from now. What damnable incompetence! What's the name of your commanding officer, Sergeant?"

"Pushchin!" Grisha shouted at the top of his lungs and started toward him. A chair overturned behind him; Chernyshev's voice rose angrily. The two guards, coming to life, intercepted him halfway across the room.

The prisoner raised his chained hands toward his blindfold and tore it off, revealing Pushchin's pale and shocked face. He shook his head, blinking, as at an apparition. "Grisha?" His voice was high with disbelief. "You here? What are you——?"

"Pushchin! Ivan Ivanitch! Pushchin!" Grisha repeated stupidly, still struggling unavailingly against the hands that were forcing him back into the chair he had left, holding him there. Chernyshev's voice, shrill with exasperation, said, "Prisoners are not permitted to converse with each other."

"Prisoners? Are you—?" Pushchin broke off. Grisha filled his eyes with the sight of the well-loved face, whose vivid darkness was now replaced by a yellowish-gray pallor; it was much thinner than when he had seen him last, cheekbones jutting out sharply above the hollowed-out cheeks. Even as he looked, the sharpened features became luminous with stark intensity of purpose. "But this is all nonsense," Pushchin spoke slowly, deliberately, every word weighted by the heaviness of a message that had to be gotten across. "It is a mistake; you shouldn't be here, you are innocent."

"Oh, let him go," Chernyshev said pettishly to the guards who still held Grisha in their big, white-gloved paws. Obediently they released him, lapsing into their former immobility at his side. Chernyshev's black eyes shifted nimbly from Grisha to Pushchin. "This is quite an affecting meeting," he said mildly, but with a distinct sneer. "However, it was not scheduled and must come to an end. Take him next door to wait."

Paying no attention to the order, Pushchin said loudly: "I wish to make a statement. Prince Volynski is not and has never been a member of the society to which I belong. I categorically deny . . ."

"My good sir, you must be aware that any such denials have very little weight. Particularly in your case. You have made denials about every one of your acquaintances. Others have tried to cooperate but not you . . ."

Grisha's inheld breath was released in a deep sigh. A sense of pride—even exultation—filled and lifted his heart. You see? he said silently to his absent father; and the last drop of poison—uncertainty, mistrust—was purged from his mind.

"Then I am punished indeed." Pushchin made a helpless gesture, raising his arms and letting them drop to his side, with a hopeless clatter of chains. "Your Excellency, it is bad enough to see friends whose culpability you know brought here; but to see an innocent boy being made to pay for a friendship formed in total ignorance of his friend's associations—Who accuses him? Let him be confronted with the man who accuses him. Ask for such a confrontation, it is your right," he said directly to Grisha.

"That'll be enough. Take him to the next room. Oh, let it be," Chernyshev added irritably, as the sergeant began fumbling the handkerchief that had served as a blindfold back on to Pushchin's face. "Now he thinks of it! Blockheads!"

As Pushchin was marched away, his eyes sought Grisha's again, commandingly. Grisha understood him as though he had spoken aloud. Tell them nothing, said those blazing eyes, that pale and wasted face.

"Well," Chernyshev said, settling himself back in the chair and painstakingly rearranging his papers with his small plump hands. "That was an interesting meeting. I hadn't realized the extent of your involvement with Pushchin. You must have been close friends."

"I have no intention of denying that," Grisha said. "He is my dearest friend."

"In fact, he might very well be the very one who had induced you to enter the illegal secret society."

"No, he didn't."

"Who then?"

"No one, your Excellency. No one had even approached me with such a proposition." He added, painstakingly: "And I am not a member."

A slight smile touched the inquisitor's rosy lips. "Very good, my boy. Quite to be expected—after all, you had just been given your instructions on what to say. . . . You do know, however, that Pushchin was one of the ringleaders of the unfortunate attempt of the fourteenth."

"So I have been told."

"And you were never privy to his intents?"

"Your Excellency, I wasn't even in St. Petersburg on the fourteenth."

"Yes, I am aware. Nevertheless, you might have been told. When there is that kind of an intense friendship between an older man and a younger one, there is usually complete trust between them. Thus it was in the days of ancient Greece, wasn't it? Damon and Pythias—Orestes and Pylades—as one who had every advantage of classical education, I am sure you are aware of this, hmmm?"

"I suppose so," Grisha answered, puzzled and vaguely uncomfortable. As Chernyshev's face moved closer, he perceived with a small shock that the rosiness of his cheeks was as unnatural as—although far more skillfully applied than—that of old Prince Yusupov's. He too was rouged and powdered. Grisha contemplated this discovery with some curiosity. The hair and the moustache, he reflected, must also be dyed. That was not as much of a surprise; quite a few army men of more mature years touched up their moustaches; but he knew no one else who wore rouge.

"Please have the goodness to answer the last question." There was a hint of shrillness again in Chernyshev's voice.

"I don't remember quite what it was," Grisha answered truthfully. What was it? Why was he being quizzed about ancient Greek personages, as though at a school examination? He was all at once overwhelmed by the absurdity and the tedium of this. Irresistibly his jaws quivered in an incipient yawn.

Chernyshev's smile grew rigid. "If you find this conversation boring, Prince," he began and stopped, his expression changing. Still another door opened; there was a simultaneous crash of rifle butts against the floor and the sentries came to attention, as did Chernyshev, leaping to his feet behind his table.

The Tsar had entered and was moving across the great room as relentlessly straight and swift as a tornado; the retinue of officers following him seemed drawn into his wake as helpless as chips. Eyes of impenetrable leaden gray slipped over Grisha, the small shapely head nodded minimally to Chernyshev, who immediately left the desk and joined his retinue. Then he was gone through the further door, into the room where Pushchin waited, and Grisha, left alone except for the guards, was able to let out his inheld breath.

Chernyshev returned in a few minutes. No longer paying any attention to Grisha, he scribbled a note. As soon as the ink was dried, he summoned the sergeant of the squad that had brought Grisha to the Hermitage and gave it to him.

Back to the guard room? The very thought of returning to that flea-infested, ill-lighted limbo filled Grisha with despair. But this time they didn't stay there long. A soldier thrust him into his coat, like a rough-handed nanny, another picked up the portmanteau that Fomitch had packed. Then he was led through many corridors, hustled outside, and put into a two-horse-drawn sleigh, in which yet another *feldjäger* was waiting.

The sleigh drew away from the Winter Palace. Smiling unconsciously Grisha gulped down drafts of winter air, as fresh and icy as chilled champagne. Bells jingled merrily in the darkness, streetlamps bloomed and faded as they drove swiftly along the embankment. Freedom! They crossed the bridge across the frozen Neva. But it was only after they began crossing another bridge, and the squat breastworks of a fortress loomed dim before him, that Grisha realized that he was being taken to the Petropavlovsk Prison.

Claire's Journal, January 15

Now that Z.N. has written to Grisha's father, there is nothing to do but wait. The worst possible ordeal for me: the natural thing for me is to act, to bend the circumstance to my will.

Lying sleepless in bed at night, I begin to build all sorts of fantastic schemes; going to St. Petersburg, somehow gaining audience with the new Tsar, making him listen to me. *Sire, you have just inherited the throne of Russia, do not dim the radiance of your new reign by the persecution of a mere boy. Since he is a Russian, half his heart already belongs to his sovereign; generosity will obtain the rest; this is a very special youth, sensitive and strong, a lovely spirit just emerging from childhood with so much before him: can even you afford to throw all this away?*

Or else somehow getting in touch with whatever members of the society are still at large, evolving some scheme to penetrate the prison where Grisha is, bribing the guards, rescuing him—oh, yes, and Pushchin too, naturally. Then flight to the border, to Europe. . . . Oh, such silly fantasies, an absurd return to childhood; they soothe me as though I were a child reading fairy tales, and I can go to sleep. . . .

I suppose my schemes for kidnaping Allegra were something like that too: a desperate struggle to stay in command of circumstance. Fantastic and practical at once, the way I went about it. Oh, very level headed. I kept Mary and P.B. in complete ignorance; even in the midst of my obsession I knew better than to involve them. But I did deliberately fascinate poor Henry Reveley all over again and then sidetracked his impending proposal into a scheme to help me. I still remember how pleased Mary was at our *tête-à-têtes.* Ah, at last the troublesome relative showing some sense, settling down!

Yes, that was Mary—so very rational and so unreasonable at the same time. My life was like a house after a storm had passed through it—the roof off, windows smashed—and she wanted me to disregard all this and start housekeeping. . . . So exactly like her.

I had it all planned. The visit to Bagnacavallo to spy out the lie of the land, the abduction itself . . . I knew Allegra would know me. Children don't forget. She would know my touch—my voice, I said. She would be only too happy to come with me. And then—then—we would lose ourselves, sink out of sight, leave Italy. I didn't think there would be pursuit once I had her: he didn't like scandal.

I even had a schedule of sorts worked out. I was preparing to tell Mary casually of my impending visit to Lady Mount Cashel, not to expect to hear from me, for a while; and then, and then. . . .

P.B. didn't have to say it. The message was as clear as though his dear face had turned into a death's head.

I remember running to the door and screaming—screaming—I can still feel that scream tearing along my vocal cords, searing them: "Murderer!"

For years I think I have carried that scream silent inside me. But now of course I see that if he was the murderer I was an accessory. I have said so to Grisha.

Claire's Journal, January 16

I still have some drafts of the desperate letters I sent when it became clear that he wouldn't let me see Allegra. Oh, hateful ones—my words seemed to turn to snakes and toads as soon as they left my mouth. I hated it and I couldn't stop. No, not true, I didn't want to stop.

As if I could ever want to hurt him with what I knew. I had written that once in this diary. But I had done just that. I used all my knowledge of him to hurt him. I, who know the repellent image of himself he had built; I, who had done my utmost to dispel it so that he would be free—I deliberately went on to build it up again. Madame Claire, he wrote furiously, that man-eating bitch, the damned whore. I very subtly let him see that, yes, there was a moral ugliness in him that was mirrored in his appearance; yes, Geordie, you were right, your wife was right, your mother was right, I was wrong, you are a monster, after all.

After he had sent her to Bagnacavallo, I wrote the worst letter yet. I said to him in it: "Are you punishing her because you have convinced yourself that she isn't yours after all? Give her back to me then. I would settle for her to have been a spawn of a sordid night's debauch if that would bring her back to me. Give her back to me, she isn't yours."

Ah, me, but that stung him. He used to complain to P.B. about my letters, but he never showed him this one, nor even spoke of it. All he did was vilify me in such terms that P.B. left him in anger. . . .

Let me write it down, let me turn that dagger once more in the secret wound where it has festered so many years and pull it out at last.

Was it because of this letter that he didn't go to see her in Bagnacavallo? Was it because of this letter that she died alone?

Claire's Journal, January 19

A miserable day. I went to the Jaenisches' to give a lesson. Took a hack back. There had been a heavy fall of snow and the streets were almost impassable. I shivered in the drozhky, staring at the brass medallion bouncing on the *izvoshchik's* back, it seemed to me for hours, as we struggled to get home. I remembered Grisha waiting for me in his sleigh. The boy's eyes brilliant with anticipation, the unconscious smile on his mouth that was just beginning to lose that touching fledgling look . . . Hands tucking the furs around me, trembling. . . . Later, the warm bed, fire flickering in the fireplace; the body in my arms, smooth, young, fragrant with that special odor of youth . . .

I have drunk lashings of hot tea and still I am cold. Can't stop shivering— . . . And so tired, like that poor *izvoshchik's* nag, with scarcely enough strength to stand up, having to struggle on to keep from falling.

Oh, how I ache for Italy—ah, to feel the blessed warmth, to stretch out in the sun and let it all dissolve in the burning, healing, indifferent rays . . .

Claire's Journal, January 20

Bad news came today. Z.N. has heard about Grisha, not from the father, but from a St. Petersburg crony, who writes him that young Prince Volynski is in prison. Not only I but everybody in the house is made miserable by this. Even Marya Ivanovna is subdued and is keeping little Johnny by her all the time. Z.N. tries to cheer us up by saying everything is so confused in St. Petersburg that the merest rumors are given out as gospel truth.

But somehow I can't feel hopeful. . . . Perhaps it's because I am feeling so ill. I keep shaking with the cold so that I find it hard to write. And there's a pain in my side.

But all that is nothing compared to the pain inside of me. I can't bear to think of my poor Grisha in prison. Chained perhaps. They say that many of them are chained hand and foot. How he would hate them fumbling about with his bad leg! And suppose he falls ill? What happens then? No one to take care of him, the bloodsucking doctors bleeding him. . . .

Couldn't anyone stop them? Don't they know what just pure commonsense tells me, it is madness to bleed a body already wasted by illness . . .? Make them stop, take those leeches away. . . .

Strangely enough, in the beginning the cell was more bearable than the guard room had been. Anything better than that bug-infested limbo, that way station on the road to nowhere, where you waited with a sickly sinking heart, not knowing what would become of you.

After he had been searched and issued prison clothing (ragged linen trousers and shirt), he was given a prison supper of *shchi* and black bread, which he ate with appetite after his two days of near-starvation. After that he wanted nothing but sleep. The night light—a green glass jar with a wick floating in oil—glimmered reassuringly on the table, bringing back nursery memories, recalling the cozy glimmering of the candles before the ikons in his own bedroom. He curled up on the hard narrow bed, drew the gray hospital-like blanket over his head, and dropped as through a trap door into the black oblivion of dreamless sleep.

Even the next morning, on awakening, he lay on his bed without feeling any special distress, as he surveyed his new quarters. A strange calm possessed him, as if he had been hurtled barely alive on to an unpromising shore and was still more concerned with survival than surroundings. The nightlamp shone on the table, but now something like blanched twilight filled the cell. This sparse illumination came in through a large window deeply niched in the thick wall. Thick iron bars criss-crossed the glass, which was plastered over, letting in some light but no view. The cell was about six feet by eight, steeply vaulted so that one could stand upright only in the middle. Bed table and chair furnished it, also a stove, with a slop pail next to it. The walls were whitewashed; but damp patches started through the paint, and the cracks, he saw with disgust, were alive with insects.

He wondered what time it was and, as though in answer, heard the chimes ringing in the distance. The brassy din resolved itself laboriously into *God Save the King*, the familiar tune percolating into his cell as diluted as the daylight that struggled through the blanketed windows. He remembered it from last night. It rang out on the hour, he supposed. But which hour? He had no way of telling, since they had taken away his breguet watch.

His unnatural serenity began to drain away. A minute tremor of anxiety started up in him, slowly expanding into a quake. The panic was delayed, as the unlikely morning erupted into a feeble spurt of activity. A soldier came in, bringing him tea with sugar; another, a gray faceless mute of a veteran, brought water for his ablutions, swept out his cell and took away the slop pail. The commandant of the prison, General Sukin, whom he had met the night before, grizzly, erect, wooden legged, came stumping in, accompanied by a taciturn prison doctor, whose examination of Grisha, to his relief, consisted merely of a stare, ranging from head to foot, and a dismissing nod.

"Well, how do you like your quarters?" the commandant asked genially. "This is one of the better cells: nice and dry." He looked about him with proprietary pride.

Grisha asked involuntarily: "What are the worst ones like, then?"

The commandant smiled, with agreeableness. "The worst are— oh, worse." He added, not unkindly, "Don't look so downhearted, my dear young sir. There are others here much worse off then you. They have to wear chains and such orders had not been given us about you. And you are allowed tea and sugar. Apparently the authorities have some hopes of you."

After he left, an unreal little priest as old as time came in to visit Grisha. A dim old voice questioned him quaveringly about the state of his immortal soul: had he been baptised? was he a believer? had he taken communion? Grisha answered obediently, bowing his head as the trembling old hand traced a sign of the cross over him.

"Pray to God, my child, He will restore you to a state of grace and soften your heart, so that you will confess your deeds to the proper authorities and thus be absolved from guilt."

Grisha straightened up in revulsion. "By you, Father? Or by General Chernyshev?" But the dim eyes blinked incomprehendingly meeting his incredulous look, and he realized that the words were a meaningless patter, learned by rote over the years and no longer even heard by him who uttered them.

Then again the squeak and rattle of the bolt, the clanking of the keys, the heavy thump of the outside bolt being dropped. Silence.

I can't get out, said the starling. Miss Clairmont—Claire—but this was before she had become Claire—said once that those were the saddest words in the English language. On the whole, he agreed.

There were some uncomfortable discoveries to be made about his living quarters. The cell was divided, it seemed, into two distinctly delineated horizontal zones of contrasting temperatures. The stove pipe running overhead and disappearing into the window exuded considerable heat, which pervaded the upper reaches, making your head ache. On the other hand, a solid layer of cold air lay along the floor, freezing your feet.

Even more disagreeable was the discovery about the judas window. In the guard room he had been made miserable by the glass door; he had felt exposed to the eyes of every passerby. Here, sealed away as he was from human eyes, he could at least have privacy, he thought. Not so. The green burlap curtain on the other side of the little window in the door could be twitched aside at any moment to enable the guard to look in on you. They wore felt boots so that the approach was unheard. What especially tormented Grisha was that there was no corner in the cell immune from their furtive stare, and he could never be sure when it was fixed on him: it could be on him even as he used the slop pail.

The discovery drove him to his bed, the best remedy both for the unseen watcher and the cold emanating from the slimy floor. A sort of stupor descended on him; he even nurtured it: the alternative might well be howling despair. He took to sleeping a great deal, sinking effortlessly into an instant drowse. On waking up he would lie quietly, thinking of nothing, incuriously observing the patches of damp on the wall; as he watched, they would change shape, become in turn lakes, grotesque faces and bodies. There was one that took the shape of a woman's body curled up in sleep; the image solidified and held. Involuntarily his eyes sought it again and again. It made him think of Claire as he had seen her last, in his bed.

Was that all over now? he thought. Would he ever again feel the answering movement of a woman's body beneath his? He began remembering how it had been; his body awakened and took over relentlessly, completing the memory by itself. He turned over and lay face down on his pallet, letting the racking urge carry him strengthless to its culmination, feeling to the last the loneliness of the unaccompanied act.

The sadness came afterward. It was so profound that it became apparent to him that he could no longer afford to remember Claire. So as not to be quite alone he summoned another presence— sisterly, tutelary, benevolent. Claire, the dear seductress, melted away, banished to the furthest confines of his mind by a stern effort of will, and in her place Miss Clairmont stepped forward, neat, clear-eyed, sweetly acerbic (but there was the mole at the right corner of her mouth—carefully he obliterated it), carrying a pile of books in her slender arms for her pupil to read. He could see the letters of a title—*Islam*—shine in faded gold on the Morocco leather.

[335]

She had been made happy, over and over again, he remembered, by his liking of P.B.'s poetry. So to please her, he began reconstructing in his mind parts of *The Revolt of Islam*: passage after involuted passage swam into his mind . . .

> Oh Spirit vast and deep as Night and Heaven
> Mother and soul of all to which is given
> The light of life, the loveliness of being . . .
> Lo, thou dost reconvert . . .

No, that was wrong.

> . . . reascend the human heart. . . .

It was a familiar sensation of toiling along a mist-filled path that led you higher and higher, toward a soaring mountain peak intermittently glimpsed. After a while, the path became obliterated, and he gave up, turning to other easier lines, that he also loved:

> Hell is a city much like London,

(Would he ever get to London now? Or to France? Or anywhere?)

> A populous and a smoky city,
> There are all sorts of people undone
> And there is little or no fun done
> Small justice shown and still less pity. . . .

And:

> I saw Murder on the way
> He wore a mask like Castlereagh . . .
> Very smooth he looked and grim . . .

Murderously angry lines clanging like a sword; they came easily to the tongue. With a sudden spasm of desolate hatred, he thought of his father walking out of the guard room, coldly prepared to purge him out of his mind.

That had been the best verse of that poem—the *Masque of*

Anarchy, it had been called—he remembered being alternately uplifted and disappointed as he read it. Miss Clairmont had said that very few poets were capable of sustained excellence. "Perhaps only Shakespeare in his sonnets . . ."

"Pushkin too," he had told her. He had tried to convey to her something of the felicitous ease, the sustained harmonious excellence that had made him special in the crop of modern Russian poets. And she had cried: "Oh, how I wish I understood Russian better." She had even talked of studying it in earnest. "I translated some Goethe once and not incredibly. Perhaps I will do better for your Pushkin one day than that ridiculous Pichot did for Albé."

Pushchin, like other friends of the poet, had in his possession a written transcript of the first three cantos. He had let Grisha have them for a few days, at the end of which Grisha had not only copied them but committed them to memory. He began now reciting them to himself, starting with the lightheartedly galloping first lines,

> My uncle, of unswerving virtue,
> When he became severely ill
> Knew how to do just what was proper
> And kept himself respected still.
> We all may learn from his behavior,
> But what damned boredom, oh my Savior,
> To stay with him both night and day
> Not moving even a step away. . . .

The poem went on, sparkling with worldly mockery, breathing tenderness, veiled with sadness, living. . . .

Sometimes a line or a word would elude him and he would scrabble it out patiently, aware of an absurd triumph when he could fit it into its proper space so that the lines could go marching on. Reluctantly the tedious hours kept pace with them, slipping away. . . .

Presently he made up a game, trying to accompany actions and memories with suitable tags. Remembering Monsieur Lachaine he would quote with relish:

> Monsieur L'Abbé, a Frenchman needy,
> Unwilling to fatigue the child
> Not so much taught him as beguiled;

For pompous pedantry ungreedy
He'd scold him gently for a lark
And walk him in the Summer Park . . .

Or say to himself, as he mopped up the last of the soup from the greasy tin plate with a piece of bread,

Ours was such bread as captive tears
Have moistened for a thousand years. . . .

The last came from *The Prisoner of Chillon*, which he used to quote *in toto* with sentimental pleasure, a grandiose work, surely capturing the very essence of man's indomitable spirit in captivity. (Miss Clairmont had listened with an air of withholding that he knew to be directed at the author rather than the work.) Certain cynical afterthought occurred to him now, as he recollected it: could there be glibness in the lines he had used to find sublime?

When Zhukovski's translation of *The Prisoner of Chillon* first came out, their drawing master, a gloomy young student hopelessly in love with his sister Sophie, then unmarried, made a drawing for her illustrating the poem. Gothic pillars emerged from the artistically executed murk; three prisoners, dressed in picturesque rags, leaned against them in various attitudes of despair. They had all admired the gloomy realism of the scene, Sophie even shedding a few tears over it:

"Oh, Monsieur Kostolyapin"—such, indeed, to his justifiable despair, was his name—"it looks so real! I am sure that's exactly the way it is in dungeons!"

Grisha smiled, remembering this. Well, not exactly. The illustrator had left out the slop pail. So for that matter, now that he thought of it, did the poet. He only mentioned the high-minded torments; he spoke eloquently of how the prisoners suffered—but not of how they must have smelled.

(That was another torture; the unclean miasma of the cell, as if the impurities of generations of prisoners had been channeled into this coffinlike space; an eternal frowst attached itself to him, so that he felt he moved in a sort of dirty cloud, smelling to high heaven. He would strip and scrub himself thoroughly when they brought the regulation ewer and basin of water and would feel clean for a short while and then it was upon him again. . . .)

[338]

But then the next line swam into his mind, smiting his heart with its curt truth:

> They chained us each to a column stone
> And we were three—yet each alone. . . .

Somewhere in this silent, smelly fortress, his friend Pushchin was immured, perhaps only a few feet away from him, in the next cell. It became another torment to think of him so close yet unavailable. *Yet each alone*—yes, the poet may not have known about the uncleanliness, but he did know about loneliness.

So he plodded doggedly through the tedious hours, telling poetry like beads, huddled in his bed, his inner eye averted from the dingy cell around him. Whenever he stopped, incredulity would descend on him. *This can't be but it is, it is; when I open my eyes, it's all there, the stained walls, the cracks alive with insects, the whitish, hopeless sepulchral light, not quite dusk, not quite dawn. Somewhere outside, there's the delicate shuffle of the guards' felt slippers; a rustle in the corner as something unspeakable scurries out of sight into a rat hole. . . .*

"You should move about a bit, your Honor," said the soldier who brought him his meals, breaking the silence for the first time. Grisha looked at him as surprised as if the rickety table had spoken up. "It's not so good to be always lying down on your bed like that."

"It isn't?" Grisha said vaguely, taking him in. Sharp nose, mousy hair, small eyes: a nondescript sketch of a face carelessly drawn and rubbed out into anonymity—now suddenly coming alive with kindness.

"No, sir. There was a gentleman in this cell before. He used to walk around and exercise every day. Then I guess he got bored; he took to his bed and died."

"Well," said Grisha with a twisted smile, "I'm bored too."

"Ah, no, your Honor, don't you talk like that. Why, you've only been here four days . . ."

Was that all? It felt like half a lifetime.

"And another thing, sir, why don't you ask them to give you a book? Gentlemen like you enjoy reading, I know . . ."

"Why, would it be any use asking?" When Grisha was brought to Petropavlovsk, all of his possessions had been taken away, including the book he had with him, his copy of the latest volume of Karamzin's *History*. Since that could hardly be considered seditious, he had taken it for granted that no reading material of any kind was allowed.

"No harm trying, your Honor. Some of the others have asked and got it, so why not you?"

"Oh, if only . . ." This was the first time in his life that he was without a book within easy reach.

". . . And the most important thing is don't you lose hope, your Honor. Things might change. The Lord has already afflicted you, looks like. Now may be the time for Him to make up for it and show you some mercy." He was looking down on Grisha's foot as he spoke, and the look was so informed with kindness that no resentment was possible, only comfort.

Grisha's lips trembled. In the blurred radiance of suddenly starting tears, the plain figure of the nondescript little soldier seemed to shine luminous. The whole cell was irradiated, as though by an arrival of an angel, by the simple words of kindness, a radiance that seemed to linger long after he had left.

On his next morning visit, the Commandant brought with him a sealed official envelope, together with pen and ink, and requested Grisha to answer in writing all the questions submitted to him. "Consider them very carefully, however, Prince. Take your time and be sure to answer truthfully." He added, with an air of making a quiet little joke, "No hurry, you know, you have all the time in the world."

Before he left, Grisha asked him about the chances of getting something to read and was pleasantly surprised at being answered in the affirmative. "Not the kinds of books you are used to, I daresay. But yes, Prince, even here we can always put our hands on the Holy Bible." He bent that fuzzy, incongruously benevolent look on Grisha. "It might help you to answer the questions in the right spirit of humility and remorse."

Grisha unsealed the envelope, and looked through the list of the questions, signed with a signature which this time he had no trouble deciphering: Adjutant General Chernyshev.

He noticed that he had been given more paper than he needed to make his answers, if he wrote small; and he immediately, automatically squirreled some of the sheets of paper away under his mattress. If they would take the ink away, he could probably make some, using the lampblack and water, and easing a splinter off from the underside of the table for a pen. He was beginning to act like a prisoner already, he thought, learning all sorts of grubby little habits like blowing his nose with his fingers, so that he could keep his handkerchief clean and use it to cover the grease-stained pillow. With time he might even learn to disregard the sentry's eye watching him through the judas window.

He addressed himself to answering to the first few questions and was aware of a sheer childish pleasure at writing his name. A submerged selfhood slowly began struggling uppermost, as he wrote. Yes, I am Grigorii, Pyotr's son, Volynski; I am eighteen years old; I have been educated privately—he listed the names of his tutors, writing them down carefully, in his best script, experiencing, as he wrote, the painful pleasure of exercising cramped muscles.

Those were all comparatively innocuous questions; but the last one brought him to a full stop: At what time and from whom did you first obtain your freethinking and liberal mode of thought? How did it become entrenched in your mind?

But of course he didn't need to answer immediately; as Commandant Soukhin had told him, he had all the time in the world.

Later in the afternoon, the soldier brought Grisha a tattered old Bible. Overjoyed, Grisha seized on it. The worn dusty cover felt as soft as Morocco leather to his lovingly patting fingers; the age-browned print on the dun pages leaped out at him with joyful brilliance. Tearing his eyes away from them, he looked gratefully at the soldier. "Thank you," he said, "thank you for everything."

The soldier answered his look stolidly, all traces of humanity again rubbed out of his gray face. "The commandant's orders, your Honor." He put the soup plate down on the table, moving so that his thickset body was between the table and the door. Then, holding Grisha's eyes with his own, barely moving his lips, he said: "*Isaiah,* chapter ten."

The next moment he was gone, the door of the cell going through its usual gamut of depressing sounds—the muffled thud of wood, the rattle of the keys, the rusty slide of the bolts—as it closed behind him.

With unsteady fingers, Grisha leafed over the book, until he came to the right page. It stared at him, mysterious, uncommunicative, the angled letters of the Slavonic script jumping erratically beneath his straining eyes. The first reading of the chapter yielded no clue. The passage in which Israel is comforted with promise of deliverance from Assyria—could that be it? It gave him no comfort. He read and reread it doggedly, in hope, in incredulity, finally in resentful despair. Could he have misunderstood; could it have been merely the little soldier's idea of comforting him with what seemed an appropriate text? Or perhaps a cruel mystification, his grubby angel turned grubby devil to plague him? The thought was only a little less unbearable than another one, stirring in him like a worm: perhaps he had only dreamed or imagined it. . . . He read the page carefully once more, tracing each line with his finger, like a child learning to read; and suddenly felt a line of minute perforations under his finger tip. His heart began thudding against his ribs so loudly that for a moment he was afraid that it would be heard outside. There *was* a message then. It teased his searching finger-tips, it hid behind the insufficiency of light. Only after a long time was he able to tip the book into the proper angle under the flickering lamp, so that the pricked out characters could be distinguished.

Nothing known against you. You are innocent. Deny steadfastly. Volunteer nothing. Do not despair.

Later, brushing his fingers again across the mutely speaking page, he came across another tiny benediction: a single perforation discreetly placed under the letter P.

He sat for a long time at his table, staring down unseeingly, tears pouring down his face. Let the watcher slyly lifting the curtain at the judas window see this unmanly spectacle, he thought with an incongruous spark of lightheartedness, and report to the authorities that the prisoner's heart was touched by contriteness, as he read the Bible.

Even without the secretive little signature he would have known who the sender of the message was. He could see his friend painstakingly limning the message with his chained hands, trusting to happenstance, yet taking his measures against disaster; taking the time to prick out "you are innocent" so that the rest of the message, if intercepted, would not sound like advice to a guilty accessory.

Nothing known against you. But there is, they do know, he told the absent advisor. They know about that meeting where we talked so calmly, so rationally about murdering the Emperor. Yes, we had been against it; but not utterly so. Yakubovich was not rejected out of hand, merely held in reserve. And he himself—his voice came back to him, stammering rapturously "A holy sacrifice. . . ." A memory followed as always by a dark backwash of guilt.

Yes, here was the danger. The creeping uneasiness, the deep perverse desire to confess it all and be absolved—that was the thread by which he could be unraveled.

But I will try. I will try. He recalled Chernyshev's petulant accusation to Pushchin: "Others have cooperated but not you." And again the flood of pride rose in him, driving back despair and cowardice. Dear Pushchin, like a good officer, protecting his comrades even as he made an orderly retreat, while all about him ran pell-mell in panic. Yes, I'll follow you along that road, I'll deny steadfastly, no threat or cajoling will draw any names from me.

Another communication came the same day, through more legitimate channels. The commandant himself brought it to him and watched with an indulgent smile as Grisha drew the letter out of the unsealed envelope.

The familiar scent, the well-known lacy script on pressed paper. "*Mon fils,*" his mother wrote, "I beg of you on my bended knees, avail yourself of the opportunity our blessed Emperor has given you in his angelic mercy. Atone for your errors by telling them whatever they want to know. Have mercy on me: I am ill, I am writing you this with the last of my strength. . . ."

Clear as clear he could see her, lying on her lounge, *souffrante,* with Nikolavna hustling about her with vinegar compresses and Hoffman's drops. Something soft and self-indulgent moved treacherously within him, responding to her weakness. Suppose . . .?

He thrust his hand inside the Bible where a splinter marked the precious page. Secretively his fingers sought the minute perforations. Deny steadfastly, they said to him, to the end.

Later that evening he returned to the questionnaire and steadily wrote out his answer to the last question. "I am not aware of possessing any specially freethinking tendencies; my mode of thought has been formed by education provided to me by Godfearing parents, whose only desire had been to make me fit for service to the Emperor."

Another lighthearted spark of self-satisfaction soared up in him: I am well fitted for diplomatic service after all, he thought.

The next day Grisha was summoned to another interview. He was given his own clothes to put on, blindfolded with his own handkerchief, taken out of his cell and out of the fortress. Again a short ride, the fresh night air, eagerly gulped, the fudged brightness of the streetlamps penetrating the thin folds of linen. He was helped out of the sledge, led indoors. Walking through interminable corridors, he guessed that he was back in the Hermitage. But when his handkerchief was removed he found himself in a smaller room than the one where he had been questioned at first. Its walls were hung with paintings of the Italian school. Directly under a big-eyed, mysteriously smiling Raphael Madonna, Adjutant General Chernyshev sat at his desk, as jaunty as ever.

Grisha took the chair in front of the desk prepared for the worst. The inquisition would be thorough, he knew, and this time a succoring angel in the shape of his friend Pushchin couldn't be counted on to make an appearance.

And indeed Chernyshev's attitude was now businesslike, without the false bonhomie that had marked the previous interview. No more genial, though malice-spiked, mentions of his father, no caressing references to the prisoner's tender years. He was now being questioned as a criminal.

"You say you are not a member. But you don't deny that you were on terms of exceptional friendship with the conspirator Pushchin. Do you persist in saying that you had no intimations of his plans?"

"I heard nothing from Pushchin after he left Moscow."

"What about before? Were you aware then that he left precisely in order to foment a disturbance in St. Petersburg?"

"But he didn't," Grisha blurted out. "I am sure he had nothing like that on his mind."

"Is that what he told you?" There was a quick oily flash in Chernyshev's eyes.

"Well, he . . ." Grisha stopped helplessly. "I mean . . ."

"You mean, obviously, that you had discussed the situation. As fellow members. Isn't that correct, Prince?"

It was then that Grisha understood the full meaning of the instructions pricked out in chapter ten of Isaiah. It wasn't merely the question of taking a heroic stance, and thus retaining your self-respect. It was the only possible strategy. Keeping silent, volunteering nothing, denying all knowledge kept you not only from incriminating your friends but also from betraying yourself. Your only safety lay in silence and denial.

"Pushchin told me that he was going to see his family in St. Petersburg, as he did the year before."

"And of course you had no suspicion . . .?"

Disregarding the sneer, Grisha answered stolidly: "None."

He was set to answer the next question in the same style. But it came from a totally different direction, as brutal as cannon shot.

"Be good enough to tell us about the meeting at which the assassination of the Emperor was decided on."

And again a wave of pure guilt swept over him. Denials, explanations crowded to his lips: but it wasn't so—it hadn't been decided—on the contrary nobody wanted to, Fonvizin even said— No. Pushchin's gray eyes blazed at him sternly, forbidding him. Deny steadfastly. Until the end.

He said in a low voice from which he couldn't keep a tremor: "I know nothing of such a meeting."

"Really? Nothing at all?"

"Nothing."

"And yet, Prince, we have a deposition identifying you as one of the members present at that meeting."

Who had named him? Fonvizin, who had smiled at him with such fatherly affection because of his youth? Nikita Muraviov, who hadn't noticed him at all? Or perhaps . . . Shivering, he remembered his father's contemptuous "writing the Tsar every day from his cell." He began to pray silently, let it be Muraviov, let it even be Fonvizin, only not Sasha, please God, not Sasha Odoevski.

"Well, Prince? Surprised?" There was a note of triumph in the query.

Grisha dragged his mind away from the sickening speculation and fixed it on Chernyshev. "I can't imagine who could have said so or why."

Chernyshev smiled contemptuously and, veering again, started asking him more questions about Pushchin.

He was beginning to catch on to Chernyshev's technique. It consisted of changing from one line of questioning to another; keeping you perpetually off balance. There was something repellent in a contact with such a mind; slippery, aggressive, sly, it dodged and feinted all about you; you beat it off the best you could, as you would some repulsive animal persistently attacking you, something slippery and ferocious like a ferret. It was tiring and disgusting. And now the creature was at him about Mitkov.

"Do you know Colonel Mitkov of the Finland Regiment?"

"Yes, slightly." Had it been Mitkov? Burly, genial Mitkov, with his thundering laughter? Let it be him—only not Sasha.

"Where have you met him?"

"At various social functions—I don't quite remember."

"At Pushchin's house?"

"Yes, I think so."

"But you also have been to his house."

"No, never." Making a truthful statement was curiously restful; like finding a firm foothold in a treacherous swamp.

"And yet it was at Colonel Mitkov's house that the meeting took place."

"What meeting?"

"I beg of you not to play the innocent, Prince." Chernyshev's tuneful tenor rasped unpleasantly. Perhaps he too was tired. Even the most assiduous of ferrets wearies of the hunting. "You know what meeting I mean. The one at which the assassination of Emperor Nikolai was discussed . . ."

The old shift and pounce. So we're back to that again, Grisha thought wearily.

". . . as the only way of freeing the participants of the criminal attempt of December fourteenth."

The words flowed by smooth as oil and then suddenly doubled back pounding at his incredulous ears. Assassination of Emperor Nikolai? *Nikolai?* Not Alexander? Had he misheard? Had Chernyshev misspoken? But he had said "freeing the participants of December fourteenth," he was talking about something that happened after December fourteenth, nothing to do with Alexander, safe in his grave. Then he didn't, he couldn't mean—Grisha drove his nails convulsively into his palms, physically reining himself in. Careful! Don't leap at it! Don't, as you were about to do, blurt out, "But if you mean *Nikolai* . . ." with that betraying joyful relief, that special inflection, totally different from before, that an experienced examiner would know only too well how to interpret.

But it took all the control he didn't know he had to say in exactly the same subdued hesitant tones as before. "I know nothing of such a meeting." Then with exquisite carefulness, testing each step in that quaking, uncertain morass, "If you could tell me, General, when it took place . . ."

An incredulous smile flickered across Chernyshev's rosy lips. "You would like to have your memory refreshed, Prince?"

"I only hope—since I have no way of knowing when it took place, as I have said before"—establishing that fact in his mind, pinning it to what had gone on before— "that perhaps I might be able to show that I was elsewhere at the time. Perhaps even out of Moscow."

"Very well." The smile broadened. I'll humor you this time, it said, but you and I know quite well. . . . "*Were* you out of Moscow on December nineteenth? That is a date you should remember: His Imperial Majesty was proclaimed Emperor in the Uspenski Cathedral on that day."

"I know. I was present in the Uspenski at the time." Stealthily Grisha fetched a deep sigh. He hadn't misheard, then, Chernyshev was not talking of the October meeting at all. "But I didn't go to any meeting on that day."

"And yet you were quite unmistakably identified; by name and by—ah"—he coughed delicately—"by a certain unmistakable characteristic."

"You mean by—by my leg?"

Chernyshev nodded, contemplating his beautifully polished nails.

"But how can that be?" Grisha said blankly. Somebody was lying. That much was clear. A furious anger rose up in him: after a second's deliberation, he decided that it was safe to give vent to it. "But that's a lie. Who says so? Who has identified me?"

"Allow me to remind you, Prince, that here *I* am the one to ask questions."

And now it was time. Now it was all right to do the other thing Pushchin had demanded. "With all respect, General, I think I have a right to be confronted with the man who has accused me."

At least one thing was sure: it wouldn't, it couldn't, be Sasha Odoevski.

"Of course," said Chernyshev, still using his humoring voice. Nevertheless he looked baffled. The black-dyed moustache twitched suspiciously, the rosy mouth puckered into a petulant rosebud. Somewhere, somehow the whole flow of the interview had been diverted; the prey had veered unexpectedly, diving into the underbrush. "Take him to the next room," he told the guards, testily.

In the next hour or so that he spent waiting, Grisha had time to be appalled all over at the narrowness of his escape. Guilt and fear—fear and guilt—who had said that? The words came floating to him from a conversation taking place in another world, eons ago—they almost did for him. He had been constantly on the brink of confessing to something with which he hadn't even been charged. Pushchin had saved him as surely as though he had been standing there at his side, proffering his quiet advice.

He was on firmer ground now. He could deny not only steadfastly but confidently, strengthened by the knowledge that at least in this particular he was telling the simple truth: he had never been a party to any plan to assassinate Emperor Nikolai as a way of freeing the participants of December 14. *If* there had been such a plan—the whole thing had an unreal sound, downright daft. He frowned: something stirred vaguely in the back of his mind, eluding him maddeningly.

Before he had a chance to mull further over it, the door opened. His heart beating erratically, his mouth dry, he was led back to the room where he had been questioned.

He looked with painful curiosity at the man who sat hunched in a chair facing Chernyshev: a burly redhead wearing the uniform of the Izmailovski Regiment. Grisha stopped short, staring. He knew the man, he had seen that shaggy red hair, that long brigand's moustache somewhere before. But how? Where?

"Sit down, Prince," said Chernyshev, indicating another chair. Grisha did so, without withdrawing his gaze from the man who was presumably his accuser. The dejected figure stirred uneasily under it. The dull eyes moved toward him, shifted away, the shaggy head went deeper in between the shoulders. There was an abject shame in the man's entire attitude.

"Well, gentlemen," said Chernyshev chattily, "let's see if we can clear this up to everyone's satisfaction."

Unfolding a document, he patted it smooth on the table before him and began reading from it.

"Pavel Petrovich Mukhanov, Captain of Izmailovski Regiment, deposes that——"

"Mukhanov!" Grisha whispered. "Why, of course, Mukhanov."

It all came back to him now; the bristling red moustache, the whirling gestures, the harsh voice holding forth roaringly in Orlov's study. But how changed now, beaten, silent . . .

"—that, on December nineteenth, he was present at a meeting at the house of Colonel Mitkov of the Finland Regiment, where he made several remarks about the possible means of assassinating Emperor Nikolai. Among others at that meeting was Prince Volynski, who was much interested and questioned him, Captain Mukhanov, about the means of encompassing such an attempt. . . ." Chernyshev paused, impressively. "Is that correct, Captain Mukhanov?"

The carrotty head nodded.

"Do you still hold to that statement about Prince Volynski?"

Another brief and hopeless nod.

"But that's a lie," Grisha said, softly, wonderingly. His voice rose. "It's all a lie!"

Mukhanov's whole body flinched at his voice as at a blow; the burly shoulders hunched even more. He even squinted his eyes shut, like a child threatened with a whipping. A pang of pity stabbed Grisha in the midst of his anger. "Captain Mukhanov," he said, in a trembling voice. "Why are you doing—why are you saying this? We don't even know each other. The only time I met you was not at Mitkov's house, it was at Orlov's after the manifesto in the Uspenski Cathedral . . ."

"At Orlov's—hmmm—yes . . ." Mukhanov muttered disjointedly, keeping his eyes stubbornly averted from Grisha.

"We didn't exchange five words there. You left almost immediately. And I never saw you again. How can you say what you—? He is lying, I don't know why he should, but he is just lying," Grisha cried out in outrage.

Chernyshev looked at his polished nails, bored with it all.

"Well, Captain Mukhanov, what about it? Do you still identify Prince Volynski as one of the members who listened to you at that meeting?"

With another quick shift of his lusterless eyes, Mukhanov nodded. A strange performance; like the fraudulent goggling of a blind man going, for some painful and compelling reason, through the motions of seeing. It was borne in on Grisha that that was exactly what it was: Mukhanov was not really seeing him; for all intents and purposes he wasn't even there; apparently his shame

[349]

and misery were so acute that he somehow managed to absent himself from the ordeal of treachery even as he went through it. Sight and hearing sealed by guilt, stuck in his error like a fly in tar, he was perfectly capable of mindlessly persisting in it to the end. All at once Grisha was afraid.

"He doesn't know what he is saying. Orlov will tell you that I was merely visiting him when this man came in and he left by himself. If you'll only ask Orlov. It was he who—"

Orlov coming back into the study, saying to him, with an irritated smile: "That madman Mukhanov. His idea for retrieving the situation . . ." It was to Orlov that that bizarre plan was confided. But of course, he couldn't say that. . . . He couldn't refresh mad Captain Mukhanov's muddled recollection in front of Chernyshev, sitting there with his odiously cheerful smile, while the two suspects bickered involving more and more people in their unenviable plight.

"It was Orlov," he said carefully finishing the phrase, "who saw you out in the hall and you didn't even say good-bye, let alone discuss anything with me. I never saw you again, until now. How can you say—? For God's sake make him look at me!" With horror he heard his own voice cracking in panic. "Look at me, Captain Mukhanov! *See* me."

Obediently Mukhanov turned his head; his eyelids rising unwillingly, on rusty hinges, he looked at Grisha. Gradually his expression changed, a faint color washed over his dough-pale face. Something like disbelieving joy came into it.

"But it's not the man," he said with an uncouth movement of his arms that was a mere echo of the violent gesticulation Grisha remembered. Blinking his inflamed eyes, stammering, he repeated: "It's not the man at all."

"But you have just identified him. . . ."

"The hell with that, it isn't. I didn't see—I understand now—oh God." With a dry sob he clasped his head with both hands. "He's right—it was at Orlov's—that's just where it was we met—Orlov introduced him but we didn't talk. . . . And then later at Mitkov's, there was another young man, same name—or maybe just like it—and he limped too, you see, so I, so I . . ." Mukhanov burst into loud uncouth sobs. "I'm sorry, I'm sorry, I'm so mixed up, so fucking confused I don't know what— This is just a boy, the other one was much older—yes, and an army man—only the name was—

Forgive me, for Christ's sake," he said to Grisha and toppled heavily off the chair on to his knees. Savagely, deliberately he knocked his head against the floor three times, and stayed at Grisha's feet motionless.

Instinctively, Grisha moved to lift him. He stopped in mid-motion as it became clear to him that this was probably the only posture in which Captain Mukhanov would be likely to find any comfort. It wasn't merely Grisha's pardon that he was begging in his characteristically immoderate manner; he was abasing himself before all the others whom he had named, betraying them out of weakness, out of stupidity, in sheer mindless funk.

Chernyshev, clearly shaken by this unforeseen development, stood up behind his desk fussily issuing orders. He called for water, directed the guards to help Mukhanov to a chair. "Call the guard to take the other prisoner back. . . . We shall certainly inquire further into this, Prince," he said to Grisha, who looked back at him uncomprehendingly; surely, now that it was clear that a mistake had been made—But at least there was a definite change in Chernyshev's voice; the indulgent sneer was gone from it, and it was merely polite.

As the detail marched Grisha away, he could still hear Mukhanov's wrenching sobs. Chernyshev's voice, matter of fact, said, "And now Captain Mukhanov, let us see if you can't remember the name of the man whom you mistook for Prince Volynski."

In some ways the next two days were the worst of all. He had expected to be released immediately; he sat on his bed the whole day, alert, ears strained for a messenger's brisk footsteps to stop at his door. Presently a wild impatience began to take possession of him. He had done everything required of him, hadn't he? He had been careful, involved no one, denied steadfastly, avoided—by a hair's breadth!—the pitfalls set for him, had been cleared by Mukhanov. Why wasn't he released, then? He wanted to bang on the doors, with his head if necessary, scream obscenities, howl like a wild animal newly trapped. When the little soldier brought him food, his first impulse was to hurl it at the wall. He restrained himself: that subdued presence, moving silently about his cell, calmed him; had it not brought messages of hope to him before? Irrationally he waited for one more. But the soldier went about his chores, silent and vacant-eyed, apparently having nothing more to say.

"What is your name, friend?" Grisha asked him at last, reaching across the silence.

The man looked at him somberly with empty eyes. "Why do you want to know, your Honor? I am a dead man. Dead men have no names."

Without another look, he left the cell, carrying the slop bucket with him.

A bad omen, Grisha thought. A dull calm despair replaced his impatience. He would be here forever. Eventually, everyone's mind would be emptied of him, annulling him, and he would cease to exist.

Surely not Claire, he told himself, trying to rally. Yes, Claire too, the deadly little voice inside his head assured him. One forgot people. Hadn't he forgotten Matryosha? He never thought he would, but he had. She had dwindled to a pathetic little ghost, slowly receding along the corridors of his mind. Remorseful, he tried to bring her back: she belonged in the thickened shadows of his cell. But try as he would she hung back, featureless; all he could summon of her was a blank white oval of a face with cornflower-blue smudges for eyes. . . .

He turned his face to the wall, no longer waiting for the messenger with the order for his release. *I can't get out*, *said the starling*. Repeating the hopeless little phrase he fell asleep.

But the next day he was after all taken out of his cell and brought back to the Winter Palace. Immediately, with a beating heart, he became aware of the slight differences in his treatment; the most important being the removal of the blindfold as soon as the sleigh left the grim purlieus of the Petropavlovsk fortress.

There was a reassuring change in Chernyshev's manner, too, as he greeted him in the great hall where he had been questioned the first time. This time he was both courteous and indifferent: the ferret was digging at another hole, no need to waste time on the escaped prey. With solemnity he unfurled an official document from which he read aloud:

"By the order of His Imperial Majesty, the Commission of Inquiry hereby attests that Prince Grigorii Petrovich Volynski, as has been found during the inquiry, had never been a member of the secret society and took no part in its malevolent actions." Breaking into a genial smile, he folded the attestate and handed it to Grisha.

Grisha took it mechanically. It was all over then, he could go home.

"A genuine mistake, Prince," Chernyshev was saying. "We do owe you an apology. The man whom that muddled idiot named—it turned out to be a Lieutenant Volkovski. Unfortunately he had fallen off his horse a few days before and was still limping. An unfortunate combination that stuck in that fool's mind. You must forgive us for keeping you in Petropavlovsk, but of course once there was any suspicion of a plot against His Imperial Majesty, there was no choice. . . . And now, if you'll kindly follow me, the Emperor wants to see you."

The Tsar's tall figure rose from behind the baize-covered table blotting out the Raphael Madonna behind him. He was huge, seeming to fill the whole room. Grisha remembered him from his sister's wedding ball as a tall, slender ramrod-straight figure, towering by a head over the dancing crowds. But now he was filled out, inflated, by the power he had acquired; it radiated from him visibly, flooding the room so that there was barely space left to breathe.

"Well," said the Tsar, "so it seems we have made a mistake about you. I'm glad, I'm very glad. Your father is an old friend."

"You are very good, Your Majesty," Grisha murmured out of a dry throat.

"I'm delighted that it turned out the way it has. But you know, I hope, that, if you had been guilty, even my friendship for your father wouldn't have helped. I would have been very sorry indeed, but you would have been punished."

"Yes, Your Majesty."

The Tsar came out from behind the desk and came strolling toward him, his big body moving gracefully, like a tiger on the prowl. "Still," he said smiling, "you can't quite blame us. It was a justifiable mistake, wasn't it?"

"It—it seems so, sire."

"That oaf Mukhanov made a mistake about you being at Mitkov's. But he did see you at Orlov's, that was how he came to make it. Well, now—Orlov, Pushchin—you did move in bad company, didn't you? Incredible that you were not corrupted." With a swift movement, almost a pounce, he was close to Grisha. He put his hands on Grisha's shoulders looking down at him from his great height. "Or were you? Are you sure there was nothing?"

[353]

His eyes bored into Grisha's, with a heavy, leaden, and entirely intimate look, that seemed to read all his thoughts. It said, "I know all about you, I just want to see if you'll lie." He had been using the familiar *thou* throughout the interview; suddenly the familiarity seemed frightful. The Tsar himself, the Tsar of All the Russias, the wearer of the Monomakh's Hat, the Anointed One! Standing within the grip of those heavy hands one felt as though one was in the hands of God himself.

"There *was* something, wasn't there?"

Grisha made a weak attempt to break away from that unswerving unblinking stare and was held as in a vise by twin leaden rods that bored through his skull. There was no escape; you had to mollify this looming presence, to fall down at his feet, weeping, to confess all and at all costs be forgiven. Grisha understood now why so many had broken down, why Odoevski wrote frantic letters from the prison, offering to do anything, anything . . . The weight on his shoulders grew, crushing him. He staggered under it and, as he did so, deliberately let himself lurch on to his bad foot. The leaden glance flickered downward, momentarily deflected, and changed, as he knew it would, as everyone's did. And that moment's respite was enough.

"I don't understand, your Majesty." He heard his voice, piping shrill, like a frightened child's.

"There had never been subversive conversations? No plots fomented?"

"No, sire."

"No mention of the secret society?"

Grisha drew a deep breath. "I can't say that, sire."

"Oh?" There was a flicker of triumph in the leaden eyes. The royal lion diminished into a huge cat playing with a mouse. A terrifying sensation but safer—oh, safer than that overpowering paternal figure leaning on him with all its pitiless majesty.

Carefully reaching back into the innocuous past, Grisha said, "Everybody talked about there being one. But nothing serious. Somebody I knew called it a—a *secret du polichinelle*." Claire's words, dredged up from his memory, coming to his hand like a talisman. "She had laughed about it, said that a secret society that everybody knows about can't be very serious."

"And what did you think?"

"I thought it probably was a—a sort of debating society. That's what everybody said it must be. . . ."

"Nobody said anything to the contrary?"

Careful now. "My father did. He talked about conspiracy. But everybody thought he was wrong, that it was a sort of obsession with him. I—I did too."

"And what about your friend Pushchin? He never enlightened you to the contrary?"

Why, he's merely a police inspector, Grisha thought. Like Chernyshev. A policeman trying to add to his record. "No, never, sire."

"Never prevailed on you to join this—debating society?"

"No, sire."

"On your word of honor?"

He would have given it unhesitatingly, anyhow. It was merely incidental that he could do so without lying. "On my word of honor, Your Majesty."

The hands on his shoulders pushed him backward, step by step, until he was brought back to the table, with the candlelight full on his face. "Yes, those are honest eyes. One must believe them." Nevertheless there seemed to be something else. "This Pushchin of yours. An unblushing, insolent rogue. A man without principles. What drew you to him, as a friend?"

The unbreakable honesty, the fatherly smile in the gray eyes, the strength unmistakably sensed beneath the mildness—he reached beyond them to the most trivial reason of all.

"Your Majesty, he is Pushkin's friend."

"I see." A faint smile flickered across the steely features. His voice changed, became indulgent. "All you youngsters are besotted about that rhymester." Letting go of Grisha's shoulders, he patted him lightly on the cheek. "Very well, I'll take your word. You may go. In the future be more careful of the company you keep."

"Yes, Your Majesty." With a feeling of utter unreality he kissed the long white hand held out to him and left the room.

Claire's Journal, January 22

Haven't written in my journal because of my illness. For a while it looked as though the cold I caught coming back from the Jaenisches might turn into pneumonia. However, I survived in spite of the attendance of doctors. Isn't it Voltaire who likens a doctor to a man standing at a bedside flailing away with a stick? If he hits the illness the patient is cured; if he hits the patient, the patient dies.

But I am indomitable, people say. They don't always say it as a compliment; in fact, it seems to reveal something a little coarse in my character. . . . *Che vuole*? Better to survive coarsely than to expire elegantly like Clarissa Harlowe.

Claire's Journal, January 23

I still get tired very easily, and when I am tired objects and people around me become transparent, figures from the past suck the reality from them and take their place. Marya Ivanovna looking in on me, as I take my afternoon rest, shimmers and seems to dissolve, and Mary takes her place at the foot of my bed to fix me with her sisterly censorious look, harboring no illusions about me. Talking to Hermann, I find myself in the midst of a silent conversation with P.B. And when I doze off, a figure comes limping into my dreams as Grisha and leaves them as someone else. . . . Someone dying alone, far away from me, calling my name. . . .

Claire's Journal, January 24

Strange; I am beginning to think of him on his sickbed at Missolonghi almost as much as I think about Grisha in his cell. I see him, alone, feverish, unable to fight off the blood-sucking doctors, dying. . . .

When the news of his death came two years ago, I wasn't affected in the slightest. Unnatural of me, now that I think of it. I was never flint hearted, an affecting passage in a book would find me all too responsive. I remember Mary laughing when she found me shedding tears over the description in *Crito* of Socrates' last moments. And *he*—he had lain in my arms, his lips at my breast—how could I not pity him? But I shed not a single tear.

Why then is my heart wrung now?

I was on his mind when he died. Fomitch said so to Mary. I don't mean Fomitch, of course, I mean Fletcher. . . . When will I finally get rid of this confusion . . .? Fletcher said he called out my name and seemed concerned about me. Wanted me there. Why? To absolve him of some new nightmare that was besetting him? Were my services in that line required again? Had he forgiven me for exorcising them so presumptuously before?

Forgiven me? What an odd thought. What did *he* have to forgive?

Claire's Journal, January 25

Poor Marya Ivanovna. A clear instance of *vorrei e non vorrei* . . . She drags me along with her to Du Loup and insists on buying me a bonnet; she glowers at me when I come down to supper. She hates me and wants me to disappear; she wants me to stay and exchange delicious memories and comparisons. When I refuse to do so—merely looking blank at her veiled hints—she flies into a rage. Then she apologizes in a torrent of tears: "Do you want me to fall on my knees before you?" No. I don't want that. All I want is peace and quiet.

All this will come to a head one of these days. She will have to precipitate the break—I feel too languid and tired to bestir myself and do so—but I shall be so grateful to her when she does.

Claire's Journal, January 26

Not a word from Grisha's father. I daresay, being what he is, he took Z.N.'s kind letter as an expression of vulgar curiosity rather than that of compassionate good will. . . .

But how cruel, to be denied knowledge about someone you love. Anything, anything better than not knowing . . .

I am thinking of enlisting Countess Zotov's aid to find out about Grisha. The Zotovs' connections in St. Petersburg, through their cousin the ex-Minister Kurakin, are considerable. And Countess Zotov will do it for me, I am sure. She is still fond of me. I remember how she wanted me to stay on as a *dame de compagnie* even after Betsy had married. I didn't because the excessive Marya Ivanovna offered me an excessive salary which I couldn't afford to refuse. And then there was Dunia . . .

Claire's Journal, January 27

Have just awakened from an extraordinary dream.

Had laid myself down on my bed to rest from a busy afternoon—I still get tired. As I lay there, only half awake, my mind wandered off and fastened on the riddle which had lately begun despite myself to occupy it. What was it he tried to say to Fletcher in Missolonghi? Claire, he had said, Claire, and the rest a mere restless babble. And suddenly I was there myself, standing in the doorway of the room in which he was dying. It was all so incredibly vivid, the brilliant sunshine outside, and the dark room where he tossed and muttered feverishly.

At first I couldn't make out what it was he was saying. Which was it?

I am sorry, I have always loved you,

I am sorry I have never loved you. . . .

You were dangerous to love. I hung dreamily in the doorway, half in shadow, half in sunlight, letting the message unfold in my sleepily recipient mind. *Unsafe to love you, dangerous, to be avoided like death itself. Once you saw deep into me—nobody could see as much as you and as little—you who walked in and out of my mind as if it were a room with an unlocked door. You went through my cluttered soul like a busy housewife cleaning house, winkling a tormenting nightmare out of my inmost self. . . . There I was clean swept of fears, absolved from my nightmares, light of heart, truly in love. And not a line of poetry left in me. You had swept out more than my dark dreams, I became a mere cipher, without meaning or purpose, impotent. The god had withdrawn from me, his gift gone—no, not quite dead—it came back, to be guarded jealously, no one dangerous to be allowed near, and most of all not you. . . .*

I? I, who would have given my life to be of use to him? And *was* of use? But the speech was wiped off my stammering lips, the nightmare held me motionless, listening while the indictment went on and on. . . . And then he rose from his deathbed and came toward me, stretching his hand to me over Allegra's little coffin that had come winging through space to light between us as soft as a moth, and said, "Let us forgive each other, Claire." And I said, "Yes, we must," and touched his hand and the touch was so cold—so burning cold that I awoke. . . .

(Written a few hours later.)

A strange dream—where did it come from? Why did it have such a ring of truth to it? It seemed to total up all the things I knew and didn't know, willfully forgot, reluctantly remembered. . . . I did know about his brief inability to write in Venice, Mary had told me that: "Albé writes P.B. that he is having trouble writing." Oh, he will, I had countered blithely, he could never stop writing for long, that cloud will pass. And it did, he sent us *Manfred* from Venice, and I thought no more about it.

There is a dark place in me, he said once, where the poetry comes from. . . . Yes, I remember that too now. . . .

But it doesn't matter any more, does it? I'll never know whether what I dreamed was true. Geordie didn't come back from beyond the grave to tell me in person the message he couldn't form as he was dying. I merely dreamed my own dream, conjectures, doubts, half-memories, self-accusations coalescing into a cloudy hypothesis, not necessarily true. . . .

The true wonder is that such a devastating dream should leave me with such a sense of peace. I think it was the thought of forgiveness. The word *forgive*—something so peaceful and refreshing about it, like dreaming of violets and cool moss in the midst of fever. . . . So I have forgiven him, it seems. But I think it had happened before, because of Grisha. It was as if I had at last done what I have always wanted to do—reached all the way back, into Geordie's unhappy youth, shared and sweetened it—I had always known I could have!—and only then was able to forgive him. . . .

Claire's Journal, January 28

A letter from Grisha! I stopped at Lenhold's to see whether there was anything for me. Nothing from England, but a letter to me addressed in Russian. I opened it and there it was: he was free, it had been a mistake, he was vindicated and set free. And then a postscript:

"You told me once to write to you in English no matter what my state of mind was. As you see, I am obeying you."

It was then that I burst into tears right there in Lenhold's music store.

"Yes," Sergey said, "this is where it all happened." With a sweep of his hand he indicated the Senate Square, dominated by Falconet's equestrian statue of Peter the Great. The snowy square lay quiet before them with the Neva sparkling frigidly beyond the buildings. To Grisha's eyes it wore that special look that clings to a place where a catastrophe has recently taken place; in spite of the placidity, something askew about it; the passersby skulking along like jackals after a battle, the heap of granite blocks for the unfinished St. Isaac's Cathedral piled up like ruins of a sacked city. The very whiteness of the new-fallen snow looked suspect, as though it was there to cover the blood spilt on cobblestones.

"We, the Preobrazhentzy, were in front of the Admiralty where we are standing right now," Sergey went on. "We were the first to come. I think I told you . . ."

Grisha had already heard how the Preobrazhentzy Regiment, after having taken the oath to Nikolai, was going about its business when the commander came to the barracks with the disturbing news—"All right, gentlemen, take your places, the Moscow Regiment is playing the fool"—and led them to the Palace Square in front of the Winter Palace where Nikolai was waiting. ". . . So the Tsar asked us if we were ready to march, and then 'Division forward, half left turn, quick march!' and we were off. He took us to the Admiralty himself; then he told the soldiers to load the rifles and he himself mounted his horse—a beautiful filly, like your Nelly, only white—and took his place before us. He was wearing the uniform of the Izmailovski Regiment, he's their chief, you know. Afterward, when it was all over, he changed into our uniform. Because they didn't show up until later, the Izmailovtzy, they wouldn't take the oath until Grand Duke Mikhail went over to their barracks himself. . . . But we, the Preobrazhentzy, came immediately, so we really got the best spot, we could see everything," Sergey said, sounding exactly as though he had been given hard-to-get tickets for Didelot's *Ruslan and Ludmilla* with Istomina dancing the lead. "We are practically on top of them. . . . I saw Governor Miloradovich coming back after they shot him down, the bastards. . . . He just lay on his horse's neck bouncing like a sack, and when he reached us he fell right off, and they put him in the sleigh and took him away. God but he looked awful—sort of little and shrunken and all bloody. . . ." From the shadowy change on his brother's face Grisha guessed that it was perhaps at that point that the adventure, 'til then not too different from performing at the maneuvers, suddenly became uncomfortably real. He asked: "And they? Where were they?"

"The rebels? They grouped themselves right around the monument. Old Peter looked as though he was riding at their head, leading them right at us. . . ."

But while the bronze emperor soared immobile over the rebelling troups, the living one, also on horseback, was apparently being extraordinarily active.

"You have to understand the genius of the Emperor," said Sergey. "What he did, you see, was isolate them. Wanted them all on the Senate Square, so he could keep track of them. While he was still waiting for reinforcements in the Palace Square, a detachment of grenadiers came through, yelling hurrah for Constantine, and he just told them, 'If that's what you want, you go that way,' and waved them on to the Senate Square. . . . And then our side started coming around: the Semyonovtzy marched along the Neva Prospect, and took their place at the Cathedral, Izmailovtzy grouped themselves near the Admiralty. The Pavlovtzy marched around to the Senate Building." Sergey's eyes shone. "There they were, the bastards, surrounded."

"And then what?"

"And then everybody just stood around for the next five hours. I tell you we froze. The only consolation was it must have been even worse for them—we at least were protected by the buildings. They stood right in the wind, with Neva at their backs. Their arses must have been frozen right off!"

Looking toward the monument, Grisha could almost see a tightly packed column, standing in perfect formation around the bronze horseman who reared up above them, as if leading an attack. An impressive, even a frightening sight; but neither the rider nor the men stirred. They were a static menace, there to endure rather than attack. Perhaps in the end, like the statue, they were merely there as a symbol.

He crossed over to the monument and stood in the shadow of the Horseman, imagining himself within the shadowy limits of the vanished carré. Closing his eyes he imagined the pressure of warm bodies around him, the cries of "Hurrah, Constantine," and the click and shock of rifles hitting the ground. But oh, yes, it was cold. He imagined them standing here for five hours, growing colder and colder, inactivity chilling body and soul, waiting.

Why hadn't they moved?

He looked up into the Bronze Horseman's face, reflective and pitiless under its laurel wreath, and it gave him no answer.

"Now if *he* had been in charge," Sergey said, "it would have turned out differently. But they had nobody important to lead them, luckily for us. No high-ranking officer showed up at the Square— nobody there above the rank of a regimental commander. Some of the civilians took command. There was one on my side of the column who seemed to know what he was doing."

Pushchin?

"What did he look like?" Grisha asked trying to keep his voice even.

"Look like? I don't know—just a civilian in a long greatcoat. But

there was a military air about him—probably a retired officer . . .
When the Horse Guards attacked, I heard him ordering the soldiers
to shoot over the riders' heads. It wasn't much of an attack—not
enough room and the horses' hooves slid on the ice. . . ." Sergey's
round face grew thoughtful. "It was touch and go. It could have
easily gone the other way."

"But I thought they were surrounded, and outnumbered."

"Yes, but even so . . . For one, the rabble was on their side.
They threw rocks at us, and they brought them food, and
everything. . . . And our side wasn't as single-minded as it should
have been. Some of our men kept sneaking over and telling them,
'Wait 'til it gets dark, then we'll come over.' I saw myself, after the
Horse Guards charged, there were the rebels helping the ones that
fell down to get back on their horses, friendly as could be. Must
have been an understanding among them, that's why that chap
ordered them to shoot over their heads. . . . So everybody waited
around. And then at three in the afternoon as it started getting dark
a battery of guns was brought out. Right there." He pointed to the
street between the Admiralty and the Cathedral. "I looked around
and there they were, three big brutes. They're what finally decided
it."

Grisha visualized the three iron snouts, slowly turning, focusing
on them, threatening.

"The first shot went over their heads. But the second one—it
went through them like a scythe through grass. Then they moved
all right—they ran. But the guns kept going—piff, paff! paff!"
Sergey smiled joyously, producing the childish sound with which
they used to punctuate their toy soldier battles. "Well, that was
more like it, action at last. They swept the Senate Square clear, and
then rolled the guns over to the embankment and kept shooting—
some of the rebels were trying to escape over the ice, you know."

Grisha looked at him bleakly. "And how did it feel to shoot down
brother Russians?"

Sergey looked back in wonder. "But what else was there to do?"
he asked. "I tell you, it was a closer shave than you know. . . . You
won't believe this, but there was no ammunition brought for the
guns—that's how confused everyone was. If they had stormed the
guns, while we were getting the ammunition, well! And, what's
more, some of them knew it. That same man I told you about—I
saw him pointing at the guns. I knew exactly what he was saying,

[363]

'Let's go get the guns, while we can.' Fortunately he was a civilian, so he couldn't order his men forward. . . . But if he had . . ."
Sergey whistled.

Pushchin? Grisha wondered again.

"Look, the Emperor didn't want to do it. He kept sending emissaries over to the other side, asking them to lay down their arms. The Archbishop went over with the ikon. They kissed it and sent him back: 'stay out of trouble, father. . . .' And old Mikhail went over to see if he could talk them out of it, and that did no good. . . . But even then the Emperor hesitated. He would order 'fire!' and then 'hold it!' and 'fire!' and 'hold!' And then finally 'Fire!' And that was it. . . ." Sergey paused. "Funny," he said in an altered voice, "how quiet it was at first. Just the cannon booming out, and people falling down without a sound. It didn't seem real, any of it. . . ."

Again Grisha saw it happen. The stillness, men toppling over in silence like figures in a nightmare, blotches of blood starting out on the snow. And then panic, rout, confusion . . . It was all over.

Sickened, he asked: "Were many killed?"

"Oh, plenty. They were cleaning up the whole next day, throwing corpses into the Neva. Near-corpses, too, I hear. . . . Yes, quite a mess it was . . ." Sergey shook his head, frowning. Then he put it all aside for a more agreeable memory. "And you know what?" he said, smiling with pleasure. "Do you know what the Emperor did after it was all over? He went and wrote the whole thing down in the palace log book just as though it had been an ordinary day and he a mere colonel on duty. Isn't that splendid?"

Grisha looked at him blankly. "Why?"

"Why what?"

"Why is it so splendid?"

"Well, because—you wouldn't understand anyhow, you're not an army man."

"And the Emperor is?"

"Every inch an army man," Sergey said proudly. "Not even being an Emperor is going to change that. That's why his reporting what happened and then signing as just simple colonel is so marvelous. Don't you see?"

Grisha shook his head slowly, bleak faced, feeling as far away from Sergey as though the whole length of the Senate Square were between them. But there was no use saying anything else. Sergey being what he was, one might as well expect the retriever Toozik to listen to a homily on the rights of ducks.

"Let's go home," he said.

From the first he had had no sense of coming home. He would have been as well suited staying at Demuth's. There, like any other visitor of rank in an unexceptionable hotel, he could have enjoyed the maximum in physical comfort; the prison uncleanliness sluiced away in a luxurious bath, cramped bowels loosened in blessed privacy. All this awaited him in his parents' house on the English Quay. But nothing more.

It wasn't even that he was angry with them. A deadening indifference had descended on him, sealing him away from them. When they all sat down for the family supper, nobody looked real to him. Anyone at that table could have changed places with the liveried footman standing behind each chair without making any difference to him; his father, coldly indolent as ever; his mother, her face made young and gay not by his deliverance but by her own long-desired return to the city she loved; his fashionable sisters with their fashionable husbands. The only one with whom he could talk naturally was Sergey, who had greeted him on his arrival with simple noisy joy, alternately embracing and thumping him on the back and proclaiming happily that he had known from the beginning and had been telling everyone that it must have been "a filthy mistake of some sort." His presence made everything easier, sweetening the strained atmosphere; when he left to go back to the barracks, staying there became unnatural and intolerable.

Are they really my family? he wondered drearily. He had met strangers to whom he felt closer; something had passed between them, a thin nourishing stream of kindness, a living spark. The motherly stationmaster's wife shaking her head over him tearfully, because he was so young; the nameless lieutenant at the Winter Palace worrying about him as he was marched away; the dim little soldier in Petropavlovsk, with that luminous look of kindness on his worn face—those are my kindred, he thought, they have reached out to me, we have looked at each other and felt briefly the affinity of our common clay. Surely Fomitch, throwing himself absurdly into the breach, is more of a father to me, than the handsome man who looks at me so unseeingly, caring for nothing but his credit with the Tsar. . . .

They were uneasy with him too; his very presence was felt as a reproach. Once a visitor talked of a Princess Troubetzkoy, whose husband, implicated in the fourteenth, was sent to the Petropavlovsk Prison. Every day she went to the Petropavlovsk Cathedral for the Mass and afterward walked around in the little park outside of it on the chance of her husband, immured behind one of the row of eyeless appertures that served for windows, seeing her there. After the visitor had gone, his mother, flushing patchily, began to describe how ill she had been while he was in prison and how the doctor had categorically refused to let her leave her bed; and even his sister Sophie found it necessary to mention how long it took her to recover from her difficult confinement. Grisha looked at them, vaguely puzzled. He had forgotten that he had ever expected anything from them.

As for the Prince, he was as inhumanly unpredictable as ever. Grisha, upon being released, couldn't help looking forward to their meeting with a feeling of malicious triumph. Surely there would have to be a scene in which he, Grisha, would have to explain away their interview in the guardroom; obviously a misunderstanding from beginning to end; his failure to proclaim his innocence entirely due to his bewilderment at being suspected. Why, Grisha thought, grimly amused, there might even be an apology forthcoming: "My son, forgive me, I was wrong about you." He would accept it, naturally, with generous forgiveness: "*Mon père*, we were both victims of circumstances." The thought of his duplicity filled him with malicious pleasure. This perverse satisfaction was however denied him. His father never even referred to their meeting or even to his brief imprisonment, preferring to forget it.

Once in the presence of company, noticing a few curious glances in Grisha's direction, he did condescend to say smoothly, "You have heard, of course, of the absurd mistake they had made about Grisha." And Grisha was all at once assaulted by a wicked impulse: what if he was to say, in front of them all, "But it wasn't a mistake." . . .

Many more visitors came to the Volynskis' in St. Petersburg than had been allowed in their Moscow house. They brought with them stories to which Grisha, keeping carefully in the background, listened silently the way a scout in the back of the enemy lines listens, crouching in the dark, to the talk around the bivouac fires.

The Emperor, it seemed, in spite of all the pleas refused to go to

Moscow to be crowned until the rebels' fate was decided in a trial which would probably take place in the beginning of the summer; the Investigative Committee was working on this night and day, and Speranski himself had been brought in. . . . A Colonel Batenkov had gone mad in Petropavlovsk and dashed his brains out against the walls of his cell. . . . Prince Alexander Odoevski was ill with brain fever and his father had come in from his country seat and was begging to be allowed to see him. . . . Mikhail Orlov would probably be let off because of his brother Alexey who was very close to the Tsar and had distinguished himself on the fourteenth: Prince Pyotr heard this with a vexed and contemptuous smile. He was more pleased by a discreditable story told about Chernyshev, who, although useful in his work, was universally disliked as an upstart and toady: it seemed that he claimed kinship with one of the conspirators with the same name as his, hoping to gain his large estate when he was condemned; but when he addressed the prisoner with the words, *"Comment, cousin, êtes-vous aussi coupable?"* the latter answered him, *"Coupable, peut-être, mais cousin, jamais!"*

With all of him Grisha longed to leave St. Petersburg. All of that stately harmonious city chilled him now. He longed for the cozy Moscow, with its extravagant cupolas and innocent white walls, unstained by blood. A loving presence waited for him there; he could see her within those walls like the illustration of a princess in a fairy-tale book, slender arms uplifted, dark eyes shedding love. . . .

But he couldn't go to her; not yet. He wrote to the authorities asking to be allowed to see Pushchin, and waited feverishly for the answer. He would walk along the Strand, stop, and, leaning his elbows on the parapet, stare across Neva's steely surface toward the blunt outlines of the prison island with the Cathedral's slender spire at its center. The white Petersburg fogs descended, obliterating everything, so that the Neva bridges seemed to run into a dense whiteness. Somewhere behind that calm pitiless white wall Pushchin waited for his trial. . . . A few times Grisha went to the Petropavlovsk Cathedral for the mass and lingered on the square, not for Countess Troubetzkoy's reason—unlike her, he knew how little one could see out of a plastered window—but simply to be nearer his friend. Once he stopped at the commandant's headquarters, feeling like a graduate returning to a particularly hideous alma mater, and left some books and food there, getting no assurance however that they would be delivered.

While he waited for his request to see Pushchin to be granted, he went to visit Pushchin's family. The father was too ill to be seen, but the sisters received him. He learned from them that they were not allowed to see their brother; as a hardened criminal he was isolated even from his closest relatives. Accordingly it was with no surprise that he received an official letter curtly denying his request.

His efforts, apparently, gained him some measure of Imperial annoyance. "I understand," his father said to him at dinner, "that you have been pestering the authorities about that damned conspirator."

"I wanted to see my friend, yes."

"The Emperor remarked to me upon it today, saying with some displeasure, that your loyalties seem to be woefully misplaced." The Prince's nostrils fluttered faintly as though a disagreeable smell had inexplicably arisen from the helping of *pashtet* on his plate. "I myself fail to see any reason for persisting in an association, in spite of everything that happened, with a proved traitor."

"*Proved* traitor?" Grisha repeated in a colorless voice. "I was not aware, *mon père*, that the trial had already taken place."

Prince Pyotr put down his silver fork and absently groped for the lorgnette. Looking into distance, he remarked to no one in particular: "Sometimes I can't help wondering if a mistake had really been made."

"About me, you mean?" A cruel joy flooded Grisha's heart. "His Majesty thought it had. If you think otherwise, *mon père*, perhaps you ought to communicate your suspicions to the Investigative Committee."

"You damned insolent pup," his father cried, half rising from his chair. The footman who was about to pour the wine into his glass withdrew the crystal decanter hastily out of the way and stood stiffly at attention, his face carefully expressionless.

Grisha sat silent, waiting for his father's anger to erupt, as one waits for the onslaught of a beast that is dangerous but can be controlled. I have faced worse, he said silently and fancied the slightest possible uncertainty in the Prince's furiously protruding eyes.

"*Pierre, je vous implore!*" his mother screeched faintly.

Prince Pyotr slowly reseated himself. "I'll tell you what, Grigorii

Petrovich," he said courteously as to a stranger. "Perhaps St. Petersburg is not really the place for you. I think you would do well to return to Moscow."

Grisha bowed. "*Avec votre permission, mon père.*"

Two days later he was in a post-chaise on his way to Moscow.

Moscow greeted him like a comfortable old nanny. Its curly streets embraced him; its gilded domes rose as plump and welcoming as breasts; a chuckling sparkle seemed to come from the icy river. As Grisha drove through the gates with their twin grinning lions, he was conscious of a joyous anticipation that had been quite lacking when he had entered the palace on the English Quay.

It was pleasant to be greeted with total love, without guilt or reservations. Fomitch and Monsieur Lachaine came trotting out of the house together, as though in double harness, and fell upon him weeping, all distinctions of rank forgotten, two elderly men lifted out of themselves by unforeseen joy. They looked smaller and older to him and when they looked up at him timidly he could see that to them too he looked changed, larger and more grown up than they expected. As he hugged them, he felt their bodies sagging against him trustingly, and a protective love rose up in him. Other servants came crowding out, some of them weeping as they kissed his hands. "My dear ones, my people," he thought, loving them.

But there was more joy to come; as soon as he could he went straight to the source of it, to where his love, the center of his being awaited him.

Both Zahar Nikolaitch and Marya Ivanovna made much of him; in their transports there was a trace of awe with which the return of Lazarus from the grave might have been greeted. He submitted to them gratefully, his eyes wandering despite himself to the doorway: any moment now that empty rectangle would be filled by the familiar slender figure, the dark eyes would enfold him, bathing him with love. . . . Marya Ivanovna's face darkened. "If you are looking for Miss Clairmont—" she rapped out ungraciously. "But of course you are. She's the one you've come to see, not us. We've loved you like a son, we've wept over you while you were away—but that means nothing . . ."

"Marie," said Zahar Nikolaitch, pleadingly. Marya Ivanovna tossed her head like a refractory horse.

"Well, she isn't here. We've parted company. About time, too—I had no use for her really after Dunia . . . Besides I will not permit immorality in my house," she said with a slight flounce, fixing her eyes on him so significantly that alarm began to beat in him: *she knows about us!* But immediately she was off on another tack.

"They are all cold, those English. They lack *largesse d'âme.* I have loved that young woman as though she had been my daughter, I treated her like one—and just because of a few words spoken in justifiable anger. . . . I went down on my knees to her, and do you think that made any difference?" She gave a short angry sob, and, with fixed eyes and poppy red cheeks, addressed herself to the task of pouring tea, paying no further heed to Grisha. Grisha stood before her in angry perplexity, trying to make sense out of all those violent contradictions. She had let Claire go—she had begged her to stay—she had upbraided her for immorality— and also for being cold, like all the English. What was the woman about? And, more important, where was Claire?

Emitting a long resigned sigh, Zahar Nikolaitch took him by the arm and led him aside. "You mustn't mind my wife. She is not quite herself." His mouth quirked wryly; he knew all too well that, on the contrary, his wife was being very much herself.

"My dear Prince, don't look so worried," said Monsieur Gambs, lifting his arched eyebrows. "Miss Clairmont has been employed by the Governor's cousin, Prince Dmitry Golitzin. She will begin her duties in a month, and meanwhile she is visiting with the Countess Zotov. Her first position here was with the Zotovs, you know, and they are very good friends still. I shall be happy to give you her direction, their house is on the Tverskaya, very near the Boulevard. . . ."

"Thank you, Monsieur Gambs. . . . But what is this about immorality?" Grisha said, suddenly shaking with rage. "How dare she . . .?"

"Oh, my dear Prince Georges! Those are merely words envious mediocrity uses to brand what it doesn't understand. Someone like Claire will always be a mystery to a Madame Pomykov." A slight forgiving smile flickered over Monsieur Gambs's comely features. Understanding, rueful, he seemed to extend enlightened forgiveness to all—including, it almost seemed, Claire.

Does *he* know about us? Grisha peered distrustfully into his handsome countenance. Benignant, complacent, curiously opaque, the tutor's eyes met his, giving away nothing.

"Incidentally, Prince," he made a slight preening gesture. "I have the honor to be invited to the soirée at Princess Zinaide Volkonski's. Shall I have the pleasure of seeing you there too?"

Grisha made a vague reply. He was eager to go home; there was a letter to be written to Claire, telling her that he was back, asking permission to call on her.

But when he came home there was a letter from Claire already waiting for him. It informed him what he already knew: that she was taking a much-needed rest at the house of her former pupil and would be delighted if he found time to visit her. A curiously formal little note, written with as much propriety as though someone stood over her watching her write it.

But underneath the signature, in a different script, fierce, urgent, digging deep into the paper, she had scrawled: *Come!*

The first moments of their meeting at the Zotovs' house had the purity of total happiness. Briefly they were together alone, out of the world's reach. Then the walls of Countess Zotov's salon, fashionably wallpapered in striped green silk, were about them again; besides them, they enclosed a handsome lady of middle years and a young girl. Claire introduced him.

"We are delighted to see you here, Prince," said Countess Zotov, extending her hand to him. She was a large calm woman, wearing a walking dress of mushroom-colored velvet. A velvet beret of the same color covered her placidly graying hair. "I understand you are just back from St. Petersburg, where you had undergone the inconvenience of a false arrest. What times we live in! Our dear Claire has been so anxious about you."

"Yes, it is a wretched thing to lose one's pupils that way," Claire said composedly. "Betsy's way is much better . . . Betsy was my pupil until she got married, you know," she said to him chattily, "and this is her little sister, Natalie."

The girl curtsied. She was thirteen or fourteen, not out of pantalettes yet; just at the stage immediately preceeding that of a *jeune fille*, but already past being a child. Her light brown hair, curled in the latest fashion to lie high at her temples, was unfashionably tucked behind her ears. The rosy cheeks, faintly brushed with peach-like down, were childishly full. But there was character in the unexpected squareness of the jaw, and her eyes, large, of a peculiar unclouded gray-green, looked at him with serene frankness.

Claire sat in the chair facing him, with her embroidery. She was paler and thinner than when he left her, her ivory pallor taking on greenish tones next to the little girl's radiant rosiness, and her dress of mustard-brown wool was not a becoming one. But the curve of her long throat growing like a lily out of her white fichu made it hard for him to keep his mind on the news from St. Petersburg that he was obediently recounting to the Countess.

After a while the Countess rose to go out. "But I beg you to stay, Prince—I know dear Claire has a great deal to tell to her pupil."

Grisha kissed her hand with special gratitude, because unlike Marya Ivanovna she said this neither censoriously nor archly. It was clear that there was no thought in her head but that she was leaving a justifiably devoted pupil to have a confidential conversation with a teacher interested in his affairs. And Claire, without saying a word, had been just that—a complete *gouvernante*, sallow-faced, quiet, devotedly embroidering, definitely on the shelf. Miss Clairmont.

"*Allons, ma petite.*" The girl followed her mother with evident reluctance; a single regretful backward look came from the green-gray eyes as she left the room. And a moment later Miss Clairmont became Claire.

"Ah, Greesha. . . ." The disciplined lips quivered, the luminous blackness of her eyes brimmed over into tears. Smiling, she mopped at them with her lacy bit of cambric. "Pay no attention, I've taken to weeping on the slightest provocation—it's a carry-over from my illness— Zahar Nikolaitch used to tease me about my newly acquired 'gift of tears.' The first step on the road to sainthood, he said. . . ."

"You were ill?" he said in alarm, catching her hands.

"Yes, the weather and you have almost done for me between you . . ." So it was because of him that she looked like that; it was his absence that had hollowed out her cheeks, and shadowed her eyelids—the disclosure delighted at the same time as it stabbed him. "I can't tell you how cold and wretched I've been."

"I'll take you away," said Grisha, "we'll go somewhere where it's warm—to Italy— No, really"—as, smiling, she gave the tiniest headshake—"why not? There is nothing to hold me here. . . . I have no family—you are my family now, you are everything. . . ."

"What is this?" she said frowning, with that attentive look he knew, that seemed to reach beyond the words, gauging the timbre of heartbeat, the tolling of blood. "Yes. You look different. Older. Not by just two months but by several years. You've grown up." There was suddenly a motherly wistfulness in her voice. "Was it dreadful? Did you suffer terribly? Tell me everything now— everything."

Nobody else in the world would ever be capable of that utter stillness, that all-canceling attention with which she listened. . . . Grisha, telling her everything in a strange room in a strangers' house, said to himself, I am home.

"So he saved you then. . . . Oh, wonderful." Her voice darkened, went thrillingly deep, as it sometimes did when she was especially moved. "How I hope he knows that he has saved you!"

"Yes."

A footman came in and, glancing at them with conspiratorial deference, began lighting the candles, forestalling the dusk. Time to go soon, and not half enough said. . . .

"I am glad now," he said, "about having been in Petropavlovsk. . . . It would have been terrible not to have suffered at all."

"Oh Greesha," she mocked softly, "how exceedingly Russian that is. I know no other nationality so much at home with suffering. . . .".

"But you see it's all so different now. I used to be so—so *green* about it all." He heard in his own voice the indulgent note with which Pushchin had murmured once, "much too young . . ," "It's so easy to say that you are ready to face death or imprisonment for your belief. And it means nothing, nothing at all. Because you don't know. . . ."

It was like reciting, with deep feeling, the opening lines of *The Prisoner of Chillon*:

> Eternal spirit of the chainless mind,
> Brightest in dungeons, Liberty! thou art
> For there thy habitation is the heart . . .

The lofty poetry both excited you and made you feel safe. In spite of yourself you took it literally, seeing yourself in some inexplicable way going to prison and remaining free at the same time.

[373]

"I suppose," he said, "that's why Plato wanted to ban the poets from his Republic. They made everything seem easy and glorious—at least to green ones like me. . . . But now I know all about dungeons. It's real to me now."

"It was real to *him* too." Her voice was low, remote. "He had never been in a dungeon, but all the same he knew exactly what it was like."

For a moment he didn't know whom she was talking about: the inner thrum of anger that had always been there behind her calm voice, when she talked about him was absent now. . . . Before he had time to be jealous of her diverted attention, she gave herself the characteristic little shake and was back with him again.

"Well, at any rate, it's over now. You are here—and here I am." She looked about herself, smiling. "Countess Zotov is kindness itself and, what's more important, a reasonable human being. You can't imagine, Greesha, what a relief that is!"

And that reminded him. "Yes! What happened at the Pomykovs? What did she do?"

"Marya Ivanovna?" Claire's smile was mischievous and, to his surprise, entirely affectionate. "Oh, she did nothing except become more and more like herself. I could have borne the quarrels; it's the reconciliations that undid me." Her eyebrows made the comic swoop he knew.

"I thought she might know about us." There was a sweetness about saying "us." His heart lunged.

But she was frowning. "Why, what made you think she did?"

"Well, it was the way she talked about immorality. And she looked at me *so* . . ."

"Ah yes. Poor Marya Ivanovna, she is obsessed with everyone's morals now. I fear"—her eyes laughed—"yes, I fear, she is beginning to feel a need for another lover."

"*Another* lover?"

"Another flirt, I mean," she amended hurriedly. "I don't really know . . ." But she did know and after a moment Grisha did too. He tried to induce in himself a proper disapproval, thinking of Zahar Nikolaitch, but in spite of himself, an unwilling grin tugged at his lips, reflecting Claire's small smile. He was conscious of a reluctant, shamefaced camaraderie. My incorrigible Pushchin, he thought affectionately.

"How dreadful of him," he said unconvincingly. "When Zahar Nikolaitch was so fond of him . . ."

"And still is, I assure you. *Che vuole*?" The shrug that accompanied the words was wholly Italian. "Have you not heard the silly woman say that she has the temperament of a Messalina?" Her teasing smile faltered, dimmed, and he guessed that, like him, she was remembering how far removed his incorrigible friend was now from such temptations. Exultation filled him: so she was not the only one who could read thoughts; her mind too was unlocked to him now, he could enter it at will; surely a dispensation granted only to lovers. . . .

"Ah me," Claire murmured, "I fear I'll miss them all sadly— Marya Ivanovna and Zahar Nikolaitch and Johnny. . . . Yes, and my darling Vasska . . . Did you see him, Greesha? Have they let his fur get into tangles, now I am no longer there to comb it out?"

But he had had enough of this. "How soon can I see you? Oh Claire . . ."

She looked at him lovingly and it seemed to him sadly. "Yes, we must meet."

"Will you come to me tomorrow?"

She shook her head. "No, impossible."

"The day after?"

To this she nodded. A shadowy smile indented the corners of her small pale mouth and he was filled with painful desire.

As he was waiting in the anteroom to have his coat brought to him, he became aware of the little girl Natalie standing in the doorway, watching him. She dropped him a little curtsey and said abruptly:

"Miss Clairmont says you were in prison. Was it terrible?"

"Yes," Grisha said. "But it didn't last long."

"Ah." She went on studying him seriously while the footman helped him on with his coat. Her eyes went down to his foot and lingered there, with not precisely a curiosity but a deepening of attention, as though she was cataloguing everything about him.

"Are you coming back to see Miss Clairmont?"

"If I may, Countess."

"Please do," she said gravely, inclining her smooth little head. He kissed her small warm paw with careful tenderness: for some reason she made him think of Dunia.

Then, as the front door closed behind him, he forgot all about her. Claire, he thought, Claire, day after tomorrow.

"We don't exactly know what romantic literature is: it begins in nature, it expands, it circulates; and luckily for us it has not yet been dissected . . ." The poet Vyazemski's voice, as crisply ironic as ever. His spectacles gleamed impishly as he addressed a circle of listeners who crowded about him, waiting for an epigram.

Nothing had changed, it seemed, in Princess Zinaide's salon. The easy murmur, the witty clamor, Princess Zinaide in her classical costume, casting her charming distrait smile about her—everything was the same. Orlov's handsome head would never be seen again, towering above others; Sasha Odoevsky was sick with brain fever in Petropavlovsk. However Vladimir Odoevski, the cousin he had wanted to convert, sanguine, plump, smiling, quite unlike Sasha, was present in the midst of his coterie of archive youths. Liveried footmen circulated among the guests, proffering refreshments on silver trays. "I do love sweets . . ." Grisha remembered. He turned to Monsieur Gambs, who, trim in his midnight-blue swallowtail coat with a velvet collar, stood looking about him happily, delighted with his entree into this Moscow Parnassus of wits and litterateurs. "Just as though nothing had happened," he murmured bitterly.

Monsieur Gambs shook his head. "Not so," he said. "Can't you tell? They are all frightened."

After a while Grisha was impelled to agree with him. In St. Petersburg, his parents' friends could talk about the fourteenth with gossipy righteousness, smugly conscious of being uninvolved.But here—the very fact that all the discussions in the salon were by common agreement confined within the safe limits of the arts, without a single gibe at the government, told one a great deal. The shadow of the Petropavlovsk spire reached into Princess Zinaide's drawing room, stilling uninihibited tongues, stamping all those animated faces with a strangely careworn look.

"Bad times are coming, and everyone knows it," Zahar Niko-laitch had told him during his visit. "In spite of all the inequities of Alexander's regime, one could at least talk about them, particularly in Moscow—if only because the repressive agencies were as inefficient as they were malevolent. But now—there's a sense of horrible efficiency about the way people have been rounded up here. You begin to know without a doubt that the Emperor isn't joking."

Grisha had nodded, feeling again those hands lying heavy on his shoulders, remembering the implacable leaden look boring into the inside of his skull.

No matter what her private worries were (Grisha remembered now that her brother-in-law was implicated), Princess Zinaide remained the impeccable hostess, offering her guests the fare to which they were accustomed. Genichsta was this evening's offering; he performed on the piano with his usual brilliance. He was followed by the famous harpist Schneider, a lumbering young man with a bovine look who embraced the harp clumsily with his huge arms and proceeded to draw from it celestial sounds of incredible delicacy. It was usual after such performances to ask the Princess, an accomplished musician herself, to play, or sing; a request usually complied with after a charming little display of modesty: "My dears, after what we have been privileged to hear? How can you? How can *I*?" This time however she did not demur, but sat down at the piano immediately, pushing her bracelets higher up her beautiful bare arms. For a moment she sat pensive, head bent, running her fingers inaudibly over the keys; then looked up, took a chord, and began to sing. A murmur rippled over the audience. This would be no aria from *Italiana in Algeria*, enjoying a vogue in Moscow this winter. The very first notes, sung in a deeper warmer register, proclaimed it to be a Russian song even before the words floated out toward the attentive audience. "Nightingale, my nightingale," she sang, and it was strange to hear the simple words of a Russian song ringing through the large room with its over-civilized French trappings. But they all disappeared, ceased to matter. The woman who sat at the piano wearing the classical costume of the "tenth muse" was utterly Russian. She might have been a peasant woman, going home wearily from the fields, singing as she went; and her song was the ancient lament, a woman's plaint over her sad fate, a moan for the man torn away from her side.

> Nightingale, my nightingale
> They have caged my nightingale
> Never more he'll sing, so free,
> Nevermore, return to me . . .

A doleful sound reached Grisha's ears; turning he saw the plump Vladimir Odoevski burying his face in his hands; his stout shoulders shook helplessly. Vyazemski's sharp face crumpled into the piteous grimace of a crying child. All about them there was the suppressed stirring of grief. . . . The singer went on, inexorably transfixing the heart with note after note of pure sorrow.

> Nightingale, my nightingale
> Bring me back my nightingale.

There was no applause when she finished. A deep common sigh passed through the great room like a gust of wind through a field and was still.

Afterward conversation was sparse and subdued. Silently champagne was passed around; silently it was drunk, glasses lifted in unspoken toasts. The gathering dispersed, earlier than usual.

Monsieur Gambs was deeply affected. The emotion he had experienced and the champagne he had drunk coalesced in the sharp winter air, and he had to be helped into the sledge, uttering doleful German exclamations.

"Ah, if only Claire had been here tonight," he exclaimed, while the footman arranged the bear rug across their knees. "It would have done her so much good. That famous English stoicism, that so sternly keeps the tears inside! *Aber nein, nicht wahr!* Sometimes it is far better to relax that stern guard and let yourself weep." Suiting action to word, he shook out a snowy handkerchief and wept into it.

Grisha almost said: "But why should she weep? I am back now." Catching himself in time, he merely nodded sympathetically.

"I have always loved her, you know," said Monsieur Gambs, removing his handkerchief from his suffused eyes and fixing Grisha with a gaze that was both stern and befuddled. "*Jeder Mann muss immer ein Ideal haben.* . . . She is the sort of woman who must always strive after the highest; and in her search she will penetrate the most unlikely disguise. . . . *Sie sieht tief in die Seele hinein.* . . . What though on the surface a man appears to be a libertine? A vulgar woman-chaser? She will guess the martyr behind the rake and give herself where she loves. . . ."

"Yes, of course, but do sit down, Monsieur Gambs. Akim! Drive slower."

[378]

"Ein Mann wer sein Alles gab—a man who gave his all for freedom—what am I compared to that? A humble tutor—a poor rhymester, some one who poetizes about the sub—sublimities he cannot perform." He thought it over and said in a small reflective voice: *"Doch ist es nicht zu schlimm."* Rising once again to his feet in the slowly moving sleigh, he began to recite, with wide gestures, what Grisha recognized after a while to be lines from the third canto of *Moïse.*

Claire's Journal, February 20

It started so well. Fomitch, amiable pander, leading me conspiratorially through the back, closing the room to Grisha's apartments with ceremony behind him, as he tiptoed away. We laughed about that and about other things. We were lighthearted. I teased him with having made a conquest: little Natalie, who asked me so much about him.

"That little girl?" But I noticed with pleasure the peacocky little inflation of his chest, the serious lips yielding to the tug of a pleased smile. It's so good for him to see himself as the object of an infatuation. Even from a bud of a girl still in her pantalettes.

"Little girls have a way of growing up," I told him. "This is your bride, you know. I don't mean specifically little Natalie, though she is a darling, but there is someone like her, somewhere, being readied for you. . . ."

"Don't talk to me about brides," he said, reaching for me with violence. "You're my bride." I can still see how the tiny twin lights at the back of his eyes grew as though candles had been brought from the back of a darkened room nearer to the windows. "I love you, Claire. Tell me you love me . . ."

"Of course I do."

That strong young body, smooth, supple, discovering more and more its powers for enjoyment. . . .

And then, only a little later, it happened. He was lying by my side, drowsy and warm, and suddenly the most charming humorous little smile irradiated his face. A laugh broke from him.

"What is it?" I looked at him, ready to join in the joke.

"Something funny the other night. Monsieur Gambs thinks Pushchin is the one."

"The one . . .?" I didn't immediately understand.

"Your lover. The one you love." He looked at me, expecting me to be amused too.

Involuntarily a gasp escaped from me, as though I had unexpectedly been drenched by a bucketful of icy water.

He hurried to reassure me. "Oh, please, you mustn't be angry at him, he didn't mean anything wrong. I was angry too, until I saw how—respectful he was. You see, he had a little too much champagne at Princess Zinaide's and he was a little *exalté*. So first he said that you and Pushchin—and then he immediately explained to me how sublime it all was and how you guessed the greatness in Pushchin, as you had in Albé. . . . He always gets everything wrong, doesn't he?"

I don't know how it is, but invariably a friend trying to explain your actions in the best possible light can be paired with an enemy blackening your character.

I said nothing; it might just pass over without questions asked. But apparently there was a certain *compressed* quality in my silence that fatally attracted questions. He gave me a quick look and his brows came together. They relaxed immediately and he said in the half-laughing voice with which one recalls a piece of nonsense—something that almost took you in for a second but was really too absurd—"It's not true, is it?"

No need to drain that cup, a voice said urgently within me. Say no, lie to him immediately and incisively, and that will be that. But I hesitated. Lie to him when everything we had was based precisely on the premise that I would always keep my promises, always tell the truth? No matter how rash the promises, how intolerable the truth? Voicelessly I debated this within myself. But by the time I opened my mouth—to lie? to confess? I no longer remember—the struggle had taken too long and he was beginning to know. Sitting up in bed, he looked at me hard, unsmiling.

"It is true," he said, no longer asking a question. I think

I still could have lied to him but—well, I didn't. I watched the warm drowsy flush ebbing from his face, leaving it pale, strained, old. The next moment he had turned away from me with a spasmodic movement and was lying with his face buried in the pillow, his shoulders hunched in misery.

"Oh, darling, no," I said helplessly. "Don't. Speak to me."

He grated out, muffled: "He loved you and the minute he went away . . ." He paused for some bitter internal arithmetic. "Three days later . . ."

"Grisha, dear Grisha . . ."

"You made me betray him. My best friend, the man I owe everything to. He saved me, and I—" Lifting his head from the pillow, he fixed me with a look of black blame, the look with which men have accused women ever since Adam took the apple from Eve. "You have made me betray him."

"There was no betrayal here, Grisha, from first to last . . ."

"All I have thought of was how to manage to see him. And now—how could I face him? After we—after I . . . I want to give him everything I have and I took away from him the woman he loved while he went to rot in prison. . . . And you," he said with a groan of revulsion. "How could you? How could you love him and then . . .?"

"But I didn't. I never loved him, and he didn't love me."

There was total bewilderment on his face.

"But you and he . . .? *Il était ton amant?*" I suddenly realized that without noticing it we had switched to French. It was another stab into my already desolate heart. Our English conversations were coming to an end, it seems. . . .

I said: "Yes, he was my lover. I slept with him. But love never entered into this."

He thought it over. Presently his lips flattened out in disgust.

"I see," he said through his teeth. "It was just another one of Pushchin's amours. . . . And it suited you?"

"Yes, it suited me. There was nothing romantic about it.

But it was honest passion—we wanted each other—and at the end it was friendship. . . . So you see, Grisha, you can see him any time you want without feeling a traitor. If he knew, he wouldn't care. He would approve. We understood each other, you see."

And, as soon as I said this, I became conscious of a change in the air. Not for the better, though. He believed me, I saw. He would no longer speak in anguish of betraying Pushchin. In a queer way, he was the one betrayed now. I could clearly read jealousy and anger in his blanched face.

Jealousy and anger can always be manipulated. There is something in the male animal that is always saying to the female: "I can make you forget him." It becomes a matter of pride. I knew that if I wanted to I could make him take me now; and then again and again. Desire could be pleasurably peppered up by jealousy; anger could become a subtle goad to fiercer transports. It would be a hold hard to break. For a moment I was tempted. I had taught him the safety, the gentleness of love; it would be fitting for me to instruct him in ferocity of pleasure. . . .

No. Let someone else teach it to him.

But as I moved away, leaving the bed, his arm shot out, his thin fingers made an iron ring around my wrist. He said, breathless, through pale lips: "So you sleep with men, but not necessarily for love. You slept with him for—for lust. And I—did you sleep with me for pity?"

And again there was the wheel spinning backward. Geordie's voice from the past asking me: "Would you have loved me, Claire, if I weren't what I am?"

If—if! Men, always asking unnecessary questions.

I answered him as I had the other one: "What does it matter how love starts?"

That time it had been the right answer. This time it was wrong.

"It matters! It matters!" he groaned and dropped his head down between his clenched fists.

I dressed in silence. The winter sun blazed obliquely through the window, the fire danced heartlessly on the hearth. I came back to the bed where he lay motionless. "It'll be all right, Grisha,.you'll see."

"No," he said muffled, "no, never."

I pressed my lips to his bare shoulder and left him.

It was still light after she had gone—days were getting longer now. Grisha ordered Nelly to be saddled. He rode down toward the river, by way of the Alexander Gardens. She cantered sedately across the snowy walks, tossing her head; her hooves left wet blue prints in the snow. A curtain of clouds hung low in the sky; the presence of the sun could be guessed at by the rays stabbing downward from behind their rim. Flooded by a sullen ambiguous light, the city acquired a strangeness, a special look that seemed to proclaim an imminent catastrophe: such a light, he thought idly, might have shone over Moscow when Napoleon was entering it. The golden domes of Kremlin grew leaden, the white walls looked livid. Turning down the strand toward the Moskovski Bridge, he saw that they were working on the frozen river, putting up the underpinnings of the great sled runs for the Butter Week. The bustling activity had a sinister quality: it might have been gallows that were being erected.

Everything seemed askew. She had taken the world in her strong pianist's hands and given it a turn. It could never be put right now.

Last night he had listened to Monsieur Gambs with an amusement that he had found difficult to conceal. Claire and Pushchin! There was only one message that flashed from Pushchin to a woman, simple, uncomplicated, going directly to the point. In the beginning he himself had seen it going to Claire, only to be deflected from an impervious surface. He always gets things wrong, doesn't he? he had said to Claire. Well, and so he did, after all. Poor Monsieur Gambs, infatuated with the Wertherian ideal, endowing a vulgar affair with all the perquisites of a deathless romance. . . .

But perhaps Gambs too . . . The loving affectionate amused looks she bent on him—she wasn't in love with him, but that wasn't needed, it appeared. A lesser feeling would serve. And what about Genichsta? She admired him as a musician—bending her long neck in homage, calling him *"caro maestro"*—what more natural than that a duet at the piano should be followed by one in bed? It all seemed possible once you knew about Pushchin.

And she had harbored no illusions about Pushchin. She knew what he was. A hero, a martyr, a dear, dear man—all that, and also a cheerful libertine, not caring where he got what he wanted. Grisha remembered her little smile when they were talking about Marya Ivanovna in Zotovs' drawing room and felt sick. There was only one inescapable inference to be drawn from her undoubtedly genuine amusement. She had known all about it and hadn't minded his coming to her from another bed.

Pushchin had said to him once, "I keep away from virtuous women as I would from the plague." But of course she was not a virtuous woman. . . .

The fact that we have unloosed ourselves from trammels of custom and tradition does not mean that we do not have a more severe monitor than those within ourselves—her clear voice chiming austere from the past. He had nodded respectful acquiescence. Deluded nonsense! To his incurably romantic eyes, she had made their way of life seem as removed from the ordinary, as lofty, as the stately motion of stars. (And what about P.B.?—did he too . . .?) But looked at realistically, it was no different from the indiscriminate coupling done in St. Petersburg or Moscow society without the benefit of the lofty philosophy. How was she different from, for example, the late Tsar's mistress, the stately and voluptuous Naryshkina, who because of her many affairs on the side was known as "Minerva in heat"? Or, for that matter, the gypsy Styosha, opening her dark thighs to anyone? He remembered his brother's cheerful, "There won't be any less of her afterward!" A horrid parallel occurred to him. Is that what happened? Did Pushchin too—? Like Sergey in his brotherliness—? A strong shudder shook him. If that was so, that somehow would be the worst of all, not to be borne. Fortunately this was something he could never find out.

Oh, but you can, he said to himself coldly. All you need to do is ask. She would be only too glad to tell you. . . . *I will always tell you the truth, Greesha.* There was no stopping her: the great eyes held you mesmerically helpless while the clear voice, uncolored by uncertainty or shame, told you what with all your heart you didn't want to know.

She should have lied to him—laboriously he began to whip up his righteous indignation—because lying would have meant at least a presence of certain moral judgment. You lied when you knew you were wrong. That meant that you knew the difference between right and wrong, and, if so, it was possible to repent and be forgiven. . . . He had a vision of a Magdalene-like Claire prostrate before him, the black pool of her loosened hair lapping about his feet. . . . But she showed no signs of repentance. She looked you in the face unremorseful with a look that said to you, my body is my own and I can give it where I want, no one has any rights over it, you least of all. . . .

Fury broke over him like a blinding flash of lightning. His heels dug hard into Nelly's side and she broke into a gallop.

"Bitch!" Grisha shouted in a high cracking voice and brought his crop down with all his force. Taken by surprise, the mare reared, whinnying and striking out with her slender forefeet.

"Would you then, she-devil!" He fought her down savagely, bringing the crop down again and again. A sharp bright madness exploded in his brain. *Keep at it then, whip and spur, no letting up, 'til both of us drop. . . .*

A whistling scream broke from Nelly. There was a human note of unbearable outrage in the high-pitched sound. For another moment Grisha hung over her, whip upraised. Then with violence he threw it away and fell forward, throwing his arms around the satiny neck darkened with sweat.

"I am sorry," he said weeping, "oh, Nelly, my darling, I am so sorry, I am a beast, I deserve to die. . . . Forgive me, my darling, I didn't mean to, it wasn't you."

Gracelessly, he slid off, landing on his bad foot. A sharp pain shot up his leg, giving him a cruel satisfaction. He stroked the sweaty neck that throbbed nervously at his touch, talking to her softly as she pulled away from him, gentling her until her beautiful eyes stopped staring, thankfully feeling her snorting breath come easier, her trembling subside.

"Forgive me," he said again, kissing her velvety nostrils, with tears pouring down his face, oblivious of the passersby staring at him curiously.

Claire's Journal, February 24

No word from Grisha. But as though I am with him, I know exactly what he is going through. He hadn't minded about Geordie. Geordie was a romantic ghost, he had passed through my willing body like a bright mist, leaving no trace of sweat, no odor of semen. I might have been one of the mythological heroines visited by a god, possessed by a storm, a shower of gold. But Pushchin, ah, that was different. That was a connection too real to be romanticized. That robust body had entered mine, had moved in me just as his did. He can visualize only too easily all the particulars of that encounter, poor boy.

I knew it would have to end. . . . Ah, but I didn't want it to end like this. Who knows, perhaps I didn't want it to end at all. . . .

Claire's Letter to Grisha, February 25

. . . I have been waiting to hear from you, during this past week, with as much anxiety as I had during the terrible time when they took you away. It would be fatuous to say that nothing has changed. I can only say that *I* haven't. If you have, I must be allowed to see in what way, I must know how you are. You owe me that, I think. One never gets beyond the obligation of reassuring those who love one.

The day promises to be pleasant. I usually manage to take a walk on the Tverskoy Boulevard at about three o'clock. . . .

Perversely, Grisha did not come that day. He stayed home, the vision of Claire waiting for him vainly on the Tverskoy Boulevard alternating with that of Claire shrugging her shoulders and giving him up, much too soon, perhaps even relieved at his nonappearance. Both tortured him equally. But he was there the next day, scanning the groups of promenaders brought out by the brilliant sun. Presently he spotted the familiar slender figure. The little Countess Zotov was with her. The two of them were walking slowly along the alley of birches planted recently to take the place of the plane trees cut down in 1812 by Napoleon's soldiers.

Grisha joined them. Claire had her usual air of nervous vulnerability to cold, huddling in her fur pelisse like some wild foreign bird caught by winter in a region where it could barely survive. The little Countess walked sedately by her side, the brilliance of her cheeks matching her crimson sable-trimmed coat. Both of them brightened with welcome at his arrival.

"Everyone assures me," Claire remarked, "that it's warmer than it had ever been in February, positively balmy, and I daresay they are all perfectly sincere in this absurd assertion. I don't know how long I can bear this."

So they would talk about the weather, Natalie's presence precluding anything else. Not knowing whether to be relieved or enraged, he stumped glumly by their side, in graceless silence.

"Aren't those the Arcarovs turning into the pavilion?" Claire asked. "Yes, it is they, undoubtedly. If you would like to talk to Barbe Arcarov, Natalie. . ."

The young girl bent her head, so that only the lower part of a rosy cheek could be seen under the sable-trimmed edge of her bonnet. But there was a stubborn look about the downy line of her jaw. She remarked in a light little voice, looking fixedly at the tips of her small boots: "I really have not the slightest desire to join Barbe Arcarov, who is a silly sort of a girl and gives herself airs. If you don't mind, I'd rather stay here with you, Miss Clairmont."

Claire stopped. Putting her hands on the girl's shoulders, she looked at her gravely: "Natalie, remember I told you when we went out for a walk, that we might possibly encounter Prince Volynski, and if so I would like to have a brief private conversation with him. . . . So, *ma petite*, if you could bring yourself to tolerate the company of Barbe for a short time. . ."

The girl listened silently, her eyelashes lying on her rosy cheeks. The eyelashes and the thickish level eyebrows had the same clean glint as the sable trimming her pelisse. "I will do anything you ask me to do, of course, Miss Clairmont." She raised her eyes as she spoke. The whites of her eyes had a faintly bluish tinge, and the gray-green irises looked clear and fresh against them. Her serious glance swerved toward Grisha, rested on him for a second. Then she went away, presently breaking into a run along the cleared path.

Following the flying figure with her eyes, Claire sighed. "One can see her growing, the way grass grows in the spring. And doesn't she make me feel old!—I try to remember myself at twelve, at thirteen, at fourteen, and I can't. My childhood just fell away from me one day and disappeared out of my memory. . . . Well,

Greesha." Her glance was as direct as the little girl's. "How is it with you? Are you still unhappy? Yes, I see you are. Have you tried not to be? Can you tell me why you mind so desperately?"

"No, I can't," he said. "All I know is that I want to die."

"Ah," she said, smiling, he thought, with utter heartlessness. "One feels that way very often when one is young. Well, at least you don't want to go into a monastery, and that's encouraging." Mute, outraged, he rounded on her: how could she? "But what you do want, I think, is for me to have been in a nunnery until last December."

He gave her a somber look. "You are treating me as though I were a child," he said. "I am not, you know. I grew up—in St. Petersburg."

"And I grew old while you were there." Her eyes softened. She took her hand out of her muff to make the familiar gesture toward his face and tucked it back again without touching him. "No, I neither think of you nor treat you as a child. But it's true, isn't it? you want to possess—not only that but to have been the only possessor. The fact that you haven't been—nor are, nor will be—lowers my value to you. Because I was something to someone else, what I was—am—to you is in your eyes completely annulled. Why must it be so? I never made claims on you, though I love you. . . ."

"You could have," he said, "you could have made any claim on me you wished. I wanted you to."

Wasn't this implicit in the very nature of love? The total claim upon each other, the exclusion of the rest of the world? In love one needed this divine insulation—or at least the illusion of it. Yes, he would have settled for the illusion.

"You shouldn't have told me," he muttered wretchedly.

Her eyes widened on him. "I promised you the truth. From the beginning. Remember."

They walked on in silence passing by the pavilion. A flash of crimson just beyond the Moorish arch of the entrance: Natalie taking a cup of chocolate as she faithfully conversed with the objectionable Barbe Arcarov.

They came to a bridge curving over the artificial canal, crossed it, paused to look down on the solid green pathway of ice lying between the banks, turned back.

"Possessiveness," she said, "that seignorial itch, that demon that had risen to confront me again and again—how I hate it! It runs counter to everything I believe—everything P.B. believed. It was totally alien to him, and to me. I have never been possessive or jealous in my life. . . ."

It occurred to him that this had been said to him in the very beginning by her; a motif that had been introduced in a beginning of a sonata was now being recapitulated in the final movement. It had a taste of finality. Their duet too was being wound up. An intolerable sorrow wrung his heart.

"Everything is changed," he said. "I thought you loved me, I thought you were mine. Now I don't know, I will always wonder—I don't know you at all. . . ."

"Nobody knows anyone, Greesha. When you love you merely take the unknown on trust. I don't know you either, it seems," she said with some asperity. "You are talking like a serf owner after all. Yours—mine—as if my body which I shared with you so happily has somehow become your property. I have never expected this of you. . . ."

All at once he saw Albé listening to her, infuriated, as she told him all, expecting only the best from him. The same fury shook him. Incensed, he burst out: "You expect too much of us!"

For the first time, she flinched.

"Yes, you do. You see us a certain way and that's how we must behave. You accuse me of playing the proprietor with your body. Well, you have played the proprietor with my soul."

"Oh, no, oh, no," she said in a quenched voice, looking up at him with great frightened eyes.

"It must always be as you want. You love truth, so it must be crammed down my throat, and I must like it. What's the use of telling me how wrong it is for me to be—possessive? Just now, at this moment of my life, wrong or right, that's how I need you to be—just for me, mine alone. . . . If you loved me . . ."

"Yes," she said, "you are right, I shouldn't have burdened you with the truth you didn't want." She stopped, turning to him, arms outflung. "Oh, I'm sorry," she cried, "I'm sorry, Geordie, Georges, Greesha—I should have lied to you!"

Her arms fell to her sides. Head bent, she walked on.

He remembered how a few months ago, near Poor Lisa's pond, she had turned to him, with the same simplicity, owning herself wrong, owning to self-deception, laughing at herself. It had touched and reassured him then. But now he was merely furious.

Conscious of nothing save a witless urge to punish, he seized on the memory as a club. "You do lie, you know. All those stories about you and *him*—" But even as he began to bludgeon her down, he stayed faithful to the old behest not to use *his* right name, and that enraged him even more. "I don't believe them any more. He never loved you, you just made it up, he didn't love you, ever. He left you because he couldn't bear you any more," he said with the oddest mixture of sorrow and cruelty. "Isn't that true, isn't that how it was?"

She gave a gasp, and her head drooped even lower. In the slightest thread of a voice, she said, "If you prefer it so . . ."

He walked silently by her side, appalled at himself, yet conscious of a sort of vindictive triumph. A small convulsion—a sigh or a shudder—passed through her slender body, and she raised to him a face from which all beauty had gone—sallow cheeked, pinched, the tip of the long nose reddened by cold. Only the great luminous eyes redeemed it from ugliness. Her pallid lips stirred into a poor sort of a smile. "You are at liberty to create your own myths about me, Greesha," she said, "now that it's over. . . ."

Over? But of course it was.

". . . Because it is quite plain, isn't it, that you at least can't, any more . . . bear me, I mean . . . Isn't that so?"

"No, I can't," he answered with simplicity, his anger gone. "You are too much for me."

He needed another element in his life, something less mysterious and volatile. She would no longer serve him—whatever it was he wanted would have to be now supplied by himself.

She gave the little punctuating nod he knew. "If you have learned that ultimately you are alone with only yourself to rely on, then I indeed have been useful to you," she said, for the last time uncannily lifting his thought. Another deep sigh shook her. "Must it always be like that? Must we use people? Draw from them the nourishment we need and then . . .?" she asked, addressing not him alone, but someone beyond him. Her eyes refocused, steadying upon him, with their old compelling intentness.

"I have served your turn, and you have served mine, dear love, and it's over. But not quite. Never quite. In everything you are, everything you do or say, there'll still be me, there will always be a little bit of Claire."

There was a certain smoothness, almost glibness about this. He felt a certainty that she had said this before. Perhaps more than once. Would surely say it again. What was more, it was probably quite true.

With a profound bow, he left her. At the end of the alley he looked back, once. The girl Natalie had joined her. Standing motionless together, their arms about each other, they watched him go.

YAROSLAVL

In your Siberian mines maintain
Proud fortitude amid privations.
Your weary toil is not in vain
Nor your high-striving meditations.

*   *   *

Friendship and love will reach you still
Despite all locks their entry finding,
E'en as through your dark warrens winding
My free voice penetrates at will.

*   *   *

Alexander Pushkin

Yaroslavl was an extremely dull town. It shouldn't have been so. Perched at the confluence of two rivers, gemmed with medieval churches, so close to the gray grandeur of Volga that the songs of the men taking the rafts down to the markets could be heard on the main square, it should have been memorable and noble. Indeed the serene sparkle of the church cupolas seen as one approached it from the south seemed to promise something extraordinary. But after you had been there for three weeks, the last bit of attractiveness was gone from it; it had become a dismal limbo of a provincial town where one waited, much too long, for the one important thing to happen.

The inn in which Grisha stayed was an ancient building in the center of the main square. It was a shabby structure, badly run down, with vermin crawling out of the cracks in the wall. It took all the efforts of the indignant Fomitch, together with the half-dozen servants he autocratically enlisted to help him, to transform the room Grisha occupied to what he grudgingly called "something like." But, although he urgently begged his master to make his presence known to the Governor of the province, who lived just outside of Yaroslavl and was a distant cousin of the Volynskis, Grisha refused to do so. He had no intention of leaving the hotel even for a day. It was the place at which prisoners bound for Siberia made a stop, to change horses and eat. Within a week the party including Pushchin would—if all went well, if there were no further unnerving delays—arrive at this very hotel. He would see Pushchin, perhaps even talk to him.

That this was possible was a miracle in itself. At first Pushchin had been condemned to die, together with the others in the so-called first class. Although the death penalty had been abolished during the reign of Elizaveta Petrovna, it seemed that the heinousness of December fourteenth merited its being reintroduced. Then Imperial kindness intervened, somewhat ostentatiously. Mercy was shown. The five who had been condemned to be drawn and quartered would be merely hanged. Others who were to be hanged would be merely sent to Siberia for their lifetime. Pushchin was among those latter. Sometime during this cold windy bleak November Grisha would see him.

How much of a meeting it would be depended on the *feldjäger* in charge. Grisha knew only too well the importance of the personalities of the couriers conducting their prisoners into exile. Some were incorruptible, preferring to satisfy their rapaciousness legitimately by setting as fast a pace as possible and pocketing the difference in the allowance allotted them. Those stopped for nothing and no one; relatives traveling for miles on the chance of intercepting the convoy at one of its stopping places would be allowed only to hear the cry of "good-bye," see the last frantic wave, as the troikas plunged by them mercilessly. Other couriers were rapacious in a more human way: they would accept the gratuities, take their time about changing the horses, and look the other way while their charges exchanged a last farewell with those who had come to see them off.

The week before a quiet little middle-aged lady, who had been unobtrusively occupying a room in the same hotel as Grisha, had stood on the stoop wringing her hands and weeping, her gray hair wild in the wind, while two chambermaids, also in tears, held her back to prevent her from throwing herself under the wheels of a chaise that was making its way out of the courtyard. "Petya," she screamed after it, "Petya." "Mamma" came back in a despairing roar. She tore herself free, made a few failing steps after the carriage, and fell to her knees. Grisha lifted her up. "Petya," she said to him, kissing him blindly, "Petya, my darling son, Petya. I've waited so long." In the courtyard a crowd stood glum and silent, watching her. Grim compassion rose from them, as palpable as the dust that had risen from under the clattering wheels of the disappearing chaise. . . . She had left Yaroslavl the same day.

After that the customary tedium closed over the town again. Clouds thickened overhead; Volga flowed gray and cheerless within its precipitous banks. Grisha, spending his time on the embankment overlooking it, would lose himself in its sluggish, perpetual, sullen flow. A long raft of timber would pass below him, its steersmen intoning a plaintive chant. A crane would go swooping downwind uttering a thin keening cry like the cry of the disappointed mother.

And then one day it all changed. They are coming—mysteriously the message spread through the town. "They're coming," Fomitch told him, coming back from the kitchen. It could be felt in the altered tempo of the life at the inn; even the help fell into a peculiarly disjointed activity, not any more useful than before but different from the usual slovenly languor. A crowd, aimless but hopeful, began gathering in the square, not doing or saying much, merely waiting. The police would clear it out of the square and presently it would seep in again, straggler by straggler, through the side streets, trickling down to the square, like rainwater gathering into a puddle.

The convoy arrived late. Three troika-drawn chaises came clattering over the cobblestones—the noise of the wheels mingled with the concerted sigh from the waiting crowd—and pulled up in the courtyard. The gates were then closed and a gendarme posted in front with a drawn saber. Grisha, keeping watch at his window (he had deliberately selected a room overlooking the court), looked down on a confused activity, sporadically lighted by a perambulatory lantern. Horses snorted and stamped; a crowd of hostlers bustled around the vehicles. Straining his eyes, he could barely see dim figures helped out of the chaises, hurried inside; he thought he heard a clatter of chains, a voice spoke up loudly: a voice he knew? He couldn't be sure; his heart beat furiously, blood drummed in his ears deafening him.

Grisha darted to the door where he met Fomitch coming in, his unruly cowlick standing up in excitement.

"It's him, your Excellency, it's him!"

"You're sure?"

"Certain-sure, Excellency—I don't know any of the others, but I could see him as they were bringing them inside! it's surely him."

"How did he—? Was he—?" Not waiting to hear, Grisha pushed past Fomitch and went out quickly into the corridor, which was now a scene of hushed activity. The host was urging a crowd of curious spectators out of the way, interlarding his polite pleas to the guests with an oath and a kick at the common people who had somehow made their way inside "to take a look at the convict *barins*."

A *feldjäger* was standing in front of a closed door, listening to a well-dressed man, who spoke to him in loud, clear, cultivated tones. "The room which you are occupying, Sergeant, is not one of the best. I should be delighted if you and your charges would take mine while you are here. . . . I should be only too honored to accommodate an officer in pursuit of his duty." The officer saluted smartly, mumbling what was apparently an acceptance of the offer.

That must mean that they would be staying for some time. But would they allow their prisoners to be seen? His heart beating, Grisha in his turn approached the *feldjäger*. He looked at him fearfully: were those the pitiless Germanic features of a Sergeant

Krueger, his erstwhile guard, correct, obstinate, undiluted by any humanity? But the simple broad face of a Russian peasant looked back at him from under the visor of the gigantic shako.

"Sergeant, I happened to hear the gentleman, and I—I too . . ." he found himself running out of breath. "You are welcome to my rooms too."

"Thanking you kindly, your Honor," said the Sergeant in a beery basso, "but no need to bother your Honor, we're well suited."

"And—I understand you have in your charge a—a certain Ivan Ivanitch Pushchin. . . . If I could . . . If we could. . . ." His throat dried up. All that day he had kept in his pocket a folded up 100-ruble banknote; now to his horror his trembling fingers could not find it in his pocket, grope as they might. Finally he dragged it out, held it up in front of the Sergeant's face; the small eyes regarded it noncommittally. "Here you are—purely as a token of my esteem," he babbled, "and another to come if you—if you . . ."

He waited, in agony. The majestic head turned slowly in all directions; a thick white-gloved hand came up slowly—to dash the bribe out of his hand? No, it closed on the banknote, folded it, put it away. A ripple ran across the immobile face; slowly, deliberately one eye closed. . . .

An hour later, Grisha, waiting in his room, heard steps approaching his door accompanied by a muted clanking of chains. He leaped to his feet, trembling. The door opened; a figure entered, moving slowly, its feet hobbled by a length of chain. The well-known face, wearing a look of cautious bewilderment, looked around, became radiant with surprise. With an inarticulate cry Grisha ran across the room and took him in his arms.

In the beginning they talked little, inhibited by the presence of the guard, who, though he accepted a glass of wine amiably enough, still kept a shrewd eye on them from his post by the door. Their first remarks to each other were in French, and that too was stopped. "Conversing only in Russian," the beery basso trumpeted officiously. Balked, they looked at each other and smiled.

A meal was brought up to the room. Grisha watched with delight and sorrow the voracity with which Pushchin attacked it. "Roast goose—*pelmeni*— You're really doing me proud, brother." Nevertheless he ate sparingly, leaving half on his plate. "Not used to rich food any more," he said apologetically.

As he ate, Grisha looked at him hungrily and fearfully: was he changed? The same and different; different and the same. He was much thinner now, in the body and in the face, skin stretched tautly across his high cheekbones. He had grown a smallish shaggy moustache. But the calm look of the gray eyes was still the same. Unchanged too was the old capacity for sheer physical enjoyment of each moment. Pleasure unobscured by any shadow shone on his face every time he looked at Grisha; and he beamed with pleasure when Fomitch, with a challenging look at the guard, brought in his mug and razor and shaved him.

"Well now, here I am ready for the ball at the Golitzins'." With evident enjoyment he touched his smooth face and trimmed moustache. "Thanks, friend." Fomitch took his outstretched hand respectfully and kissed it.

After he had eaten, he took a turn around the room, and Grisha saw with a pang the shortened, almost shuffling steps he took, accommodating himself to his fetters—so different from the soldierly stride he remembered. "No, it's all right, really," he said soothingly, catching Grisha's distressed look. "I don't mind—I've got used to them, and they are much lighter than the ones I used to wear in Petropavlovsk. Besides, he"—he nodded to the Sergeant on guard at the door—"he is a good fellow; when we stop anywhere overnight he lets us take off our irons. . . ."

"Well then . . ." Grisha reached into his pocket.

"No, don't bother, let's not take the time, I am happy as it is. Just tell me everything you can, all the news. . . ."

In preparation for this meeting Grisha had gathered together all the news he could. He recounted it all now, saving the best for the last. "Your brother Mikhail is very well; he has been promoted to captaincy."

Pushchin's broad chest rose and fell in a deep sigh; he crossed himself. There was a minute tremor in the firm mouth. "Thank God. You know the worst about this is not so much what happens to you, but what it does to your people. . . . That's a heavy burden to carry, brother. When I saw you in the Hermitage that time—that was a black moment indeed. And then the relief when I learned that you were out of it. . . . Oh yes, one gets to know things. Even in prison news somehow filters in. I heard about your release, Mukhanov and all. . . . Extraordinary business . . . By the way, he is here too. He's in our party."

"Oh no," Grisha said with revulsion, dismayed at the bracketing of the man who kept silent with the traitor who told all. But Pushchin shook his head with a quiet smile.

"No, my friend Grisha, that's all behind us. Everything that happened during the investigation must be erased from our memory. No reminders, no reproaches. We're all agreed on that. How else could we live together? . . . But enough: tell me about yourself. How is it going with you, Grisha?"

"Well, there isn't much to tell—of course, I am now attending Moscow University."

"My happiest days were spent in the Lyceum." There was an upward questioning lilt in his voice. Grisha realized that Pushchin was really asking if he, Grisha, was happy, and that it was important to his friend to be reassured on that score. Laboriously he proceeded to do so:

"Oh, it's most interesting and I am learning a lot. . . . My one chance to wear a uniform, too! Of course, everybody is being pretty cautious now, some of the classes I had wanted to take were discontinued, but still it's—rewarding. The professors do drone on, rather. . . ."

"But you do find some things of value there?" Pushchin asked, watching him closely. "You're making friends?"

"Oh, yes indeed. . . . As for friends—" There was the *feldjäger*, after all, a few feet away. From the expression on his simple broad face you couldn't tell whether he was listening or not. Still, it would not do to let him hear you say that the only friends he cared to have were on their way to Siberia. He went on brightly: "I've taken to circulating in the Moscow society a bit. All the Moscow mammas have decided that I have now reached the age when I should be looking for a bride, and am besides a good catch, so I am showered with invitations. . . . Oh, I go everywhere, and all kinds of eager young ladies are paraded before me. . . . I don't dance, of course, because of my leg, but there are always young ladies kind enough to sit out dances with me—very intellectual some of them, since I have a reputation of being an intellectual young man. We discuss Kant and Hegel . . . It's dull, all the same. . . ." The words escaped him before he could stop. He tried to make light of them, shrugging his shoulders, twisting his mouth into a deprecatory smile. "You know what Moscow society is like. . . . Remember in *Woe by Wit*? 'And really the world is turning stupid. . . .' Anyhow, I shall be going abroad soon."

He stopped short, cursing himself. There was an unforgivable indelicacy in flaunting one's ability to go wherever one wanted before a man condemned to immobility for the rest of his life. But the gray eyes lighted up with pleasure. "Really? Where do you plan to go?"

"I don't know yet. I should like to attend some lectures at the University of Göttingen, I think."

"And when? Soon?"

"Yes, soon. Now that I have seen you. . . ."

For months that had been the only thing he had looked forward to. He had focused on it like a traveler, making his dogged way across a flat and monotonous plain, always seeing ahead of him a light, a shape of a house to give him brief refuge. When this is over—his heart fell. With desolation he saw himself starting out to traverse another plain of equal monotony and dullness, but this time without a goal in view.

Pushchin looked at him reflectively. With the new moustache blurring the line of his smiling mouth, it was harder than ever to see what he was thinking. "You don't seem utterly overjoyed at the prospect of traveling." And in a lower voice, "What is it, then?"

"Oh nothing really. Boredom is a national illness, you know. We are all infected with it. Once I get away. . . ."

But Europe seemed as dull as Moscow, Moscow as dull as this dull town briefly irradiated by the long-awaited encounter. He said, trying to smile, "Sometimes I think, it might have been better if Mukhanov had stuck to his—error. . . ."

Pushchin looked at him silently, brows drawing together, and he added hastily: "All I mean is that I might be going with you now and I can't think of better company to be with—far better than the Moscow *haut monde.*"

"*Merci,*" Pushchin said dryly. He poured himself more champagne, swirling it gently so that the bubbles swam around and around in the glass. "What year is it? Eleventh year, by God, year of the comet . . . You *are* doing me proud. . . ." He drank it down slowly, his eyes dreamy. "We were wrong, you know," he said.

"Wrong?" Grisha stared at him dismayed.

"No, listen. We were people who tried to build a structure against all the rules of architecture. A building should be erected slowly, brick by brick. And, more important, from the ground up. But we didn't. We started up in the air, with the third floor."

"And came down with a bang," came suddenly from the immobile presence at the door. Pushchin burst into loud ringing laughter, unaffectedly amused by this interruption.

"No, he's right," he said, wiping his eyes, "we must all listen to the Sergeant. His present profession notwithstanding, he is basically a Russian. Russia itself speaks through his lips. And that's what I mean—the building must start from the earth—the good solid fertile Russian earth." Laughter faded away from his features, which presently became slowly illuminated by a light whose intensity Grisha recognized from before. It had shone in Pushchin's face in the Hermitage. But he said almost casually. "You know I didn't plan the fourteenth. It was upon me before I could think, and I—all of us—were whirled away as by a hurricane. . . . And the results were precisely what a hurricane leaves."

"You can't mean that it was of no use," Grisha said almost angrily.

"Everything is of use," Pushchin said, "or can be made so by a thinking man. . . . There has to be built up in Russia a class of men who will stay quietly riveted to the idea of reform, who will unobtrusively go on about their work, to make things better for the people. Men who can use everything at hand, learning, influence, position, who can bend under adversity and then rise up again to go on. Men who are capable of learning the art of timing. That is the most important thing in everything—including lovemaking," he interpolated with a sudden merry smile. "And in the long run such men are as important as those who perish on the barricades—and perhaps more useful. . . . But enough of this lecturing—much too solemn. Tell me—I have heard that they've let the Cricket out and that he came to Moscow? Did you see him? How was he?"

They stayed together for the next two hours talking, while the night wore on and the *feldjäger*, settling deeper into his chair, began to nod comfortably. A knock at the door brought him to his feet. He went to answer it.

"Well, gentlemen," he said to them, after a minute of low-voiced conversation, "it's time, the horses are ready."

It was over.

Was this what I came here for? Grisha thought, following prisoner and guard into the courtyard. To be told what to do with my life? Knowing that I couldn't disregard instructions coming

[401]

from such a source, just as I couldn't but obey the message pricked out in chapter 10 of *Isaiah*?

Following the muted jingle of chains into the darkness outside, I'll try, he said to himself, as he had that other time, I'll try.

Outside the usual bustle of departure was going on. The other prisoners had already been put into their chaises. The hostlers were still working on Pushchin's.

Pausing on the steps Pushchin looked about him, breathing deeply, filling his chest with the fresh night air. "That's one good thing about being penned up—the air tastes so good when they let you out." His profile shone serenely against the night: lips faintly pursed to taste life; the forehead clear. He put his arm around Grisha's dejected shoulders. "Don't look so sad, my dear boy. One can make a life anywhere." His chains' jingling subdued, he began easing himself into the carriage, with the *feldjäger's* help.

"Is there anything I can do? Dearest Ivan Ivanitch, can't you give me any errands?" Grisha said, with tears in his voice.

"You've done enough for me, just being here. However, if you think you could . . . Tell my sister Annette not to use the lemon in her letters any more, they know all about invisible writing, and all it does is annoy them—let her just write news about the family and that will be fine, that's all I want. . . . And, yes, Mukhanov's sister lives in Moscow—her married name is Shahovski, she lives somewhere on Prichistenka—tell her he is in good shape. . . . And the same thing to Nikita Muraviov's mother. . . . Give everybody I know my greetings. . . ."

"Anything else? Anyone else?"

Pushchin thought about it. An extraordinary smile, imbued with rueful sweetness, flickered on his face. "Say good-bye for me to my little Englishwoman."

Grisha's heart gave a painful little jolt. There was no need to tell Pushchin that Claire was no longer there; that she had left Russia, she was back in London or perhaps Italy, picking up old threads, weaving in new ones, making a new skein of her life. It didn't matter. He said merely: "I'll tell her."

He had tried to keep all expression out of his voice. But something must have been there—a flatness, a tremor. Pushchin looked at him sharply, his forehead wrinkling. Apparently he was reassured by what he saw. With another rare smile, tender, self-mocking, sensual, he said: "She was my last woman—" And, with a shadowy reversion to his earlier cockier self, he added, laughing a little: "So far."

"And my first," Grisha echoed him silently. It was borne in on him that perhaps that was precisely the essence of her: to be one man's first, another's last, to be there to punctuate the significant moment, put her seal on them, and leave them to life for the rest.

He saw her again as he had known her at first, moving at his side with a swift step that denied his lameness, weaving her charmed past into his present, saying to him with every story she told, Look how varied and impossible and chancy life can be. See how it glitters.

The gates swung open; bells jingling, the three chaises rode out into the dawn-streaked night.

Author's Notes

Prince Grigorii Petrovich Volynski (Grisha) is a fictional character. The other two protagonists—Claire Clairmont and Ivan Pushchin—were real people.

Claire (née Mary Jane) Clairmont was indeed the stepdaughter of William Godwin, the author of *Political Justice*. She and his own daughter, Mary Wollstonecraft Godwin (later Mary Shelley), were brought up as sisters. When Mary and P. B. Shelley eloped in 1814, Claire joined them on their famous tour of Europe. She remained a member of their unconventional household, off and on, until Shelley's death in 1822. There are intimations of jealousy in Mary's letters and diaries. Shelley's poetical references to Claire in *Epipsychidion* ("Oh Comet, beautiful and fierce . . ." etc.) and elsewhere have strongly romantic overtones. Biographers have hinted at a love affair—something not inconsistent with the Utopian principles of their circle.

In 1816 Claire contrived to meet Byron and become his mistress before he left England. She was not quite eighteen. ("At eighteen," she wrote, "one knows all about life and love.") Later that year she persuaded the Shelleys to go abroad again. They met Byron in Geneva; the affair was resumed. By that time Claire already knew she was pregnant. This summer also marked the beginning of the lasting friendship between the two poets.

Claire's affair with Byron did not last beyond Geneva, and many of his biographers disclaim any serious attachment on his part. Yet there is also evidence to the contrary. His *Stanzas for Music* are commonly thought to be addressed to Claire. When he was dying in Missolonghi, her name, according to his devoted valet, Fletcher, was on his lips. The very violence of his later dislike for her suggests an ambivalence in his feelings. Even allowing for his mistrust of intellectual women, one must wonder at his inexplicable cruelty to a girl who loved him and made few demands on him. There was something deeply neurotic in his avoidance of her, as though he felt her a threat rather than a mere nuisance.

Claire's "gamble" with her little daughter Allegra has psychological plausibility, notwithstanding that, according to all sources, she was passionately fond of her. Claire certainly never expected their separation to be as complete as it turned out to be. (For dramatic purposes I have left out the one short meeting at Este Byron allowed—at which, incidentally, he took care not to be present.) Her letters begging to be allowed to see the child make affecting reading. Byron's persistent and irrational rejections of those pleas, as well as his placing Allegra in a convent to be educated, turned her love for him into a hatred that persisted even after his death in 1824.

Of course, Claire owes her immortality to her relationship with Byron and Shelley. But she was a fascinating person in her own right. A young contemporary described her as "a girl of great ability, strong feelings, lively temper, and though not regularly handsome, of brilliant appearance." We know about her lovely voice; Byron had paid tribute to it in his *Stanzas for Music* (". . . and like music o'er the water/Is thy sweet voice to me . . .") as, even more movingly, had Shelley in *To Constantia Singing*. She was also an accomplished pianist. Her diary, with its running comments on persons she encountered and books she read, shows her to be a voracious reader in four languages and indicates an original and inquiring mind. Apparently she had a gift for pedagogy and made something of a name for herself in Moscow. She kept her Godwinian background pretty well hidden while in Russia, but occasionally it cropped up to embarrass her.

An impressive list of men who cared for her bears witness to her attractions. Henry Love Peacock, the author of *Nightmare Abbey*, proposed to her in England; a Henry Reveley defied a possessive mother to propose to her in Italy; the picturesque and adventurous Trelawny avowed his love before leaving with Byron for Greece. In Russia there was Hermann Gambs. Several volumes of his poetry were published under the pseudonym of C. Clairmont; others are dedicated to her. Despite these opportunities Claire never married. At the end of her long life, she intrigued yet another literary figure, Henry James, who based his *Aspern Papers* on an episode occurring in her old age.

After the double tragedy of Allegra's and Shelley's deaths, Claire left Italy and joined her brother Charles Clairmont in Vienna. She accompanied a Countess Zotov to Russia. Later we find her with the Pomykov family, who emerge in her journals very much as I have portrayed them (particularly the egregious Marya Ivanovna). Her special charge here was little Dunia, whose untimely death at the age of five did indeed tragically parallel Allegra's.

Claire was in Moscow in 1825. Since the Pomykov household was a liberal-minded one, she must have encountered there many of the participants in the December Revolt. (Later they came to be known as Decembrists.) Ivan Ivanitch Pushchin was one of that group. There is nothing in Claire's Russian journals to indicate an affair with him, but his name does appear constantly—"M. Pushchin called"; "M. Pouchine stayed for dinner." There are many varied spellings—apparently she found it a hard name to Anglicize. It may also present difficulties for the reader who must take care not to confuse it with that of his old schoolmate and dearest friend, the great Russian poet Alexander Pushkin. The last entry in which his name appears is that of December 5, presumably, his last call on the Pomykovs before he went off to St. Petersburg to participate in the fatal revolt.

There is a great deal of historical material on Pushchin, as there is on all the Decembrists; December 14 is an attractive subject for the Soviet historian. The indications are that he was not a hard-core revolutionary. His preference was for constitutional monarchy. However when the confusion of the interregnum, lasting from November 19 when Alexander died to December 14 when Nicholas I was officially proclaimed Emperor, provided a chance for a coup, he did not hang back but joined his comrades in Senate Square. According to some sources, he was offered an opportunity to leave the country after the revolt was put down, but turned it down, preferring to share his friends' fate.

Pushchin was one of the very few conspirators who were able to sustain the grilling without breaking down and naming names. The verbatim minutes of his inquest show his answers, in contrast to the hysterical outpourings of poor young Odoevski, to be terse and unemotional, giving away as little as possible. Called upon to disclose the man who recruited him into the society, he first invents a fictional character, then names a man who is no longer alive. His advice to Grisha is therefore completely in character. The way this advice reached the latter is based on similar episodes described in the Decembrists' memoirs.

In Siberia Pushchin remained true to his character, kindly, enterprising, optimistic. He was a sort of father figure to the other exiles, always taking pains to keep in touch, transmitting messages, using all possible outside sources to improve their conditions. Other traits likewise remained unchanged: he had many love affairs and fathered several illegitimate children while in Siberia, but remained a bachelor until almost the end of his life. After the general amnesty of 1850 allowed him to return to Russia, he married Fonvizin's widow.

I have tried to adhere as much as possible to actual events. The timetable of Claire's "secret journal" follows that of her actual journal. It is of course a fictional device; however Claire did briefly use code in her journals and in her Moscow entries she inverts Trelawny's name, calling him Ynwalert. The story of Byron writing a repentant letter to his wife is based on the fact that in Geneva he had been persuaded to attempt a reconciliation through the good offices of Madame de Staël, who lived nearby.

All the Decembrists portrayed in this novel are real people. The liberties taken are minimal; e.g., the meeting with Nikata Muraviov took place earlier than November, and young Odoevski was not present at it. On the other hand, Mukhanov's visit to Orlov and his demented proposal are authentic; confessing to it later, he implicated a considerable number of other prisoners.

The author would like to express her thanks to the Pforzheimer Institute, that valuable repository of materials dealing with Shelley's circle, and to Kenneth Neill Cameron, the well-known authority on Shelley, who has kindly looked over the Shelleyan section of this book. I should also like to express my special gratitude to Marion Stocking for her kindness and encouragement; her beautifully edited and lucidly presented *Journals of Claire Clairmont* started me on this project, and provided valuable background to the book.